IN HER EYES

ERICA ALEXANDER

In Her Eyes
Copyright © 2022 by Erica Alexander
All rights reserved.

This is a work of fiction. Any resemblance to actual persons living or dead, businesses, events or locales is purely coincidental.

ISBN: 978-1-7324215-8-5 (ebook)
ISBN: 978-1-7324215-9-2 (paperback)

Developmental editor: Nicole McCurdy at Emerald Edits
Editor: Paula Judith Johnson
Proofreader: Lawrence Editing
Cover design: Kari March Designs
Formatting and interior design by Erica Alexander at Serendipity Formatting.

DISCLAIMER: The material in this book is for mature audiences only. It is intended only for those aged 18 and older. Trigger warning: murder, kidnaping, violence, loss of a family member.

BE STILL. LISTEN.

The ghosts have voices.

FOR AVALON
(2013 - 2020)
YOU LEFT TOO SOON.

IF A CAT COULD BE A SOULMATE, SHE WOULD BE MINE.
THE MAIN CHARACTER IN THIS BOOK IS NAMED AFTER HER.

ORIGINAL WATERCOLOR PAINTING BY GISELI VARGAS.

A NOTE FROM THE AUTHOR

This story takes place in Ocean Cove, a fictional, small beach town in New Hampshire. This town is based on several other real coastal towns in New England.

I spent a crazy amount of time doing research on missing persons for this book. Read dozens of articles, reports and official documents. I also talked to police officers, detectives, and others experts in law enforcement. Once thing that stuck with me was this sentence:

Being missing is not a crime.

And because being missing is not a crime, the police will not actively search for a missing person unless they are a minor under thirteen, elderly, senile, or a person with a mental disorder. The police will investigate if the person disappeared under suspicious circumstances, regardless of age or mental status. Teenagers are assumed to be runaways. And there's no law that says an adult can't just walk out.

According to the National Missing and Unidentified Persons (NamUS) database, which is funded by the US Department of Justice, over six hundred thousand people go missing annually. This is for the US alone. That number is staggering. And while most missing persons are found or recovered eventually, there are thousands still that never are.

Missing persons' reports are also handled differently from city to city. Some large cities may have a dedicated unity, and some don't have anything at all, and local law enforcement officers or detectives handle those cases in addition to their normal duties.

Another fact that surprised me was that, on average, seventy-five percent of missing persons are males. According to statistics, Alaska has the highest number of missing persons per capita, and California has the largest number overall. Rhode Island has the least.

There's a myth that a person has to be missing for 24 hours before they can be reported. This is not true. If someone is missing, it should be reported as soon as possible. The experts' advice was to call 911. Every minute counts.

PSYCHOMETRY

Noun: (in parapsychology) the ability to deduce facts about events by touching objects related to them.

PROLOGUE
AVALON

THE FIRST TIME I DIED WAS AT MY BIRTH. NO OXYGEN entered my lungs as my mother expelled me into the world. My tiny body didn't shiver as it met cold air for the first time. No cries passed through my blue-tinted lips.

But I had luck and medicine on my side. Doctors and nurses hovered over me and unwrapped the umbilical cord from around my neck. Pressed fingertips into my chest, and butterfly-light touches pumped life into my heart.

My first gasp of air was followed by my first cry.

There was laughter and celebration in the delivery room. But it was short-lived, for one life was traded for another that day. My mother never had a chance to hold me.

I was five the second time I died—a cardiac arrest resulted from some absurdly high fever. They worked on me again. Cooled my body, pumped me full of drugs, machines breathed air into my lungs. The fingertips pressing into my chest, less butterfly, and more thumping bird. They blamed it on a virus—the catch-all culprit doctors blame for all the ailments they cannot explain.

The third and last time I died, I was thirteen. We were at the beach. I loved the sand between my toes, the tug of the water, the scent of sea and salt in the wind, the distant line where dark green met blue sky on the horizon. The ocean called to me with a siren's whisper.

I didn't scream or try to escape when the first wave took me in, lifted my feet off the ground, and robbed me of breath. I didn't know how to swim, but instinct had me kicking my legs, moving my arms, seeking the light just above the watery prison.

I kicked and kicked, but the ocean didn't let me go.

Not until he dragged me out of it.

Not until again there were hands at my chest, pressing harder this time. And lips against mine, pushing air into my lungs until *his* breath was my breath, and *his* gift of oxygen forced the water away. I sat up coughing, saltwater burning my throat, coating my mouth as it left my lungs and stomach.

I opened my eyes to the beautiful face of a young man. A young man with two different-colored eyes. One green like the sea and one blue like the sky. The first time someone's lips touched mine was to give me the gift of life. I was just a child, on the cusp of womanhood, but I knew I would never forget those eyes.

CHAPTER 1
AVALON

"COME ON, PLEASE? COME WITH ME. YOU DON'T HAVE TO touch anything." Lynn holds her palms together as if in prayer. Eyes wide and lips in a pout, like she's a first grader instead of their twenty-eight-year-old teacher.

She's lying. And she knows I know she's lying. She'll want me to touch everything.

My gaze bounces between her and the antique shop across the street from the café we're in. Morning light streams through skylights. The low hum of conversation fills the bright space. Hanging flower baskets filled with begonias, fuchsias, and lantanas add pops of color throughout the room.

I inhale the heavenly scent of coffee before taking a sip from my mug. "Don't beg, Lynn. It doesn't look good on you. No one with working eyes would ever believe you really mean it."

Lynn points at herself. "Wrong. These baby blues and pink pouty lips work wonders to get what I want."

I snort. "With horny guys, maybe."

5

"Hey, they're eager to please me. Don't diss until you try it."

I roll my eyes. If I could put a mileage counter on eye-rolling, mine would be in the thousands—every single mile caused by my best friend.

"I don't want to go in there. I'm on vacation." My words mean nothing. Lynn can always bully me into doing what she wants.

She cuts her stack of blueberry pancakes in half and gives them to me. "Only you would call driving aimlessly through New England a vacation."

I trade her pancakes for half of my avocado and cheese omelet. "Not aimlessly, carefree. No schedules, no set dates. And we're here now, in this quaint beach town." I gesture at the window and the tree-lined street and its colorful storefronts, each more inviting than the next. People walking their dogs and cars driving by slowly. It's a postcard-perfect little town. "When I told Grandma I wanted to go on a road trip with you, she suggested we go to Ocean Cove. Give it a chance. It's only day one. We have nearly two months to do whatever we want before we both have to go back to work. If we get bored here, we can just go somewhere else."

Lynn sighs and slumps back in her chair. "Yes, but when you said we should go on a summer-long vacation together, I was thinking of Paris or London."

I cut into the pancakes. "I know, but I wanted to take the same trip Grandma took with my mother when she was a kid. Do the kind of stuff I've never had a chance to do." Lynn makes a sad face at the mention of the mother I've never met. Her absence shouldn't bother me, but sometimes it does. This trip is in part a way to connect with her.

Lynn breaks into a big smile, and I know trouble is

coming. "I'm calling the best friend card." She holds an imaginary card above her head like we've been doing since we were ten.

I slouch into my chair. Stay still. Try to blend in with the furniture. My gaze finds the exquisite pastries lined in neat little rows behind the glass case.

She waves a hand in front of my face. "I'll buy you walnut maple ice cream next time we go to an ice cream shop."

I smirk. "I'll go if you come running with me."

"Heck no! I'll buy you ice cream every day for a week instead."

I release a mock-exasperated huff. "Okay, I'll go." I've been trying to get her to jog with me for years. She always says no, but we play this game anyway. She tries to bribe me with food, and I try to get her to run with me.

She points a fork full of pancakes at me. "I would agree to buy you ice cream for a month before I agree to go running."

I love running. I need the asphalt under my feet, the steady rhythm of jogging steps, one after the other, the burn in my thighs and calves, and the rush of air in my lungs. That's how I clear my head. How I wash away troubles and center myself. "One of these days, you'll say yes, Lynn."

"No, thank you. This girl does not run."

The antique store welcomes us with that smell all antique stores share—a bit dusty and moldy. It's the smell of old things, attics, and the back of closets. It's the scent of memories and history.

I hesitate by the door, and Lynn tugs at my arm, but I hold my place and stand in the opening. Sunlight at my back and the darkened and cluttered space ahead. I'm on the threshold between the past and the present. I still myself, ground my feet, and inhale deeply. The smells of the past mingle with the fresh breeze coming in through the open door. The palms of my hands tingle. That familiar anxious pressure in my chest makes itself known. I ready myself, step in, and let the door gently close behind me.

The past calls to me like it always does whenever I enter an antique store, an old place, a church. The art historian in me rejoices in finding old objects, little treasures long-lost in time, and my soul rejoices in learning the history and in reading the memories each object holds.

Lynn bumps into my shoulder. "I don't know why you always put up a fight. You love this."

I smile. She's right. I love this. I've lived my entire life surrounded by old things. I have the privilege of working with objects most people can only admire from behind a glass pane in a museum. An antique shop is nothing compared to my job. But I spend so much time trapped in the past, sometimes I wonder if I forget to live in the present. But that's not something I want to voice out loud. "Because I get paid to do this, and I'm on vacation," I whisper, as if we were in a church and not a store. The place demands a certain reverence.

"Yeah, yeah, yeah, they pay you a shit-ton of money to travel all over the world. You get to see and touch treasures, art, and objects that very few people even know exist. This is all I have." She gestures around.

I laugh. There's no real animosity in her words. "Gosh, I wish Grandma were here." I've lost count of the many times she and I visited antique stores just like this one. Driving around with Grandma, sleeping in tiny bed-and-breakfast places, with no direction other than whatever called to Grandma next.

Lynn wiggles her fingers. "Do your thing," she whispers.

My thing . . . psychometry. My gift. The ability to know the history of an object simply by touching it. A secret only shared with Lynn and my grandma. It has served me well in my job. I'm glad I took Grandma's suggestion to go to Ocean Cove. If Grandma tells you to do something, you do it. In all our travels, we've never come this way. I guess it holds too many bitter memories for her and her falling-out with my mother.

Grandma's abilities are far more potent than mine. My gift, as grandma calls it, clamors for something else. It wants more. More than reading objects for their history or authenticity. There's an empty spot in my soul, and it is hungry, but I have yet to discover what it hungers for.

"Come! This way." Lynn waves at me and walks down an aisle.

I follow her voice. Find her near a huge shelf holding dozens and dozens of small blown glass figurines. Nothing about them draws me in.

"These are so cute." She reaches for a large figurine of a dolphin. I take her hand and point at the sign on the shelf.

You Break It, You Buy It

"Let's look with our eyes first. I'll let you know if something grabs my attention." But something in this store already has. There's a buzz in my solar plexus, and it—whatever it is—calls to me.

We walk around under the vigilant eye of the shop owner at the back of the store and the security cameras discreetly set into the ceiling. We're not doing anything wrong, but the extra attention we're getting, in addition to the pull in the pit of my stomach, unsettles me. The stale air is suffocating. It weighs heavily on my lungs. I make a conscious effort to breathe.

The pull gets stronger with each step I take into the store. The unease grows, and I want to leave, but I don't. I won't. I can't deny the pull. I follow Lynn, who's completely unaware of my struggle.

Lynn points at a gun. The sign beside it says it's a Colt 1860 Army .44. The revolver is secured to the display but not encased in glass. I touch it, close my eyes, and wait. Cold metal and smooth warm wood meet my hand. Nothing. A soldier never touched this gun. I open my eyes and shake my head at Lynn. "It's a replica."

Her eyes go round, and she gapes at the two-thousand-dollar price tag.

I lower my voice. "That's worth around three hundred at most."

"Holy crap."

I grin. "I know."

Lynn looks around for the next object. "Okay, find something. Get your spidey senses on."

I look around the store and smile when my gaze lands on a small picture frame. The black-and-white photo is yellowed with age. It's a wedding day picture. The woman is seated, gloved hands on her lap. She's wearing an elaborate gown. Multiple skirts are layered over one another, and delicate lace covers the fabric on the bodice and high neck. Flowers are braided into her hair and a delicate veil is draped over one shoulder. The man is standing next to her in a dark suit and holding a hat in one hand. His other hand is on her shoulder.

A flower in his lapel. They look happy. A love match, and not an arranged marriage. The cast-iron frame is gilded with gold. My hands tingle when I brush my fingertips against the top before I pick it up.

My eyes close, and my mind floods with images. My smile gets bigger.

An English countryside flutters before my closed eyelids. Purple-blue wildflowers spread amidst grass and rocks. A dirt road marred by the twin ruts of carriage wheels extending down the path. The giggle of children. A massive stone house with tall windows and heavy draperies. A wall of leather-bound books. A floral settee. The very same picture with someone writing something on the back. The picture frame sitting on a mahogany desk. The frame wrapped in newspapers and the pitch-black from inside of a trunk. A trip across the ocean. An old map of Virginia. A new home, whitewashed walls. Older kids now. The images move through my mind, one after the other, like the pages of a book being flipped until the last image dissolves with the words on a sign: Estate Sale.

I open my eyes, blink a few times, look around, and allow the present to settle into me. It takes a couple of seconds to get my bearings after the vision. The past never wants to let go. I take a deep breath and shed the wash of faint emotions that always linger with the images—the visions attached to the picture frame were happy and bittersweet. That's not always the case, and I can't tell what I'll get until I touch something. The earlier pull I felt is dulled by the lingering effects of this vision. But it is still there, waiting for me.

Lynn bounces on her feet, all impatience and contained energy. "So? What did you see?"

"If someone could figure out how to harness all of your enthusiasm, I bet they could power a small country."

"Ava!"

My smile grows large. I'm enjoying my little power trip and making her wait.

"Avalon Mitchell Bloom, if you don't tell me right now, I swear—"

"Oh-oh, she's using my full name. I'm in trouble now."

Her hands fist a few inches from my face in a mock fight stance.

I put mine up in surrender. The sound of a throat clearing and a chair dragging on the wood floor grab our attention. The shop owner is none too impressed with our antics. He faces us, head tilted down to look over the glasses dangling halfway down his enormous nose. I turn my back to him and repress a laugh. "Shh, behave. We're nearly thirty, not teenagers."

She pushes her shoulders back. "No, we're twenty-eight, and that's not thirty. I know math because I'm a teacher."

I grab the picture frame. "Let's go. I'm buying this. It will look great with my other antique frames."

Lynn follows me around the shelves as we put some distance between the man and us. I tell her everything I saw.

She sighs. "It's so romantic. I'm so jealous. I wish I could do that."

"It's not romantic. It just is. Not all memories are happy ones." I've had my share of unhappy impressions.

Lynn picks up a teacup and sets it back. "I know. But you have this gift, and it's such an amazing thing."

"So do you. You bring joy to kids every day, and they learn to read in the process. You're creating smart little minds."

"Fancy words, but at the end of the day, I'm just an elementary school teacher. I do love my first graders and my school. I wouldn't trade it for the world."

I hug the frame to my chest. "Of course, June, July, and August don't hurt either."

She nods. "Can't complain about having summers off. If I had any other job, I wouldn't be able to come with you on your impromptu summer vacation."

"Let's go." I tilt my head toward the cash register at the back of the store. "Before that guy calls the cops on us." That pull gets stronger again, but something in me is resistant to the idea of touching it, whatever it is.

I smile big at the man behind the counter and place the picture frame on top of the neat pile of butcher wrapping paper. He looks older than some of the pieces in the store.

That pull I felt when we first entered the store takes hold of me again and doesn't let go. My knees nearly buckle. Lynn's hands come to my back and steady me. I glance at the old man, but he's distracted, wrapping the picture frame. I turn, orienting myself toward the call pulsing in my chest. To my right, in a glass case behind the counter, on a hook, hangs a necklace. Two large blue stones dangling from a long silver chain. The stones sway ever so slightly, as if they're trying to get closer to me.

I point at the necklace. "May I see that, please?"

The man looks behind him and back at me. His eyes glint. I cannot hide the eagerness in my voice. He's already calculating how much he can charge me. I try to tone down my interest. "It's such a pretty blue."

"Ah, yes, I got this a few days ago. Pretty, eh? I think the stones are lapis lazuli and turquoise."

He grabs the necklace from its perch, and I want to swat

his hands away. Keep him from disturbing the imprints that so strongly call to me.

He dangles it inches from my face, and my hand trembles when I close it around the stones. I'm instantly assaulted by images, even before I can close my eyes. I turn my back to the man and lean into the counter. Lynn shifts at my side but doesn't touch me. She has seen me do this most of her life. Never touch me while I'm reading an object.

I hold the necklace to my chest, and in an instant, I'm falling backward, falling, falling, arms extended, body stiff, bracing for impact. My hair flowing around my face—no, not my hair. Hers. The owner of the necklace. She's beautiful, around my age. Long brown hair with hot pink streaks. Huge amber eyes. A beauty mark at the corner of one eye. Then she's being dragged across the ground, a masculine hand around an ankle. Her emotions flow through me like a whitewater river. Fast and chaotic. She's grasping at . . . anything, trying to get a hold, trying to stop him, but the only things under her hands are dirt and leaves. Her clothes are dirty, bloody, and tattered. Black slacks, white blouse, a pink floral scarf.

Cold water splashes on her face. She gasps, then moans in pain. Ropes around her chest. She's tied to a chair. A gray metal chair. She tries to swallow. It hurts. She's thirsty, so thirsty. And terrified. The man walks around her. Taunts. Grabs at her hair and pulls her head back. She sobs. He slaps her. A glint of silver. He sees the necklace. Tugs at the chain and looks at the stones. Pulls it over her head gently so as not to break it. The stones look small in his hand. There's a small, jagged scar on his wrist.

The girl whimpers. He wraps the necklace around his palm twice. His hands go around her neck and squeeze. The necklace dangles along his wrist. The metal digs into her skin. She gasps and thrashes, her eyes widen, blood vessels break in the sclera, and her mouth gaps open as she tries to suck air that will never fill her lungs again. Then nothing. Darkness fills my vision.

She doesn't come back this time. I know she's dead. This poor girl was murdered, and the necklace was hers.

When I open my eyes, I'm sitting on the floor, back against the counter, Lynn kneeling in front of me and rubbing my arms. My heart thunders so loud it pulses in my ears. I'm shaking, hands still clasped around the necklace and pressed to my chest. The taste of salt on my lips. My face wet with tears.

Lynn digs a tissue from her purse and wipes my face. The man peers from the other side of the counter, his shadow momentarily blocking the overhead lights. "Is she okay?"

"Yes. It's a dizzy spell. She has them sometimes." Thankfully, Lynn is talking because I'm not sure I could manage it just now. I take a deep breath and count to seven, exhale and count to seven again. Do it two more times, the way Grandma taught me. The shaking recedes. My vision clears, and my heart slows down to a normal pace. I move my hands from my chest, open them, flex my fingers, and allow the silver chain to slide, dangle from a thumb—the imprint of the stones against my palm—a temporary brand.

"Help me up?"

Lynn holds my elbow and helps me to stand, keeping both hands on me and making sure I'm steady on my feet. Her always happy and smiling expression is gone.

I turn to the counter, the necklace back in my palm. "How much?" As terrible as the images were, I can't part with this. I need to find out more. I need to help her, somehow.

The glint of greed waned. The man seems more worried than calculating now.

"How about a hundred bucks for everything?" He points at the frame and my hand.

"That works." I open my purse and fish a crisp bill from my wallet.

"Want me to wrap it?"

I don't want to part with it, not for a second. I don't want to have his touch taint the impressions. "Do you have a small box?"

"Sure." He searches under the counter and opens a small navy-blue cardboard jewelry box. I peek at his wrists. No scar. He's not the killer. I don't give him the necklace but grab the box instead. Set the chain inside, arrange the stones, and close the lid. The top is too loose, but I don't say anything. I want to get out of here.

Lynn grabs the bag with the frame and the receipt. We walk to the door. I stop at the threshold and turn back to him. He's still eyeing me wearily. "It's Shattuckite and Larimar."

"What?" He clearly has no idea what I'm talking about.

"The stones. You said they were lapis lazuli and turquoise. You're wrong. They're Shattuckite and Larimar."

The man glares at me.

"And that Colt 1860 is a replica," I throw at him as we leave the store.

CHAPTER 2
AVALON

WE MAKE OUR WAY BACK TO MY CAR IN SILENCE. LYNN'S gaze is on me the entire time. She's staying close, probably anticipating another fall.

She stops at the driver's side door. "Maybe I should drive?"

I don't fight her. My hands still tremble when I dig through my purse, looking for the car fob.

Lynn takes the fob, and I walk around and get in the passenger seat. She turns the ignition, the Porsche Cayenne purrs, and she purrs right along with it.

She caresses the steering wheel like a lover. "I love this car. I want to marry this car and have its babies."

I click my seat belt on. "Ouch. Little Porsche babies? That's gonna hurt."

She laughs, but her gaze turns serious. "What happened back there?"

I look at the objects I purchased, now lying on my lap. "It was . . ." I suck in a breath. "It was terrifying."

She waits while I gather my thoughts. The images flash back in my mind, and instead of fading like they usually do, they intensify. The acrid smell of metal, blood, damp earth, and fear burns my nose. The sting of scratches and scrapes on my skin. I'm in the mind and body of a dead woman.

"The necklace. I saw the girl it belonged to. And how she died."

"Oh." Lynn's hand goes to her mouth. "I'm sorry. I should have never pushed you to go in there."

"No. It's not your fault. This is our game. You ask me to read something. I pretend I don't want to, but I do it anyway. That's what we do, what we have always done. And it's not the first time I have seen someone die. It's just that . . ." I don't know what to say. I can't put words to it.

"What?" Her voice is gentle, barely a whisper over the low hum of the car's engine.

"This is recent. This girl, she just died. Days." Phantom fingers press into my throat, and I swallow, trying to dislodge the pressure building there. "A week at the most and it was so intense. The energy is so fresh."

Lynn's eyes widen. "How do you know it just happened?"

I search my mind for any clues to timing. There's no tangible indication of any kind of timeline. But the energy . . . it's so strong, so raw. Nothing like the artifacts I usually work with. "I don't know. I just do. This will sound insane, but time has a certain flavor and smell. That's not the right description, but the closest thing I can think of. The older an object is, the more pungent the flavor and smell are. This necklace? It's fresh, and new, and strong." The certainty of it sits on my chest like a boulder.

Her hand finds mine, and she squeezes. "Want to talk about it?"

"No." I want to forget what I saw. "But maybe it will feel better if I do."

I tell Lynn everything and leave out no detail. With each horrific description I give, her face goes whiter, her eyes widen, and her mouth drops. She wipes her face with the heels of her hands. "Jesus, she was murdered. And this just happened?"

I inhale deeply and answer her with the exhale. "Yes."

Her watery gaze searches my face. "What're you gonna do?"

I look away, the weight of the vision suffocating me.

Lynn puts a hand on my shoulder. "We have to go to the police."

"I know, but what will I tell them, Lynn?" I run my hands through my hair, strands getting caught in the ring Grandma gifted me. I yank at the curls, shove my hands into my hair again, lean into my fists, and close my eyes. The images come back, one after the other, demanding to be seen, heard, and acknowledged.

Lynn rubs my back. "Maybe we can call in an anonymous tip?"

We. I love her for that. For letting me know she's in this with me. I shake my head. As much as I hate exposing myself, revealing my gift, I know I must do this in person. And it twists in my stomach like a hot knife. "I must talk to the police face-to-face."

She nods once. "What're you gonna say?"

I tap the gear shaft. Hell if I know. "Drive. Let's find the police station." Something will come to me. It has to. And if it doesn't, there's always the truth.

In a small town like this one, and with the help of Siri and Navigation System, it takes less than ten minutes to drive to the police station. Lynn parks across the street and digs in the cup holder for quarters to add to the meter.

She looks at me. "Now what?"

Now what indeed. "Now we go in."

She lingers, hand on the door handle, and waits for me to do the same. Lynn's giving me time to change my mind. As much as I want to leave and forget I ever saw that necklace, I know I won't. I can't. The images imprinted in the necklace are as real as my own memories. And they won't go away. I can't save the girl in my visions, but maybe I can help the police catch whoever hurt her. And perhaps prevent it from happening again.

I leave the picture frame in the console between the seats and put the box with the necklace in my purse.

She searches my face. "You sure?"

"Yes, we'll just go in and ask to talk to someone in charge of homicides, give them the necklace, tell them what I saw, and leave. They'll do the rest. That's their job. We're not cops. That's the plan." I can hear Grandma's voice in my head now. *Make plans if you want to give the universe a good laugh. The Fates just love messing with plans.*

"Wait!" Lynn grabs her phone. "Let's Google it."

"Google what?"

"Google the police station. Let's find out who's in charge. This way, we can ask for them directly." Her fingers fly on the screen.

I shake my head. "I don't think police stations have a directory with the names of their cops."

"Found it!"

"What? No way."

Her smirk hits a ten on the smug scale. "Told you. I know these things."

She shows me the screen, and indeed there are a dozen or so officers listed by titles followed by names, which appear to be a decreasing rank. "No homicide detective, though. This town is too small."

Lynn scrolls down the screen. "I don't think we want to go directly to the top. Every chief of police in movies likes to yell."

"Okay, who's next in line?"

"There's a deputy chief, a detective sergeant, a sergeant, a K-9 cop, and a bunch of officers."

"Let's go with the detective sergeant. High, but not too high."

She points at the screen. "Then, we want to ask for Jake Knox."

My stomach churns. Here goes nothing. "Ready? Okay, let's go."

She nods, and we open the car doors at the same time. The warm June breeze blows my hair across my face. I close my eyes and take a moment to settle my nerves while Lynn feeds the meter. I push a hand into my solar plexus and take three deep breaths. Imagine myself inside a bubble of protection. Nothing can hurt me in here. We cross the street together. This side of town is a little less touristy but still lined with charming stores, cafés, and restaurants. It's the kind of place that makes you feel safe. So very different from NYC.

Lynn bumps into my side. "Jaywalking right in front of the police station and all these cops. You like to live dangerously, my friend."

I'm grateful for her attempt at levity. "I'm following you."

She steps around a pothole. "Dude, if you're following me, we're so screwed. I have no idea where I'm going. I thought I was following you."

I laugh, but the sound is hollow. I know she's trying to distract me from the mounting tension in my chest. But experience has taught me that the anxiety will dissipate as soon as I confront my fear and do what I set out for myself.

Gray steps lead up to a red brick and cement building. The words CITY HALL and POLICE are engraved on the wall. People come and go through the wood and glass double doors. A couple of cops linger on the sidewalk talking, hands on belts heavy with gadgets and guns.

One of them has a police dog, and the German Shepherd wags his tail at me, then takes a short step in my direction, his eyes tracking my progress as I near the building and go up the steps. I smile at the dog and the tail wags faster. The K-9 cop notices and smiles at me. He scratches behind the dog's ear, says something to the dog, and his tail wags faster still.

"He's cute," I whisper to Lynn.

"Which one? The dog or the cop?"

"Both, I guess, but I was talking about the dog."

Lynn giggles. "You did it again."

"Did what?"

"Charmed that dog. Animals love you."

"I love them too," I say as we walk through the front doors.

"Yeah, but you could be like a regular Disney princess with all the forest animals following you."

I shrug. She's exaggerating. There was that one cat who hated me, but he hated everyone, so there's that. Lynn's not too far from the truth, though. Animals do love me. They can

22

sense something in me. I'm not sure what. Grandma is the same way. "I wish. If I were a Disney princess, they would be cleaning my house and doing my laundry, too."

The doors open to a long hall. The sound of distant voices echoes in the large, open space, and a few yards down, a sign over a door points to the police station. We walk through the door and make our way to a reception area. The air conditioning is set to Alaska in winter. I rub my bare arms and try to hold to some body heat without much success. Lynn gets closer to me—whether because she's nervous or just trying to stay warm, I can't tell.

The space is small, maybe eighteen or twenty feet long, with a wall-to-wall counter framed by glass going up to the ceiling. At the end is another door, and on it, the words AUTHORIZED PERSONNEL ONLY are printed in red. Three desks fill the space on the other side of the thick glass. And behind them is the chief of police office, if we go by the words etched on the closed door.

An older man watches us as we approach the front. He nods and leans into one of the two small openings at face level on the glass. "How can I help you ladies this morning?" He's all small-town smiles and charm.

"Good morning, Officer. May I speak with Detective Knox, please?"

The charm takes a back seat to curiosity, and an inquisitive expression chases away the crinkles on the corners of his eyes.

"May I ask what this is in regard to?"

"I prefer to speak with the detective directly. Thank you." My tone is firm, but my smile is friendly. I know I look younger than my age, not that twenty-eight is old, but people, especially older men like the officer on the other side of the security glass, tend to look at me in one of three ways: like I'm a lost kid who needs help, like someone they can bully, or with lust. In this case, it's mostly the first option with a touch of the second.

He stays silent, hands on his belt like the cops outside. The seconds stretch between us. I smile bigger, friendlier, and more confident. Lynn shifts from foot to foot just behind me.

The officer nods. "Let me see if he's in." He steps back, picks up a phone from a desk, pushes a few numbers on the dial pad, and speaks with someone. And with the glass between us, I can't hear anything he's saying. He comes back. "He'll be right out. Take a seat, please." He points to the hard plastic blue chairs behind us. Chairs attached to iron bars set into the floor.

"Thank you, Officer." I walk away, and Lynn follows me. But I don't sit. Those chairs look as inviting as a jail cell.

Lynn fidgets next to me. "Are you nervous? I'm freaking out a little."

"You have nothing to be nervous about. I'm the one with the visions."

She grabs my arm. "I'm nervous for you. What if they think you did it? Oh, man. This was a bad idea—we should leave right now."

"Look around. There are cameras everywhere, and it would look far more suspicious if we chickened out now." Whatever I face here will be nothing compared to what that poor girl suffered.

She looks up. "I didn't even think of the cameras."

"Don't worry. You don't have to say anything. Leave it up to me. Everything will be fine." It has to be. I must trust that we are here for a reason. Just then, the PERSONNEL ONLY door opens, and a man in dark jeans and a light blue shirt, sleeves rolled up to his elbows, steps out. He's not in uniform. He's gorgeous—chiseled cheekbones and a strong jawline. What one could call universally handsome. Thick hair with a slight wave, broad shoulders, the muscular lean build of an Olympic swimmer. And tall. So very tall. He looks more like a movie star than a cop. I was expecting a crumpled, bald guy with a mustache, like the detectives in the old movies Grandma made me watch with her.

His face is all sharp angles, and his eyes are hidden behind dark sunglasses. Indoors. He doesn't smile. If I had to take a wild guess, I'd say he's not having a good day. Annoyance radiates from him. Lucky me.

The closer he gets to me, the faster my heart beats. I remind myself why I'm here and order my heart to slow down. Half of me wishes I had never stepped a foot into this building. The other half wishes I had met him somewhere else, and for a reason that didn't involve a police station and a murder.

He stops a couple of feet away from us. "I was told you want to speak with me."

"I want to speak with Detective Sergeant Jake Knox. Is that you?" I emphasize the name. And smile. I don't want to talk to a random cop and have to do this all over again.

An eyebrow peeks just above the sunglasses.

"Come with me." He walks away without looking to see if we're following. It takes me a second to gather my courage, but I follow him, Lynn right at my heels. Someone buzzes him in, and we go through the door. The smell of stale coffee hangs in the air. We walk along a wall flanking all the desks, down a hall, and past a couple of closed doors. He stops at a door with a keypad lock and blocks our view with his body while he unlocks it. He pushes the door open and motions for us to walk in. The office is small. Institution-gray walls. A desk covered in folders sits in the middle. Tall metal filling cabinets line an entire wall. On the opposite wall is a giant corkboard covered in pictures, newspaper clippings, and sticky notes with calligraphy so bad whoever wrote it could be a doctor. And hundreds of colored tacks. The wall is organized chaos. Barred windows face the parking lot behind him. He points to two chairs, thankfully not the hard plastic kind from the front area, but they don't look much more comfortable.

He sits behind the desk, his chair squeaking under his frame. It tilts back as if trained to the motion by uncountable hours of use. His broad shoulders hide the chairback, and it looks like he's floating.

The sunglasses stay put, and I have the childish urge to dig mine from my purse and put them on. I sit, and Lynn follows, sitting on the chair next to mine.

"How can I help you, Miss . . . ?" He drags the S. Is he mocking me? With his eyes covered, I can't read his expression, but his jaw is tight, and his posture guarded. Not the friendly kind, then.

"My name is Avalon Bloom. You may call me Ava. And this is Lynn Reynolds."

"How can I help you, Miss Bloom?" He ignores my nickname.

"I want to report a murder." I've never imagined I'd say these words.

He leans in now, a hand resting on the desk between us. "Okay. Start from the beginning. Who was murdered?"

My heart does its best to speed out of my chest. "I don't know."

"Where and when did this murder happen?"

"I don't know." I have to force the words out. I look more and more like an idiot with each question.

He grabs a pen and twirls it on his fingers. "Did you see this happen?"

"Not exactly."

"Did you overhear someone talking about it?"

I fist my hands in my lap to stop them from trembling. "Not exactly."

He drops the pen to the desk and leans back with an exasperated huff. "What do you know?"

"I know that a woman was murdered. She was kidnapped, dragged through the woods, beaten, and then strangled."

He leans into the desk and braces his arms on it. "How do you know this?"

"I saw it."

He drops back to the chair again. "You just said that you didn't see it. Now you're saying you saw it. Which is it? Did you see, or did you not see what happened?" Hardness coats his voice.

"I saw it, but not with my eyes."

His head tilts to the side, not unlike a confused dog.

"I saw it with my mind. I can see things, and I saw this young woman being killed." Did I seriously just blurt that out? I sound like one of those side-show psychics. *Someone close to you whose name starts with either A or M wants you to know they're okay.* I could punch myself.

He stands up. "So, you're a psychic. Thank you for stopping by, but as you can see"—he points to the pile of yellow folders on his desk, which tilts precariously close to the edge—"I'm swamped, and I don't have time to chase after the visions of psychics. I work with facts and evidence." He points

27

at the door—a clear command for us to leave. Lynn starts to get up, but I press her hand back into the chair arm.

"Please, sit, Detective. I understand this may be hard to believe, but I have proof. Or evidence, as you call it." He stands for another ten seconds. Then sits, elbows on the desk, hands stippled partially blocking his face, lips pressed into a thin line.

"What's the evidence?" His tone is dry and challenging.

I reach into my bag, and he stiffens. I slow down my movements and take out the small navy-blue box the antique owner gave me less than an hour ago. How can so much happen in such a short time? I place the closed box on his desk, making sure the loose top stays on. He looks at me.

"This belonged to the murder victim." I nod toward the box. "Open it."

He pushes the box back with the tip of the pen, glances back at me for several seconds, and then uses the pen to nudge the cover off the small box as if it were full of snakes.

He looks at it, and all color drains from his face. He pulls his sunglasses off, lays them on the corner of his desk, and they drop to the floor. He's on his feet, fumbling through the pile of folders. Half of them slide across his desk, and a few follow the sunglasses to the floor like a paper waterfall. He pulls a folder from the remaining pile and sets it on the desk next to the box. The typed name on the sticker faces him, but it's big enough that I can read it upside down.

ALICE THOMPSON

He opens the folder with a slight tremble, shuffles through the papers, and finds a large picture. It's the same young woman from my vision. Same brown hair with pink streaks. She's wearing a black T-shirt, and very visible against it is the necklace. The one-of-a-kind necklace because it is made of natural stones. He places the picture next to the box and spends what seems like an eternity looking back and forth between the two items. "Where did you find this?"

When he looks at me, I see his eyes for the first time. Two different colors—one green like the sea and one blue like the sky.

THERE'S NOTHING LIKE THAT FIRST SLICE. THE GIVING AWAY OF THE FLESH WHEN I MAKE THE FIRST CUT. NO MATTER HOW SHARP THE KNIFE, THERE'S ALWAYS RESISTANCE . . . THEN THE BLADE SLIDES IN. IT'S . . . INTIMATE.

CHAPTER 3
AVALON

GREEN AND BLUE. THE DETECTIVE'S EYES ARE GREEN AND blue. My brain rearranges his features into a much younger one. Everything snaps into place like a Rubik's cube when all the colors are in their correct position. I stare at him, and instantly I'm back at that beach in North Carolina, so far away from here. I'm thirteen again. I'm drowning. The taste of salt coats my tongue, the touch of his lips, the pressure of air being pushed into my lungs. My throat dries and constricts. My mouth moves, but I'm incapable of sound. I choke on unspoken words. It's him. The boy from my teenage dreams. The boy who saved me.

Lynn grabs my arm, and I force myself to turn to her. Every cell in my body fights to stay locked on his face. I drag my gaze away from him and finally meet hers. Her eyes are wide, and they quickly slide to the detective before turning back to me. Her face speaks to me with the language of a friendship so deeply rooted in a lifetime of knowing each other that words are not needed. She's asking all the questions I'm already asking myself. *Did you see his eyes? Is that him?*

She was not at the beach that day. The day I died for the third time, but she's heard this story a thousand times over the years. It's her favorite. When we were kids, we'd be awake into the night during sleepovers giggling over our many imagined lives for the man who now stands in front of us. Even now, well into our twenties, every so often, one of us asks the other, "What do you think he's doing now?"

The answer is always something crazy. *He's training to be an astronaut. Or he's a champion surfer living in Australia.* We created many versions of who he was and what he did. But we never pictured this.

I give her a warning look, and she reads my meaning. No, I don't want to bring this up right now. It is not the time nor the place.

He stands up, his body braced by fists on the desk between us. "Where did you find this?"

His posturing is intimidating, but I'm not sure if he intended it to be. He's intense, and I want to shrink away from the unspoken menace in his voice but hold my ground as he leans over the desk and erases the space between us. "At an antique store. About a ten-minute drive from here. I just bought it."

He stands tall now, his body less tense, but the sharpness of his eyes increases. "Why did you bring me the necklace?"

I've dealt with my share of intense men who think they can intimidate me—pompous, self-important men—but never anyone like him, never someone so intrinsically a part of my life. And he has no idea who I am. I swallow and dig in, find some cojones, as Grandma would say. "Because I know the owner of it was murdered. I saw it happen."

"Because you saw it. In a *vision*." His lips curl at the last word. As if saying it leaves a nasty taste in his mouth.

My fingers grip the strap of my purse. "I saw it, yes."

He drops to the chair, and it squeaks again under his weight as if protesting the six-foot-plus and two-hundred-pound man sitting on it. He swivels back and forth, arms lazily draped over the chair as if he didn't have a care in the world. But his eyes are locked on me. He may be trying to look casual right now, put me at ease, so I drop my defenses and reveal more than I want. A cop trick, I'm sure. But his gaze is calculating and cold. He's trying to read me and is coming up empty.

"You actually saw it?" he asks again.

"Yes." How many times will I have to repeat myself?

"And you know for sure she's dead." His calm, casual, almost slouched sitting is a trap. This is a man who misses nothing. But then again, neither do I.

"I watched her die."

He's skeptical. He looks between me, the necklace, and the picture of the young woman wearing the same necklace.

He leans into the desk again, fingers steepled. "Explain."

Lynn fidgets next to me. His gaze goes to her. "Did you see this murder as well?"

Lynn shakes her head so hard she makes me dizzy.

I touch her hand. "No, she didn't see anything. Just me."

He's not buying it. I don't blame him. There are two kinds of people in the world: those who believe in the supernatural and those who don't. He's clearly in the latter category. I'm sure we'd be out on the street already if it weren't for the necklace. But after a long and silent stare, he grabs a yellow legal pad and a pen from the mess of folders and papers on his desk. Flips the pages on the pad until he gets to a blank one and looks back at me.

"Names?"

"Ava Bloom—my first name is Avalon, but everyone calls me Ava."

He looks at Lynn. "And?"

"She saw nothing." I have the irrational need to step in front of Lynn as if doing so could keep him from seeing her.

"And yet she's here. Name?"

I attempt to keep my features smooth. "She was with me when I found the necklace."

"I thought you said you bought it. And I still need a name."

I poke the inside of my cheek with my tongue and then bite it before speaking again. "Yes. I bought it. After I found it. In the store." I smile with the warmth of a glacier. If he wants to play the asshole game, I can play it too. "Listen, I know you don't believe in visions. That's clear. But I had one about this necklace. And I'm never wrong."

He raises an eyebrow at me. I can't stop staring at his eyes and trying to match up the sweet boy of my teen fantasies with the cynical man sitting a few feet across from me.

Lynn clears her throat. "It's Lynn. Lynn Reynolds."

He scribbles on the paper. "Name of the store where you found the necklace?"

His mouth moves in exaggeration when he says, 'found.' I stare at his lips. And back at his eyes. They're so beautiful. It's such a distraction. I guess that's why he hides them behind sunglasses, even indoors. He's nothing like I imagined him. I'm a jumble of conflicting emotions, and right now, the predominant one is irritation.

I look at Lynn in question. I didn't pay attention to the store's name.

"A Stop in Time," she replies.

Lynn gets a genuine smile from me. "That's the store name? Really?"

"Yes. It's cute, isn't it?" Lynn reverts to her easy, good-natured self, her guard down for a moment.

I try to tamp down my temper. I should be used to skeptics by now. Detective Asshole taps the desk with his knuckles. Like a judge reining in control of a courtroom.

"Address for the store?" There's not an ounce of pleasantness to him.

I shrug. "I don't know the exact address. We don't live here. It's off the main road. I'm sure you can just Google it and find out." I show him my perfect teeth in a mock smile again. I'm pretty sure antagonizing the police is not smart, but he started it.

He opens the drawer, grabs a small device from it, and pushes a button. "Mind if I record the rest of the questions?"

"Yes, I mind it." This is hard enough without having a recording of my voice.

He turns the device off. "Miss Bloom, you're in possession of an object that belongs to a missing person. A person who vanished without a trace and this necklace"—he nudges the box with the pen again—"is the first clue—the only clue we have. I need to know every detail related to your finding the necklace. I ask again. May I please use a recorder? So I don't miss any details that might help me to locate the missing woman?"

Well, damn it. When he phrases it like that—I hate being put in this position. Where saying 'no' makes me feel selfish or unbending. I don't want my voice or anything that can be traced back to me made public. I can only imagine the pompous old farts at the museums getting a hold of the recording. It would destroy my career. I'd be a laughingstock. Who would trust a psychic to authenticate artifacts?

"Who else would listen to this recording? I'm not comfortable having my voice on it."

For several silent seconds, he looks at me with those mismatched eyes. "It would be for my ears only."

"What guarantees do I have that this recording won't make it into the news or social media and that my name won't be dragged all over?" Why am I even considering this?

"You have my word." This is the first time he doesn't look at me with some variation of disdain.

His promise lodges itself under my skin. I have no reason to believe him, but I do. He saved my life once, and something inside me says he would risk his own to save me again if it ever came down to it.

"But I don't know you. Or the worth of your word. What I do know is that my job and my career would be on the line should any of this information, and my involvement in helping you, be made public."

His lips press into a thin line when I challenge him. "Miss Bloom, it's not only *your* career on the line here. Taking advice from psychics is not exactly respect-earning in my line of work."

I want to tell him I'm not a psychic, but that's not entirely true. I hate the negative connotation that comes with it. Images of sideshows on fairs and boardwalks come to mind.

I drag in a deep breath. "I don't think it's the same."

He drops the pen on top of the yellow pad. "Why not?"

"I'm a historian. I deal with facts, proof, and tests. If word of this . . . *ability* got out, it would have consequences for my career. Everything I did, all the years I put into my job, would be doubted. They would ostracize me. I want to help you find whoever killed that woman, but I can't be publicly involved."

He stands, hands bracing his weight on the desk, reduces the space between us, and traps my gaze with his own. I could not escape him if I tried.

"I'm a detective. I deal with facts, proof, and tests. If word got out that I have a psychic giving me tips on a case, it would have consequences for *my* career. Everything I did, all the years I put into my job, would be doubted." He throws my words back in my face and sits down. "I'm willing to take that risk to find this woman. To protect other lives."

The room temperature drops to freezing under that stare. I suppress a shiver.

We glare at each other in a silent war. I nod my agreement very much against my better judgment. Nothing happens by chance. There's a reason I'm here, right now.

He pushes the record button again. "Today is Monday, June twenty. Please state your name and tell me what happened. Start from the beginning."

I close my eyes, gather myself, and step back to this morning. The images are fresh in my mind. I look at him again. "My name is Avalon Bloom. My friend Lynn Reynolds and I were having breakfast at a coffee shop and saw an antique store across the street."

"A Stop in Time," he confirms.

"Yes. We finished our food and went into the store. Walked around for a few minutes until I saw the necklace." I hesitate. Here comes the hard part.

He waves his hand at me. "Go on."

I swallow. "It was in a glass case, and I asked to see it."

"Why did you want to see this particular necklace?"

"I was drawn to it. It's hard to explain. I felt a powerful pull toward it and had to touch it."

"Is this strong pull something you feel often?" His voice softens, inviting me to open up to him. An eyebrow rises with the question.

I inhale through my nose, delaying the answer for a few seconds. "Yes, I've had this ability my entire life. I don't question it."

His head dips once in a silent push for me to continue.

I swallow the nervous knot trying to tie itself around my vocal cords. "As soon as I touched the necklace, the images started."

He leans in. "Images?"

"Images, visions. Call it what you want. It's all the same to me." My voice rises a bit. His lips twitch, and he cocks an eyebrow again. Is that amusement? Is he entertained by my irritation?

I roll my lips together. "Have you ever heard the term psychometry, Detective?"

He stares at me for several seconds and then shakes his head in slow motion as if it costs him a vital body part to admit he doesn't know the meaning of the word.

"A little louder, Detective. For the recording because I don't think it can capture head shakes." My smile is all teeth and promises of biting back.

His eyes narrow. "No, I'm not familiar with the term psychometry."

"In simple terms, psychometry is the ability to sense or read the history of an object by touching it."

He sits back, tapping the pen on the desk. "So you can go around and touch anything and tell the history of that object? What happened to it? To whom it belongs?"

"Yes and no. It's not as simple as that." My hands tremble, and I press them into my thighs, fingers spread wide.

He props his elbows on the desk and laces his fingers, tapping them to his chin. "Explain."

I prepare myself for a sneer or condescending remark, but neither comes. His head tilts, and interest shines in his eyes.

Lynn shifts in her seat, squirming like a kid eager to raise her hand and shout the answer.

"Objects, people, plants, animals, everything is made of energy."

His eyes shift to the side as if he's trying to curb an eye roll.

"This is not my opinion. This is quantum physics. This is what the universe is made of. Matter, dark matter, and energy. You can look it up on your own time." I didn't call him any names, but the asshole at the end is implied.

I hold his gaze for a long moment before speaking again. "Objects hold the energy of the person they belong to—some more than others—jewelry, stones, metal objects like coins or a letter opener. Even pictures can hold that energy. The amount of energy is directly related to how often the person held or wore it. But also, by the situations in which the object was involved."

He frowns. "Situations?"

"Yes, an object involved in a traumatic situation is likely to hold more energy. The more energy an object holds, the easier it is to read."

The detective looks at the necklace nested in the jewelry box. "So something like this necklace that the owner wore often would be easier to read."

"Exactly. And that necklace was also part of a traumatic event. It holds the last impressions of the owner and the man who killed her because he held it while he strangled her. Normally just touching an object briefly would not leave that person's imprint on it, but in this case, because of the violence and the intensity of his feelings, I got them both. At the end, I saw what happened through his eyes."

He pushes the recorder closer to me. "Tell me everything."

And I do. I reach for the box and take the necklace out. He moves like he's going to stop me and then sits back. I close my eyes and shield myself against the onslaught of emotions. I'm better prepared now that I know what to expect.

The images come again, more vivid somehow. Less gray, more colorful. I repeat everything I told Lynn and more. Some details become clearer as I speak. When I open my eyes and look at him, his face is expressionless. He's a mask of self-control. His eyes are as cold as ice. I set the necklace back in the box. A shiver runs down my spine. The little hairs on my arms rise. I rub my palms against them to erase the sensation.

"Where were you on the night of June fifteen?" His words are casual sounding and yet measured.

"June fifteen?" That was a week ago. "I was in London."

"For how long?"

"London itself, five days."

"And before that?"

"Paris. I was in Paris for four days. London for five days and after London, I went to Amsterdam for a day. I came back last Friday, the seventeenth."

"Vacation?"

"No, work."

"Can you prove it?"

"Yes, I can prove it. There are stamps on my passport, hotel reservations in my name, people I met."

"Here," Lynn says, shoving her cell phone across his desk. "See, she sent me this picture from London Bridge."

He looks at the picture. And I know what he's seeing. Me, wearing a gray pencil skirt and a white blouse. Black Louboutin heels. I look older and more sophisticated in that picture. I need to. It's hard enough being much younger than the other art curators, but to also be female? Well, that's just too many strikes against the old boys' club. If it wasn't for Grandma having paved the way for me, I would have never had the chances and opportunities so early in my career. He looks back at me, at what I'm wearing. Cutoff jeans shorts, a Metallica T-shirt, and sneakers. Real-life me and work me are worlds apart.

"That picture could have been taken at any time."

"Why do you want to know where I was, anyway?" I know the answer as soon as the words are out of my mouth. How could I have been so naïve? "You think I had something to do with the murder?"

"I didn't say that. And this isn't a murder investigation. This is a missing person investigation." His poor excuse of a denial doesn't put me at ease.

"But you do. You don't believe a word I said. You think I'm involved somehow." He doesn't deny it. "Does that thing work?" I point at the computer on his desk. "Can you access the internet on it?"

He gazes at me for longer than necessary before turning to the monitor and tapping on the keyboard. The machine comes to life after several seconds. No background picture, just a boring, solid dark blue color.

"Go to Google," I order. An eyebrow pops up, and he waits an extra second in defiance. Then, he opens a browser and goes to Google.

"Type in London, British Museum, my name, and June fifteen."

Google does its magic, and several hits show on the screen.

"Click on the first one." It's an article showing the unveiling of a new Egyptian exhibit. In the first picture on top of the page, you can see me along with several other important names in archeology. Our names are tagged in the article. He reads it. Looks at the picture and back at me. Looks at what I'm wearing again. The lack of makeup and the completely different version of me in front of him.

"How old are you?"

I don't see why it matters. I look younger than I am, so this is a question I get a lot. Especially dressed like this. "Twenty-eight. And you?"

He ignores my question. "What exactly is it you do?"

"I'm a curator and authenticator. I work with museums worldwide, examining ancient artifacts. I organize exhibits, assist the local curators, sometimes work as a liaison between different museums."

Lynn's chest poofs out like a proud mama hen. "She's lowballing you. She's a double major in Art History and Archeology with a master's in Historic Preservation."

"Lynn." I try to stop her. After Grandma, my best friend is my biggest cheerleader.

"But that's nothing. Ava was already working with museums all over the world when she was a teenager." There's no stopping Lynn.

He tilts his head back and raises his brows above those mesmerizing eyes. "Is that so? You were working all over the world as a teen? Even before you got all the fancy degrees?"

His response drips with sarcasm. He may not have said it out loud, but the word liar coats everything he said.

I dig my nails into my palms and control the urge to throw something at him. Assaulting a police officer would not make a good entry on my résumé. "Yes, my grandmother worked with these same museums. I just followed in her footsteps. She paved the way for me. When she retired, it was a natural progression for me to take over since I learned everything I know from her."

He stares me down. Glances at the computer screen and back at me. "Do you have any siblings?"

"No, I'm an only child. What does it have to do with anything?" I don't even bother to mask the exasperation in my voice. "Oh, I get it. You think I'm impersonating someone. That I can't possibly be the person I say I am? Why? Because I'm not dressed the same way as in those pictures?" I point at the monitor.

He turns off the recorder. The corner of his lip twitches again. He *is* enjoying my irritation. Am I a joke to him? Did any of this get through to him, or is he just humoring me now?

I dig into my purse, pull out my wallet, and then my driver's license. If it weren't for the desk between us, I would shove it into his face. As it is, I hold my arm straight, the plastic ID a foot away from him.

He looks at my license before taking it from me, his fingertips grazing mine for the briefest of moments. My entire body goes on alert. Shivers start at the back of my hand, and like a tidal wave, run up my arm and all over my skin. I look at him, searching for a reaction. Did he feel that surge of energy, or is it one-sided? There's a slight tremble in the hand holding my ID. But his body is completely still, as if he's holding his breath.

I've felt this before—this overwhelming sense of unrest and recognition, like an old memory trying to come to the surface. It also happened the first time I crossed paths with the detective fifteen years ago. The day he rescued me and breathed life into me again.

CHAPTER 4
AVALON

I suck in air, and his gaze lifts to mine. The jolt of electricity still dances on my skin. He looks away after a heartbeat. Did he feel that too? Or is it just me?

If the detective is aware of my inner turmoil as his fingers fly on the keyboard, he doesn't show it.

He has the perfect poker face. He's checking my driver's license, but he won't find anything nefarious. I've never even had a parking ticket.

He returns the license—his face is a mask. If he's disappointed or relieved for not finding anything, I can't tell.

His gaze lands on Lynn next.

She squirms in her seat, then squares her shoulders and raises an eyebrow. "I guess you want to check my license, too. See if I have any prior arrests? Speeding tickets? Sorry to disappoint, but you won't find anything on me either."

She bats her eyelashes at him in such an exaggerated way. I snort and then cough to cover it up. I didn't fool him, though. His eyes narrow on me. Guilt prickles at my conscience, and I look away. This is no laughing matter. A girl is dead at the hands of some psycho. *Maybe even more than one girl,* a voice whispers in my mind. And it seems I might have the only clue to the murder.

He takes Lynn's driver's license and checks it on the computer. Like mine, he gets nothing. But that's because Lynn has the incredible ability to avoid tickets with that sexy girl routine of hers, while I always follow the rules.

The detective clears his throat and returns the license to Lynn.

He taps the necklace box with his pen again. "I'll have to keep this. We need to test it for prints and confirm with the family that this is the same necklace in the picture."

I shrug. "I figured as much. But my prints will be on it. And possibly the store clerk, too."

"I'll check into the store myself." He says this as if he doubts my account of where I got the necklace.

"Can we go now?" I may have phrased that as a question, but I wasn't asking for his permission.

His eyes narrow. "I'll need your phone numbers. You two need to be available for contact in case I have other questions."

I give him a business card with my number and email on it. "My information is here."

He takes the card, looks at it, and gives it back to me. "Write your friend's number on it, too."

I want to refuse, but I don't. I write Lynn's number on the back of the card and give it back to him. He takes it, checks the back, and sets it to the side. "Your IDs say you two live in New York. Where are you staying?"

"We have an apartment in the Seahaven building by the beach." I exchange a look with Lynn. An entire conversation passes between us in a fraction of a second. My apology for dragging her into this mess and her seeing it as some exciting adventure.

He leans back in his chair. "How long are you here for?"

"We have the summer off, so it could be a couple of weeks. Maybe more, maybe less. The apartment belongs to a friend of my grandmother and is on loan to us for as long as we need it. We don't really have a fixed plan."

He frowns. "Please don't leave town without talking to me first."

"Listen. I won't mince words. I know you think I had something to do with the murder—"

"Missing person," he corrects me.

"I already told you everything I know. I can't help you. I can't tell you any more than I already did. I didn't have to come here and do this. But something tells me that poor girl is not this man's first victim, and she won't be the last. I hope the information I gave will help you get the guy. But we're not killers."

I get up and push the chair back. Lynn starts to follow me.

"We're done here."

"Sit down, Miss Bloom. You will sit and comply, unless you want to spend the night in a nice little cell out back." His voice is harsh and clipped.

I hold my ground. "You have no reason to hold me. You have nothing that ties me to your case."

"I have this." He points to the necklace. "And your confession to a murder."

Lynn gasps.

My heart skips a beat. He's fishing. Trying to rattle me. "Murder? You're crazy. A second ago, it was a missing person. I wasn't even in the country on the date you mentioned."

"Your friend was. Maybe you have an accomplice. I don't know. But I will find out how you got the necklace and how you know so much about this girl."

"I already told you how."

"Ah, yes." He makes air quotes. "You're psychic." His tone couldn't be more condescending.

I lock my knees and fist my hands around my purse strap. "I don't know what games you're playing, acting all casual one second and like a jerk the next, but this one-man good-cop-bad-cop act will not hold. You've got nothing, and you know it. Yes, you can try to intimidate me, dig around, try to push me and scare me, but here's the thing you don't know about me. I've been dealing with much bigger assholes than you my entire life. You have a lot to live up to."

He scowls.

Lynn tugs at my shirt. Damn it. I dragged her into this mess, too.

"Ava, you're gonna have to show him. He needs proof."

Proof. The last thing I want to do is show him anything—to perform like a circus monkey for his entertainment. You know what? I'll gladly play this game. I can't wait to wipe that smug, condescending look out of his face.

I sit back down. "Okay, then. Give me something."

His eyes scrunch. "What?"

I wave my fingers in a come-on motion. "Give me something. Any object, and I'll read it for you."

He leans away. "I don't need a reading."

"No, you don't. What you need is proof. Because you don't believe anything I've said. But I'll happily change that." I smile the fakest smile I can manage.

He swivels the chair back and forth. His shoulders are stiff. He huffs. Then opens a desk drawer and grabs something from it. Something small enough that it fits in his closed hand. He holds it out for me and opens his hand. In the center sits a small gray river rock with a white stripe through the middle, smooth, flat, and a nearly perfect circle.

I open my hand, and he drops it into my palm. At once, the images start, and I close my eyes. Smile. He's been carrying this rock with him for most of his life. I see a progression of images. A timeline of events.

"You're seven or eight years old. You're fishing with an older man. He gave you the rock to skip on the lake, but you wanted to keep it instead because of the way the rock looks. He has a full head of white hair. He's your grandfather, and he's wearing an old baseball hat. It used to be black but now it's gray and sun-bleached. The fishing pole has your initials carved into it. Three letters. JHK. You love spending time with him more than anything."

The images leap. He's older now. "You're fourteen. And at a funeral . . ." I'm overwhelmed by the sense of loss and emptiness. The urge to cry stings my throat, and I squeeze my eyes to stop the tears. "Your grandfather died. A man yells at you to stop crying. It's your . . . father? He says men don't cry. You're not allowed to grieve."

Devil's eyes. That's what his father called him. What a horrible thing for a father to do to his own child. His father is not a good man.

I drag in a breath. "You try to put the rock in the coffin with him, but someone stops you. A woman. She's your grandmother. She tells you that Pops would want you to keep it with you always, for luck and to remember him and the good times."

A squeak from his chair is the only other sound in the room.

"You're older, maybe sixteen, and at a high school baseball game. You're anxious and waiting for someone. A girl. And a first kiss." I smile at this.

"You carry this rock with you everywhere you go. You keep it on the night table at home, and you touch it every night before you go to sleep."

The images leap again. Several years. "You're in the military. They discharged you with honors and just came back home—"

A crashing sound rips me off the vision, and I open my eyes, but the images still play in my mind, like a film in the background.

His chair is flipped and lying on the floor. He's standing, his arm stretched and hand open in wait.

"That's enough." His voice is rough and terse.

I place the rock on his palm, and he returns it to the drawer.

We stare at each other. I didn't tell him everything I saw. I kept what I saw about his little sister to myself. I wish I could feel smug about putting him in his place, but the weight and guilt he feels for the loss of his sister isn't something to feel smug about. He carries so much pain. For his sister, his mother, and never measuring up to his father, never a kind word from that cruel man—the images of what he had to endure still flash in the back of my mind. How could anyone see evil in his eyes? I see only beauty. Sky and sea. But also hope and despair.

"Okay!" Lynn claps her hands and snaps me out of my trance. She stands up. "Now that we got that out of the way, and he's a believer, can we go?" She tries to steer me to the door.

The detective doesn't move, and neither do I. When he

does, he rubs a hand over his chest and turns his back to me. His breaths are shallow, and his hands have a slight tremble. He fists them. A much more muted version of his pain reaches out to me like invisible fingers, a subtle and dissipating connection.

He faces me again. His careful mask of indifference has cracked. Raw pain darkens his face. His jaw ticks with the effort he makes to pull it all in and reassemble his features back to what they were before.

I can't stop staring at him, at his momentary loss of control, and the vulnerability in his eyes. It speaks to something inside me, my own loss, pain, and fears. And the mask I, too, keep in place.

CHAPTER 5
JAKE

WHAT THE FUCK.

My heart is running laps in my chest. That familiar hollowness echoes with the memory of all I lost and what she voiced. I don't understand. How could she know any of it just by touching a rock? I open my hands and flex my fingers, try to suck air into my lungs, but it seems to be stuck in my throat.

I don't believe this shit. There's no psychic power, no visions, no ghosts, and sure as hell, none of this crap. If there were, Pops would have found a way to save Emily.

The room is closing in on me. I need space. I pick up the chair, set it aright, and shove it back until it hits the wall with a soft thud. I take a step to the side and keep some distance between the wacko and myself. Push the hair falling over my forehead off my face. It flops back in defiance. "It's not possible."

"And I spoke too soon." The friend plops back in her chair. "He's not a believer."

The crazy woman heaves a deep breath, and her shoulders rise with the motion. "Were my descriptions accurate?"

I press my lips together rather than give her an answer. I'd sooner bite my tongue off than confirm the things she said. I was fooled by this bullshit once. Never again.

Her chin juts out. "Denial doesn't make it any less real."

I say nothing.

Her head shakes with minuscule movements, and she releases a breath. "We could do this all day. You could give me object after object, and I could read them for you, and you would still believe it's some kind of trick."

She gets up, grabs her purse, and hitches the strap over her shoulder. "Let's go, Lynn. We're done here." There's disappointment in her voice. And for some reason, I care.

Her friend gets up and follows her to the door, and I'm still stunned into silence.

Miss Bloom stops at the door and opens it. Small, delicate fingers hold the edge. She lets her friend go out first, then leaves. A second later, she pops her head back in—messy brown hair falls around her shoulders.

"It doesn't have to be like this, you know. Whatever preconceived ideas or beliefs you may have, I'm not it." She closes the door quietly.

Did she see that too? Did she see my reason for not believing?

I drop to my chair. But it's no longer there because I pushed it out of the way. The ground meets my ass, but not before my flailing arms knock more papers to the floor.

"Fuuuuck!"

I get to my knees, and the first thing I see is the necklace she left behind. I'll send it to forensics, but I know they won't find any prints on it. At least no prints other than Ava's—

Miss Bloom's—or the store owner. Every other piece of evidence we found before was wiped clean.

"Jesus! What am I doing?" This is the first break I've had in months. I have to stop her. I search for my sunglasses, but I can't find them. I hate the stares, the squinting, and questions that come with the realization I have different-colored eyes. "Fuck it. They already saw my eyes."

CHAPTER 6

AVALON

"WHAT AN ASS." THE EARLY SYMPATHY THAT FILLED ME during the detective's vision burned to ashes.

"Yes, he has a great ass."

I roll my eyes at Lynn. "That's not what I said."

"That's what I heard." She waggles her eyebrows.

Even in the middle of a worst-case scenario, I can count on her for comic relief. "I envy your ability to find humor in everything."

Lynn shrugs. "That's how I deal with stress."

We get back to my car, and I dig in my purse for the key fob. The jingle of metal against metal comes from the other side of the car. Lynn holds my key chain. She lobs them into a wide arch over the hood. I step back to catch them and bump into a hard-muscled chest. A hand that's not mine catches the key fob over my head. I turn to see who the thief is.

The detective.

What the hell? I step away from him with an extended arm, palm up, and wiggle my fingers.

He closes his hands around the fob, enclosing them

tightly in his fist, and glances away before returning his gaze to me.

"Listen. I don't know what happened back there . . ." He squeezes the back of his neck with his free hand.

Day-old stubble shadows his square jaw. Glints of gold highlights in his hair make it look more blond than brown. He's what one could call jaw-dropingly handsome. He reminds me of a young Robert Redford or Harrison Ford—two of Grandma's favorite actors. I miss spending time with her and watching old movies.

"But I need you to do it again." His voice comes out as if someone is strangling him. As if it costs him to say the words out loud.

Of everything he could have said, this is the last thing I expected. "W-What?"

His free hand goes through his hair, pushing the strands away, only to have them fall back on his forehead.

I have the strangest urge to brush his hair away from his face. My fingers twitch with the need, and I curl them into a fist. What the hell? I should have the need to punch him for being a jerk, not to pet him.

"I must be fucking insane," he says under a breath. "Okay." Both his hands come up, my key chain dangling from one of them. "I can't believe I'm saying this, but can you do the psychometry thing again? With something else?"

I cross my arms. "You've got to be kidding me."

"That means yes. She can do it again." This comes from Lynn, who is still standing on the other side of my car.

"Lynn!"

She walks around the bumper and puts both hands on my shoulders in a side hug.

"What do you need Ava to put her hands on, Detective?" Lynn smiles. "She'll be happy to touch all the things."

I push her off me with my elbow. I'm going to wipe that smile right off her face—with my fist.

The poor detective blinks at her. Lynn has mastered the art of standing on the line between deadly serious and overtly flirtatious. One can never tell if she's being polite or a tease.

His gaze is back on me. "Three women went missing in the last six months. All three disappeared without a trace and no clues as to what happened to them. That necklace and your . . . visions are the closest things I have to a lead."

"How often does something like this happens?"

"For us, not often at all, and when it does, it's usually a runaway teen, and we find them in a day or two."

"Three missing women? Isn't that a lot?"

"Currently, there are reports of thirty-five missing persons for the whole state. Is it a lot for us? Maybe. For a state like California, which has over two thousand missing persons this year alone, no. It varies by location."

Wow. "I had no idea so many people go missing. How come we don't see this on the news? Shouldn't everyone be talking about it?"

He shakes his head. "More than six hundred thousand people go missing every year in the US alone. Each state has its own procedures, and within the states, the towns handle those cases differently, too. Unless it's a child, someone who's mentally or physically impaired or in need of medical attention, or there's suspicion of a crime, there isn't much that can be done. Being missing is not a crime."

"So, nothing happens? That's crazy. No one is really looking for them?"

His eyes go hard. "I am. I'm looking for them."

A shiver runs down my spine. I clear my throat. "Are the three women local?"

"Two are from here. The other is from a couple of towns over."

"And you have no idea what happened to them."

A muscle ticks in his jaw. "No, and that's why I need your help."

My defenses are cracking. God, what if there are more? What if I see something that can help him? Help the women? "What do you need help with?"

He looks around before speaking again and lowers his voice. "I need to know if you can do the same with other objects. If you had access to some objects that belonged to the missing women, do you think you might find out more?"

"I can—if the objects have something to show me. That's not always the case. Or the objects might hold images that have no bearing on what happened to the owner at all."

"It's worth a try." He looks away again, hands on his trim waist, and then nods to himself. "I can't pay you for it. The department would never approve, but you would do the missing women and me a huge favor if you could give it a shot with the touching thing . . ."

Lynn grabs my arm. "Your first case. I've always told you that you should do this."

True. She has told me to work with the police dozens of times. Hundreds even. "Lynn, this is not an Alex Cross book and I'm not changing careers."

I turn to the detective, tilting my head up to meet those mismatched eyes, even more startling and beautiful in the sunlight. "What do you have in mind?"

"Before you say yes, you need to know that doing this wouldn't be exactly . . . legal."

Not legal? If anyone at my job finds out . . . apprehension skitters across my chest like a bug and I squash it. "How not legal are we talking about? Get yelled at illegal? Or get thrown in jail illegal?"

He presses his lips together and then exhales. "The second one."

"Let me get this straight. You want me to help with your case, and doing so would be illegal because . . ." I wave my hand.

He shoves his hands in his jeans pockets. My fob with it. "Technically, it could be said it's tampering with evidence."

My eyes widen. I'm not up on all the laws involving evidence, but I have watched enough cop shows to know that's a serious offense. "You can't be serious." There's a swarm of bugs in my chest now. "Don't the police use consultants all the time? I thought as long as the evidence has already been processed, detectives can sign it out and show it to consultants or people they're interviewing."

"That's true. We can bring in an expert for certain cases, but a psychic is not an expert."

"And yet you expect me to do this?"

He curses under his breath. "I know what I'm asking is a lot to deal with, but I'm desperate enough to try anything. Even this touch psychometry thing." He says psychometry as if the word has teeth, and it bites his tongue.

Great! He's trying to get me to do some illegal shit, and he's not even a believer.

"You're right. This is a lot to ask of me. It's not just the fact that it's"—I step closer to him and lower my voice—"illegal. But it's also my name and career on the line."

His hands go deeper into his pockets, and my gaze tracks the movement. This is so not the time for me to notice how muscular his thighs look in those jeans or the bulge behind the zipper. I snap my gaze up.

His head dips. "You don't know me—you have no reason to trust me or help me. I get that. But I'm asking you to do this anyway. I need to find them, and I need to find the man doing this and stop him before another girl goes missing. And if she's dead, as you say, odds are the other two are also dead. The families of these women need closure, and they need to know the guy who did this to their loved ones won't do it to anyone else."

I stare at him. I can't believe I'm even considering doing this. I'm not a cop. I should just walk away. But his words get to me. If I can use my gift to save someone, isn't that much more important than dating some old piece of pottery? And he saved my life . . . even if he doesn't remember me. I might be the only thing between the next girl and death.

I square my shoulders. I don't want to let him know I'll help just yet. "Hypothetically, if—and this is a big if—I was to help you. How would we go about this?"

He smiles at me like I'm a cute puppy, and he wants to pat me on the head. "We have one thing on our side. My office also doubles as the evidence room. All the evidence for open cases is locked up in my office."

My nose scrunches. "Aren't you supposed to have special rooms for that? With locked doors and someone to sign stuff in and out?"

"In a big city with a big police department, yes. In a small town like ours with a small police force, no. We have a space where evidence for cold cases is stored. But all current case evidence stays in my office. I'm the only detective in our department and the person in charge of any and all evidence for anything that happens in this town. Everything goes through me."

Well, that's convenient. "Is that normal? To be a jack-of-all-trades like that?"

"Again, what's normal in a big city doesn't apply here. Small towns with small budgets and not a lot of crime make do with what they have. It's common for evidence to be in an office or even a locker."

This is crazy. "Why isn't everyone freaking out about it? What's happening to all those missing people?" I gesture toward the picturesque buildings, flowerpots in every corner, and baskets hanging from old-fashioned lampposts.

He inhales, his chest expanding with the deep breath. Then exhales. "The majority leave on their own, or at least that's what the statistics say. But I don't think this is true for these three women."

"I can't believe more people aren't talking about it."

"You might see speculation in local papers from time to time. But with adults, it gets less attention than when a child goes missing. And people have short memories. Something else happens, and that's where the focus goes."

So, this is it. I'm his last resort. "How long would you need my help?"

"That depends on you and what you find out—maybe a week or two?"

"Two weeks?" My voice goes high.

"We have the time," Lynn pipes in, ever so helpful.

I give her a warning look and turn back to the detective. "Why would it take two weeks to look at some evidence?"

"It takes time for me to follow up on whatever you find out."

Okay, that makes sense. "How would you justify my

presence? Wouldn't people ask questions if we keep going back in there again?" I gesture toward the building.

Lynn steps closer. "Oh, I know."

The detective crosses his arms over his chest and fixes his attention on Lynn.

"You can be his girlfriend." She claps her hands, shoulders lifting nearly to her ears, and smiles.

"What?" My voice rises again. I press my lips together to keep from saying something I don't want him to know. She's trying to set me up with him.

The detective's only reaction is a raised eyebrow.

Lynn puts both her hands up. "Stop. Listen to me."

I take a deep breath. I know my best friend is crazy, but her ideas usually have a way of working out.

"Okay." I exhale. All the air exits my lungs, and my shoulders drop. "I'll listen."

"If we—you keep going back there to look at stuff, it will look suspicious and raise questions. But if you two were dating, and you stopped by during lunch and brought your boyfriend a sandwich, well, no one would think much of it. And since the evidence is in his office and that door has a lock . . ."

Damn it! She has a point.

The detective has one arm crossed over his stomach while rubbing his bottom lip with his free hand. Back and forth that thumb goes, his gaze lost in thought. He blinks, and his eyes find mine. His hand freezes, thumb pressed into his lip, creating a dimple. I can't stop staring.

He clears his throat, and his hands go to his back pockets.

I drag my gaze from his face, from that mouth, from those eyes, and glare at Lynn. "Except his wife or girlfriend won't be too happy about that. You didn't think of that when you turned him into Detective Cheater, did you, *Lynn?*" *Please be single.*

He shakes his head. "I don't have a wife or a girlfriend."

It's hard to believe that a guy with his looks is single. "Oh, you have a boyfriend." Oh my God. What's wrong with me? Stop talking.

He looks at me, both eyebrows raised. "No, I'm not gay. Just not seeing anyone right now."

Shit! My face heats. I squeeze my eyes shut and run a hand over my face. I can't believe I said that out loud. "Sorry, I'm a little stressed right now." My voice comes out in a mousy squeak. "I didn't mean to be rude. It's been a day . . ."

An amused smirk softens his features. "This could work. Maybe don't say girlfriend outright. There would be questions, but a friend who's visiting for a while . . ."

"From college!" Lynn adds. "A friend with benefits from college." She nods in agreement with herself.

My fingers curl around an imaginary neck. I'm going to kill her.

He returns my key fob. "Are you free around five tomorrow afternoon?"

I glance at Lynn, and she nods. "I am."

He dips his head. "I'll be in touch."

CHAPTER 7
AVALON

"Ava? Ava? It's the middle of the afternoon. Wakey-wake!"

Lynn's voice, followed by a light tapping on my shoulder, drags me from my slumber. Hmm. I guess I fell asleep. The visions yesterday took a bigger toll than I expected. I slept like a rock through the night too.

He didn't text me yesterday or this morning. I'm mildly disappointed. I don't know what I was expecting. He probably already dismissed everything I said. That's for the best—even if he's the guy I've dreamed about for half of my life. We are so completely different. If I go down that road, I'll get my hopes up and get invested, and then what? Go back to my life in New York and never see him again?

"Man, going to the beach this morning knocked you out."

I stretch. I didn't tell her I'm still recovering from the toll the visions took on me. "I had fun, and the weather was perfect." I try to blink away my stupor and reach for the water bottle on the night table between our beds. With the first sip come flashes of a dream. I'm back at that beach in North

Carolina where Jake saved my life. His mouth is on mine. He's kissing me. But I'm not a teen anymore, and he's not a young man either. It is us as we are now. A shiver skitters from the base of my head down my spine. A frisson takes up residence in my chest. I'm not averse to the idea of kissing him, not at all. I'll have to tell him who I am eventually, but not yet. When the time is right.

Lynn sits on the bed across from mine. "You slept a long time."

"How long was I out?"

"Almost two hours."

I rub my face, trying to wipe away the last dregs of sleep. I hate afternoon naps. It always leaves me groggy and disorientated for a while. "What time is it?"

She reaches for her phone. "Two-fifty-two. The detective texted you. You were sleeping, so I answered for you. He'll be here at five. You have two hours to shower and get ready for your—"

"It is not a date."

"Meeting with the detective," she continues as if she intended to say *meeting* all along.

She pulls her legs up on the bed. "Can we talk about him now that you had a whole day to process everything?"

She knows me too well. All morning she pestered me about this "date" with the detective and what I'm going to wear. As irritating as it was, it did help to get me out of my own head. "Yeah, I'd like to."

"How are you feeling?"

I let her question wash over me and search through my web of emotions, separating what is real from my perceptions and expectations. I have not given myself a chance to really feel and delve into the meaning of meeting him after so many years and under these circumstances. Is it really him? A part of me doubts it—the part that's afraid to believe I finally met him again after all these years. He didn't recognize me. But how could he? For him, I was a kid, and he had to have been nineteen or twenty. Probably doesn't even remember saving me at all. Surfers rescue people all the time, don't they? I read somewhere that they save as many lives as lifeguards.

I close my eyes and give in to everything that happened yesterday. Breathe.

I open them again. "I feel . . . ready. Whatever may happen, I'm ready for it."

She rolls her eyes at my evasive response. "That's not what I asked."

I know that's not what she asked. "A little confused—excited—I want to see him again and make sure I didn't hallucinate the whole thing."

"You know you didn't. I mean, I'm sure there are other people in the world with eyes like his, but it's him, right? You're sure of that?"

"I'm sure. It's more than the eyes. It's his face too. And the tingles."

Her eyes widen. "The tingles?"

"It's hard to explain. It's almost like when I touch an object and can see its history. When his fingers brushed against mine, I got that same feeling of knowing."

A pillow flies across the space between the beds and smacks me in the face.

"You had tingles and didn't tell me!"

I laugh and put my hands up when she reaches for another pillow. "When did I have a chance to tell you? I'm telling you now."

She puts the pillow on her lap and props her elbows on it. "Please describe in detail."

I laugh again. "It's like a shiver, but more intense, almost like a low voltage electric shock. But not unpleasant. It doesn't hurt."

She tilts her head down and pouts. "I want tingles. I've never had tingles before."

"You're doing pretty well without them. But they will come. I'm sure you'll get your own personal Lynn version of tingles."

"Are you going to tell him you're the girl he saved fifteen years ago?"

My stomach twists with knots and butterflies at the same time. "When the time is right."

She looks down, her hands twisting the fabric on the pillow. "Are you really going to help him?" Her voice loses the excitement from before.

I take a deep breath. "If I say no, I might not see him again. And then there are the missing women. If I can help find them, I need to. I could never live with myself knowing I had a chance to stop this guy from killing again and didn't take it. So, yes, I'll help him. I have to."

The emotional dam cracks, and I burst into tears. That girl and the horrifying way she died. I've been blocking the images since yesterday. A muted version of everything she felt assaults me. My heart races as if trying to escape my chest. I'm paralyzed with fear so intense it's hard to breathe. She held on to a glimmer of hope the entire time. There was so much light in her. She believed she'd survive this even through the terror, even as she took her last painful, strangled breath.

I gasp for air. The press of phantom hands around my throat robs me of breath. My chest locks up. My mouth opens, and I try to suck in non-exiting oxygen. I experience her death again. I'm both the observer and her—*Alice*—I know her name now.

Lynn's panicked and distant voice reaches to me, her hands on my shoulders, trying to shake me out of the vision. But the images won't let go. Not until she's dead, the light gone from her eyes and the horror she went through etched on her face. Alice is no more.

Air fills my lungs, and I choke on it. A water bottle presses into my hands, and I take greedy gulps. I stand up. Rub my hands on the back of my head and neck. Flicker my fingers as if trying to get rid of cobwebs. I mentally cut the cords that connect me to Alice. Close my eyes and regulate my breathing. Push the images away. Separate myself from what happened to her.

When I open my eyes again, it's not just Lynn and me in the room anymore. A chill sinks into my skin, like death running its icy fingers down my spine. Well, this is new.

Alice is here, too.

A gray wisp.

A faded version of her former self.

Her lips move, and she says a single word. "Help."

One may not think of stabbing as an intimate act, but it is. You have to be close. Close enough to touch, to smell, to taste. You'd think there would be a lot of blood.

And there is, but not at first. Not until I pull the knife out. It's like a crack in the wall of a dam. Slow at first, as if the body is denying the inevitable. But then, with the second stab, there's a complete splintering. It is never as good as the first, but still sweet enough to make me want to go back for more. The metallic scent of blood filling the air, coloring my hand, coating my tongue. It's a thing of beauty, all that crimson liquid spreading, dripping to the floor, like a blooming flower of death.

CHAPTER 8
AVALON

THE GHOSTLY IMAGE DISAPPEARS. IT DOESN'T VANISH AS much as it dissipates, like fog in the wind. My shivers subside.

This is not the first time I've seen a spirit, but it is the first time one has asked me for help.

My eyes fix on the empty spot. I look at the floor, half expecting to see muddy footprints.

"What is it?" Lynn's hands press into mine. She stares at the vacant space too. Then blanches. "I-is there something in there?" Her voice trembles.

"There was…"

Shudders rattle her from head to toe. She steps away from me and rubs her arms. "No. Stop it. Nope. No, no, no. Please tell me it's not what I think it is."

"If you're thinking of a ghost, then yes. It was the girl from my visions." *Help*. Alice asked for help. There's no turning my back now. I need to assist Jake in finding whoever killed her.

Lynn whimpers. "I don't want to see dead people, and I don't know why you're not terrified of them."

I shrug. "Because there's nothing to fear. Spirits are always around. They can't hurt us. Seeing them is part of the gift. You like the other stuff I do. It comes with the package."

"Yes, but that's cool. Dead people, not so much." She walks back, shaking her hands as if it could get rid of her heebie-jeebies, and sits next to me. Bumps into my shoulder. "You okay?"

I shift and look at her. "Yeah. Just tired." Weariness digs into my bones and my limbs weigh a thousand pounds.

"Maybe you should cancel your"—her eyes go wide—"meeting with the detective."

I shake my head. She's impossible. "No. I need to do this. I need to help him find this girl. The sooner he finds her, the sooner I can put all of this behind me."

"Us. You're not alone in this. I may not have all your woo-woo mojo, but I'll stand with you, no matter what."

"Thanks, friend."

She squeezes my hand. "Are you going to tell him about the gho—about what you saw?"

She can't even say the word. I snort. "Yes. No reason to hide it. He already thinks I'm crazy. May as well go all in."

Her eyes narrow. "He doesn't think you're crazy."

"He doesn't think I'm normal either."

"Who needs normal when they can have you?" She gestures at me. "A strong, intelligent, and beautiful woman. And what's normal anyway? Normal for you is not normal for me. And vice versa."

I smile at her.

Lynn gives me a light push. "Why don't you go shower, wash the day away, and I'll pick something for you to wear."

I jab my finger at her. Add a glare for emphasis. If she tries to pick a "this-is-a-date" sexy outfit...

Her hands go up, and she rolls her eyes at me. "Something nice and casual. I promise."

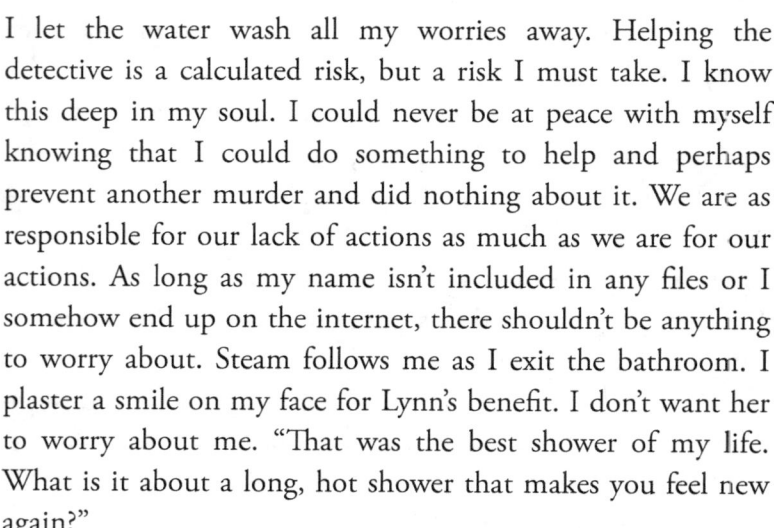

I let the water wash all my worries away. Helping the detective is a calculated risk, but a risk I must take. I know this deep in my soul. I could never be at peace with myself knowing that I could do something to help and perhaps prevent another murder and did nothing about it. We are as responsible for our lack of actions as much as we are for our actions. As long as my name isn't included in any files or I somehow end up on the internet, there shouldn't be anything to worry about. Steam follows me as I exit the bathroom. I plaster a smile on my face for Lynn's benefit. I don't want her to worry about me. "That was the best shower of my life. What is it about a long, hot shower that makes you feel new again?"

Lynn laughs. "You look like a toddler wrapped in a king-sized blanket. Glad to see you're feeling better."

I tug at the ends of my robe belt, making it tighter. The hem nearly touches the ground, and the long sleeves hang several inches past my hands.

She steps to the side and waves at the bed, showcasing the outfit she picked for me like one of those women in a TV game show. "Tada!"

Lying out on my bed is a long turquoise blue dress. One of my favorites. It's a perfect summer dress, the fabric soft, breezy, and barely there. I love the way it brushes against my legs when I walk. It's pretty and feminine, but not overtly sexy. It will look great with my newly tanned skin. "This will do."

"And this too, in case it gets chilly later." She holds up the light cardigan I often pair with this dress. "And you can borrow my silver flat sandals. I know you love them."

I run my fingers through my wet hair, shaking the loose curls. "Thank you. You did well. What are you gonna wear?"

"Me? I'm not going." Lynn drops the cardigan on top of the dress.

I squint at her. "I told you it is not a date."

She rolls her lips together and looks away. A sure sign that she's afraid to say something that will hurt my feelings. "I know, that's not it."

"What is it then?" My voice softens.

She wrings her hands. "Honestly? I can't hear you talking about all that stuff again."

Guilt nudges at me like a poking finger. I should know better. Lynn loves hearing about the old stuff. But anything recent or current spooks her. She needs the distance of decades or centuries to feel safe. "Aww, sweetie. I'm sorry. It was a bit too much, wasn't it?"

She rubs her arms as if the friction could dispel her anxiety. "I feel like such a fool. You're the one who had to see all that, and here I am being a chicken shit about it. You know that normally I love all that stuff you do. But this one . . . this one is too much."

I step closer and squeeze her into a hug. Lynn is always so upbeat it's easy to forget she's not immune to the sadder side of what I do. "It was the ghost, wasn't it?"

She nods against my shoulder. "Yeah. Seeing you break down like that, and then the ghost . . ."

That makes me laugh. "Got it. No ghosts for you. You prefer them alive, six-foot-two, and sexy."

Lynn steps away. "Maybe *your* hot detective has a friend."

"He's not my detect—" My phone chimes. It's a call, not a text message.

The detective's number flashes on the screen.

My hands tremble. "Hello?" Why am I reacting this way? Am I nervous about getting involved in the investigation, or is it about him?

"Miss Bloom?"

I swallow against the sudden dryness in my mouth. "Ava."

"Ava . . ." His voice softens at my name—the sound settles low in my belly. "I'm running a little late. Can you meet me at your building lobby at five-fifteen?"

I press the phone closer to my ear—as if doing so I could capture more than the sound of his voice. As if I could somehow hold a part of him closer to me. That old longing for him, for the young man who saved my life and lived in my dreams since I was a girl, scratches at my chest. "Will do." I sound unsure.

"See you then."

He hangs up before I can say anything else. I stare at my phone as if it holds the answer to my reaction to Jake. All the years of daydreaming about him didn't prepare me for this.

Lynn peers at my phone. "What was all that about? You sounded so formal."

"That's him. Wanted to let me know he's running late and to meet him at the lobby at five-fifteen."

Lynn peers at me, her eyes trying to read what I'm not saying. "Are you sure you want to do this?"

I sigh. "I'm not sure of anything. Jake makes me unbalanced. One moment I'm annoyed and the next, I want to run my fingers through his hair. He's so . . . what's the word I'm looking for?"

Lynn smiles and waggles her brows. "Hot?"

"No. That's not it." But there's no denying that. He's hot AF.

Her smile turns into a smirk, and the waggles go crazy. "Sexy?"

I shake a fist at her and follow it with a finger—the middle finger.

She ignores my mock insult and claps her hands. "I know! Fuckable! He's so fuckable."

"Lynn . . ." I try to hold a laugh and snort instead.

"What?" She's all wide-eyed innocence. "Well, it is true. He is."

Yes. She's right. "I don't know how they allow you to teach first-graders. If only they could see inside your brain. But you're right. Jake's a total DILF."

"Detective I'd like to fuck?" She doesn't miss a beat. There's no hesitation at all in her response.

I tilt my head back, look at the ceiling, and groan. "You know me too well. I can't hide anything from you. And the word I'm looking for is irritating. Which also applies to you right now."

"Awww." She side-hugs me. "You love me. I love you, too."

CHAPTER 9
JAKE

I WAIT NEAR THE ENTRYWAY. THE ELEVATOR DOORS OPEN with a ding and Ava walks across the lobby in a long blue dress. The fabric sways around her legs, a muscular calf peeking in and out through a long slit. Her eyes are wide, her gaze darting around the open space. There's a fresh glow to her cheeks and a touch of gold to her skin. She's been in the sun since I last saw her. I drink her in. Her brown hair falls just below her shoulders in soft waves. She's slight but strong. Her arms are toned. I flashback to the way she looked in the cutoff shorts yesterday. It's easy to imagine her tanned and slender legs wrapped around me. I wish we had met under different circumstances because I would love to get to know her better. Much better. But she's just passing through, and I'm not going anywhere. I can't leave. Even if I could, getting involved with a psychic? I scoff at the thought.

Her gaze finds me, and her step falters. A touch of pink colors her face. Her features are feminine and delicate. She looks younger than her age with her large hazel eyes and pert nose, but her full lips betray the innocent look and conjure up all the things I'd like to do with her mouth. I push away my stray thoughts. This is not the time to give in to fantasies. I wave hello, glad she can't see the lust in my eyes hidden behind the sunglasses I always wear. "Ready?"

She nods, her hands twisting around a white sweater and a small purse.

I glance around. We have caught the attention of a couple of people. The man at the front desk tracks us with watchful eyes. Someone lounging in the lobby has given up on his newspaper, finding us much more interesting than whatever he's reading. In a small town, people are always watching. Except when you need a witness. Then nobody sees anything.

We walk outside and across the parking lot. I slow my pace to match her shorter stride. A breeze ruffles her hair, and the scent of green apples wafts toward me. I inhale deeply and hold it for a few seconds, trapping her smell inside me before letting it go.

We walk in silence—the low hum of traffic fills the space between us. I unlock and open the door of my truck for her.

She hesitates by the open door. "Where are we going?"

"I don't know. We'll drive somewhere and talk."

She holds her place for another second before stepping into the SUV. Is she worried about being alone with me? Or about her safety? Cop or no cop, I'm a stranger to her. I give her a smile, a genuine one, and try to get her at ease.

I close the door and walk around. When I get in, Ava's seat belt is already fastened, and she holds herself still, eyes looking forward. Her hands are clamped around her purse and the cardigan on her lap.

I allow myself to look at her for longer than I should. I clear my throat as if it could also evict the not-so-professional thoughts from my mind and start the engine. It comes to life with a smooth rumble and the radio plays a classic rock song. We leave the parking lot.

She glances my way.

I look at what I'm wearing, jeans and a polo shirt. I didn't have a chance to go home to shower and change. Why the hell am I thinking about this? I don't have to impress her. She will be gone and out of my life, back to New York. The thought of never seeing her again pokes at a lonely corner of my heart. But my job takes priority over everything else. Trying to solve my sister's cold case consumes me. No relationship has ever lasted more than a few weeks. No woman can compete with the ghost of my sister and me trying to find who killed her. I won't rest until I do.

"Sorry I was late."

"That's okay." She gives me a tight-lipped smile.

I lower the radio. "I had an interesting afternoon."

She turns her body my way and stares at me. "Did you find anything?"

"Yes and no. When I'm not driving, I'll tell you more." I take the main road out of town. The prickly fingers of a headache poke at my temples. I know where I want to go now. "Are you hungry? I haven't eaten all day. I need to grab something."

"I could eat."

I reach into the middle console and pull out a menu. "This place is pretty good. We can get something to go and then talk."

She looks through the menu. "Want me to call ahead and place an order?"

My stomach grumbles. "Yes, please. Get me the bacon burger special with all the fixings and fries."

As I drive to the burger place, I listen as she makes the call. She gets herself a veggie burger.

She hangs up. "It'll be fifteen minutes."

I glance at her and back at the road. "You don't eat meat?"

"No." A head shake accompanies her reply.

I slow down for a red light. "Vegetarian or vegan?"

"Vegetarian. I love cheese too much to be a vegan."

I smile and take a quick look at her. She's settled into the seat, her shoulders relaxed, her hands playing with the strap of her purse. If the small talk makes her more comfortable, I can do small talk. "What's the next stop on your vacation?"

Her head tilts to the side. "Not sure. Keep going north. Vermont, maybe. I want to stop by Riggins."

My head snaps to her. "Riggins?"

"Yeah, I did my undergrad at Riggins University. Have a couple of friends who still live there."

We come to a red light. "I went to Riggings."

She searches my face. "Really? My grandmother would have a lot to say about this. Us going to the same university. And meeting again, like this."

"Well, not meeting again. I was there a few years before you, I'm sure."

Her head tilts, and she looks at me with curiosity. "Yeah, I misspoke."

If I believed in fate, destiny, or anything like that, I might think this is some kind of sign. "You're going to visit your friends, then?"

"Maybe." She moves her hand in a graceful wave. "I don't enjoy making plans when I'm on vacation. I just go with the flow, land where the wind takes me."

The light turns green, and I drive again. "I don't know you, but you don't strike me as a go-with-the-flow type." She seems far too competent and I can't imagine someone so accomplished being fickle about how they live their life.

She laughs. The sound is husky and melodic. "You're right and wrong. You're correct in that you don't know me, but intuition has guided my entire life. If that's not living on a whim, I don't know what is."

We pull into the parking lot. "Hard to imagine. My life's one of order, structure, and laws." The one time I strayed, there were horrible consequences.

"Even before you were a cop?"

I park. "I come from a military family, and we can track our ancestors' military service back to the Civil War." I reveal more than I intended, but I think her questions are more curiosity than an intrusion.

"That's cool. I've done some work with Civil War artifacts. Which branch did you serve with?"

The effect of her full attention on me is like a drug I want another hit of. My pulse speeds and my head spins. It's like an adrenaline high.

"The Army." I leave the SUV running. "Lock the doors. I'll be right back." I'm grateful for the chance to step away, clear my head, and give other body parts a chance to relax. But her presence follows me all the way to the restaurant. And again, I wish we had met under different circumstances. I pay for the food and walk back. Her gaze is on me as I exit the place. Her shoulders drop as if she was watching the door the whole time.

She unlocks the doors as I approach, and I put the bag of food in the back seat. The vehicle immediately fills with the smell of fries.

Ava shifts to look in the back seat, inhales deeply, and licks her lips with a soft hum. I fix my gaze on her mouth—

the sexy sound she made skips my ears and goes straight to my loins. So much for relaxing body parts. I start to click my seat belt when she looks back at me.

She tucks a curl behind her ear. "And then, after the Army, you became a cop?"

What? Army? Cop? Oh, she's picking up the conversation where we left off. I miss the seat belt on my first try like I'm a green boy on his first date.

I back out of the parking spot. "After the Army, I went to college for Criminal Justice, then the police academy."

"How long have you been a detective?"

"Three years as a detective. Before that, I was in the force for seven years." She's full of questions I'd normally evade, but the longer we talk, the more I want to open up to her. There's a sense of familiarity like I've met her before. But I know I didn't. I would not forget a woman like her.

Her head tilts, brows scrunched, and lips parted. "How old are you?"

I hesitate. I feel so much older than the seven-year difference between us. Ava's untarnished, and I'm too jaded. "Thirty-five." Some days, the weight of time pushes down on me with crippling pressure. Today is not one of those days.

"You've been in the protect-and-serve business for nearly half of your life. You look younger than thirty-five." She bites her bottom lip and nods her assessment.

Cheese on crackers, as my grandfather used to say, so as not to take the Lord's name in vain. I lower the AC temperature and move the vent toward my lap. *Just keep driving, Jake. Just keep driving.*

She crosses her legs, and one calf peeks through the slit in her dress. "Where are we going?"

I make a left into the State Park. "We're here."

She leans forward, looking at her surroundings. "A park?"

There are joggers, people walking dogs, kids playing ball and throwing Frisbees on the grass. I drive farther through an access road, deeper into the woods, to a place I like to come to when I need to get away and think. I find a spot under the shade of a tree, turn off the ignition, and get the food. Then I open my door, wait for her to get out, and then lock it. The loud beep is a dissonant sound in the quiet rustle of trees and singing birds.

I point into the woods and away from the trails. "There's a picnic table just ahead. We can eat and talk there."

She walks next to me beneath the trees. The breeze flutters the skirt around her legs and molds the fabric to her curves. The green apple scent makes another appearance. I suppress a groan. I'll never be able to look at or smell a green apple again and not be turned on.

"Watch your step." I gesture at a spot on the ground where tree roots crisscross the ground, making it uneven. She almost trips and takes my hand to steady herself. A zing of awareness ricochets throughout my entire body. The hairs on my arms stand to attention. They aren't the only things on my body trying to stand. Her fingers flex, and her breath catches. Did she also get hit with the same jolt of electricity?

She snatches her hand away. "It's so beautiful and peaceful here. It feels like I'm miles away from everything."

Tall bushes and taller trees hide us. There's no official trail to this spot. I have never run into someone else while in this particular area.

"Here, just after this bush." I move the foliage so she can get through. She steps around me, and I follow her. She walks in a circle, taking everything in.

The clearing by the lake is small and completely hidden

from any paths. Only someone on a canoe would be able to see us, and the park stops access to the lake after 5:00 p.m.

I sit at the weathered picnic table and set the food bag on the wooden top.

Ava walks to the water's edge. "How did you even find this place? Wait! This is the place you came to as a kid with your grandfather."

My head snaps up, and a chill runs down my spine. "How did you know?"

"It's the same place from my vision with your grandfather. There are more trees and bushes, and the water's edge looks smaller, but I recognize it."

I want to ask more questions about what she saw when I gave her the rock, but I acted like an asshole then, and I don't want to remind her of that.

She picks up a rock and tosses it at the water with a flick of the wrist. The stone skips once, twice, three times before sinking to the bottom. She brushes her hands off. Tilts her face to the sun, eyes closed, lips parted.

My fingers itch to touch her, to make sure she's real and not something I imagined standing in my favorite place in the entire world. Her blue dress flutters in the breeze, with the sun hanging over the tree line and against a cloudless sky. It's a perfect summer day.

She stretches her arms up, her palms connect above her head, and comes down to touch her heart. She stays like this for a few more seconds. I can't take my gaze away from her. I drink her in, making note of every detail, how her hair curls at the ends, the rosy color on her cheeks, the curves of her body, how petite she is.

She opens her eyes and smiles. I'm caught staring, but wearing my sunglasses, she can't tell if I'm looking at her or the lake. She walks to the table and sits opposite me. "Can I ask you a question?"

"Sure."

"Why do you always hide your eyes behind sunglasses?"

Well, fuck. I wasn't expecting that. I grind my molars and stare her down, even if she can't see my eyes behind the mirrored lenses. But instead of backing off like everyone else does when I fix my anger on them, she leans over, gently removes my glasses, and then brushes my hair back.

"There . . . you shouldn't hide your eyes. They're beautiful."

I'm hit with something I can't name—it slides between my many layers of protection and wraps around my chest. It fills me with warm comfort. Her words are like a salve for an old and painful wound. I want to her touch back. "Beautiful has never been a word I associated with my mismatched eyes."

Her gaze flits all over my face as if trying to devour every feature, every line, and nuance all at once. "Why not?"

I'm not immune to her questions or how she makes me feel. I want to open up to her, unload all my burdens, release all the hurts if it will get her hands on me again. I could give her my standard answer. It's annoying having people staring and answering questions all the time. It's just easier to wear sunglasses and avoid both. But I don't. I tell her the truth instead. "My father hates my eyes. He could never stand to look at me. And he was very vocal about it."

She frowns. "That's terrible. It's not like you have any control over it."

"Didn't stop him from blaming me or my mother." I was called many things because of my eyes—*evil* and *devil eyes* were at the top of the list. "Wearing sunglasses everywhere became second nature."

"Your mother went along with it?"

"She tried to protect me the best she could, but she's a timid woman who never stood up for herself." Or me.

"But what about kids your age? They didn't think it was cool?"

I scoff. "Other kids bullied me. And if I tried to defend myself, I got into trouble for it." It doesn't matter how many years have passed. Being called names throughout my childhood left a mark. My grandfather was my only friend. I look away. I'm not used to being this open or exposed.

Her frown deepens. "I don't understand why anyone would act like that."

"The town was even smaller then. We had a church with a pastor who loved the idea of hell more than God. He preached a lot about all the evil in the world. Anything that didn't fit his ideas of normal and godliness was a work of the devil. I guess having different-colored eyes made me a target."

She shakes her head. "I hate people sometimes. There's nothing evil about Heterochromia Iridum. Your eyes are beautiful and I love them. It's like looking at the sky and the ocean at the same time."

There's not an ounce of flattery or coquetry in her voice. She really means what she says. She loves my eyes. And she knows the name of my condition. I don't know how to respond, so I give her a water bottle and her meal instead.

I take a long drink of water from my bottle, going back to what she said before I turned into a sappy idiot. I tip the water bottle toward to lake. "It is the same place, but a lot more overgrown. I'm surprised you can recognize it from a . . . vision."

She unwraps her burger and takes a healthy bite. Covers

her mouth, chews, and swallows. "It's the energy. I recognized the energy first. And it also matches the images I saw."

I take a bite of my burger and consider what she said. "So, places and objects have energy?" How did I end up in a conversation where I sound like I'm actually buying this crap? Maybe it's because she seems to believe it. Maybe it's because I'm attracted to her, or perhaps it's because if what she says is real, then Grandpa and Emily still exist somewhere.

"Everything has energy. Places, objects, people, animals, plants. We're all energy vibrating at different speeds. But you don't have to take my word for it. As I told you before, look up quantum physics."

"People? You can touch someone and read them?" Can she read my thoughts?

"Not exactly. It's not the same as reading an object, but in theory, depending on the person and situation, if I tried really hard, I could. But it is not something I actively do or even try to do. Sometimes it happens spontaneously."

"Like what? You shake someone's hand and see something?"

She nods and picks up a french fry. "Something like that."

We sit quietly for a while, thoughts buzzing through my mind like a swarm of bees. If all Ava's saying is true, the possibility of finding more clues would be invaluable. But I don't like the idea of someone being able to read me like a book.

I check the time on my phone. It's almost six. We should have at least another two hours of sunlight.

She wraps her leftovers in her napkin and tosses them in the bag. "Can you tell me more about Alice?"

This surprises me. "You didn't look her up on Google?"

"No." She shakes her head. "I don't want to be influenced by any outside sources." She gestures for me to continue.

"Alice disappeared a week ago. Her roommate reported her missing in the morning when she realized Alice didn't come home the night before and wasn't at her job either. We confirmed that Alice worked the day before and left at five. Her car was found on the side of the road about an hour outside of town, with a tire blown out. The car was empty, except for the key fob, which was left inside."

"Is she local?"

"Yes."

"How old was she?"

"She was twenty-three."

"And her family?"

"Her mother died when she was fourteen and she has no other family. Grew up in a group home."

Ava gazes at the water. "That's terrible."

"It is."

Her gaze drifts to the lake. Ava squints as if in deep thought. "Did you go back to the antique store?"

"Yes, that's what I meant before—about having an interesting afternoon. The owner confirmed what you said. And he was quite angry about a civil war revolver?"

She laughs. "Did he say where he got the necklace from?"

Why am I telling her all of this? If anyone at the station finds out, I'll not only be a laughingstock, but I'll probably get fired. But she's the first lead in the right direction I have, and my gut tells me to trust her. "Yes. From a small-time, local thug who's been in jail once or twice for petty crimes."

"How did you find that out?"

"Security cameras."

"So, you watched Lynn and me go into the store . . ."

"And I watched the video of the thug selling the necklace to the store owner."

She crosses her arms over the table. "Now what?"

"Now, I'll pay our guy a visit and ask some questions."

Her eyebrows scrunch. "Our guy?"

Why did I say that? We are not a team. I shake my head, more for myself than for her. "Did you remember anything else?"

She shivers. "No new information. But I had the visions again, and—"

"Is that normal? To have visions a second time without touching anything?"

"No, it's never happened to me before. But I think I know why I had the visions again."

"Why?" I lean closer to her, my torso halfway over the table.

"Because right after I had the visions, I saw Alice's spirit standing in my room. And she asked for my help."

Every muscle in my body tenses. My jaw locks, and I force myself to smooth my features. I push the words out. "What do you mean, you saw Alice standing in your room?"

CHAPTER 10
AVALON

His eyes narrow, and his face hardens. A muscle ticks in his jaw. Within two seconds, his features smoothen to neutral. Had I not been intent on reading his reaction, I might have missed it altogether. He seems like a man who likes to be in control and has had little of it since we met yesterday morning.

"What do you mean, you saw Alice standing in your room?" His voice is low and cold, calculating. Gone is the easy and open tone of our conversation. What is it that makes him so angry at the mentions of anything paranormal? His reaction feels like more than just being skeptical.

"Just that. I saw Alice in my room, and she asked for help."

His hand squeezes the water bottle, and it crackles under the pressure. "Asked for help, how?"

"She said, 'help', and then dissipated like smoke in the wind." I don't like the way he's looking at me. And the image of his father calling him devil eyes comes back to me. As beautiful as his eyes are when he's relaxed, being under their scrutiny right now is unsettling.

His shoulders are rigid. "You saw her ghost."

It's not a question, but his tone holds a challenge. He may as well just call me a liar.

I curb my irritation. Snapping at Jake won't help, even if it would feel good. And it'd be a bit like hitting a dog when it snarls at you because it's in pain. That stone in his office showed me more than he realizes. "Seeing spirits comes with the territory. I've always been able to see them, but it's not something I can control or do at will. Spirits are all around us, and sometimes they show themselves."

He grinds his teeth, his jaw moving from side to side. "You didn't mention seeing ghosts before."

"It wasn't relevant information then. Like I said, I can't control when I see them, and it's not like you were exactly welcoming to my presence and what I had to say."

Jake lets go of the tortured water bottle, and it topples, no longer fit to stand. His gaze cuts away to the lake, and he takes a deep breath, then looks back at me with some kind of resolve in his expression. "Any idea why this ghost is asking you for help?"

I don't really have to think about it, but I hold back my response for several seconds. The knowing has been poking at the edges of my awareness since I saw Alice's spirit. "She wants to be found so her friend can have closure."

His fist goes to his chin in a repetitive tapping, and he looks away again.

Something in his discomfort emboldens me. I reach across the table and pull his fist down. Hold his hand between both of mine. His eyes widen, and his mouth opens.

"Listen, I can tell this whole thing makes you extremely uncomfortable. You've already told me you don't believe in supernatural stuff. And I get it. It's hard to believe. But I'm not a fake. I'm not asking for nor expecting any kind of compensation. I have nothing to gain by talking to you or helping you, but I have a lot to lose. My career—my professional reputation—is at risk."

"Why are you helping me, then?" His eyes soften, but his voice is still challenging me.

"I need to help you because I can't walk away from this. I can't allow what happened to Alice to happen to someone else. That someone else could be Lynn or me. And when this guy tries to take another girl—and believe me, he will—I need to do everything I can to prevent it."

His eyes narrow. "You think he killed before and will kill again?"

"Yes, I know he will."

"Serial killers are rare. What makes you so sure he will do it again?"

I close my eyes and wish I could purge the killer's bloodlust from my mind, but I can't. "It's hard to explain. But the glimpse I got of him, how he feels when he takes someone, it's like a drug high, and killing is an addiction. He feeds off it, enjoys his victims' fear, and lusts after the power it gives him. Killing makes him feel like God."

Jake's hand flinches between mine, and he pulls away. Something I said disturbed him. "What is it? Did anything I say ring a bell with the case?"

He grabs the paper bag with the remnants of our meal and balls it. "If you're free sometime in the next few days, I'd like you to meet me at the impound. We have Alice's car there. It's been checked and dusted for prints, but we got nothing. Perhaps you can check it as well and see if anything comes to you?"

He ignores my question, and I let it go. He's protecting more than just details for this case. It's personal to him, even if he met none of the missing women. I can feel it. The information will come to me. It always does. "Yeah, sure. Let me know when."

He nods. "I'll call you when I have a better idea. Maybe in a couple of days?"

He's creating distance between us again. With his words and tone of voice.

"That's fine."

He stands up, and I guess that's my clue to do the same. I get up, and my gaze gets snagged by the figure near the lake. I walk to the water's edge and search until I find the perfect rock. *Like this?* I ask in my mind. The stone is oval and thin.

That's perfect. The reply comes from the ghostly figure now hovering between Jake and me. I hand the rock to the detective. "One more time before we go."

His feet eat the space between us until he towers over me, his face inches away, his gaze searching mine. His posture is more desperate than threatening. The sun, low on the horizon, shines on him and makes the color of his eyes nearly translucent, like an invitation to peer into his soul. So much pain hidden away in the corners of his heart. "What did you say?" His voice is low and urgent.

I hold the rock out to him. "One more time before we go."

He steps back, turns away from me, runs both hands through his hair, and faces me again. I hold the rock on my open palm.

His hands go to his waist, and he stares at the rock in

some kind of internal battle. Then steps closer and takes the stone from my hand. Walks to the water and positions himself sideways, bends at the knees, and flicks the rock over the water. It skips, and I silently count. One, two, three, four, five times before the lake claims it.

He watches the water until the ripples die away, then walks to the table and grabs his forgotten sunglasses and the balled-up paper bag. He waits for me to follow him.

I smile at the figure beside him, the old man who told me to find a rock and what to say. His grandfather.

CHAPTER 11
JAKE

MY FEET POUND THE GROUND. I SLOW DOWN MY JOG AS I turn onto the beachside trail toward my SUV. The scent of salt and sea coats the breeze. The grass around the path is wet with dew—it shines like diamonds under the early morning sun.

Up ahead another jogger joins the path from one of the many tracks that spill into the main one flanking the beach. Ava. I allow myself to enjoy the view, and I'm not referring to the ocean. The small shorts she wears showcase a nice round ass, strong and lean legs. The crop top matches the bottom. The hot pink color shouldn't look good on anyone other than a flamingo, but she can pull it off. Her ponytail bounces with each stride she takes.

She checks her watch and slows her pace. I do the same so as to not overtake her. She looks over her shoulder, and I glance down, so she doesn't feel threatened.

"Jake?"

She turns and jogs backward so she can face me.

I come up next to her, and she turns forward again. I match my paces to hers. "You like to run?"

She glances at me and smirks. "That's why I'm running." She's not even breathless.

I'm an idiot. "I meant . . ." I don't know what I meant. "Just surprised. I didn't know you ran."

"I do. Every day unless something gets in the way. Like snow or work."

We are nearing the parking lot, and I point at my SUV. "Want some water?"

"Sure."

We jog to my SUV. I reach for the cooler in the back seat, take a bottle out, and give it to her. She presses the ice-cold bottle to her neck and face. I can't take my eyes off her. The gesture is both innocent and alluring. The image will be permanently burned into my brain. Arousal awakens a part of me that the thin shorts will fail to hide. I remove my damp T-shirt and use it to wipe my chest, making sure to hold it in front of me.

Her eyes widen. She stops mid-sip and drinks me in instead. Which doesn't help the situation in my shorts. I grab my water bottle and dump half over my head. Drain the rest in one go and hope it will tame the situation below my waist.

What the hell? I have better self-control than this. I'm not a green boy. This is the third time I've met her, and it's been a constant battle between being annoyed, angry, or turned on. Sometimes, all three at once. I need to get a grip.

She steps to the side and starts doing cool-down stretches. I know I should do the same, but my dick can't decide if it's going to behave or not. She bends down and touches her toes, her flexible body bent in half. That's definitely a no on the behaving part. I should get out of here before I embarrass myself.

She keeps stealing glances at me. I step to the side and do stretches as well. "How long do you usually jog?"

"Usually six miles, give or take. I don't always have a view as beautiful as this one." She points to the sea. "When I do, I might go a little longer. What about you? Been jogging for a while?"

I toss my shirt into the back seat of my SUV. "Today or in general?"

She's doing side lunges now. "Both?"

"I don't run as often or as far as you. Usually, three or four miles a few times a week. I was never a runner until I joined the Army. Got used to it. Keeping fit goes with the job, and I enjoy it now."

She brings a knee up to her chest. "Hit me up next time you go for a run. Maybe I can get you up to six." Her smile is teasing, like a dare.

"You got a deal."

She holds out her hand, and we shake on it. Looks like I'll either double my running average or make a fool of myself when I puke my guts out.

I rummage through my SUV, find a clean T-shirt, and put it on. "Do you think you can meet me at the impound Monday morning?"

She tilts her head. "What's today? Thursday? Yes, I think so."

"Thank you. I'll text you the address. You'll be free of me for the weekend. I don't want to take too much of your time." That means I won't see her for three days. Why does that bother me?

Her smile fades. "You're not. Taking too much of my time, that is."

Does she want to see me again? Am I reading too much into this? "Do you want to grab some breakfast?"

She looks at herself, her skin glistening in the sun. "I'm not really dressed for it."

"For the place I'm thinking about, you don't need to be."

She tilts her head. "And what place is it?"

I point down the boardwalk. "See that blue truck down by the pier?"

Ava shades her eyes with both hands. "Yes."

"They have the best burrito breakfast in town. Take a walk with me?"

She pats herself. "I didn't bring any money."

"It's on me."

She stretches her back now, and her chest rises. "You already bought me lunch this week."

I try my best to keep my eyes on her face. "You're helping me. The least I can do is feed you."

She smiles. "Next one's on me, then."

Her smile makes my heart twitch. And something else, too. "Okay."

"Let's go. I'm not turning down a breakfast burrito."

CHAPTER 12
AVALON

"SORRY FOR BREAKING OUR PLANS BECAUSE OF THIS TRIP to the impound."

The GPS chimes, warning us that our destination is two hundred feet away. The car lot is enclosed in a tall chain-link fence with barbwire at the top. This is definitely not the kind of place one expects to visit while on vacation. I park in front. Jake's cruiser is the only other vehicle I see in the small parking lot. Next to the fenced area, there's a small building with ugly green walls. Three steps lead to a door with two windows on either side, one of which is occupied by a dented AC unit that rumbles, shakes, and clicks like it's on its last legs. Water drips onto the pavement like goodbye tears.

The trees growing along the sidewalk are little more than twigs, with a few leaves hanging on for dear life. The area has an industrial vibe, with warehouses lining both sides of the street, no people walking around.

I peer out the window. What was I thinking? Investigating a murder is completely out of my league. I should turn around and head back the way I came. We'd still have time to do everything we'd originally planned for the day if we left now. But if I did that, and Alice's ghost returned, how could I explain why I abandoned her? I have to do the right thing. I shelf the unease deep inside and look at Lynn. "Is this what you were expecting?"

Lynn unlocks her car door. "Ask me again later."

I nod at the fenced-in lot. "Still thinking you're gonna find a hot country boy in there?"

She smiles. "You never know, got to be in the game to play and win."

I turn off the engine and open my door. The crunch of gravel under someone's shoes grabs my attention. The detective stands a foot away. He pulls my car door open all the way, and I just sit there, frozen for a moment, one shoe on the ground, and the other inside my car, my butt half on and half off the seat. His crotch is at eye level. *Look away, Ava. Look away!* I take him in—tight jeans hug his legs, and a black T-shirt molds itself to his chest and abs like a second skin.

Holy mother of hotness. I can count his ab muscles through the fabric of his shirt. Somewhere in the world, a calendar is missing Mr. June. My mouth goes dry, and I lick my lips. Lift my gaze to his face. The expected sunglasses hide his eyes. A brow peeks above one of the lenses, and the corner of his mouth hitches with an amused smile.

He holds the door open for me and gives me his hand. I don't need the help but take his offering anyway. That now familiar tingle grazes over my skin like an invisible touch. Heat flushes my face and pools in my belly. What is it about this man that has me either aroused or irritated or both? Is it because I've been daydreaming about him for the last fifteen years?

Jesus! I shake off the feeling and close the car door. Lynn catches up to us and salutes the detective like she's a soldier or something.

He smiles and looks back at me with a set of heavy-duty keys dangling from his hand. "Ready?"

I stuff my hands in my back pockets. "Yeah."

Lynn laces her arm through mine.

He tilts his head toward a smaller gate in the fence. "I came in earlier and signed in for the keys." He unlocks a heavy-duty bolt, removes the chain holding the gatepost closed, and pushes the gate open, gesturing for Lynn and me to go through.

I step into the lot. A weight settles on my shoulders. Too many impressions calling for my attention. The air sizzles with regret and desperation. Past bad decisions hang over the lot like a low cloud. "No crazy dog named Cujo to protect the place?"

That earns me a laugh. "No dogs on the premises. The security cameras are better at keeping people out than a dog would." He points at several poles spaced around the perimeter. Small pods on the tops glint in the sun.

I stop. I didn't think of the cameras. "Wait. If the cameras are recording us right now, how will we keep this—me—a secret?"

He presses his lips together. "Yeah, about that. I was thinking of everything you said, and there might be times like this right now where we will be seen together in a situation that can't be explained as just meeting an old friend."

I cross my arms. "When were you going to tell me this?"

He scratches the back of his head. Is that a touch of color on his cheeks? "I . . . didn't think of it until I saw the cameras when I got here. Yes, we are being recorded right now. But there's no reason for anyone to suspect anything. People come here often enough to get their cars."

I raise an eyebrow. "Don't you have to sign in or something? Give a name? Give my name?"

"I signed my name only. And if anyone asks or anything comes up, I'll say I have an informant, or it was an anonymous tip."

"Just like that, and the questions will go away?"

He clears his throat. "For the most part. I can't be forced to reveal the name of an informant without a lot of heat from the DA or a court order, and even then, I can still refuse to speak."

"Wouldn't that mean being in contempt and going to jail?"

His only response is to press his lips together. I'm not okay with this new twist on our agreement, but I'm already here. What am I supposed to do? Just walk away? No, I'm going to see this through. But that doesn't mean I have to go passively. I stare at him, and he stares back.

Lynn gets between us and waves at the several dozen cars parked along the back and side. "So, anyway, how do you guys get all these cars in here?"

With the connection broken, we both take a step back.

The detective clears his throat. "It varies. Some cars are seized from impaired drivers, who are drunk or under the influence of drugs. Some from drivers with suspended licenses or other similar issues, and a few are found abandoned." He looks at me when he says the last part. My vivid imagination has him on his knees, apologizing for the underhanded way he got me here.

Lynn shields her eyes with her hand and carries on as if

she wasn't in the middle of a war of wills. "And how do the owners get their cars back?"

He resumes his walk, and we follow. "Depending on the reason the car was impounded, the owner can pay a fine to get it back. Sometimes the value of the car is less than the fine, and they just leave it. Non-claimed cars get sold at auctions once or twice a year. This lot services a few different towns. In a big city, there would be hundreds, maybe even thousands of seized cars."

"Wow." Lynn points at herself. "New Yorker here. I don't even have a car."

He looks at me and his face softens. "You've lived in New York your whole life?"

A breeze blows my hair across my face. Jake lifts his arm as if intent on brushing my hair away but drops his hand a second later and glances down.

"Yep, my grandma has a brownstone on the Upper West Side. I lived with her my entire life."

Lynn claps her hands. "Her house is so beautiful. You should visit sometime." She slides that invitation in like a baseball player stealing home.

If the detective heard her, it doesn't show—he touches my elbow and directs me to the back of the lot. "You live with your grandmother still?"

I sigh. I miss her. She's my only family. The one constant in my life besides Lynn. Having her go into assisted living was like accepting that she won't be in my life at some point. I already ache for the loss I know will come. "Not anymore. Well, I still live in the same place, but Grandma insisted on moving into an assisted living place. Her health has been iffy for the last couple of years, and New York winters are hard on her. I didn't want her to go, but I couldn't care for her with all my traveling."

Lynn laughs. "Grandma will outlive us all. No one can make her do anything she doesn't want to." She turns to Jake. "She moved to Florida, and the place she lives in is like a continuous, fancy vacation."

"True. Trying to make Grandma do anything against her will is like trying to move the Great Wall of China." A sweet ache nibbles at my chest like the bites of a tiny sharp-toothed puppy. I miss my grandma. "We spent just about every day together from my birth until I left for college."

His head tilts my way. "You traveled with her? What about school? And your parents?" He doesn't ask about my parents like most people do.

The memory brings a smile to my lips. "No parents. Just Grandma. I was homeschooled, except my homeschool was all over the world. And I had tutors to help out. Grandma is a big believer in a well-rounded education."

He smiles. "You must miss her." Something passes between us—a kinship brought by our love for a grandparent.

"I do. After graduating, I went back to working with Grandma until two years ago when she retired." And now she left me with the only place I can call home. Time has not lessened the empty spot she left, even with my frequent visits.

I slow my pace and follow behind him, lost in thought and memories. He stops suddenly and pivots to face me. I trip on my own feet, trying not to smack into him. My hands come up, and I brace myself, preparing for a fall, but he's faster than gravity and hauls me up by the elbows. My face smashes into his chest, and my hands grip his T-shirt and dig into his sides. His scent is a lure, and I inhale deeply. He smells like fresh, clean air after a rain shower, woods, and pine with a touch of citrus. I don't know what kind of cologne this is, but I want to roll in it like a feline with catnip.

His obliques flex under my hands. My fingers open, letting go of the fabric and spreading over his stomach instead. He releases a breath with an almost inaudible moan. Holy crap, are his abs for real? There are ridges. Ridges! I've never touched ridges before.

His hands slide up my arms and squeeze, holding me in place for a second, and at that moment, I don't think either of us knows if he'll pull me in or push me away. His thumbs move back and forth in a tender caress. Gently but firmly, he nudges me back.

My brain catches up to whatever hormonal overload I just experienced.

Oh. My. God.

I'm feeling him up. I just molested him. With my hands. On his body. I swallow and take a deep breath, catching his scent again. It's like being hit with a shot of an aphrodisiac. I'll have to hold my breath for the rest of my life now.

I clear my throat, step back, and break the contact. My face flushes with heat. "T-thank you. That was a close one. I'm usually not this clumsy." I can't look at him, so I stare at the ground instead. My face burns.

CHAPTER 13
AVALON

AFTER TEN THOUSAND YEARS, MY FACE STOPS BURNING, and I look at him. His expression is bland behind his sunglasses. For once, I'm glad I can't read his eyes. I couldn't bear to see any kind of judgment directed at my unrequited attraction to him.

Jake points over his shoulder with a thumb, still watching me. "This is it." A small silver sedan is parked a few yards behind him.

I gather my wits, regulate my breathing, and prepare to do what we came here for. "I'm ready."

He fishes a small plastic bag from his pocket, and inside it, there's a single key fob with a tag attached. Handwritten on the paper tag, the license plate, and another series of numbers.

He gives me the bag. "Not sure if you can pick up anything from the keys. A lot of hands have probably touched it by now. But the car was towed here, not driven."

I remove the key fob from the bag. Faint images pop through my mind. Mundane things. "Nothing of value on the keys. Just regular stuff."

He grabs his phone, taps a few times, and then shows me the screen. The recording app is ready to go. "I'll record, anyway. You never know. What seems to be nothing could be a clue in disguise."

I nod. Jake taps the red button on the screen.

I close my eyes. "The key doesn't show me anything out of the ordinary. I see it placed in the cup tray in the car. It's on a key chain with a green frog. Cartoony looking with big round eyes. And a few images of the same key on a wood desk or granite countertop. It has other keys attached too. The kind of keys for a house." I wait, searching for more clues, but nothing comes to me. I open my eyes to show I'm done.

He taps the recording button and saves the file. "The fob was found by itself on the driver's side floor mat. There was no key chain or other keys."

"Do you think he took the key chain and the house key?"

He squeezes the back of his neck. "No way to be sure. Some criminals take souvenirs from their victims."

Shit. This is not good. "If the keys are missing, the roommate may be at risk, too. We need to warn her. And tell her to change the locks."

He taps away on his phone. "I'll call the roommate after we're done here. Perhaps we can stop by her house, and you can look around."

"Wait." Lynn steps closer and puts herself between Jake and me. My five-foot-two protector. "Let's see how Ava feels after she's done with the car. This stuff drains her."

Jake's head snaps up. He looks at me over Lynn's messy bun. "It drains you. Why? How?" He frowns. I can hear the worry in his voice.

Lynn puts her hands on her hips. "No free rides in the universe, buddy. There has to be an even exchange of energy.

Ava uses her energy to read the object's energy. The more juice an object has, the more it drains her." Lynn's shoulders pull back. She speaks with the authority of someone who has watched me do this hundreds of times. And the one who cares for me during many of my brain dumps, as I like to call the completely drained and empty feeling I get sometimes.

"It's okay. The key doesn't have much of anything to it. And if I start feeling drained, eating something usually helps ground me."

His brows scrunch behind the mirrored lenses. "Helps ground you?"

"Yes. It's a little like having a sugar low. And I rarely eat much before I do a reading. Being a little hungry makes for a stronger connection."

He tilts his head. "Why is that?"

"Because food is grounding, and it helps restore my energy." I inhale deeply and release my breath. "I'm ready for the car."

He holds his phone out. "Okay, go ahead."

I walk to the car, press the fob to unlock it, and open the driver's door. "Can I sit inside?"

"Yes, it's been scrubbed for evidence and will be released to the family once someone comes to pick it up." He stands at the door.

I sit behind the wheel but don't touch anything yet. The car is spotless. I close my eyes and open my senses. "Whatever happened to her, it was not in the car. I detect no violence here."

With eyes still closed, I touch the steering wheel. Images flood my mind. "She was a careful driver. The kind you hate to be stuck behind because they always do the speed limit."

"Like someone I know," Lynn interjects and gets shushed by Jake.

I filter through the myriad of impressions, searching for something—anything—that will give me a clue. Nothing. "I'm not getting anything of value."

I blindly trace my hands across the dashboard but stop when my fingers brush against the air vent. Wait. Something is off. "This feels different." An undefinable feeling of wrongness takes over me, like sweat-sticky skin on a frigid day. It doesn't belong.

Gravel crunches under a heavy foot, and Jake's loud breath rushes past me.

I search for what's different. For what doesn't belong, instead of searching for clues about Alice. Then I see it. "A male hand reaches for the vents and turns them all off. He's wearing disposable gloves. Like the ones you see at a doctor's office." I mimic the phantom hand tracing his movements. "He turned off the AC, cleaned the car, and removed everything from it."

More crunching sounds. "That's correct. The car was clean when we found it. Not a spec of dirt, no prints." His voice is closer.

The images flash in an almost organized manner. "I think he was wearing a hazmat suit or something like that. I see an arm in some kind of white papery sleeve and a gloved hand." I wait, but I get nothing else. Opening my eyes, I blink against the bright morning light.

Jake is squatting just inside the open door. Phone in hand, still recording.

With his face so close to mine, I resist the urge to remove his sunglasses like I did in the park. "When did you say she went missing? June fifteenth?"

"Yes."

I trace the steering wheel. "Lynn, look up the weather for that day in this area."

She taps her phone. "It was eighty-two degrees that day and pretty much the same for the days before and after."

I touch the car's dash again and meet my reflection in his glasses. "Was the AC turned off and all the air vents closed when the car was found?"

His head tilts. "I can double-check when I get back to my office, but I'm pretty sure it was."

"Interesting . . . why would anyone drive with the AC off and all the vents closed on a hot day?" I ask, more to myself than him.

He turns off the recording. "You think whoever took Alice messed around with the car vents?"

"I think he moved the car from its original location and cleaned it up. He turned the air off and closed the vents to prevent it from blowing any stray hairs, fibers, etc. He wore gloves and a protective suit over his clothes for the same reason. Bet he also wore a hair net or cap. And then he cleaned the entire car to make sure there was nothing linking the car to him. This guy is careful and methodical." My chest tightens like a wind-up toy under too much pressure. Faint energy vestiges linger like an invisible scuff mark. I have never encountered anything like this. "This man is almost robotic in the way he acts, yet underlying every action is a sadistic anger."

Lynn pokes her head around the detective. "I keep saying you'd make a great PI."

Jake stares at me. "You got all of that from touching the car?"

"No, not all of it. Psychometry is like a puzzle. Some

puzzles have thousands of pieces, and some have a few. The complexity is different depending on the object. I see the many pieces, not necessarily in order, and put them together. It's part reading the visions, part connecting the images, and part filling in the blanks."

His brows arch over the lenses. "So . . . sometimes you have to guess?"

I squint, trying to see through the mirrored shades. "Guess isn't the right word. It's more of an educated conclusion based on evidence, experience, and also a knowing."

He rubs his forehead as if soothing a headache. "A knowing?"

"That's what I call it. I just know. You would probably call it a gut feeling or a hunch. It's part intuition and part experience. A cynic might say it's the subconscious connecting the dots behind the scenes while waiting for the brain to catch up."

He stares at me for a long moment and then concedes with a slight dip of his head. "I'll cross-examine this with what we found in the cars of the other missing women and see if the same was done to their cars. Until now, these have been investigated as separate cases. We never had a reason to think they were linked."

I nod in return. "You didn't find Alice's phone, right?"

He adjusts his position. His legs must be hurting from squatting for so long. "No."

I make a move to get out of the car. "Can you hack into her Find My Phone app and track her locations for the day she went missing?"

He stands and steps back. "Not without a subpoena. I'm trying to get one. The privacy laws are pretty strict, and without a body, there's always the possibility that she isn't missing, but somewhere she doesn't want to be found. In most cases, the missing person shows up after a couple of days."

"What about the other missing women? All three of them just wanted a vacation from life?"

He presses his lips into a thin line. "No, I don't believe that. When Lena disappeared back in January, there was a chance she left on her own. When Victoria went missing in March, I suspected a connection was possible, but without any evidence to link them, each case is investigated individually. But now, with Alice, I'm convinced they are connected. Three missing women, three months apart, but I have no proof."

I stand next to Lynn and nod. "What else have you found of hers? Do you have anything else?"

He locks the car and turns his back to it. "We have nothing."

"What about where she lived?"

He runs a hand through his hair, grips at the ends, and lets go. "I already talked to her roommate, and she had nothing to add. No clues."

"Make that call to the roommate. If she allows, I can check the house. It may give me some clues."

He crosses his arms, feet set wide, drags a deep breath in, and releases. "I'll call the roommate about the locks and try to set up something."

"What about the other missing women?" Lynn asks him and then looks at me. "You might be able to see a connection the police didn't. Find that link he's talking about."

A rush of foreboding runs down my spine with icy fingers. As soon as Lynn suggests it, awareness settles over my shoulders like a weighted blanket, confining and calming at the same time. I'm certain the other missing women are linked to this case. And if Alice is dead, the other two probably are, too.

Jake nods. "That's a good idea."

He faces me, and my fingers itch to remove his sunglasses so I can see his eyes. I stuff my hands in my pockets instead.

"What's next?"

"Can you come to the station in a day or two and check what I have on the other missing women?"

I turn to Lynn, reluctant to abandon her when this is supposed to be our vacation.

She puts a hand on my shoulder. "Don't worry about me. I'm going to tan myself by the pool and eat my weight in ice cream."

"That's a yes, then. I can come either day, tomorrow or Wednesday."

Jake removes his sunglasses and squeezes the bridge of his nose. "Can you meet me tomorrow around noon?"

The impact of seeing his eyes hits me anew, and my response gets lost in his green and blue gaze. I clear my throat. "I-I can do that. And I'll bring lunch this time because that's our cover story."

He turns to the gate and opens it for us. We exit the lot, and he weaves the chain back in place and secures the lock. "I'll turn the key in. See you tomorrow."

"Sure."

He walks into the building. I get in my car and keep the passenger door locked for a few extra seconds. Lynn peers through the window and sticks her tongue out at me.

I let her in. "If you ever decide to give up on teaching, I think you'll have a brilliant future as a pimp."

CHAPTER 14
AVALON

I PARK IN FRONT OF THE POLICE STATION. ODDLY enough, in the same spot as before. I feed two dollars' worth of coins into the parking meter and call Jake. The phone rings twice.

"Detective Knox." He sounds hurried.

"Hi. It's me. I'm outside." My stomach does a figure-eight.

"Hi." His voice softens. Maybe he's starting to trust me. "Come in. I'll meet you in the lobby."

"Okay, bye." I hang up and take a deep breath. Grab the bag with our lunch and cross the street.

No friendly dog to welcome me with a wagging tail. I walk up the steps, dreading it less than the last time I was here. It's been twenty-four hours since we parted ways at the impound, but something fluttery makes a nest in my chest at the idea of seeing Jake again.

He waits for me in the hall and opens the door to the police station when I get closer.

"Thank you."

His hand goes to the small of my back. He guides me to

his office under the watchful eyes of two uniformed police officers and a man in a suit whom I think is the chief of police. I'm glad we didn't contact him. The man is huge and scary-looking.

Jake unlocks his office door and pushes it open for me. I miss the warm contact of his hand on my back.

He closes the door behind us, shutting out the low conversations and curious gazes. "Are you feeling okay?"

I set the food bag on the seat next to mine. "Yes, thank you. Why do you ask?"

"Your friend said that sometimes you get tired after one of these . . . what do you call it?"

I lift one shoulder. "I don't really have a name for it. Sessions?"

"That works." He sits on the other side of the desk, with one foot resting on his knee. His shoulders relax. There's an openness to him that wasn't there when we first met a week ago.

I break eye contact and grab the bag next to me. "I brought lunch. I hope you like BLT."

He removes his sunglasses, drops his leg to the floor, and wheels his chair closer. "Thanks, you didn't have to, but my stomach is happy you did."

"It's only fair—you've fed me twice. Now it's my turn." I hand him the wrapped sandwich and a bottle of water.

"Will eating first get in the way of your—" He gestures at me.

"Not with this kind of food. No sugar or animal products in it. Over the years, I've learned which foods ground me and which don't."

"Hmm, interesting." A dimple pops in his cheek when he smiles. "And I love BLTs."

God. No wonder he keeps the sunglasses on all the time. The smile and uncovered eyes combination has my heart working at full speed. I swallow and drag my gaze from his with the excuse of finding my sandwich. I resist the urge to fan my burning face. The heat spreads down, and I casually hold my water bottle to my chest.

I scratch at a non-existing itch on my shoulder. "Well, since we might be here for a while, I thought we should eat, and then we can talk about whatever else you have for me."

He unwraps his sandwich, picks up a half, and takes a bite. He groans with satisfaction, and the heat on my face and chest spreads into my belly. I press my lips together to hide my smile. I knew he'd like a BLT.

He opens his water bottle, eyeing my wrapped sandwich. "What did you get?"

Slow down, foolish heart. "I got an ALT."

"What's that?" His neck muscles move as he drinks.

"An avocado, lettuce, and tomato sandwich."

An eyebrow pops up in response. "Never had one of those. Good?"

I take a small bite, chew, and swallow. "Delicious. Want to try some?"

"I'll stick with the bacon."

We eat in silence, looking at each other. No small talk to fill the space. I like this comfortable quietness. The heat on my face dissipates as I get used to looking at him with no barriers.

It may have only been a week since I met Jake, but I've been dreaming of this moment for years—making up stories in my head for more than half my life. It doesn't feel like we just met.

He cleans up the wrappers, tosses them into the paper

bag, and takes a long drink of water. His eyes find mine. "Can I ask why you're staying in town for so long? Most people's vacations are for a week, not a whole summer."

Is this a curiosity question, or is he digging for information? I hold the urge to scoff at myself. He's a cop. Of course he's always digging for more information. But I have nothing to hide. "Lynn's a teacher, and I make my own hours. For years, since we were in school together, we've planned long summer vacations. My grandmother used to drive through New England with my mother when she was little. They used to rent a house at the beach for the summer. I'm sort of retracing their steps. But with my best friend instead."

He taps his fingers on the desk between us as he absorbs my response. I can almost see his brain working, sliding pieces together like a Rubik's cube. He leans into the desk. "But you didn't plan on spending the next two months here?"

"No, we didn't. As I told you before, we have the apartment for as long as we need. The owners are spending the summer helping their daughter with newborn twins in Colorado."

He nods, and his gaze drifts to the side. "It's not fair of me to ask you to change your vacation plans or to stay here indefinitely while I piece together the few clues I have."

No, it's not, but I would stay if he asked me. The answer in my head jolts me. Where did that come from? "We haven't made up our minds about the rest of the summer yet. It's wide-open. We don't have anything on our schedule until September."

The blue-green gaze softens. "I'm very grateful to you for taking a chance and coming to the police station, not knowing what kind of response you'd get. It took guts. And I also owe you an apology for how I behaved when we first met."

I run my hand through my hair, look down, fidget with the ends, and then face him again. "It's okay. I get it. It was a lot to take in. And I wasn't exactly polite either."

He shakes his head and rests his elbows on the desk. "No, that was all my doing. I was already frustrated with this case. Anyone who walked through my door that day would have gotten the tail end of my exasperation. You didn't have to come here and give me the necklace. Didn't have to stay and help me today, either. And I appreciate that."

"Yeah, but I called you an asshole."

"You did." He chuckles, and a corner of his mouth lifts a little. "But I deserved that."

He looks down again and aligns the already perfectly aligned folders on his desk. Then, looks back at me. "I have a question and a favor to ask."

Yes. I want to say yes, even though I don't even know what he wants. Once I read whatever evidence he has, my reason to stay here, to see him again, is over. "Okay . . ."

He scratches the back of his neck, and his shoulders hunch a little. "I know I've already asked a lot, and I flip-flopped back and forth between believing you and thinking you're the best scam artist I've ever met." He winces at the last part.

His candor eases the knots in my stomach, and I smile. It's easy to read his honesty and discomfort, making him even more alluring. I get a feeling he's not a man who likes being vulnerable or who shows his hand easily. "Okay, go on."

"I don't want to keep bugging you and end your vacation by dragging you into this mess, which I'm sure is the last thing you want, either. But I'd like to ask if I can keep in touch with you and get your input on whatever else I find."

Disappointment makes a cozy little nest in my chest. I wish he'd want to see me for more than what I can do for him, but the eagerness and urgency in him are centered on his job. "This case is more than just a job for you."

He jolts back as if my words are a physical blow. His body goes rigid. His eyes are ice-cold, and even if I'm not the cause of whatever is eating him, the force of his gaze makes me want to recoil. Instead, I hold firm and wait. He presses his lips together and nods once.

Perhaps I should be more careful with my words. But if I'm to help him, I need to get past his many defenses. "This is personal, isn't it?" My voice is soft but not pitying. He's not a man who would gracefully accept someone feeling sorry for him.

He doesn't respond this time. His face closes behind a mask of indifference. His eyes harden even more in a silent warning for me to stop asking questions. He's a picture of contradiction. He wants my help but has a hard time accepting it. And I can tell it has cost him a lot to ask me. I can read all of this in his body, his face, in the energy blasting from him.

"That's okay. I'm not asking you to tell me why. But to answer your question, yes, I'll help you in any way I can."

He swallows, looks down, and then back at me. Those eyes—like the sky and the sea—undo me. I'll do anything and everything to help him. He saved my life once—even if he doesn't know it was me. It's my turn to rescue him. I don't know how I'll do it, but I know that somehow his life, his very existence, hangs on solving these cases. Perhaps a way to redeem himself because of what happened to his sister. But that's not something I can bring up. He has no idea that I know. The truth in this thump in my chest with every beat of my heart.

He stands up, reaches for the wrappers from my lunch, and tosses them into the paper bag with his and then under the desk, where, I assume, is a garbage pail. "Thank you."

It's just two words. Words we say every day, but there's so much more in those two words than the simple token of gratitude.

He stands there with hands on his waist and eyes fixed on me. An internal battle rages inside him, all too clear in the stiff way in which he holds himself and in how carefully his face rearranges into a detached expression.

I get that because I haven't completely earned his trust yet. But I will. "Where shall we start?"

CHAPTER 15
JAKE

PERSONAL? DAMN RIGHT THIS IS PERSONAL. I STAND there, my back so tense that every muscle screams in pain. My biggest failure stares me in the face and taunts me every time another woman goes missing. Each passing day without answers is a constant reminder of my sister. For fourteen years, I've been searching for her. How could she disappear without a trace? I failed to keep Emily safe, and it eats at me every single day.

Ava has no idea how personal these cases are to me. Everyone moved on—I'm the only one still looking for Emily —I'll never stop.

Ava watches me, and not for the first time I wonder if she can read every thought in my head. It's disconcerting. But how do I keep her away when all I want is to be near her? This is insanity. I barely know her, and everything she is and does goes against my beliefs, my nature. And yet …

I force myself to breathe and relax, each muscle easing in turn. I step back and unlock one of the evidence drawers. Go back and clear my desk. Return to the drawer. Remove a plastic container. "This is from—"

"Don't tell me anything else." Her hand comes up to interrupt me. "I don't want you to plant any seeds that might influence me."

I set the clear box on my desk, remove the cover, and take out two sealed evidence bags. "Okay. How do you want to do this?"

She rolls her shoulders and shakes her hands. Takes a deep breath. Her chest expands and snags my gaze. She catches me looking at the swell of her breasts. There's amusement in her eyes. I blink and look away, fixing my eyes on the items in my hands.

"I'm ready. Just give me one object at a time. I assume I can't remove them from the sealed bags?"

"You—" My voice cracks. I clear my throat. "You assume correctly. Will you be able to work this way?"

The corners of her eyes crinkle with her smile. "Yes. It just takes a bit more concentration. I'm used to wearing cotton gloves to handle artifacts."

I place the first bag on the desk in front of her. Ava examines the watch through the clear bag for several seconds before touching it.

"Sometimes I pick up a vibe before I touch something." She reaches for it, and her hands cocoon the small evidence bag. Her gaze drifts and becomes unfocused. "This was a gift from her . . . mother."

I'm so distracted I nearly forget to hit the record button on my digital device. "A gift from her mother, you say?"

"Yes. She was a lovely girl. I see her face. She's opening the gift box. She has olive skin, big brown eyes, crazy curly hair.

She loved her hair." Ava smiles, as if the missing woman is standing in front of her.

The description matches the photos given to me by her family.

She closes her eyes now, no longer smiling. "There's a man. She meets him at a bowling alley. She doesn't seem to know him—this is not a date. He's bowling, and he makes her uncomfortable. She keeps looking at the watch. She wants to leave but can't, not yet. She's not there for fun. She's working. She's nervous, but not really scared." Ava opens her eyes. "Was she a waitress?"

I open and close my mouth. How can Ava possibly know these things? It shouldn't be possible. I could watch her do this a thousand times, and it would never seem feasible. "Yes, she was a waitress, and your description matches her."

She gives me back the watch. "What else do you have?"

I reach into the tote and retrieve the only other object we found. A blue stainless steel water bottle.

Ava frowns. "I've never read a water bottle before." She shrugs and reaches for it. "Oof." Her face immediately changes. One of her hands goes to her middle, she doubles over, and grunts like someone punched her in the stomach.

I rush to her side, but she puts her free hand up, and I stop.

"I'm okay." Her voice is strained. "I wasn't expecting that. Jesus. This bottle literally packs a punch."

I'm frozen in place. I don't know what to do.

Ava drags in a deep breath and straightens her shoulders. "I'm good," she whispers, then closes her eyes.

"The man is gone. She's still unsettled, but she's relieved he's not there. The place is empty. She turns off all the lights, steps outside, and locks the door. Stays by the locked door for a moment. She scans the parking lot."

Ava pauses, eyes still closed, breathing a little shallower now. "It's cold and starting to rain. Her breath condenses in the air. Her heart is beating so fast. She tucks the bottle inside her jacket and zips it up. Car keys in her hand, a key between her fingers like a weapon."

Ava tilts her head and moves it to the side as if she's watching a movie behind her closed eyelids. "The parking lot is empty. She speed-walks to her car. Someone calls her name and startles her. She looks over her shoulder. The outline of a man in the shadows. She runs to her car and opens the door. Something shoves at her back. It's him. The car door closes before she has a chance to get in. She screams."

Ava opens her eyes—they're rimmed with tears. "Can I have the watch again?"

I hand the watch back to her, and she holds one object in each hand. Closes her eyes.

"His arms go around her middle, trapping her to his chest. She stomps on his foot. Her feet leave the ground. He picks her up. She slams the back of her head into his face. He drops her. She tries to run. A bloody hand grabs her arm. She head-butted him hard enough to make him bleed. She turns, then tries to impale his face with the key in her hand. He blocks it. It's raining harder now—it's hard to see. She tries to get away. He grabs her again. Yanks her back and punches her in the stomach. She doubles over. The bottle slips out of her jacket, hits the top of her foot, and rolls under the car. She screams again. A hand covers her mouth. She bites it. He slaps her. She claws at his face. Her head slams against the car. She drops to the ground. Cold, rough asphalt abrades her face. Her vision blurs. She tries to push herself up. The watch comes undone. Hidden by her body. No fear now. Only rage. She pushes herself up on her knees and shaky hands. Scraped fingers. Chipped pink nail polish. She reaches for the watch. Slides it under the car, fills her lungs with air, and screams. Blinding, burning pain to the side of her head. Darkness."

Ava flinches, opens her eyes, blinks a few times, and sets both objects on the desk. "I think he kicked her in the head, and she passed out." She rubs her hands on her legs and then wipes her eyes with the heel of her palms. "He didn't notice the watch or water bottle. He's too careful and meticulous to leave anything behind. He didn't expect her to put up such a fight. He lost control. He didn't seem well prepared. Maybe this wasn't a planned abduction."

I may be standing still, but my heart is running a marathon. I can't catch my breath. Every muscle in my body is locked and rigid, and the bones in my spine grind with tension. As much as I want to deny everything Ava said, she has again confirmed something I already knew. And now she's giving me some insight into how this guy's mind works. If the disappearances are related, as I suspect, and these women are indeed dead, I might have a serial killer on my hands.

She curls her hands into fists and presses them to her lap. "That sick bastard. We have to stop him. Did you check the bowling place where she worked? Do they have security cameras?"

We. My stomach flips. Ava's made herself a part of this investigation. At my invitation, I know. This is temporary, a one-time thing. But Ava's a sliver of hope. The only hope I have right now. I've exhausted every other option. "No cameras in the parking lot. And the only cameras inside were over the cashiers. It's an old place. And the owner is more concerned about an employee pocketing some money than any other safety measure. No prints other than hers were on the car, and if anything else was on the ground, the rain washed it away. Nothing to go by except the watch and the bottle."

"Tell me about her now."

I know the information by heart but grab the file, so I have an excuse to do something with my hands. "Her name is Lena Greer. She's twenty-five. She has worked at the bowling alley for the last two years. She lives with her family. They went looking for her when she didn't make it home and didn't answer calls. Found her car and called the police. Every avenue I've tried failed. I have nothing. Just like the other two."

She brushes a trembling hand through her hair and drops to the chair behind her. Her face is pale, and a sheen of sweat beads on her forehead. She swallows and closes her eyes. A shiver runs through her body.

I don't know what to do, but I need to do something. I sink to my knees in front of Ava and take both her hands between mine. She's shaking. I thought what I witnessed Ava do before, with my rock and the car at the impound, prepared me for whatever else she had coming. I was wrong. This is way more intense than I imagined.

I rub the back of Ava's hands with my thumbs, trying to soothe her. Her face is hidden behind a curtain of loose curls. I want to wrap my fingers in those curls and tug, tilt her face up to mine, and . . . Jesus! What am I doing? There's no excuse for behaving this way. I need to stop this line of thought. Get myself under control. Nothing good can come from allowing my attraction to her to take over.

Ava tilts her head up. Her lips are inches away from mine. Big hazel eyes look up at me, wet with unshed tears. Shades of green, brown, and gold flecks in her irises. I drag in a breath and with it the scent of apples. Her scent. I lean a little closer and her lips part. A soft, nearly inaudible gasp escapes.

The phone rings, the sound like an alarm going off inside my head and asking me what the hell I'm doing. I pull back and let go of her hands. Then, straighten up as the ringer goes silent. I clear my throat. Search for something to say. "Apples . . ." What the fuck! What am I saying?

Ava stands up. "Apples?"

"Hm, yes. I smell apples." I'm an idiot.

"Oh." She smooths her hair, fingers combing through those curls I admired a second ago. "It's my shampoo. Green apple scented."

"It smells nice." Shut up.

She smiles. Her cheeks go pink. "Thank you."

The phone rings again. I walk around my desk. "I have to take this. Call you later?"

She nods and lets herself out of my office. I stare at the closed door while the phone continues to ring.

I answer the call. "Knox?" My boss's voice comes through. His usually unflappable tone is more urgent than I've ever heard. "There's another report of a woman gone missing."

CHAPTER 16
AVALON

"Hey, you're back!" Lynn's smiling face greets me as I enter our apartment and kick off my shoes by the door. I walk to the sofa, sit down, sigh.

She sits in the corner. "What's the matter?"

There's a war inside me. "I feel terrible for all these poor women and, at the same time, excited to be near Jake. It's like being on an emotional roller coaster."

She pats my calf. "Well, look at it this way. You're helping him and helping the missing women, too."

I grab a pillow and hold it to my chest. "I'm so attracted to him. I feel guilty. I shouldn't be having all these thoughts about him. This is serious stuff, yet my mind goes there."

Lynn shakes her head. "You're not a robot. You can't turn off how you feel about him."

"But there should be a more appropriate time to feel this way, right? One second, I'm in the mind of this poor murdered woman, and the next he's kneeling in front of me. And he's so close—all I want to do is lean in and kiss him."

"Next time, do it. Kiss him."

I throw the pillow at her.

Lynn catches the pillow and sits on the other end of the sofa. "Tell me what happened?"

"Well, we ate lunch and talked a little. Then Jake showed me the evidence for the first missing girl—her name was Lena. She was just twenty-five." I take a deep breath and close my eyes. "The images are so fresh in my mind." I shake my head and open my eyes again. "This is harder than I thought it would be."

Lynn reaches out to me and squeezes my hand.

I squeeze back, thankful for her reassurance. "I know I've done this stuff a million times before, but it was never like this."

I need to move. I get up and pace. "I've seen people die, and I've seen people do horrible things, but they have all been in the past. Hundreds of years ago, sometimes even more, but this is different. It's too fresh, too close, and it feels like I should be able to stop it, but I can't because it already happened."

Lynn tracks my back-and-forth. "I can't say I know how you feel because I don't, and I never will. You know there's nothing you can do to change what already happened, but what you're doing right now—it makes a difference, Ava."

She waits until I stop moving and look at her again.

"With your help, the cops can stop this guy. They'll catch him. And you'll help bring closure to those women and their families. You'll be their Avenging Guardian Angel." She says the last three words with a smile on her face. Lynn can never stay serious for too long.

She pats the sofa. "Come sit down and tell me what you found out."

I do as she asks. "He took this girl from her job. She

worked in a bowling alley. I think I want to go there, check it out, get a feel for the place, see if I can find anything else."

"That might be a good idea. Did you plan that with the detective?"

"No, I think having a cop walk into the place will automatically put people on the defensive. I was thinking . . . Maybe you'll come with me. Tomorrow? And then we can be just two girls for a night out. It's been six months since she disappeared, but I want to see the place myself. Maybe find a clue the police didn't."

Lynn puts both her hands up. "You mean, you want me to go with you to a place where somebody was kidnapped and murdered, hoping to see if the killer's back there?"

I wince. "Well . . . when you put it like that, it sounds terrible, but yeah, that's kind of what I was thinking."

"Okay, I'll do it for you"—she sighs exaggeratedly and loudly—"but in exchange, you have to go out to a pub with me this Friday. We need to shake this whole dead people thing off. You're buying, and I'm planning on drinking and eating a lot."

"A pub?"

"Yes, I found this place in town, down Main Street. It has pool tables and live music. We are going to have fun, fun, fun."

"God knows I need some fun after this last week." I put my hand up, and she high-fives me. "Deal."

"That's what you've been doing when I'm with Jake? Walking around town?"

"Yes, this town is adorable. All these colorful little stores and the locals are so friendly and welcoming. I guess it's easy to see how someone could have been taken. None of the distrust we get in New York."

129

"I feel less guilty knowing you're at least enjoying yourself."

"I am. Did you find any new clues about the guy?"

"Not really. What I saw was more of a confirmation of what Jake already knew, but at least it shows he's on the right track. I hope I can find something soon."

"What's next then?"

"Jake is getting in touch with Alice's roommate to arrange a time for us to stop by so I can look around and see what I can find. After that, I guess I'll keep looking for clues."

Lynn sighs. "I guess I'll be doing a lot of stuff alone this vacation."

"I'm so sorry. But we can still do lots of things together. I mean, helping Jake shouldn't take all my time."

She puts the back of her hand on her forehead and falls back into the sofa like a fainting old-time movie star. "I'll just have to do a lot of shopping and flirting with the local guys while you're busy saving the world."

I grimace. "I promise the next vacation will be the best one ever."

I love watching them as they realize the God they've been praying for isn't coming to save them. The hope vanishes from their faces with each ragged breath. The life dimming in their eyes, the clouding of their vision, is almost as satisfying as the first cut.

Almost. But not quite.

That first cut is like losing your virginity. You can only experience it once. I still remember my first time. That first cut was the sweetest of all. I've been chasing it all these years, but no one was ever as sweet as my first one.

CHAPTER 17
AVALON

JAKE DRIVES IN SILENCE. THE ONLY SOUND IS THE HUM of the motor. I steal glances at him. He's staring at the red light, lost in his own world.

I clear my throat and shift my body so I can face him. "I went to the bowling alley with Lynn yesterday."

He whirls his head to me. "You did what?" His voice is like the crack of a whip.

I ignore the trace of anger in his tone. "I went to the bowling alley with Lynn."

The lines around his mouth deepen. "Why would you do that? Do you have any idea how dangerous that could be?"

I cross my arms and stare him down. I know he's glaring at me, even though those damn sunglasses hide his eyes. "Lena went missing six months ago. I doubt the killer will strike in the same place twice. He's not stupid. We were perfectly safe."

A light beep sounds behind us. I glance at the now green traffic light and back at him. He doesn't make a move. The beeping is a little louder now. His hands squeeze the steering

132

wheel. The beeping increases and is accompanied by others. I raise one eyebrow, and an image of Grandma giving me the same look flashes in my mind. Gosh, I need to call her. It's been a few days since we talked. She might have some insight into these cases.

He turns to face the road and drives. Someone passes us and gives him the finger. I laugh. I have to.

He grinds his molars. "What's so funny about that?"

"I'm a New Yorker. Flipping the bird is practically the official state salutation."

The corner of his mouth twitches. His chest expands with a deep breath. He glances at me. His face resigned, but no trace of anger remains. "Why did you go to the bowling alley?"

I lift a hand as if the gesture could explain my reasoning. "I had to go and see for myself. I hoped that something else would come to me."

His eyes are fixed on the road. "And did something else come to you?"

I shake my head, but he's still not looking at me. "No. Nothing."

He glances at me. "I could have come with you."

"Yeah, I thought about that. But it would have been a cop and me, and cops tend to make people wary. I figured if I went with Lynn, it would be just two girls having fun. People might have talked. But no such luck."

He nods once, the steering wheel sliding through his hands as we come out of a turn. "This is a small town, and people like to talk, but usually not to strangers. And to them, you're a stranger."

To them? "I'm not a stranger to you?" My voice is small and unsure.

He chuckles without humor. "It's been, what? Not even two weeks since you walked into my office and turned everything I believe upside down. You told me things about myself that even I'd forgotten and then said more things no one should know."

He parks in front of a townhome and turns off the engine. Then, looks at me. "No, I don't think you're a stranger to me. We are way past that."

My pulse beats so loud it drums in my ears. "What am I then?" We have so little time together, and none of this time is what I hoped it would be when I dreamed about meeting him again. Could there ever be more than just this awkward professional truce between us?

He looks at me for a long time, his gaze traveling all over my face and body. "I have no idea."

Ruby opens the door to Alice's bedroom and steps aside. "The room is as she left it. I can't bring myself to go in there and touch anything."

"Thank you, Ruby." I try to give her a reassuring smile, but don't quite make it. She wears her sorrow like a mantle.

"I'll leave you to it." Ruby walks away.

I walk into the small room alone. Jake stays at the door and watches me. I don't touch anything yet. There are drawings on the walls, some pencil sketches, and some in full color. Beautiful renditions of dragons, unicorns, and other fantasy creatures. Each piece of art has her name and date in one corner. A small desk holds paper pads, pencils, and other art supplies. She was an artist. A good one, too.

Across from the desk is a twin bed, a purple blanket

messily pulled over it. Pillow askew. Folded laundry on a chair. Open curtains over a single window. A small bookshelf with a couple of dozen paperbacks. Most with stickers from a used bookstore.

I drag my fingers over her desk, catching glimpses of her working with her art. "She loved this, loved sitting here and escaping into her drawings. She was so full of hope. But also pain. She felt so alone all the time."

I sit at her desk and splay my hands over an unfinished drawing of a man. He's wearing armor, thick bands around his wrist, dark bat-like wings at his back. His features are blank. "She was working on this piece. It was the last thing she worked on. I think she was drawing him, but I don't think they had met yet."

"I'm getting flashes of her talking to someone on a phone. Not a cell phone. One of those phones you see in an office with multiple lines. What did she do for work?"

"She worked as a receptionist in a real estate company."

I grab a pencil next. "Hmm . . . she spoke with him on the phone. More than once, and she was keeping it a secret because of her job."

Jake walks into the room. "Could it be someone she worked with?"

"No, I don't think he worked there. I think he was trying to pass as a client to get her to trust him. She was hesitant the first few times he called, but she warmed up to him."

"Both her roommate and the people at her job said she was not seeing anyone."

"She wasn't. I think he took her the first time she met him."

I stand up and walk around the room, allowing my senses to guide me. Brush my fingers along the walls, the bed, and the dresser. "I don't have anything else. She was quiet. Went to work, read, and drew her pictures."

Jake nods, and we leave the room, closing the door behind us.

Ruby waits in the living room, a cup of tea in her hands.

I sit across from her. "I'm sure the police have already asked you this, but do you know if she was talking to someone? Perhaps someone at work. Did she even mention anything like that?"

"No, Alice kept to herself. We met in tenth grade and became fast friends—the two girls who didn't really fit with any of the school clicks. She had a rough life, you know. She didn't trust easily, but she was my best friend. I still can't believe she's gone. I keep expecting her to come in and show me a new picture. She loved drawing."

I nod and look around the condo. "How are you managing without a roommate?"

Ruby's gaze goes to her teacup. "Oh, she rented this place from her job. They told me not to worry about her half of the rent. They changed the lock, too. I should move. It's too hard being here. But I don't want to lose hope that she'll come back. If I go, then this is it. She's gone forever."

I meet Jake's eyes and stand up. "Thank you for letting us come in, Ruby."

She nods.

"We'll see ourselves out."

CHAPTER 18
AVALON

THE BLACK AND GOLD SIGN ABOVE THE DARK WOODEN doors makes me snort. *The Lady and the Ghost.* I side-eye Lynn. "Leave it up to you to find a pub with this name."

She brushes her nails on her blouse and blows on them. "I'm that good. What can I say?"

"Modest, too."

She laughs and pushes the door open, and I walk in ahead of her. The place is all dark wood paneling, like an old English tavern. Colorful stained-glass frames hang from the ceiling and divide the space into two uneven areas. To the left, a few people mingle around pool tables set on a platform a couple of steps higher than the rest of the space.

Lights hang above each table, two of which are empty. A floating shelf with scattered drinks atop lines the wall behind the tables. High stools are nested under the shelf.

Classic rock music blends with the murmur of conversations and clinking glasses. The smell of different foods entices me to go in farther.

The hostess approaches us. "Welcome to The Lady and

137

the Ghost. Do you want a table, or will you two be at the bar?"

Lynn looks at me and decides for us both. "The bar, please."

"You can go right in. There are a few spots open still."

We thank her and walk across the pub. The main area has several tables and booths. Rich, dark leather and wood make the large space feel cozy and intimate. The massive bar takes nearly the entire back wall. Deep, dark mahogany and two pillars with intricate carvings flank each side. A collection of alcoholic beverage bottles fills the back wall, interspersed with landscape paintings evenly spaced. Copper sconces shed a soft light over each framed picture.

Lynn points to the side, closer to the pool tables. "Let's take those last two chairs at the end. I want to watch them play."

I give her a look she knows all too well. Lynn is a pool shark. She'll come in all petite and sweet, ask for tips on how to play, and then clean the table in two strikes. "Maybe don't call attention to us with your pool skills tonight?"

"What? I didn't do anything." She sounds so innocent. I can almost see a halo over her head.

"Yet. You didn't do anything yet."

She takes the chair closest to the wall, which leaves me to sit next to a chair occupied by a man in a baseball cap. Luckily there are several inches between us, so I don't feel crowded.

I take a seat and turn to Lynn, who's already sizing up the very cute bartender. Bet she's eyeing the tattoos peeking from under the rolled-up sleeves of his black shirt.

He gives her a dazzling smile and sets two paper napkins in front of us. "Good night. I'm Marcus."

Lynn taps her lips with her index finger while looking him up and down. She leans into the bar top. "Oh, let me see your tattoo."

He shows her his arm. The tattoo is an intricate bird cage, the door open, but the bird inside is dead at the bottom of the cage. Lynn frowns at it.

The bartender smiles. "It's a reminder to escape our traps and not die with our dreams still caged. What can I get you ladies tonight?"

"I would love a Screaming Orgasm. Can you give me that, Marcus?" Lynn unleashes her inner vixen on the poor bartender.

The guy sitting next to me chokes on his beer. I laugh-cough-choke right along with him. He nearly drops his bottle. Then catches it, but not before spilling some on the bar. I grab the napkins the bartender gave us and try to sop up the mess. Our hands brush, and a zing of awareness climbs up my arm and settles on the back of my neck. Our eyes meet. And even in the dimmed light and partially obscured by a baseball cap, the two different colors call to me. Green and blue.

The detective is sitting next to me. How did I not notice him until now? One of grandma's favorite movie quotes comes to mind. "Of all the gin joints in all the towns in all the world . . ."

"She walks into mine," Jake finishes the quote.

We just stare at each other. None of the animosity from our initial encounter in his voice. His eyes are soft, and his shoulders are loose. He seems more relaxed than I've ever seen him. Not that I have a lot to go by. But something of that boy who saved my life comes through in the soft smile playing on his lips. It's the same smile he gave when I opened my eyes and locked gazes with him all those years ago. It makes him look younger and carefree. I can't help but respond in kind.

Still grinning and giving Lynn hot, smoky glances, the bartender finishes cleaning up the spilled beer. "And for you?"

I drag my gaze back to him. "A Mojito. And some water, please."

Lynn looks around me. "Well, well, well. Look at what we have here."

Jake tips his beer bottle in her direction in salutation.

Marcus brings us our drinks and a fresh beer for Jake. Lynn's cocktail looks more like a dessert than a drink. Rich and covered in whipped cream and a maraschino cherry. She takes a long pull through the straw while keeping eye contact with the bartender.

He smiles. "Good?"

She pops the cherry in her mouth and looks him up and down. "Delicious."

I'm definitely going back to the apartment alone tonight.

I turn to Jake, who's watching the exchange with a frown. I lean a little. "Will she be safe with him?"

He takes a sip of beer. "I don't know him very well, but I've never heard anything bad about him other than he gets a lot of dates. She should be all right, as long as she doesn't expect him to call her tomorrow."

"No problem there. Lynn has zero interest in settling down."

"What about you?" He presses his lips together as if trying to rein the words back in.

His question pokes at something inside me. My heart squeezes. The question surprises me and perhaps it surprises him too. He looks down at the bottle in his hands and traces the label with his thumb.

"I don't know. I haven't put much thought into it." I take a sip of my drink. "Haven't had any good role models for lasting relationships."

He tilts his head. "You mentioned living with your grandmother. What happened to your parents?"

"My mother died giving birth to me."

"I'm glad you had your grandmother to care for you."

"Grandma is all I've ever known."

"And your father? Isn't he in your life?"

"I don't even know who my father is. All I know is that he left when he found out my mother was pregnant. And she died giving birth to me, so I'll never know him." Or my mother.

His eyes soften. "I can't imagine walking away from my child. Even if I didn't want a relationship with the mother, I would never abandon my kid. It must have been very hard on you, growing up without your parents."

Some old ache inside me eases a little. It's been years since I thought about my parents. I don't spend much time and energy thinking about what could have been or how different my life might be if my mother was still here and my father stuck around. "I think it would have been harder if I had known them and then lost them."

He taps the side of the beer bottle with his thumb. "That is true."

"Grandma raised me. It's been generations of single mothers raising daughters in my family. The gift is passed on from mother to daughter. None of the fathers stayed long. My great-great-grandmother was the last one to have a long marriage. I guess the men couldn't take being with a woman with those kinds of powers." I laugh.

"So, this . . . ability is something your whole family shares?"

"Only the females."

"That's fascinating. Everyone has the same abilities?"

"No, it varies. Grandma said my mother had a gift too, but she resented it. She blamed her gift for everything that went wrong in her life. I don't think she ever planned on being a mother, and sometimes I wonder if dying was her choice. If she just decided to give up on living the moment she gave birth to me. Maybe the idea of raising a child with the same gifts as hers was too much to bear. But her gifts were much crueler than mine. She saw deaths, accidents, and diseases every time she touched someone. She saw it all. Sometimes I'm sure she died so she would never have to touch me and see what was coming my way."

CHAPTER 19
AVALON

Jake's eyes widen, and his lips part, but he says nothing. I just dropped a bomb on him. I have no idea why I'm sharing so much. Maybe because I want him to trust me. To understand me and where I come from. I want him to like me. To be the man I've been dreaming of for half my life.

Silence falls between us, and background noise fills the space left by unsaid words.

Lynn nudges my shoulder. "Want to play some billiards?"

Gosh. I forgot Lynn was there for a second. Jake's gaze flits all over my face, as if he's trying to read my mind. "Yeah, sure." I can use the distraction. I take a sip of my drink. The refreshing mint and lime taste center me.

I look at Jake again. "Want to join us? Since we are *old* friends and all."

He hesitates for a second and pushes his chair back. The three of us walk to one of the empty pool tables. Lynn goes straight to the wall holding pool sticks and carefully inspects them as if they are surgical instruments, and precision is essential for this operation.

143

She returns with three sticks and hands one to both Jake and me. "There are three of us, so we can play eight-ball, and the loser gives up his spot to the next person, or we can play cutthroat with the three of us. What will it be?"

I've never played with three people before. "Cutthroat? What's that?"

Jake points at the rack in the center of the table. "We each get five balls to protect. Instead of pocketing your balls like in a regular game, the objective is to pocket your opponent's balls. Wipe them off the table."

Lynn smiles. "That's right."

"How do we know which ball belongs to who?"

Jake adjusts the balls, moving their positions inside the rack. "We go by numbers. One person gets balls one through five, the next six through ten, and so on."

Lynn saddles up to the table and nudges the rack a hair to the left. "I'll go first."

I point at her with my cue stick. "No, you won't. The game will be over before we start. Jake, you can go first."

He shakes his head and takes a step back. "No, ladies first."

"Okay, I'll go first, but Lynn will go last."

Lynn touches my elbow and stops me before I can hit the racked balls. "Let's make it interesting, though."

Oh no, here it comes. "Lynn . . ."

She ignores me. "Loser buys dinner. And I agree to go last. That's fair."

Jake narrows his eyes at her. Her relaxed demeanor, one hand at her hip, cue stick in the other. Her eyes wide and innocent as she waits for an answer. "Why do I feel like I'm about to get swindled?"

She places her free hand on her chest. "What? Why, I'm

offended." Her thick Southern accent has me nearly choking on my mojito. She's a yank. A New Yorker through and through and there's not an ounce of a Southern belle in her.

Jake laughs. "Maybe I should just hand over my wallet while I'm ahead."

The sound of his laugh is melodic and unexpected. Warmth spreads into my chest as I see him smile and the tension ease off his shoulders. But there's also a little unwelcome sharp burn, like the prick of a heated blade. I want to be the one making him laugh like that. I shove the feeling away and force myself to relax, stop thinking, and be present. Enjoy this moment, enjoy the truce between us, and take what he's offering. I mentally thank Lynn for dragging me here today. I step to the table and break the rack.

Solid and striped balls roll and settle. Four balls hit the sides and the cue ball sits in the middle. I study the table and make my call. "I'll take six through ten."

Lynn looks at the spread. "Good call. I'll take one through five. And *your detective* can have eleven through fifteen."

I glance at him. A raised eyebrow tells me he too caught the inflection in Lynn's voice when she said *your detective*. I might have to beat her up with the pool stick. I take a deep breath and go after her balls instead. Pocket one.

"Hey? And you call yourself my best friend?"

I smile and go for another one of her balls. I miss this time, and Jake steps in. He pockets two of her balls and misses the third. It's Lynn's turn now.

She swaggers forward. Grabs a chalk cube while she studies the table. Then tosses it over her shoulder, and Jake grabs it mid-air while I flinch. She laughs and winks at me. "Prepare to be amazed."

She goes after Jake's first. Pockets all five balls in rapid succession. Someone whistles and someone else says, "I want her on my team."

We have a small audience now. The bartender comes over to watch—a dishtowel draped over his shoulder. He crosses his arms and smiles at Lynn. She saunters around the table, her back to him, leans over, and gives him a fantastic view of her ass. I have to laugh. The poor guy has no idea what's coming for him.

She sinks four of my balls and misses the last one on purpose. The hit is so wild there's no doubt she cheated. "Oops. It's your turn again, Ava."

Jake walks behind me and whispers into my ear, "Your friend is a hustler."

Every tiny hair on the back of my neck stands. A shiver runs down my spine, and my nipples go painfully hard. I fight the urge to cross my arms over my chest, and I bring my elbows in, holding the stick between my laced fingers instead. Drag a slow breath in. Gosh. I didn't expect my body to react like this.

Lynn narrows her eyes at him. "What did you say? It was about me, wasn't it?"

Jake stands next to me now. Barely an inch between us. He smells so good, like fresh laundry and sunshine. I want to bury my face into his chest and inhale deeply. Instead, I hold myself stone-still. He studies the table and then glances at Lynn. A corner of his mouth tips up. "I said you're a hustler."

She shrugs. "I've been called worse."

I sink one of her balls and miss my next shot. Jake is out, so it's Lynn's turn again.

She sinks the rest of mine, and the game is over. She saunters back to the bartender. "Can we have three menus?

Our friend here"—she tilts her head toward Jake—"is buying tonight."

I mouth *sorry* to Jake.

The bartender's gaze never leaves Lynn. "My shift is done for the day, but I can grab you a booth if you want?"

She rewards him with a smile. "Sure, we'd love that."

The three of us settle into a half-circle booth, with me in the middle and Jake and Lynn on either end. Not five minutes later, Lynn excuses herself, and two minutes after that, I get a text message from her.

Lynn: Enjoy your dinner. Ask Jake for a ride. I took your key fob.

"What the heck."

Jake shifts closer to me. "Is everything okay?"

"That little scheming thief. I'm going to kill her."

He frowns. "Who?"

"Lynn. She took my car."

His frown deepens. "She left without you. Why?"

Lynn: And don't worry about me drinking. I didn't even finish half of it. I'm good, I swear.

Because in her mind, she's doing me a favor by leaving us alone together. I look at the bar, and Marcus is nowhere to be seen. "Where's the bartender?"

Me: JFC, Lynn! Did you leave with the bartender? There's a serial killer out there. What are you doing?

Lynn: I'm fine. I'll be safe, I promise.

I'm typing an angry message back to her when my phone vibrates again, and a string of emojis comes through. A taco, eggplant, tongue, the peace sign, water drops, and multiple flames. I delete my typed text and send her a dozen knife emojis instead.

"I can't believe she did this. I'm going to switch her coffee to decaf."

His hand gently wraps around my wrist. It's warm and comforting like it belongs there. Like his touch belongs on my skin. "You didn't answer my question. Why did she leave you behind and not say anything?"

My face heats. Hopefully, Jake won't notice it in the dim lights. "Lynn's a jokester."

"That's not funny. And not safe either. How does she expect you to get back to your place?"

"She believes I'll be safe with you, and you'll give me a ride."

His hand is still wrapped around my wrist. His thumb moves once, twice in a gentle caress. The tender touch reverberates up my arm and into the back of my neck, where chills dance on my skin. I squeeze my thighs together and make a conscious effort to keep my breathing even. The booth works like a cocoon, isolating us from the rest of the place. He's so close, his gaze so intense. My body leans into him without my permission. My lips part and—

A waitress stops with menus. Jake releases my wrist and shifts a few inches away from me. I take a menu and keep my gaze fixed on it. The waitress rattles the specials. I don't hear a thing she's saying. Jesus, what was I about to do? Kiss him? This is insanity.

"Thanks. We'll need a few minutes." His voice reaches me as if from a distance.

No, not a few minutes. A lifetime.

CHAPTER 20
JAKE

SHE HAS YET TO LOOK AT ME. SHE'S HIDING BEHIND THE menu, but I doubt she's actually reading anything since it's upside down. I don't like the way her friend left without saying anything. I want to believe Lynn is trying to give us a chance to be alone away from the police station. And as much as I like the idea of having Ava all to myself without any of the investigation crap between us, I worry about her distracting me from what I need to do. I believe her and yet a small part of me still doubts the whole thing.

You don't have to let a dog bite you in the ass to know it has teeth.

My grandfather's voice sounds in my mind as clear as if he's standing next to me. That's something he used to say to me often. I haven't thought about it in years. Ava snorts a laugh and drops the menu. She looks past me, and I follow her gaze, half expecting to see Grandpa walking between the tables. I look back at her in time to see her flipping the menu right side up.

I cross my arms over the table. "Something funny?"

She blushes. "Yeah, me trying to read the menu upside down." Her gaze flicks over my shoulder again, but I resist the urge to look.

My mind is playing tricks on me. This whole situation with the missing women and Ava's psychic abilities has me on edge. I came here to get away and relax, and that's what I'm going to do. "Find anything vegetarian?"

She goes back to looking at the menu. "I did. Thanks. You know what you want?"

What a loaded question. You, in my bed. "Yeah."

The waitress comes back with water glasses. "Ready to order?"

I tilt my head at Ava.

"I'll have the veggie quesadilla. Can you add guacamole, please? Thank you." She tries to give the menu back to the waitress, who's smiling at me and ignoring Ava.

The waitress looks vaguely familiar. I glance at her name tag. *Renee.*

Not a name you see every day. "You look familiar. Do I know you?"

Her hand goes to my shoulder and stays there. "Yes, we had one class together, freshman year of high school. I moved away, but I'm back now."

I reach for the water glass and her hand drops.

Ava waves the menu at the waitress. "You can take this now, thanks." She smiles, but it's the smile a dog gives you just before the bite.

I take Ava's menu and mine and hand them back to Renee. "I'll have the steak and fries. Cooked medium, please."

The waitress leaves, and Ava watches her. "I don't think she likes me."

"What makes you say that?"

The look she gives me suggests I'm a dozen crayons short of a twelve-pack box. Another thing Grandpa used to say. Her presence is making me think of him. For a moment, I could almost swear I smelled his aftershave.

"She didn't look at me once."

"Maybe she's shy?"

"There was nothing shy about the way she was looking at you." She picks up the water glass and her lips wrap around the paper straw.

My imagination paints X-rated pictures in my mind. My stomach clenches and I shift in my seat. I swallow and clear my throat. I want to ask her if she's jealous, but this is a line I can't cross. I should not cross. Oh, fuck it. "Jealous?" I laugh to make it sound like a joke.

Ava sets the glass down. "If I were your girlfriend, I might be jealous. But that's not the point. She doesn't know what kind of relationship we have. We could be friends or lovers. And her behavior was deliberate. She's not shy, she was coming on to you."

She's right, but I'm not ready to concede yet. "Maybe she's friendly?"

Ava laces her fingers and props her chin on them. "Is she shy or friendly?"

I smile. I can't remember the last time I enjoyed myself like this. "Both?"

Her hand comes up in a *give me* gesture. "Come on, Detective. Hand it over."

"Hand over what?"

"Your badge. You just lost it. I'm demoting you for being clueless."

I laugh—a real, head-tilted-back laugh. "Maybe I'm not

being clueless. Maybe I'm ignoring her"—I make air quotes—"coming on to me."

"And why would you do that? You're single and she's pretty. Is she not your type?"

"I'm not sure I have a type."

"No?"

"No, but I'm looking forward to finding out." What the hell? Am I flirting? I *am* flirting. I can't even remember the last time I flirted with a woman. "What about you? What's your type?"

She takes a sip of her drink. "I'm not sure I have a type, either. Not a defined physical type, at least. I can appreciate a handsome face and fit body, but the things I find really attractive in a man are not tangible."

"What do you mean?"

"I'm attracted to intelligence, a sense of humor, confidence without arrogance, and kindness. A pretty face and hard body can be fun for a while, but if that's all there is, it will get boring fast."

I'm about to respond when the waitress comes back with our food. She places the dishes on the table. Her body turns in such a way that her back is to Ava. And this time, her hand goes to my bicep. "Can I get you anything else, Jake?"

I look at Ava and she mouths, "Watch me." Then she flickers a spoon off the table. It falls behind Renee with a loud clatter.

"Oops. I'm such a klutz." That smile with a bite is back.

Renee picks up the spoon, her eyes narrowed. "I'll be right back with a clean one."

Ava waves a hand at her. "Oh, no need to come back. I don't need the spoon. Thanks, though."

I disguise a laugh into a cough.

153

Renee walks away, and Ava grins like someone who just had her cake and ate it, too.

I grab the beer bottle and take a sip. "Okay. You're right. She's coming on a little strong."

"Told you."

"Let me make it up for you. In a place without interruption by an overeager waitresses. Have dinner with me Sunday night. At my place. I'll cook." Wait. Where did that come from? Did I just ask her out?

Her lips part and I want nothing more than to slide my tongue between them and taste her. But not here. Not with so many eyes on us. The gossip brigade will have lots to talk about this weekend as it is.

She's at a loss for words for a few seconds, then a shy smile. "Yes, I would like that."

CHAPTER 21
AVALON

My phone rings, and I smile when Grandma's face shows on the screen.

I accept the FaceTime call and plop on my bed, phone in one hand and a comb in the other, as I try to tame the mess of wet curls rioting on my head. "Hi, Grandma—"

"So, you met a boy. Tell me everything about him."

I pull the phone back and stare at Grandma. Her silver-white hair just touches the top of her shoulders. Her trademark power red lipstick is perfectly applied. Her all-knowing gaze is on me. Lynn steps behind me and waves at the phone.

I twist to look at her. "Did you tell Grandma about—"

"No, she didn't." Grandma interrupts me again. "Lynn, you can stop waving now. I can see you."

I shake my head. No matter how often Grandma does this, it's always a bit of a shock. She claims she can't see or hear well anymore, but she always knows everything. Her gift of foresight is sharper than ever.

155

"Let me prop the phone better so you can see both of us." I set my phone down against a couple of pillows.

Lynn steps in front of me. "Hi, Grandma. Yes, she met a boy."

I nudge Lynn to the side so I can see my phone. "Yes, I met someone. He's not a boy. He's a grown man and a local police detective."

Grandma's voice softens. "He's one of the good guys."

"Grandma, when you told me to come here on vacation, did you already know what would happen?" The thought has been needling at me for a while now.

Grandma pats her perfectly coiffured hair. "He'll be good for you. But he needs to let go of a few things first." She ignores my question, as she tends to do in situations like this. But I'm not giving up so easily.

"Grandma! Can you please answer my question? This is way more complicated than the errands you've sent me on before, where I find a rare book or a lost piece of art. People are getting killed."

She looks at me for a long time, and I hold out for an answer.

She sighs. "You know I can't tell you everything I see. The future is not defined. There are paths within paths, and the choices you make will determine what happens. I can only guide you, but the choices and the paths are yours alone."

"And yet you sent me here. To find these missing women."

"I sent you there to find *him*. The one you've been dreaming about all these years."

Her words hit me like a blow to the chest, momentarily robbing me of breath. "H-how?" I'm lost for words. She knows I met Jake that and he's the boy who saved my life fifteen years ago?

Her shoulders sag. "Locating the missing women is his fate. Not yours. But you chose to do this, and now you two share the same goal."

Thoughts whirl in my mind like debris being scattered around by a tornado. "What will happen?"

"What do you want to happen?" She throws the question back at me, kindly.

What do I want? "I want him *and* my career. I want my life the way it was before I stumbled on that necklace. I want to erase all those terrible images from my mind."

She smiles. "You can have him and your career. But I'm afraid what you saw is forever a part of you. You'll need to learn to live with it, and in time it'll fade like all things tend to do."

Lynn takes the forgotten comb from my hand and tackles a section of my hair, unsnarling the tangles with expert hands.

I don't see how I can have it all. "No, Grandma, this is temporary. I'll be leaving soon. He belongs here, in this town, and I belong . . . nowhere."

Grandma huffs. "Nonsense. He's not a tree—he can move —he can take his roots with him wherever he goes. And you? You belong everywhere. The world is yours for the taking. You two can make it work *if you* choose to."

My heart tries to escape through my mouth. I swallow it down. "Grandma, you can't just say something like that and then tell me it's my choice. I'm freaking out over here."

Silence reigns. I wait. And wait.

She looks at the delicate watch on her thin wrist. "I have to go. There's a game of mahjong starting soon, and I'm going to win today."

And I know she won't say anything else about Jake. But maybe . . . "Grandma, before you go, can you tell me anything about this killer and the missing women?"

She presses her lips into a thin line.

"Please, Grandma?"

"Be careful. Both of you. Be very careful and trust no one. Except for your detective— you can trust him and only him." She hangs up before I can say anything else.

CHAPTER 22
AVALON

"You have a cat?" A huge orange tomcat stares at me from the top of the kitchen island. He looks like he's been through a few rounds. He's missing the tip of one ear, and the other ear looks like it was nibbled on by rats. There's a scar on his nose. But his fur is bright, clean, and long. He looks like a Maine Coon mix.

"Yeah, that's Kojak."

"Kojak? Like the old detective show from the seventies?"

He walks to the cat, rubs his head, picks him up, and puts him on the floor. "Yes, like the TV show." The cat immediately jumps back onto the counter in a move so smooth he doesn't jump as much as materializes on top of it.

Jake sighs loudly. "I can't keep him off the counters, tables, or any place he decides to be."

I laugh. "Well, that's what cats do. I pictured you more of a dog person than a cat person."

Jake scratches Kojak just behind his ear, and the cat tilts his head, eyes half-closed in bliss. "I didn't really have a

159

choice. He decided this was his home, and that was that."
Jake walks to the fridge. "Something to drink?"

"Just water, thanks."

He gets a beer for himself and a bottle of water for me.

The scent of garlic and fresh bread makes my mouth water. "It smells delicious in here."

"Hopefully it will taste good, too."

We sit at his dining room table. Kojak promptly jumps on the table, walks across it, and then settles on a large empty wooden bowl in the center.

Jake points at the bowl with the beer bottle. "I used to put fruit in there. But he'd take everything out and lie inside it. I gave up. It's his house now, and I just pay the bills."

I'm enjoying this too much. It's a side of Jake I hadn't seen much of yet. Sweeter, more relaxed, jovial. "How long have you had him?"

Jake's smile is unguarded. "Two years this summer."

"And you said he just showed up at your door?"

"Not exactly my door. At the barbecue grill. I was making hotdogs. Put the grill on and set a plate of hot dogs next to the grill. Went back inside because I forgot the tongs. Came out, and there he was with a hot dog in his mouth. He hissed at me, hotdog in mouth and all, and took off."

I'm laughing, picturing the huge cat stealing hotdogs. "So, it was love at first hotdog?"

"No, I think the grilled salmon did it."

"The grilled salmon?"

"Oh, he showed up a couple of days later. I had grilled some salmon for dinner and was eating outside, enjoying the nice weather. Next thing I know, he jumps on the table and sits right in front of me. I gave him a little piece of the fish and he tried to steal the rest right off my plate."

Now I'm laughing so hard I have to hold back a snort. I swear the cat is smirking at us.

Jake smiles. He looks years younger. The closed-off vibe he always projects is gone.

I reach over to pet Kojak, and Jake holds my wrist to stop me. "He doesn't like to be touched. I'm the only person he tolerates. He has the vet terrified of him."

"I don't know. I'm pretty good with animals." I reach for the cat again and give him the back of my hand to sniff. Kojak pushes his head into my hand, and when I scratch his neck, he purrs so loud that he sounds like a little engine.

Jake huffs. "Traitor. Is that all it takes? A pretty face, and you turn coat?"

The sideways compliment makes me blush. The cat rolls onto his back inside the bowl and gives me his belly.

Jake shakes his head. "I've never seen him do that before."

An alarm goes off. Jake stands up and pushes his chair back under the table. "Let me get that dinner I promised you."

"What can I do to help?"

"Nothing." He takes a large pot from the stove, takes it to the sink, and pours the contents into a colander. "I prepped ahead of time."

He drops the contents of the colander back into the pot and takes it to the stove.

The cat moves and lies on his side right in front of me, purring away. "So, what's for dinner?"

"Pasta primavera."

"Oh, that's one of my favorites."

"I know. I asked Lynn. It's also safe because Kojak never tries to steal any vegetables."

The cat sniffs as if offended.

"It's like he can understand what you're saying."

"Maybe he can. Can't be much crazier than the stuff you do." He stops. "I'm sorry. I didn't mean it like that. I don't think you're crazy."

I know he didn't. I like this. That he's letting his guard down and talking without censoring his every word. "No offense taken, and no need to apologize. I know what you mean. I think animals know a lot more than what we give them credit for. We're the ones who can't understand them. Not the other way around."

He stirs a pot on the stove. "Wish they could speak. Probably could solve a lot more crimes if they did."

Jake picks up a large tray and adds plates and bowls. "I thought we could eat outside?"

"Sure, sounds good to me."

I follow him through French doors into a beautiful, covered porch. It wraps around the entire back of the house. The wide blades of ceiling fans move lazily above. At one end of the porch, a hammock begs me to grab a book and lie on it. There are two sitting areas. One with a love seat and a couple of rocking chairs, and the other an outdoor tiki dining table that seats four. A candle flickers in the hurricane lamp set in the middle of the table. It's already set with placemats, silverware, and wine glasses. A bottle of white wine chills in an ice bucket. A wall of rhododendrons lines the sides of the property. The pink blossoms scent the air. The yard slopes down into a lake. A huge tree occupies one side of the yard. Not a bare spot in the perfectly manicured lawn. This is the kind of backyard you see in the after picture of a garden makeover show.

"This is absolutely beautiful. I might park myself in that hammock and never leave."

Jake sets the dishes on the table. Salad, pasta, and garlic bread make an appearance. "You're welcome to stop by anytime. I don't make enough use of the yard. I'd be happy to have someone else enjoy it."

"I might just leave our place and spend the rest of my time here. Do you have a spare bedroom?"

"There are three of them."

"That's settled then."

He pulls my chair out for me. This feels more and more like a date than just having dinner together.

"Thank you. Everything looks delicious."

Jake taps his phone, and a song plays from hidden speakers, soft and unintrusive. We talk and share stories from childhood, high school, and college. The conversation flows easily like we've done this dozens of times.

Dinner is long finished, the plates moved to the side. The sun is setting over the lake, painting everything in yellow, orange, and pink. The water ripples like liquid gold.

I inhale deeply. "Thank you for inviting me here." I gesture toward the lake. "This is absolutely beautiful. I'm jealous you get to see this sunset every day. That's not a view I can get in New York with so many buildings all around."

He smiles, his features soft and open. "You're welcome to come over and enjoy the sunset anytime. I confess I don't enjoy it as much as I should. Half of the time, I'm not home."

I want to ask him if I'm also welcome to enjoy the sunup. But I don't. What would it be like to wake up next to him? That old, bitter-sweet ache of longing for the man sitting across from me rises in my chest. I take a long drink of water and force it back down into the corners of my mind that dare dream of moments like this.

The first cords of "You and Me" by Lifehouse play over the speakers. "Oh, I love this song. Such pretty lyrics."

He stands up and holds out his hand. I'm not sure what he's doing, but I take his hand. He pulls me to my feet and takes both my hands, then walks backward down the steps and into the grass. He pulls me closer, embraces me, and we dance. My heart fills to the brim and then overflows. Something in my soul snaps into place, like a final puzzle piece finding its way home. My body melts into his, seeking to be closer still.

Fireflies dot the evening like stars playing hide and seek along the reeds that line the lake's edge. The sound of lapping water keeps the beat with the chirping crickets. The night is alive with nature's symphony playing along with the song. But none of this can compare to the sound of Jake's breath in my ear, the feel of his day-old whiskers as he rubs his cheek on mine, the scent that's uniquely his and now so familiar to me. Or the heat of his hand at the small of my back and the press of his body against mine as we sway to the song coming through the speakers.

The cadence of our bodies moving to the rhythm of a song of our own making. In synch to the beat of our hearts, and a need as old as time. My skin burns under his touch. Warmth pools low in my belly against the press of his erection. My breasts ache, and I push my chest into his. The sound that escapes his lips is half-moan, half-grunt.

"Ava . . ." He traces the line of my neck and up my jaw with his nose and inhales deeply. "Apples. This damn scent. I get aroused every time I smell apples now. And it's all your fault."

I giggle. How could I not? But the giggle turns into a gasp when he nibbles at my neck.

Then his mouth finds mine. And I'm lost.

Lost in his taste.

Lost in his touch.

Lost in the heat of his embrace.

We move against each other, our bodies melting together. "Too. Many. Clothes," I say between kisses.

His hands slide down my sides and slip under my blouse, skin-to-skin contact. They brush my sides and splay on my back. But that's not where I want his hands. I push my breasts into his chest again, rub against him, and try to soothe the ache. But it has the opposite effect and only leaves me wanting more.

He smiles against my mouth, and his hands come to the front. His thumbs brush the underside of my breasts. The barrier of my silk bra is the only thing keeping his hands from my bare skin.

"Please, Jake."

His mouth travels down to my collarbone and then to the center of my chest. He tugs at the buttons on my blouse with expert fingers. The buttons open for him, one by one as if they have a will of their own and are as desperate as me to feel his hands on my skin. He pulls me up and places open-mouthed kisses on the exposed skin, licking at the swell of my breasts and tracing the edge of my bra with his tongue.

I have never been this turned on. Jake finds the front closure and releases it. The bra falls open, and night air meets my bare flesh—my skin pebbles under his stare.

He traces the curve of each breast with his fingertips. "Beautiful."

Right now, I don't want gentle. I need his hands on me. I take charge, grab both of his hands, and press them against my breasts. Jake squeezes just hard enough to be on this side of intense pleasure. Then he lowers his head and takes a nipple into his mouth. I fist his hair and pull him into me, arching my back to give him better access.

He doesn't disappoint me. Skilled hands. Skilled mouth. Skilled tongue. Fuck! I have to fight the urge to tackle him to the ground and have my way with him, right here in his backyard—neighbors be damned.

Jake seems to read my mind because he wraps both arms around me, picks me up, and carries me to the sofa on the porch. He lays me down and hovers over me for several seconds, his gaze fleeting all over my body. I look down at myself. I'm a wanton mess. Skirt hiked up to my thighs, blouse open, bra hanging loose.

He moves a knee between my legs to make room for himself, nestles on top of me, and resumes kissing me. I tug at his shirt, eager to feel his skin on mine. He lifts just enough to pull it over his head in that sexy way guys do and settles back on top of me.

I touch him. Splay my hands on his back, trace his sides. His stomach muscles contract under my hands. I slide my hands down his hips and grab his ass. Tilt my hips up, lock my legs around his. He groans. A hiss escapes his mouth when I tilt my hips up again.

He kisses me deeply. His tongue tangles with mine. He sucks, nibbles, and bites.

My core aches for him. I need him inside of me now. Right now. I tug at the sides of his jeans and make my intentions known.

Jake covers my hand with his and stills me. Our kiss becomes less frantic. He's slowing us down. My racing heart and panting breath become more even. Why is he stopping?

"What?" I'm breathless, and I can't hide the frustration in my voice.

He brushes a lock of hair away from my forehead. "I'm sorry."

"Why? What happened?"

"Someone's knocking on my door."

My entire body protests at the interruption. "Now?"

"Yes, I'm sorry." He stands up and pulls me up with him. Then, he arranges my bra, hooking the two sides, and starts to button my shirt. I take over. My fingers shaking.

He finds his shirt on the floor and pulls it over his head. "Give me a minute to find out what's going on." He takes a step back and points at my blouse. I missed two buttons, and it hangs sideways off my shoulder.

Jesus. I'm a mess. I take a deep breath and redo the buttons. Comb my hair with my fingers. Return to the table and pour a glass of water. My heart is still beating faster than normal.

I'm cranky and frustrated and . . . mad at whoever interrupted us.

Low voices come through the small gap left by the nearly closed door. But I can't make out what they are saying. I press the glass of cold water to my face and neck. I'm overheated.

I find my phone on the table and use it to look at myself. Bright eyes and flushed skin meet me. My lips are red and swollen. My hair is sticking up in all directions like I just woke up. There's redness along my neck where Jake rubbed his face. I look like they interrupted me mid-coitus. Well, not quite. Five more minutes, and they would have. I sit and try to tame my hair again. Then, drink the whole glass of water. Fan a hand to cool myself.

Jake comes back. Pulls out a chair and sits in front of me. Our knees are nearly touching. "I'm sorry."

"Is everything okay?"

"No. There's something I have to deal with."

"Is it another woman?"

"No. Wait. Are you asking about a missing woman or another woman?"

Now he has me thinking. I never even asked if he was seeing someone else. I know he said he was single when we first met, but . . . "I was asking about the missing women. But now I'm wondering—"

"No to both. No new missing woman. And I would never be here with you if I were seeing someone else. Even if it was casual. I don't do that. Date multiple people at the same time." He lowers his gaze and then looks up at me again. "You? Probably something we should have talked about before . . ."

"No. Never. I mean, I've dated before. But never two guys at the same time. Same as you." The words rush out. I'm relieved that the interruption has nothing to do with other women, missing or not. But now I'm curious. Who would come to his house this late?

I look over my shoulder toward the house and back at him. "What happened?"

He sighs. "A minor family emergency. I have to take care of something. I wish I could delay it, but it can't wait. I need to go. I'll walk you to your car."

My shoulders drop, weighted by disappointment. "Okay, I'll grab my stuff. Do you want help cleaning up the table?"

"No. I can do that when I come back."

We walk outside, and he locks the door behind us. There's a cop car parked across the street. A police officer leaning on it, arms crossed. When he sees Jake, he opens the cruiser's back door, and a man stumbles out of it. He leans heavily on the car, holding on to the trunk. His shirt is in disarray, half tucked in and half hanging out of his pants.

He's partially in the shadow. The light from the lamp pole distorts his features.

Jake opens my car door and leans in for a chaste kiss. "I'll call you soon."

I drive away slowly—looking in the rearview mirror—I see him cross the street. The drunk man takes wobbly steps toward Jake. It's all I catch before I have to make a turn.

CHAPTER 23
AVALON

WE'RE SITTING ON A BENCH AT THE PIER AND ENJOYING our burrito food truck breakfast. There's an air of excitement all around. Red, white, and blue flags and banners decorate the pier and the buildings along the beach. The sea breeze brings some relief to the already too-hot morning. Not a cloud in the sky. It's a perfect summer day.

Lynn shows me the screen on her phone. "So, according to this, the fireworks start at nine p.m., and the pier is the best spot to watch them."

"It will be very crowded."

She takes a long drink from her juice. "Fourth of July fireworks always draw crowds, no matter where you are."

"That's true." I'm not a big fan of crowds. I'm much happier in quiet places. But Lynn is an extrovert and feels right at home among a few hundred or a few thousand people.

"Anything new with the investigation?" She's nearly finished with her burrito.

"Not that I know of. It's frustrating and feels like trying to build a puzzle in the dark."

Lynn looks up, a clear sign she's thinking. "But that's just it. You don't have all the puzzle pieces, and it is not a single puzzle. You're working with multiple puzzles, all at the same time, and the pieces are all mixed up."

The light bulb goes off in my head. "Oh my God, Lynn, you're a genius!"

She flips her hair over her shoulder. "Duh, I know that. But what genius accomplishment are you talking about?"

"I've been looking at each of those cases as individual puzzles." I look around and whisper to her, "But what if it's just one giant puzzle? I know people go missing every day, and the police don't automatically link them. Jake thinks they're related, and I think they are related, but I'm not looking at the big picture."

"Okay, stop for a second. You're making me dizzy. And you lost me." She looks over her shoulder. No one is paying attention to us. She lowers her voice to match mine. "You looked into two missing women, right?"

"Kind of? I found Alice's necklace and checked her car. That was it for her. And the reading for Lena at Jake's office. I didn't find anything at Alice's house. I need to look at all of them at the same time."

"Whoa, hold your horses there." Her hands come up high as if she's trying to stop a runaway horse. "All of them? At the same time? No, no, no. That's not a good idea. It would be too draining. You'd get sick and have headaches for days."

I avert my eyes and pick at a non-existing chip on my nails. "I can do it. I can pace myself and not get burned out. It won't be much different from when I go into a museum and curate artifacts. I work on several at the same time." It's not the same. Not at all. The violence of the images linked to this case takes a much bigger toll on me, but I'm not about to tell her that. She would mother-hen me, and I don't need that right now. I push my hair away from my face. "This guy could already be preying on the next girl."

Her voice softens. "But it is different. You know that. Looking into those missing women is affecting you differently. These . . . feelings and emotions never followed you before. Not to mention the ghost." She visibly shivers.

I take in a big breath and release it. "I didn't know what to expect and wasn't prepared for it before. But I am now."

Lynn raises a single eyebrow.

My hands come up together in an appeasing gesture. "Now I know what to expect, and I can protect myself by turning off my emotions."

She twists to face me. "Can you? Can you really turn off your emotions?"

"I can dull them." It's a lie. It will be impossible to open myself to the images while closing myself on the emotions they bring. The two are the same.

Lynn stares at me for a long moment and sighs. "Okay, but promise me you'll slow down if it gets to be too much."

"I promise." I'm not sure this is a promise I can keep. Time to change the focus from me to her.

"Whatever happened to the guy from the pub? What's his name again?"

"Marcus. Nothing happened. I wasn't going to leave with him, you know. We hung out outside the pub a bit, but as pretty as he was, the flirting was more fun than our conversation. I thought all bartenders were supposed to be skilled conversationalists. Not this dude. Got a weird vibe from him. He kept calling me a *little bird* and looking around like he was worried someone was watching us. Then wanted me to follow him to his place. I noped out of there."

"Why didn't you say anything? I thought you spent the night with him." Should I have picked up on something? I didn't really get creepy vibes from the bartender. I rely so much on my intuition. What if I miss something?

"Nah, I went for a drive and hung out by the lake. There was a bonfire, and I spent some time there. When I got back, you were sleeping. I didn't want to wake you, and then you were off with your detective the next day. Nothing happened. It wasn't worth mentioning."

This investigation is taking over my life. I can't believe I didn't ask Lynn about the bartender or that I missed her discomfort about him until now. "Please be careful, Lynn. With everything that's happening, maybe it would be best if you didn't see anyone while we're in this town. And I'm sorry I've failed at my best friend's duties since we got here. I suck."

"You haven't failed. You're busy and doing something important. I'm sunning myself, window shopping, and drinking margaritas you're paying for." She grins.

I take our empty bottles and walk to the recycle bin a few feet away. Seagulls swoop above the pier. I shield my eyes and watch as they screech and fight for scraps of food someone is tossing in the water for them. When I turn back, Jake is there, walking toward me, his form standing out among the dozens of people milling about. Oh, sweet baby Jesus, he's shirtless. Golden skin glistening under the sun. Hands on his hips. Chest heaving as he catches his breath. Muscles everywhere. A dusting of hair on his chest, abs for miles, and those indentations . . . the magical V. I want to run my tongue down them. Like always, his eyes are hidden behind sunglasses. Thank goodness. I don't think

I can handle all that's on display and his eyes at the same time.

My face gets hot as images of last night replay in my mind. Us dancing, his hands on me, the kisses, the intensity. I stay frozen in place until he's standing right in front of me. "H-hi."

He takes a step closer. "You didn't go running today?" He sounds disappointed.

"No, I woke up late." Was he looking for me? It took me hours to fall asleep. Who knew being horny would turn me into an insomniac?

Behind him, Lynn tilts her head to check his ass and gives me two thumbs-up. I should get an Oscar for being able to keep a straight face right now.

He pushes the sunglasses to the top of his head, his gaze traveling over my body, intimate, hungry. And there it is. Those eyes are my undoing. My skin pebbles under his stare. He inches closer. "What are you doing today?" His voice is low, just for my ears.

I point behind him, and he turns. Lynn waves at him.

I resist the urge to fan my heated face. "We're just talking about it. Watch the fireworks, I guess."

"That doesn't happen until nine tonight. You have a long wait until then." There's such an intensity to his gaze.

I fidget, rolling the beads of my bracelet between my fingers. "Any suggestions for what we can do until then?" Oh my God. Why did I say that? It sounds like I'm propositioning him.

He smiles and rubs a hand on the back of his head. His bicep flexes. "They always have a few fun events throughout the day at the beach."

Never in my life have I had the urge to bite someone's biceps before, but here we are. I swallow. "Oh, like what?"

"There's a sand sculpture competition."

I laugh. "That's definitely outside my wheelhouse."

He crosses his arms, and those biceps bulge now. "Kite flying and an ice cream eating contest—"

"Ice cream eating contest? Now that sounds like fun."

He wipes a bead of sweat from his pecs. "Not as fun as you would think."

I force my gaze back to his face. "Why not?"

"Brain freeze, and I speak from experience. I competed when I was fifteen or sixteen." He grins. "Was trying to impress a girl. Let's just say it didn't end well."

We laugh. I love seeing this side of Jake. His sense of humor shows now that his guard is down. "I want to try that. Ice cream is my weakness." I point at Lynn over my shoulder. "Want to join us for the ice cream eating contest?"

His smile fades. "I can't. Fourth of July is a busy day, and I'll be on call from two until the morning. It's an all-hands-on-deck kind of day."

I press my lips together to keep from pouting like a toddler. "Hope to see you around while you're doing cop stuff."

"I'm looking forward to it."

Silence stretches, neither speaking and yet the memory of last night's events fills every nook and cranny of my mind like a hologram playing between us. He heaves a breath, and his broad chest expands. Another bead of sweat runs down his bare chest and gets caught on the ridges of his stomach.

My breath gets caught in my throat, and I have to force it down. Everything around us fades away. There's only Jake and me standing under the sun, the scent of the sea on the breeze, the call of distant seagulls, and eyes filled with unfulfilled desire.

We inch toward each other—the screech of car tires on asphalt followed by a horn and curses invades our bubble, and we both take a step back. On the street, a man tosses insults at someone in a black sports car and points at the white pedestrian stripes on the ground. A cop appears and disperses the small crowd of curious onlookers.

Jake sighs. Tilts his head toward the commotion. "It'll be a long day."

Then, he turns and walks away. My gaze is fixed on his back until he disappears among the hundreds of people on the boardwalk.

I walk back to Lynn and plop on the bench next to her.

"I thought you guys were about to make out right here in the middle of everything and I was getting ready to take a video on my phone."

Lynn . . . I look at her and brace myself for the barrage of jokes and teasing. "Okay, go ahead, say it. I know it's coming."

"No one is coming yet, but if you two had had two more minutes—"

I shove her playfully. "Let's go find that ice cream contest. Maybe some brain freeze will cool me off."

CHAPTER 24
AVALON

THAT SAME COP WHO ALWAYS LETS ME INTO THE BACK waves me to the security door as soon as he sees me, and I go through without having to call Jake. The entrance to his office is open, and I step in, then close the door behind me.

He stands, eyes wide at my unexpected visit. We didn't run into each other yesterday after all. There were thousands of people watching the fireworks. Even if he was looking for me, the odds were against us meeting by chance again. And he was working. Texting or calling didn't happen either.

"I need to see all the evidence together. At the same time." The whispered words spill as soon as the door clicks shut. "And sorry for just showing up without calling first."

He walks around his desk and stops. Jake stares at me as if memorizing each inch of my skin. Silence grows until it becomes awkward, and I regret my rushed decision to just come without talking to him first. "I shouldn't have come. You're busy. Of course you're busy. I'll go. We can do this later. Another time." I step back and grab the door handle.

He moves fast. His hand closes over mine—warm, rough, and soft at the same time.

"Stay."

He's so close the tips of his boots touch my sneakers. I tilt my head to meet his gaze. His eyes are free of those damn sunglasses. I sway a little. God, he's so beautiful. My heart races like the rat-a-tat-tat of a machine gun.

Jake reaches around me, and the sound of the lock being engaged booms loudly in the silence. His hands come to my waist, and he presses against me with the heavy wooden door cool at my back. His eyes search my face. His head lowers. His lips on mine are sweet agony. I open for him and invite him in with a flick of my tongue against his. Jake accepts my invitation.

Heat spreads everywhere, pooling low in my belly and pulsating between my thighs. My nipples harden, and my body reacts to his like a magnet being pulled closer and closer. I want to melt into him. I want to rub on him like a cat in heat.

One of his hands travels up my side to hold the back of my head. He deepens the kiss, and I moan into his mouth. My hands find purchase on his shoulders, and I go up on tiptoes, needing more. His grip on my waist pulls me even closer to him. He's hard against my belly.

More. More. More. My body screams at me. I want his hands everywhere and his mouth on me. I moan again, frustration and need nipping at me.

My hips move, rocking against him. A distant part of me is watching, wide-eyed, and asking what am I doing? This is not me. I'm never this forward, this wanton.

Shut up, brain.

The hand on my waist lowers and cups my ass. Jake pulls

me closer to him, and I wrap one leg around his knee. *Yes, yes, yes. Oh, God, yes.*

The friction between us increases, and the hand behind my head falls to my breast. He squeezes the nipple, his tongue toys with mine. This is too much. Too much and not enough. I need a little more—just a little more. My body arches back. I break the kiss and gasp for air. His mouth falls to my neck and suckles there.

Wave after wave of pleasure spreads throughout my body until I'm limp in his arms. My head is cradled on his heaving chest. I drop my trembling leg to the floor. Jake's arms around me are the only thing keeping me on my feet. Minutes tick by, and we don't move. My heart slows to a normal tempo, and my breath evens out.

Jake tilts my head up, kisses my forehead, and looks at me, his eyes dark with lust.

My desire-clogged brain clears.

"Oh my God." My face burns. I squeeze my eyes shut as if doing so will somehow erase my embarrassment.

A low rumble comes from him. "We probably shouldn't have done that. Not here, at least, but I don't regret it, and it was not a mistake." His voice is husky and sensual, like a caress. "Please don't say it was a mistake."

I keep my eyes closed. Avoidance and denial taking charge.

"Hey?" He kisses my eyelids.

I don't respond.

"You okay?" He cradles my face.

I nod but keep my eyes closed.

"Did I . . . hurt you?"

His worry pulls me from my pool of embarrassment. I

open my eyes. Look at him. "No, you didn't hurt me. I'm—I've never—you know, done anything like that before."

He smiles. "Like what? Make out like horny teenagers inside a police station?"

I chuckle. "Yes, that."

His lips gently brush mine, then he steps back, pulls me with him, and directs me to take a seat. He turns his back to me, his walk a little stiff, pained. He tries to be discreet about adjusting himself, but I catch it. I avert my gaze until the sound of the creaking chair tells me he's sitting down and then meet his eyes.

Yearning stretches between us like a tangible unspoken thing. My legs are shaky, and I'm glad I'm not standing right now. My entire body still vibrates. Dear God, if this is what it feels like with all the clothes between us, I can't even imagine what it would be like if we were naked and actually had sex.

"I…" His gaze goes to the door. He runs a hand through his hair. "Sorry. I don't know what happened. I didn't plan on jumping on you . . ." His voice is hoarse.

My cheeks burn. I force myself to hold Jake's gaze. "It's . . . hmm . . . okay. I think I jumped on you, too."

He smiles. His hands go to his lap. My gaze follows his hands. They don't disguise the bulge in his pants. He wheels the chair closer, and the desk blocks the view. "You said you want to look at all the evidence at the same time?"

I clear my throat. "Yeah, I think if I look at all the evidence at the same time, I might be able to get a better picture."

He tilts his head. "Will that make you tired or worn out?"

"I can handle it. We just need a space large enough to lay everything side by side, so I can try to read it the same way I would a book."

His eyebrows arch over those mesmerizing eyes. How can anyone look at his face for more than a few seconds and not get lost?

He gets up and looks around the space. "I can't remove anything from this office." Hands on his hips, Jake turns in a circle and looks down at the gray carpet. "The space behind my desk could work."

"Yes, as long as you have enough room to lay everything out, it'll work."

He looks at his watch. "I have a meeting in a few. Tomorrow morning. Can you do it then?"

I'm half elated with the promise of seeing him again tomorrow and disappointed I can't spend more time with him now. "Yes, tomorrow morning is fine. Nine?"

"That works." He walks around the desk and stops a few feet away from me. My stomach tightens with each step he takes my way.

I stand up. The pull toward him grows. I force my feet to stay in place and not throw myself at him again. "I'll bring coffee. And donuts."

A dimple appears on his cheek. "I like chocolate glazed."

Who doesn't? I walk to the door with him at my back. He unlocks and then opens the door for me. "I'll walk you out. I've got fifteen minutes yet."

We exit the station in silence. That gatekeeper cop smirks at us like he knows exactly what happened in Jake's office.

A warm breeze ruffles my hair when we step outside. We cross the street to my parked car, and I unlock it with the key fob, then turn to him.

Jake stands next to my car, hands on his trim waist and head tilted to the side. He looks at me. His eyes linger on my face as if searching for something. Golden skin peeks through the first few open buttons on his shirt and the muscular forearms displayed by his rolled-up sleeves.

"There's something about you . . . I don't know what exactly, but it nags at me. I feel like we've met before, and yet, I know we haven't."

Now. This is the time to tell him the truth. I drag in a breath. Air scented with pine fills my lungs. "Fifteen years ago, you rescued a young girl from drowning on a beach in North Carolina. You pulled her out of the water, put her on your surfboard, and paddled to the shore. You gave her CPR and saved her life."

His eyes widen. He takes a minuscule step back, then stops himself. "How do you know that?"

I want to step closer to him but hold myself in place. Grind my feet into the ground. Tamp down the rush of emotions clawing up my chest and swallow them, blinking away the threat of tears. "That girl is me."

She's a pretty thing. So open and trusting, fluttering around like a sparrow, not a care in the world.

It will be easy to take her.

She doesn't know she's already lost.

She doesn't know she's already dead—she won't know until it's too late.

No one to hear your screams, little bird. I can pluck you feather by feather until there's nothing left of you but eyes filled with terror and an empty shell.

CHAPTER 25
JAKE

Wait. What? Flashbacks flood my mind. Snippets of a memory long forgotten come to life. Part of me always wondered if I imagined the whole thing. I thought about the girl I saved from time to time, but less and less over the years, and not once since Emily went missing.

Summer in North Carolina. I wasn't even supposed to be at the beach that day. Something needled at me to go. The hairs on the back of my neck stand. "To this day, I don't know what happened or how I even knew where to look."

"What do you mean?"

I shake my head. "I don't know. I wasn't even supposed to be there that day. But something told me to get my board and go, so I did. And then, when I was in the ocean, I heard my name . . ." The same sense of urgency that chased me then claws at me now.

"You heard your name?" Ava asks me when I go silent.

I meet her eyes. Run a hand through my hair. Consider the insanity of what I'm about to reveal, but if anyone can understand this, it's her.

"I heard my name being called from the water. Not around me. From under the water. I know it's impossible. But I did."

"I never called for help."

"No, it was not a call for help. It was my name. Jake. Clear and urgent. The ocean called to me with a feminine voice."

Her lips move, but no words are said. Her eyes mist, and she blinks.

"I dove. I dove into the ocean and found you, floating, eyes open and unseeing, your hair flowing around your face. I grabbed your arm, pulled you onto my board, and paddled to the shore as fast as I could. I never understood what happened. Then, over the years, I shoved it away, chalked it up to my imagination."

Tears run freely down her face now. "You brought me back. You saved me. And I never even said thank you."

I wipe a tear with my thumb. "No thanks are necessary. I was glad to be in the right place at the right time. And then, once you were breathing again, the lifeguard showed up and took over, so I stepped away. You didn't have a chance to say anything."

Ava rummages through her bag, finds a packet of tissues, and uses them. Her face is dry now, but her lashes are still wet, and her eyes are brighter.

I search her face for clues but find nothing. "What does all of this mean?"

She drags a deep breath. "My grandma would say that it was meant to happen. All of it. My drowning, you saving me, and me being on vacation here and finding that necklace that somehow brought us together."

No. I back away from her. My jaw goes tight, my stomach

twists into knots. Everything in me rejects this idea. That means those women went missing and possibly died for us to meet again. It also means Emily had to die for me to be here right now. I never would have chosen to do what I do if not for my sister's disappearance.

Ava takes a step forward and reaches to me, her soft palm on my face. "I know. It's hard for me to believe, too. I hate the circumstances that brought us together, but I can't regret being here with you."

This is too much. I step out of her reach again, and Ava's hand drops away from me. A flash of hurt crosses her face and fades away as Ava smooths her features.

She hugs herself. "Everything is connected. Whether we believe it or not. Whether we like it or not, we can't escape it. Cause and effect are the building blocks of the universe."

I just nod, unsure of what I can say. Fuck the universe and its building blocks. What the hell trade is this? The life of my sister and others for the chance of meeting a woman I could love but not have? She'll be gone soon enough, and I'll still be here. Alone.

CHAPTER 26
AVALON

Something just changed. Jake reverted to his closed-off self. That invisible wall is back. I'm not sure which part of what I said made this happen.

Unease unfurls inside me. "What is it?"

He frowns, presses his lips together, and looks at me. "I don't know if I can reconcile the idea that all that happened to be with you now."

"What do you mean?" Unease spreads its wings like a bird sunning itself.

"Saving your life fifteen years ago and then meeting you again by chance. I can deal with that." He rubs at his chest as if trying to dislodge an uncomfortable weight. "I cannot reason or justify the idea that so many people had to go missing or die for this to happen."

I want to reach out to him but hold back—dig my fingers into my arms as I embrace myself. "I don't think it's as simple as that. I think my drowning, the missing women, and us meeting again is just a small part of a much bigger picture. A picture we have no way or means or the ability to see."

187

His face darkens, and the corner of his mouth curls into a sneer. "So what? We're all just puppets, our strings being pulled this way and that by some kind of God?"

I take a step closer but refrain from touching him. I don't think my touch would be welcome. "No, not puppets. Puzzle pieces. I think, we"—I wave my hand around, at the people walking, and in their cars, and at the trees—"and everything around us, we are all puzzle pieces in a much bigger picture. We are puzzles within puzzles, pictures within pictures, and not one person can see the entire image. We can only see a few pieces of the puzzle at a time, and if we're lucky and our eyes are open wide enough, we get to see a few pictures, too."

He drags both hands up his face and into his hair and then drops them. His hands go to his pockets, a motion now familiar to me, a sign of his discomfort.

"I have to think about this, Ava. I have to figure out a way to be okay with all of this and what it means for us." He waves his hand between the two of us. And then puts it back in his jeans pocket. "And I have to figure out a way to be okay with everything else that's happened."

What is he saying? What else happened? "I understand." But I don't. Not really.

He tilts his head back, his gaze fixed on the sky and clouds above. He looks back at me. Nods. "I'll call you." And then he walks away, leaving me there on the side of the road. I track him as he dodges a passing car and then takes the steps two at a time into the police station. I watch as he pulls the heavy door open with ease and disappears behind the wood, glass, and brick. And I keep watching for minutes more, afraid to move and make everything worse than it already is.

"Lover's quarrel?" The voice startles me.

I turn, and that K-9 officer is at my side. His dog watches

me, head tilted and tail slowly wagging. The cop gives me a friendly smile and pets his dog. The skittering of a thousand spiders crawls up my back. "Excuse me?"

He rocks back on his heels, then squats next to the dog and pets him. Loose dog hair gets caught in the breeze. The officer's posture is casual. He seems friendly, but it hits me the wrong way. Maybe it's because of the lover's quarrel comment.

He tilts his head toward the police station. "Looked like you and your boyfriend were having an argument."

I force a laugh. Widen my eyes and twirl a lock of hair in my fingers. Play the innocent girl game. "You mean Jake? Oh, no. He's not my boyfriend. Just an old friend."

He buys my silly girl routine. Most men do because they underestimate me.

He laughs. "That's not what the gossip around town is saying."

"I wouldn't know. I'm just passing through and will leave soon."

"You should stay longer, enjoy the town, lots of fun things to do."

I force a smile. "That's a German Shepherd, right?" I try to deflect his interest with the question.

He stands up and pats the dog's head.

"Yes, this is Duke." That too friendly smile comes back. Too perfect. Too crafted, and like he practiced it in front of a mirror a thousand times.

I need to get away. "What time is it? I have a hair appointment and don't want to be late." I use the question to glance at his wrist and check for a scar.

He looks at his wrist and shows me his watch, but a thick watch band prevents me from seeing if a scar is present or not. I look at it without noticing the time. "Oh yes, I've got to go.

Nice talking to you." I turn on my heels, open the car door, and get in, locking it before turning on the ignition.

The K-9 officer crosses the street, forcing a car to slow down as if he has all the time in the world. I check over my shoulder and pull into traffic just as he gets to the other side of the street. His figure reflected in the rearview mirror as I drive away.

CHAPTER 27
JAKE

I'm an ass. And I hurt Ava and there's no denying I didn't handle this whole thing well.

But I can't accept that my sister's death plays a role in bringing us together.

And yet I know it does.

I drop to my chair, and it screeches in protest. I need to replace the old thing, but it's one of the few tokens I have from my grandfather, and I refuse to give it up. I spent many hours sitting on his lap as a boy on this chair while he read me books or taught me how to make sailing knots. I reach for the drawer, pull it open, and grab the rock made smooth by time and friction.

"What should I do, Pops?" I swivel in his chair, half expecting him to appear, but only silence greets me.

I close my eyes and lean back. The chair creaks again, and the sound is followed by a knock on my door. Ava? My heart punches my chest from the inside. Idiot. *Of course it is not her, not after how you left her on the side of the road. You'll be lucky if she comes back to see you at all.*

191

I put the rock back in the drawer and close it. "Come in."

Jeff opens the door and steps in. Makes himself comfortable in one of the chairs across from me, and Duke lies on the floor next to him. He slouches and crosses one leg over the other. Smiles. "Trouble in paradise?"

I narrow my eyes at him. "What do you mean?"

He scratches the side of his nose. "I saw you out front with your girlfriend. It looked like you were having a fight. Everything okay?"

He's fishing for information, but why? Is he interested in Ava? If he is, it will be over my cold, dead body. I clench my hands at my sides. Guess that answers my lingering question about whether I want to be with her. I slide into my friendly cop skin.

"Fight? No fight. Not sure what makes you think that." Did he hear anything we talked about?

Jeff uncrosses his legs and slouches further down like he's settling in for a long stay. "I don't know. It looked intense from where I was."

I laugh. "And where was that? I didn't see you outside."

He scratches his ear. It's one of his tells. He's getting ready to pounce. "Oh, you wouldn't. I was in my car."

He didn't hear us then. Relief washes over me like a retreating tide, taking away the worry with it. I grab a couple of files and tap them together on my desk. It's more subtle than *get the fuck out of my office*, but still pretty obvious I want him gone.

"She said the same thing. No fight. She's a pretty little thing, isn't she? If you're not together, is she single?" Jeff smirks.

I won't take the bait. I drop the files on my desk. Recline again. "How long have we known each other, Jeff?"

"I'm not doing that math, but since middle school, if my memory serves me right. Over twenty years, I reckon." A smooth smile follows.

I stand up, brace myself on the desk, and lean in. "Have I ever volunteered information I didn't have to or gossiped about anyone in those twenty-plus years?"

"Nope. You're still the same old good boy, Jake. Never tell lies, never tattletale, never say a word if silence will do. You'll be taking a lot of secrets with you to your grave." It doesn't sound like a compliment. He gets up then and glances at my desk. His eyes widen, and he shakes his head.

Fuck! Emily's case file.

He looks at me with pity. "After all these years, you're still looking for her?"

I loathe the bitterness rising in my chest.

He walks to the door. Stops. "Why? Some cases can never be solved. Past time you let it go. It can only bring more pain. Emily is gone. Forever."

I bite my tongue to keep from cussing him out and prove him right in one thing. I let silence be my answer.

CHAPTER 28
AVALON

I DON'T REMEMBER THE DRIVE BACK TO THE APARTMENT. My mind is a hurricane of thoughts. I wasn't prepared for Jake's reaction and never expected him to take the revelation of how we originally met the way he did. But it was more than that. I kick off my shoes and drop onto the couch.

The bathroom door opens, and Lynn steps out wearing my robe, followed by a cloud of steam. "Hey, you're back. How did it go?"

I meet her eyes.

She rushes over and sits next to me. "What happened?"

My shoulders go up, I open my mouth, and nothing comes out. I get up, walk to the fridge, and get a bottle of water. Drain it. Toss the empty bottle in the trash.

I stare into nothing. "I don't know. I'm still trying to figure it out. One minute we were making out like teenagers, the next he's walking away because he can't deal with the reasons we've been brought together—the missing women."

Her hands go up. "Whoa, whoa, whoa. Back up a minute."

"What?" I force myself to focus on her.

"Go back to the part where you two are making out like teens. Let's start there and leave nothing out."

Oh, Lynn. I try to smile, but my lips tremble—I press them together and lift a shoulder instead.

She crosses her arms and raises an eyebrow.

I'm not getting away without telling her something. "I don't know. One second, I was knocking on Jake's door, the next, the door was locked, and he had me against it, and his mouth was on mine. And..." My face heats at the memory of that kiss, the grinding, the orgasm. Nothing like that has ever happened to me before, at least not without a lot more foreplay.

"And?" Lynn waves her hands at me, fully invested in finding out as much as she can.

My gaze meets hers. "I had an orgasm." My voice lowers, even though there's no one else here to hear us.

Lynn's eyes widen, and she squeals. "Did you have sex? In his office?" Thank God she keeps her voice low.

"No! It was just kissing. And..." Ugh, am I really about to say this? "And some, you know, dry humping."

"Oh my goodness, that's so hot."

I crack a smile at her enthusiasm. "It was."

Lynn, ever observant, tilts her head. "Something else happened. Something not good. What was it?"

"After"—I wave my hand—"the make-out session, we talked. I told him."

She gasps, her hands coming up to cover her mouth. "About the drowning and how he saved you?"

"Yes, he walked me to my car and said that he felt like we had met before, but he knew that wasn't true."

"That was the perfect opening."

"It was, and I took it. But now . . . now I'm not so sure."

"He didn't take it well?"

"He was okay at first, not upset, just in awe and curious about all the coincidences." I make an *air quotes* gesture when I say coincidences.

"So, what got his balls on fire then?"

I snort. Leave it to Lynn to come up with something no one else would just to make me laugh. "The idea that those women had to die for us to meet again. I think he feels somewhat responsible. I don't know."

Lynn nods to herself. "I get it, though. Think about it. All the things that happened to bring you two together again." She gets up and starts pacing in the space around the couch. "Of all the places to stop for breakfast, we picked a restaurant across from an antique shop. And I badgered you to go in there."

"You did."

She stops pacing to shoot me a glare. "And then you found that necklace . . . which took us to the police station. What are the odds?"

"Where fate is concerned? The odds are always a sure thing."

"No surprise the poor guy is freaking out. He couldn't even take the psychometry thing, and now his brain can't handle that many coincidences."

"Synchronicities," I correct her. Grandma's voice echoes in the back of my mind.

She waves me off and now expands the pacing to the rest of the room. No wonder she hates it when I pace. My neck's getting slow-motion whiplash watching her.

"Dude, he's a cop with a bunch of missing women, and

now he thinks that somehow their disappearance is related to having saved your life all these years ago."

Wait, what? "What do you mean?" Even though I already know.

"I mean, this story—the two of you getting together—it doesn't start with the women going missing and you finding that necklace. It started when you were thirteen, and he saved your life. And now you're here, and all he can think of is that if those women didn't go missing, there would be no necklace for you to find, and there would be no making out in his office."

"I don't know about that. I think we were meant to meet again. I've always felt that. Somewhere, somehow, our paths would cross again. I just never envisioned it happening this way."

Lynn sits on the other end of the couch. "No one would. I mean, you were thirteen, and that's a lot of years ago."

I grab a pillow, hold it to my chest, and rest my chin on it. "Why can't things be easy and simple? Why couldn't I just meet him again in a bar or something like normal people do?"

Lynn snorts and holds a hand up, fingers spread. "One, you hate going to bars. Two, you're far from normal. Three—"

I toss the pillow at her to stop her countdown. Lynn snatches it and throws it back across the couch. "Now what? Are you still going to help him? Are you going to see him again?"

I roll my lips together and exhale. "Before the whole disaster happened, I told Jake I wanted to see all the evidence together. Unless he tells me otherwise, I will show up in his office tomorrow morning at nine as we agreed."

She nods. "Make sure you're careful and don't exert yourself."

Her words uncoil some of the tension in my chest. The knowledge that Lynn will always have my back, be at my side, and care for me takes some of the sting out of Jake's rejection. "I will. I promise. I'll get some dark chocolate and dried mangoes to nibble on after."

"And don't forget the water, lots of water."

I smile. "I won't forget. I'll even let you pack a snack bag for me, Mamma Lynn."

"I will do that. Now, what do you want to do? Go somewhere? Take a walk? Shop?"

I shrug.

"Go antiquing?" She suggests with a waggle of her perfect eyebrows.

I toss another pillow at her.

CHAPTER 29
AVALON

WELL, HERE GOES NOTHING. JAKE DIDN'T TEXT OR CALL to cancel our meeting, so I'm standing outside his closed office door. And it's not like I can retreat, either. I had Lynn drop me off so she could have the car. The cops behind the front desk smirked at me and waved me into the back.

"They probably think I keep coming back for booty calls," I mutter. They wouldn't be entirely wrong now, would they?

I inhale deeply. The scent of dust and stale coffee lingers in the air as I knock on the door.

"Who is it?" His voice comes through, the tone dry and irritated.

I swallow. "It's me, Ava."

The door opens a few inches, his body blocking the view inside. He looks over my head and widens the space just enough for me to slip in.

"No one told me you were here." As soon as I clear the opening, Jake glances out and locks the doors.

"They waved me in." A nervous flutter sets itself in my stomach.

Jake has yet to meet my eyes. He shakes his head. "So much for security."

I lean on the door, cross my arms, and fight the urge to hunch my shoulders to make myself smaller. When he looks at me, his gaze travels down my body and back up again. Heat darkens his mismatched eyes to a deeper sea-green and twilight sky. Too late I remember that this is the same spot we were making out just a day ago.

Jake blinks away the tendrils of lust hanging between us and takes a step back. He gestures behind him, and I see why he was guarding the door.

He set up a long gray folding table behind his desk, a foot or so off the back wall. Sunlight comes through the blind-covered window, painting light and shadow stripes over the table and the objects on it. The table takes nearly the entire width of the small office. All the collected evidence in plastic bags is neatly laid out with numbered sticky notes next to each.

I push away from the door, drop my backpack on a chair, and step around his desk. Jake must have moved it to make more space. His old, creaky chair is pushed to the side, as well.

I walk around the table, touching nothing, yet the past reaches to me with a near physical presence. It's like walking through spiderwebs. I resist the urge to swat away the tingling energy dancing around me like dust motes in sunlight. I curl my fingers into my hand.

"You have the recorder ready?"

Jake leans over his desk and grabs the small digital recorder. His gaze darts to the locked door behind me. A bead of sweat forms on his temple. His chest expands with a deep breath, and he nods.

These objects want to be read. They scream for my touch. Pressure builds at my back, like invisible hands pushing me forward. The hands of the victims, perhaps, in need of closure, justice, and peace.

I hope I can provide it to them.

I take the recorder from him and look it over. "Ready?"

He nods and steps back, giving me space to move around the table. I turn on the recorder and set it in the middle of the table.

I breathe in, roll my shoulders, and then hold my hands together and blow into them to dispel the settling cold.

I don't follow the order in which the objects are laid out. I follow the pull of energy and reach for a small bag in the center of the table. Inside is a pair of sunglasses. I close my eyes and open myself. The images start.

"The young woman has a brilliant smile. Long, straight brown hair. Vivid brown eyes. She's the kind of person who's always happy." *Was* always happy. "A man reaches for her, takes the sunglasses off her face, and tosses them in a car through the open window. It's a sunny day. He's wearing a baseball cap and sunglasses. His face is shadowed by the sunlight behind him."

I set the sunglasses down and allow the pull to grab my attention again.

A bigger bag this time. Fabric. A sweater. "Fabrics are hard to read. They don't hold energy well."

He frowns. "Why is that?"

"Because they get washed. Water is a natural cleanser. But traumatic events amplify the energy."

He nods, and I close my eyes. Open myself more, reach deeper, and invite the images to come. These images feel older than the sunglasses. "Fall. Late fall. I see trees, and most are bare. There are leaves all over the ground. They are outside. The day is cold and windy. She keeps moving hair off her face. Brown hair with soft curls. It's the same woman. The man reaches for her and tucks a lock of hair behind her ear—" I gasp.

"What is it?" Jake's voice is low but intense.

"The scar. It's the same scar I saw when I found the necklace. It's the same man. I'm sure of it."

My body moves and sways a little. I allow the image to take over. *I'm her now.* I tilt my head up, cross my arms over my chest, and hug the evidence bag with the sweater to myself. I'm cold. The image flashes, and she's somewhere else with the man. "They're walking. She's standing by a blue car. It's quiet wherever they are. He gives her a to-go cup. She takes a sip, but the lid is not secure, spilling the light amber liquid on herself. Maybe tea?"

Heat flows into my chest as if I, too, have been doused with hot liquid.

"She's embarrassed and pulls the sweater away from her chest. The man takes the cup from her. He tells her to take her sweater off and put on his jacket. She refuses, but he insists."

I stop and dig for more. There's something there, just out of sight. "Damn it."

The floor creaks under Jake's feet, but he stays quiet this time.

I frown and search the images flashing behind my closed eyelids. "I see . . . it's a sign. A wooden sign. There are painted words in red and green. Three letters—D E R." Come on, move, look up, show me. "Cider. The sign says HOT CIDER."

I open my eyes and place the bag back on the table and slump against the windowsill.

Jake takes two steps toward me and then stops himself. He drops the notepad on his desk and opens a mini fridge I had never noticed before. Takes a bottle of water from it and hands it to me.

I take the bottle, open it, and take greedy gulps. "It was cider. She spilled cider on herself. And he made her take the sweater off and gave her his jacket. These things don't belong to Alice or Lena. Where did they come from?"

Jake leans against his desk, his long legs crossed in front of him. "The items were found in a duffel bag about a hundred yards from where Alice's car was located when a perimeter search was conducted. I had no idea whether it was linked to Alice or not. It looked like someone tossed the bag over the railing, and it should have fallen all the way down an embankment. But the bag got caught on some branches. Otherwise, it would have never been found."

My mind races. "So, that means more people are missing."

His posture seems relaxed, but his shoulders are rigid. "It's likely there are reports of others missing in surrounding towns."

"Why isn't everyone freaking out over this?"

His head drops. "Because we don't really search for missing people. I told you that."

I don't know what to say to this. It seems crazy. I turn my back to Jake and focus my attention on the table again, hovering my right hand over each sealed bag. Memories reach out to me like spiderweb tendrils and tickle the palm of my hand. I reach for a small bag. A lipstick tube. Images flood my senses. "This is a different woman. There's a trail in the woods. It's narrow in some spots and wide in others. It's well-marked. Many footprints on the ground. Some are well-defined, like people were running in mud and the tracks kept their shape after drying in the sun. Others are mere smudges."

My heartbeat speeds, and my thighs and calf muscles ache. Like I've been running for miles. I know this burn well. "She's running. There's a race or marathon. I see other runners ahead of her. There's a chill in the air, and the trees around aren't quite leafed out yet. It's early spring."

My feet are firmly in place, my eyes still closed, but I allow my body to mimic hers. My arms come to my sides as if I am running alongside her. My breaths come in shorter bursts. "Someone jostles her. The impact makes her lose her footing, and she trips. She tries to regain her balance and twists her ankle." Sharp pain wraps itself around my ankle. I gasp.

The floor creaks and I put a hand up, anticipating Jake's approach. My eyes are still closed, and I lower myself to the floor. Then, I wrap my free hand around my lower left leg.

"What's her name?"

"Victoria. Victoria Welsh."

I call to her in my mind. *Talk to me, Victoria. Help me find you.* "She's hurt. She's on the edge of the trail. Other runners pass by. She pulls herself off the trail and sits to the side. Someone checks on her, a woman, but she waves her away, says she's fine, just needs to catch her breath."

I move my body on the floor the same way she moved hers. "Someone else stops and squats in front of her. I don't think he's a runner. I don't see a number tag on his shirt. She knows him. She's comfortable with him. He helps her up. The tube of lipstick falls out of her pocket. Red lipstick. She always races in red lipstick. It makes her feel powerful."

I open my eyes. "It's the same man I saw before in my other readings."

His eyes widen. "Did you see his face?" There's so much eagerness in Jake's voice.

"No. Just his hands when he helped her up. Same scar. I'm starting to recognize his energy, but it's odd. Sometimes it changes."

Jake rubs his chin. "I don't understand. How can you recognize something like that, and how does it change?"

"It's hard to explain. Energy has an imprint."

He frowns. "An imprint?"

How can I explain it better? How can I put in words something so wholly intangible? "Like a . . . scent. Like when someone wears the same perfume all the time, and you can recognize it. Sometimes the smell is stronger because they just put it on, sometimes softer because it's been a few hours, and sometimes it changes because that person is sweating, but you can still detect that faint smell."

He nods slowly. His forehead creases as he tries to process what I'm saying.

I put the lipstick bag back on the table. "Was the lipstick found near a trail?"

"Yes. There was a marathon. A First-Day-of-Spring marathon. When the race ended and she didn't appear, her husband, who was waiting for her at the finish line, reported her missing."

"First day of spring? That's March twenty. It's been four months then."

"Yes. And when it went public, a woman came forward and reported seeing her fall and sit on the side of the trail.

That's where we found the lipstick. The husband confirmed it was hers."

"No one else saw what happened?"

"No, we had dozens of volunteers search the park but found nothing. Got a rescue dog to come in, but there was a huge storm later in the day, and whatever scent was there got dispersed."

"Dispersed?"

"Light rain and moisture are optimal for scent tracking. Dry, hot days make it more difficult. But with heavy rains, the scent disperses, gets moved around with the water and wind, making it more difficult for a dog to track it."

"I didn't know that." I run a hand through my hair. I'm so frustrated with myself. Why can't I see more? See his damned face. An urge to leave the room tugs at me like a tethered string to my chest and I need to follow it. "Take me to the place where you found the lipstick."

He glances at the table and back at me. The silent question is clear in his gaze.

"Now. We need to go right now."

CHAPTER 30
AVALON

WE WALK SIDE BY SIDE. THE GRAVEL CRUNCHING UNDER our feet gradually turns into dirt and muffles the sounds of our steps. All around us, a symphony of forest sound soars. Birds chirp, and insects buzz in the distant background, the gurgle of water a constant melody. Cool wind rustles in the trees. The temperature drops under their canopy. The deeper we get into the forest, the denser the foliage becomes. Sun dapples the uneven ground here and there, wherever it can find a break between the branches, leaves, and evergreens. The forest closes in on me. That pull in my chest is like a compass directing my steps.

The air is rich with the scent of pine and earth. But underneath it all, the stench of death reaches me every so often, carried by the breeze. My insides twist.

I stop. "Can you smell it?"

Jake turns. A nod is his only response. He gives me his hand. I step closer and take it. His fingers lace with mine, and his touch settles the unease in my stomach by a fraction.

We're not near the marathon trail. There's no footpath in

this part of the forest, but here and there natural trails appear, with clear deer tracks in the mud. I open my senses.

Come.

This way.

I heed the call whispering for me to follow. Her voice is soft, calm, and loving. I tug at Jake's hand and veer off the deer path. He resists at first, but I tug again. "She's this way."

"How do you . . ." He doesn't finish the question, shakes his head, and follows me. His hand squeezes mine a little tighter.

We walk for several minutes, pushing low branches and vegetation away, being careful of our steps, and picking through leaves and rocks. The deeper we get into the forest, the quieter it gets. I expected the nature sounds to grow louder. But even the sound of water is gone now, as if the forest holds its breath. It's also darker, the canopy of trees denser. Little sunlight gets through.

A movement to my right catches my attention. A dark shadow speeds by. My heartbeat pounds in my ears like primordial drums.

I stop.

Tears fill my eyes, and pressure builds in my chest. I gasp with the need to breathe.

There's no air.

My knees buckle, but Jake catches me before I hit the ground.

He holds me to his side, strong arms around my waist to keep me upright. "What is it? What happened? Are you hurt?" The urgency in Jake's voice grows with each question.

My mouth has gone dry. I swallow and lick my lips. "I'm —I'm okay."

He releases a breath. His chest shudders as he inhales

again. "What happened?" His voice is gentle, and his hands are gentler when he pushes a lock of hair behind my ear.

I find the strength in my legs to stand on my own feet. "She's here. She's close by."

His gaze leaves my face to search our surroundings.

I blink away the wetness in my eyes and focus again. There are signs all around us. Small things that would go unnoticed if we were not looking closely.

"Look." I point at a snapped branch and some large rocks that appear to have been moved around. Footprints follow them from their original place to the new one.

He puts a hand up. "Stay here."

The wind shifts. The stench of death and turned dirt gets stronger. The low buzz of flies can be heard now. I cover my nose and mouth with both hands. Hold my breath. Jake reaches for his shoulder holster and pulls out his gun. My body goes numb with cold despite the mild temperature. He steps carefully, the gun trained on the ground as he scans the entire area.

There. The voice speaks in my head again. *Behind that fallen tree.*

The fallen tree is enormous. A person could easily crouch and hide behind it. There's a huge hole where it used to stand. Broken roots reach into the air like the tentacles of a bizarre forest monster.

"Jake?" I call his name in a whisper.

He stops and glances over his shoulder.

I point to the trunk.

Jake makes a wide turn around the roots. When he appears on the other side of the tree, he closes his eyes and his head and shoulders droop. A shape takes form next to him.

Victoria.

209

She smiles. Bright red lipstick coats her lips. *Thank you for finding me. My family can be at peace now.*

Tears stream down my face and I'm flooded with a relief that's not mine. Victoria turns and steps away. Fades into a stream of sunlight breaking through the trees.

"Jake?"

He holsters his gun. "Stay there. You don't need to see this." He walks back to me, takes me into his arms, and tucks my head under his chin. Holds me for a moment and then lets me go.

My throat aches. "Is it her?"

He nods.

I need confirmation. "Are you sure? It's been four months . . ."

"It's her."

"What did you see? I don't know much about this, but a body in a forest after four months . . ."

"The body is mostly intact. She was not here long."

I blink at him. "What?"

"Come on, let's go back to my cruiser. Get Lynn to come and pick you up. Once you leave, I'll call dispatch and report the body."

My first reaction is to say no. But Jake and I shouldn't be here when the rest of the police shows up. "What are you going to say?"

"That I got an anonymous tip. Someone was hiking and saw the body but was too scared to identify themselves."

"Then what will happen?"

"The OCME will come and check for themselves. Talk to me. Check the area."

I sniffle and rub the wetness away from my face. "What's the OCME?"

"It stands for Office of the Chief Medical Examiner. They'll send a medical examiner, and then the body will be transported to the OCME autopsy facility at Concord Hospital."

"You think they'll believe it was a tip?"

He tugs at my hand, walking faster now. "I don't see why not. Hikers and hunters walk the forest often enough and they're usually the first ones to find bodies in the woods."

My gaze darts around as if I'm about to find more bodies. "What about my tracks? Won't they see our tracks?"

"They might. But that can be justified as the tracks of whoever made the anonymous call." He looks at my feet. "You should probably get rid of those sneakers, just in case."

I look down at my own feet and nearly trip. "I'll get rid of them when Lynn picks me up."

The way back seems a lot shorter. He lets go of my hand when we reach his cruiser. "Call, don't text because text messages can be subpoenaed."

I call Lynn, and we wait inside his cruiser. The low hum of the air conditioner is the only sound. He's closed off again and thinks I was following my intuition, and I debate telling him what I saw and then go for it. "I saw her . . . behind that tree."

His eyes widen. "How? Her body wasn't visible from where you were."

"Not her body. Her spirit. She told me where her body was and then thanked us for finding her. She was happy her family can have closure now."

He runs a hand through his hair and then holds the steering wheel. "Okay. This is something else. This is way above reading energy in an object. Now you have a ghost telling you where to find her body."

"I know."

His knuckles go white around the steering wheel. "Help me understand. How does this work?"

"I've always been able to see spirits—and hear them. They can hear us, too. But it's not something that happens at will like the psychometry."

"And the ghosts just show up?"

I shrug and try to hold it together, not show Jake how shaken I am on the inside. If I let go of my ironclad hold on myself, I'll crack wide-open. I can't let this happen. I can't allow myself to give in to the urge to cry and run away. I won't be like my mother. I breathe in, close my eyes for a moment, release the air in my lungs, and then face him. "Not exactly. When I held the lipstick, I asked Victoria to help me find her. I guess she listened because I felt the pull to come here."

His hand drops to his lap, and the back of his head hits the headrest. Once. Twice. Three times. "I can't believe I'm going to say this—" He shakes his head and looks up at the ceiling of his cruiser. Shakes his head some more. Drags in a big breath and releases it. "Can you ask the others where they are as well?"

CHAPTER 31
AVALON

Lynn envelops me in a bear hug. Her fierce loyalty and strength slip into me as if by osmosis. I never underestimate the power of a hug. Lynn has been one of the few constants in my life. A sense of calm eases the weight off my chest. She lets go and walks me to the car with her hands on my shoulders as she would one of her students. I haven't said anything to her, yet she can read me well enough.

My gaze locks with Jake's as we drive away, then I close my eyes and rest my head against the seat. I release the emotions and cut the cords that still connect me to Victoria. Peace for her. But for her family, anguish at losing their last shred of hope that Victoria was alive and sorrow at her passing.

Lynn's gaze searches my face, her keen eyes looking for answers without having to ask the questions.

"I'll tell you everything later, okay? I need to process what happened first."

Lynn squeezes my forearm. No words are needed right

now. She starts the engine, and we drive away from this place. If only I could leave the images in my head behind too.

All I want to do is take a hot shower and wash away this day. There's a part of me that wishes I never walked into that antique store and found the necklace. A part of me wants to give in to anger and blame Lynn and Grandma for the role they played, so I can distance myself from all of it. But I can't and won't blame either of them. There's no blame to be placed on anyone but the evil asshole preying on these women.

This whole mess is heartbreaking. Even knowing I'm doing something good, knowing I'm helping the victims and the families, and hopefully also helping to catch the bastard who's doing this—God knows how many more he has hurt. I find it hard to believe that it's only the four Jake told me about. And in a small town like this, I would expect people to be more alarmed. But missing is not dead, and without proof of foul play, there's always the possibility that people just left. All of it will change now. There's a body. And once the experts do an autopsy and figure out what happened, they will definitely know she was murdered.

I close my eyes to the blur of green speeding by outside my window and start a counting meditation. Counting down from ten to one and then reverting from one to ten. Again and again, until the whirl of thoughts in my head gives way to the numbers, and I can block everything else.

I jolt awake when Lynn parks the car outside our building.

"Did I fall asleep?"

"You did."

I twist my head from side to side and squeeze the back of my neck. An ache has settled deep into my muscles, more from tension than falling asleep in the car. "Thanks for picking me up."

Lynn pats my knee and gets out. I follow her, and we share the elevator with three other people. I'm grateful for their presence, so I can't say anything. Not that Lynn would pressure me, but I'm still processing everything that happened.

When I get out of the shower, Lynn is waiting in the kitchen. "I figured you'd need some food, so I ordered from that little Mexican place down the road. Got you a sweet potato quesadilla."

My stomach grumbles as the rich scent reaches me. "Thank you. I didn't even know I was hungry until now."

"Dig in! Then you can take a nap."

We eat and talk with Lynn telling me all about her morning and learning to kayak at the lake.

"Kayak? I never knew you had an interest in kayaking."

Her smile gives me the answer before she speaks. "I wasn't until I saw the instructor."

"Of course. My boy-crazy best friend. Why else would you do anything remotely in the neighborhood of sports?"

She grabs her phone. "Did you know kayaking requires a lot of core strength?"

"I do now."

She grins. "I took pictures of his abs."

I nearly choke on my food. "You did what?"

Her grin grows bigger. "What? I asked."

I stop eating. "You asked to take pictures of the instructor's abs?"

"Well, not the abs. I asked if I could take a picture of the kayak. I can't help if he was standing beside it and shirtless, can I?"

She shows me the picture. "Those are some exceptional abs."

She looks at the screen again and sighs. "They are, aren't they?"

"So, what else did you do? Go anywhere? Do anything fun?"

Lynn puts her phone on the couch. "I went into town. You know that cute K-9 cop we saw outside the police station?"

I lean back into the chair. "Yep."

"I ran into him, and we grabbed a coffee together. His name is Jeff Donavan."

Wait. What? "With the dog?"

She laughs. "No, silly. He was off duty. I was walking and window-shopping, and he came up to me. He said he remembered seeing me before. He asked how we knew *your* detective."

"Really?"

She pokes at her food. "Yes, but no worries. I didn't give anything away. I told Jeff you and Jake were friends in college but lost contact over the years. When you ran into him the other day, we stopped by to say hello."

My stomach clenches. "Did he believe you?"

"Yes, I think so. Why wouldn't he?"

Uneasiness prickled at my neck. "Hmm . . ."

"Hmm, what?"

"Nothing. Just be careful. I'm probably overthinking everything. So, how was it? The coffee date, I mean."

"It wasn't really a date. We just walked into the place and ordered coffee, talked for a few minutes, and then he had to go. He's nice, though he seemed a little shy."

"Shy?" I didn't get a shy vibe from him.

"Yeah, he asked how long we were staying in town and how we liked it so far, but none of the questions guys usually ask when they want to get in your pants, you know?" She waves her hand as if I know what she's talking about.

"No, not really."

She huffs. "You can read objects and talk to ghosts, but you can't tell when a guy wants to sleep with you?"

"You know I'm not good at that stuff."

She rolls her eyes. "They look at your body, make excuses to touch you, ask questions with sexual innuendo, you know, stuff like that."

"The guys I dated before didn't do any of that."

Her sigh is loud and dramatic. "You've got to stop going out with those stuffy museum types."

I point at myself. "Hey! I'm a stuffy museum type."

"No, you're far from it."

I scrunch my nose. "So . . . this guy didn't ask questions like that or check you out?"

"Nope, he was pretty generic and polite. A little distant even. Oh, well, his loss. He'll never know what all of this"—Lynn gestures at herself—"can do when properly motivated." Her eyebrows wiggle. "Now, go take that nap. You look exhausted. I'll clean this up, and then I'm going to watch rom-coms on Netflix."

"Rom-coms sound good. I could watch some with you. I'll probably fall asleep halfway, though." I don't want to be alone right now. I don't want to be alone with my thoughts or my mind filled with memories that don't belong to me. And definitely not images of dead women calling for help. I'm drowning all over again. Barely keeping my head above water. And this time, I have to save myself.

"Okay then. You pick something, and I'll clean this up. Be there in five."

I drag myself to the couch and find the remote control. Scroll through the listings, trying to find a movie we haven't watched yet. I'm already half asleep when an icy coldness envelops me like a wet blanket and a voice rings loud and clear in my ears.

"He's dumping another body."

CHAPTER 32

JAKE

Someone leaked information. The police station is in chaos. Word got out fast, and both the local and city press are conglomerating outside, throwing questions at anyone who comes in or out of the building.

I can't get the image of that poor woman's body out of my mind. Victoria. She's been missing for four months. There were signs he kept her body frozen for a while. Whoever took her killed her months ago. Why dump her body now? What is he planning? Maybe it's what he does. Dumps the body in the woods, and the animals take care of the rest. If Ava had not been here, Victoria's body might have gone undiscovered for months, maybe forever. There are enough big predators in the area to take care of a body, for sure.

Thank God Ava didn't see it. If we find any others, I have to make sure she doesn't go anywhere near them.

"Congratulations." Frank's slap on my back snaps me out of my head and the nightmarish images rooting in my mind.

I bite my tongue and smooth my face before the sneer

trying to take over has a chance to set. Congratulations. On what? Finding a body? Crushing all hope her family had of finding her alive? I didn't solve the case. I didn't catch the bastard, yet this is not the first time I've heard the word today. It feels out of place. And it's not my credit to take.

I know Frank means nothing by it. He's old-school and has been in the station longer than anyone else.

"How did you find the body so fast?"

Fast? I wouldn't call four months fast. His question puts me on edge. More so than I already am. I widen my stance, resisting the urge to cross my arms. Stuff my hands in my pockets instead. "What do you mean?"

Frank rubs his bald head and wipes his hand on his uniform pants. Beads of sweat shine under the bright fluorescent lights. "Heard you got an anonymous tip about the body being in the woods. There are miles and miles of woods. How did you find it?"

I stare him down longer than needed. "I followed my nose. Hard to miss the smell of a dead body baking in the summer heat."

He grimaces. "Yes, but how did you know where to drive to?"

I cross my arms now. What is it? Simple curiosity? Is he fishing for information? Or accusing? "Got a tip with the location. They gave me a mile marker and directions from there."

He shakes his head. "Was it bad?"

Was it bad? No, Frank. It was a fucking picnic. I shrug. Where is he going with this? I check his wrist for scars. Nothing that I can see.

He rubs his head again. "I don't miss that part of the job,

and I'll be glad to finish my days behind a desk and never see another dead body again."

The chief waves to me from across the room and saves me from having to give Frank an answer. He nods toward his office, and I follow him. He closes the door and lowers the blinds on the large window facing the main area. Then he drops into the chair behind his desk. "Out with it."

I hold my place, still standing, shoulders relaxed. I loop my thumbs on my waistband. Tilt my head. "Sir?"

"Don't bullshit me, Knox. There's more you're not telling me. I'll go along with this tip story. It works for the press, but we both know that a simple check of your phone would reveal no one called with a tip."

The chief is a viper. I've had him riding my ass for months about the missing women. "I never said I got a phone call, Chief."

He narrows his eyes. His gaze goes cold and calculating. "You didn't, but that's what everyone is saying. That you got an anonymous call?"

"I can't help what they gossip about."

He's on his feet in an instant, and it takes everything I have not to flinch. I hold my ground, and a staring match ensues.

"Don't fuck with me, Knox. I want this bastard. I want his ass behind bars until the day he dies. I need an airtight case. No loopholes, no doubts, no escape route—"

"I want the same thing, Chief."

"Then you better make damn sure that whatever comes out of your mouth about this investigation is fucking clean and will hold because if anything happens to give this bastard a chance to get away, it will be your ass on the line. If I don't get him, I'm coming for you."

"Understood, Chief."

He drops back to his chair. "Now, are you sure it's the jogger's body?"

"Yes, it's her. But of course, we won't notify the family until we have dental records confirmation." I've stared at those missing women's pictures for so long that I've memorized every freckle and line on their faces. "I think he kept the body frozen."

"Jesus! The phones are ringing nonstop. Between the families calling and the journalists, we need to come up with something to tell them. What do you plan to say to those hyenas sniffing for blood outside?"

"Me?" What? I don't want to talk to the press. "I thought you would address them, sir."

He rolls the chair back and crosses one leg over the other. "It's your case, Knox. I'm not in the habit of stealing anyone's thunder."

"I would rather not talk to the press. I thought you would do this as the chief of police."

His scowl is instantaneous. "Get out there and get rid of them. I don't want any journalists sniffing around my station. You hear me?"

"Yes, sir."

"And make sure not to say anything that can hurt this case."

"I won't." I leave before he can give me any more orders.

Fuck. I need a minute of respite and get away from everyone watching me. I go to my office and lock myself in. "Shit!" All the evidence is still out on the table, left out since this morning when Ava said we had to go right away. I put everything away, fold the table legs, and lean it against the wall. A knock on my door startles me.

I take one last glance around, make sure nothing is out of place, and open the door. Jeff is on the other side. "What?" My voice sounds harsher than I intended.

Jeff smiles. "The chief said you're talking to the press and sent me to get you."

I move and force him to take a step back, close my office door, and wait for the click of the lock.

Jeff and the chief flank me like I'm a prisoner being taken to the gallows. The rest of the station follows behind as if they have nothing better to do.

As soon as we step outside the building, the shouts and camera flashes start, like in a scene of a movie. Metal barricades contain the dozen or so journalists and several more onlookers.

I raise a hand, and they fall mostly quiet. The murmur of traffic is present again.

I take a step forward. The shouts start again.

"Is it true you got a tip with the location of the body?"

"Where was the body found?"

"Has the body been identified yet?"

"What are you doing about all these missing women?"

"Could it be a serial killer?"

Each question is like a punch to the gut. I have to protect Ava. She can't be exposed to this—to them. Once more, I put my hand up and wait until the questions stop.

"This is what we know so far. A body was found in a section of Bear Brook State Park. It has been recovered and transported for further examination. We have not yet identified the body. This is an active investigation, and we are not taking questions at this time." As soon as I say the last word, the questions return. Louder and more aggressive. The chief nods at the other cops, and they disperse the press and onlookers.

I go inside and the chief follows me. "You did good out there. But now you need to be alert and watch your back more than ever because they will be watching you. And so will the bastard who killed that woman."

224

CHAPTER 33
AVALON

I STARTLE MYSELF AWAKE. TIREDNESS CLINGS TO MY bones and weighs me down, but sleep is gone. I have to talk to Jake. I check the time. It's been nearly six hours since Lynn picked me up. He has to be thick in the middle of this investigation. I don't want to distract him, but this is important. Another body. But who? And where?

No response comes to my silent question.

Lynn stands in front of me and presses a hand on my forehead. "Are you okay? You look . . . off."

I sit up on the couch. "Yes, I'm fine. No fever. Just tired."

"I thought you'd be napping by now. Did I wake you?"

"No. I was half-asleep, but . . ."

She sits on the couch arm. "But what?"

I shake my head. I don't want to scare her.

"Come on, tell me. If you don't, I'll assume there are ghosts everywhere in here and will start to pack to go back home."

I try to smile but fail. "No ghosts." None that I can see, at least. "But I think he's dumping another body."

She slides onto the couch and crosses her legs. "How do you know that?"

I squeeze the remote control and accidentally start a show. I stop it. "I heard a voice. Someone told me he's dumping another body."

She jumps out of the couch so fast that pillows go flying. She's halfway across the room before they hit the floor. "You said there were no ghosts!"

"There aren't. I heard a voice. In my head and that's it." Well, technically, I heard with my ears. But that will only freak her out more. "It could have been just a random thought. From all the stress, you know."

She points at me. Index finger-wagging. Goes into the kitchenette and comes back with a saltshaker.

"What are you doing?"

"I'm doing an exorcism." She shakes salt all over the room.

And she's serious about it, too. My shoulders shake with the effort not to laugh. "I don't think that's how it works."

She walks a circle around me, saltshaker half empty now. "I've watched *Supernatural*, and it works. I'm buying some sage, too."

"Lynn." I stop her in her second circle around me. Take the shaker from her hand. "Sit down. Relax. Let's watch a movie. Something light and funny. There are no ghosts here. I swear."

She gives me the side eye. Then relents and sits down. Grabs the pillows from the floor and arranges them around her like a fort. Then she takes the remote control and turns on the TV.

I stand up and slide my phone into my pocket. "Find something for us to watch. I'll be right back."

I walk to the bathroom and close the door. Step into the shower, close the curtains, and text Jake.

Me: I need to talk to you.

I don't expect an immediate response, but floating dots appear on my screen.

Jake: Is everything OK?
Me: Yes. Let me know when you can talk freely. Maybe we can FaceTime.
Jake: I'll FaceTime you now.

The phone rings a second later, and I answer it before the sound can alert Lynn.

His face fills the screen. His hair's in disarray, as if he's been running his hands through it. "Hey. How's . . . everything?" I keep my voice low.

He sighs. "It's a clusterfuck." His voice is as low as mine.

"What? Why?"

He leans back in his chair. "Someone tipped the press. There were journalists with cameras at the station when I got back. They knew about the body."

My hand goes to my mouth and covers a gasp. "How?"

"No fucking clue. I've never seen anything like this before. The local paper reports on town events, sports, and minor violations or traffic accidents. Whoever tipped them made it sound like it's a serial killer."

"Serial killer? How could anyone know?" Even if they are not off the mark.

He shrugs. "There have been reports about the missing women and I guess someone is connecting the dots."

My stomach lurches. "This is not good, Jake."

He fists his hair. Lets go. "I know. My boss is riding my ass and made me talk to the press."

Talk to the press? I don't want to ask. I don't know what I'll do if the answer is yes. But I have to ask. "Do they know about me?" My voice is a whisper.

He shakes his head. "No, I said nothing to anyone about you. You know I wouldn't."

Relief floods me and weakens my legs. I slide to the floor and sit against the tiled wall. "But how could they know about the body?"

His lips thin. "It could have been anyone in the chain of information. The only person I know for sure wouldn't leak the information is the chief because he hates journalists."

"Who else knows about it?"

"The medical examiner, other cops, the funeral home who retrieved the body. It's safe to assume that any of them could have gossiped about it and said something to a friend or spouse, and it got spread from there."

I'm biting my nails. A habit I quit years ago. "I don't like this. If it's out to everyone like that, it means the killer also knows."

He sighs again, sounding tired. "I know. And with the attention I'm getting because of the press, and families asking for information, and the gossipmongers, it will be a lot harder to get you here."

"We'll have to lie low for a while."

"Worst fucking timing. Just when we have a break."

"Maybe I can—"

"No. The last thing we need is some photographer taking your picture going into the building and someone recognizing you and making speculations. I promised no one would find out about you, and I intend to keep that promise."

My eyes fill with tears. The emotions of the day catch up with me. "Thank you."

His gaze searches my face, tenderness in his eyes. "Are you crying?" His voice softens.

"No." I swallow the knot in my throat. "Just tired and emotionally drained."

The familiar squeak of his chair greets me. It's a comforting sound. "I'm sorry for dragging you into this mess. I really am."

"No. I don't regret it. I want to help."

Silence. No words are exchanged, just the sounds of our breathing and our gaze locked on each other. He leans back in the chair and runs his free hand down his face.

"Jake?"

"Yeah?"

"I think he's dumping another body."

WELL, WELL, WELL.

HE FOUND MY LITTLE GIFT FASTER THAN I EXPECTED.

HE SPOILED MY GAME. IT MAKES ME MAD.

THE DETECTIVE MAY BE SMARTER THAN I THOUGHT.

NAH. HE'S NOT THAT SMART. HE HASN'T FOUND EMILY YET, HAS HE?

HE GOT A TIP. BUT HOW? AND FROM WHOM?

I'LL FIND THEM, WHOEVER THEY ARE. I HOPE IT'S A WOMAN.

I'LL HAVE FUN RIPPING HER TATTLETALE TONGUE OUT.

THE DETECTIVE JUST GOT LUCKY.

GOOD LUCK FINDING THE NEXT ONE, PAL.

THIS IS MY GAME. AND MY TURN TO ROLL THE DICE.

WHO WILL BE THE NEXT ONE? SO MANY CHOICES.

CHAPTER 34
AVALON

THE SQUEAKING OF HIS CHAIR TURNS INTO A SCREECH when he moves. "What?"

"I think he's dumping another body." I squeeze my eyes shut and wait for his response. What will it be this time? Anger or doubt again? Or is he finally in all the way?

"Jesus. Who?"

Acceptance then. I look at Jake again. "I don't know yet. And I don't know if it's already happened or if he's planning on doing it soon. All I know is there will be another body for us to find—and soon."

"Did you have another vision?"

"No. It was a voice."

"A voice? Is that . . . normal?"

I laugh. The sound is unintentional and broken. Normal? "I don't know what's normal anymore. Unusual for me, yes. But not something that hasn't happened before."

"Okay . . ." The word is dragged out, slow and careful. He's silent.

I wipe an errant tear. "What's next?"

231

He sighs. "Notify her family. Wait for autopsy reports."

"It will get the press into a frenzy again."

"Yes, but it will go away like every other horrible event. Other things will hit the news-and people will forget."

I search his face, looking for answers to questions I haven't asked. "Not everyone. Victoria's family won't ever forget it."

"No. They'll have to learn to live without her."

Like he learned to live without his sister. He doesn't say it. He doesn't know that I know. But I hear it in his voice anyway. "The press won't go away. There will be the next body. The question is, why now? Why is he dumping bodies now? And why did he keep them this long?"

He rubs his face. "We'll have more information once they release the autopsy results. Maybe something in them will give us an answer."

I lean my head against the wall and adjust the phone in my hand. "How long will that take?"

"An autopsy usually takes a few hours to perform, depending on what they have to work with. We should get some preliminary results by tomorrow, but the full report could take weeks. Months even."

"That long?"

"Yeah, especially if they need to do DNA testing or toxicology. But I think they'll find the cause of death pretty fast."

"Why?" I sense a hesitation. "Why, Jake?"

"You're not gonna let this go, are you?"

I shake my head. "No, I need to know."

"It—the body had ligature marks on her neck. And . . ."

"And what?"

A loud exhale precedes his answer. "Freezer burns. There

were indications of freezer burns on her skin. He kept the body in a freezer."

I cover my mouth to prevent a sob from escaping. Close my eyes and drag in a deep breath. "God."

He runs a hand through his hair again. "I think he might be dumping the bodies because he's leaving the area. Maybe he's selling his home or moving."

"No. He's not leaving or moving."

"No? What makes you say that?"

The certainty hits me like an arrow to a bull's-eye. "He's making room for more."

CHAPTER 35
JAKE

Fuck. "Are you sure?"

"Y-yes." Ava's voice is shaky.

I hate asking her these questions. Hate getting her involved in this mess. Hate that she's hurting because of me pushing her to help me. But I keep going anyway. "Anything else?"

She's biting her nail again. "No, not right now. Maybe something else will come to me when he makes a move. Or when I look at the evidence."

A knock on the door is followed by a muffled voice.

She looks away from the phone. "I'll be right out."

And back at me. "It's Lynn. I'm hiding in the bathroom. This stuff is freaking her out."

I want to punch myself. "Maybe you two should leave. Go back home."

"No." There's no tremble in her voice now.

I'm an ass for wanting her to stay. "Let me figure out the rest. Now that we have a body, maybe we'll find some clues."

"I'm not leaving. I made a promise to stay and help."

Relief and fear for her battle inside me. I need to give her an out, a chance to get away. "I'm releasing you from that promise."

"Not to you."

"Not to me?"

"I made a promise to Alice. I'll find her and bring closure to her friend. I'm staying."

"Ava . . ."

A hand comes up. "Don't. You can't talk me out of it. I'm in too deep. They are coming to me without the aid of objects, and my leaving won't make a difference."

I don't know how to respond. "I made a promise, too. To keep your name out of the investigation, and now that the press is interested and fishing for information, we have to be even more careful."

"We will be."

"Someone could recognize you."

"I doubt it. I'm not known outside the museum circle."

"They could easily find your name and start there. They have resources."

"You have resources, too. And you have me."

"Do I?" The question escapes before I have a chance to rein it in. I'm not asking about her staying to help me with the case. And the extended silence that follows my question shows that she knows it, too.

"You do." Her response is almost a whisper.

My chest goes light and immediately heavy. This is wishful thinking. Ava has a richer and far more fulfilling life than anything I could ever offer her. "For how long?" It's my turn to whisper.

"As long as you'll have me."

I close my eyes, drag in a breath, and open them again. "But you're leaving."

The screen shows her sad smile. "You can come with me."

"Or you could stay." Fuck! "I'm sorry. That's not fair of me to ask you that."

She sighs. "No more unfair than my asking you to come with me."

"We are at a crossroads."

"We are."

I swallow the growing knot in my throat. "I won't hold you back."

"I know you won't, but maybe I want you to."

I could never do that. Hold Ava back. Watch her life grow small by being attached to this town and the promise I made to my sister. "What are we going to do, Ava?"

"I don't know. But I'm not worried about it."

"No?"

"No, the universe doesn't give you a problem without also giving you a solution. We just need to get out of our own way and allow life to unfold."

"You know, I don't really believe in any of that stuff." I did once but swore to never believe again. Yet I can't deny I'm starting to.

"You didn't believe in me, either, but here we are."

"Indeed. Here we are. Complicating everything and hurting ourselves in the process." The words taste bitter on my tongue. "I'm sorry, that wasn't necessary. I'm tired and frustrated and . . ."

"It doesn't have to be complicated, Jake."

"But it is."

"You're looking at it in black and white. Either or. And neither option in your mind works. You say you can't leave your job and this town. And I can't give up my life in New York and my job."

"What other options are there? Some long-distance relationship where we see each other on summers or holidays or whenever you're not flying all over the world?"

"That's one option, yes."

"You'd tire of it. And resent me. And I can't ask that of you. I can't ask you to give more than I'm capable of giving."

She pushes a lock of hair behind her ear. "You're not asking."

"And I never will."

"It's my choice, though. If I want to travel to some small town and spend my time with a grumpy cop, I will."

I laugh. The sound a bark of joyless discontent. "Grumpy cop?"

She grins. "As grumpy as they come."

"My life is ugly. Hopeless. Every day, I deal with the worst of humanity, and I don't want to bring that to you."

"You won't. Your life is not ugly. Or without hope. It's the opposite. What you do is important. You're not just dealing with the worst of humanity. You're giving hope and closure to the families. And stopping those ugly things from happening again."

I shake my head. "Don't romanticize my life. You don't know everything."

Her gaze shifts down before meeting my eyes again. "I know more than you think."

"What do you mean?"

She looks away again. "Nothing. I spoke out of turn."

"What do you mean, Ava?" My voice is louder than I intended.

She sighs. "I know about your sister."

"What?"

"I'm sorry. It wasn't intentional, but I knew about it that first day. When you gave me the rock. I've known all along."

"And you said nothing?" Anger coats my tone.

"No, it's not like that. I saw your sister was missing and that—that you blame yourself for it. That's it."

"All this time, you're withholding this information from me?"

Her eyes narrow. "What was I supposed to say? By the way, Jake. I know about your sister. How would that fly with you?"

"You should have said something."

"There was nothing to say. What I saw didn't give me any clues. I don't have any answers for you. And saying anything before would just have had you throwing me out faster. It wasn't my place to say anything."

I need to end this conversation before I say something I'll regret. "I have to go."

"Jake?"

"I have to get back out there, find out what's happening, and put a rush on the medical examiner."

She leans forward, her face filling more of the screen. "Don't do this, Jake. Don't go away mad."

I hang up.

CHAPTER 36
AVALON

THE SCREEN ON MY PHONE GOES DARK. I KNEW THIS would happen. There was so much pain in the glimpse I got about his sister. I told him the truth. I don't know anything else. Only that she disappeared years ago, and he feels guilty about it. But I don't know why.

There's a soft knock on the bathroom door. "Ava? Can I come in?"

I drop my head against the cold tile and close my eyes to keep the tears at bay. "Come in."

The door handle jiggles and opens slowly, and Lynn's head pops in, her eyes wide. She walks in and sits on the closed toilet bowl. "Strange place for a nap."

I try to smile and fail. My lips tremble, and the tears come rushing down my cheeks.

Lynn grabs a hand towel and gives it to me. I bury my face in it and have a good cry.

She shifts, lays a hand on my shoulder, and rubs back and forth. "Let it all out."

I do. I cry. Sobs wrack my body. My chest constricts and

makes it hard to breathe. I cry until the sobs turn into coughing and I choke on despair, pain, loss, fear, and hopelessness. This is not my pain alone. These aren't my tears alone. I share in the loss of each of those missing women. It's their tears and pain my body expels. Their wails move through me. I'm their gateway to freedom. I'm their salvation. And their last hope.

I cry until my eyes swell shut, and my head pounds with the stabbing of a thousand ice picks.

Everything goes hazy and muted. There's a gentle hand guiding me out of the bathtub and down the short hall. A glass of water and painkillers are thrust at me. A soft voice tells me to take the pills, and everything will be all right. I want to believe her.

Lynn tucks me into bed and wraps a blanket around me. Her hand rubs my back. I inhale deeply and my chest aches like I've run a marathon. Sleep takes me in, and I welcome the dark oblivion.

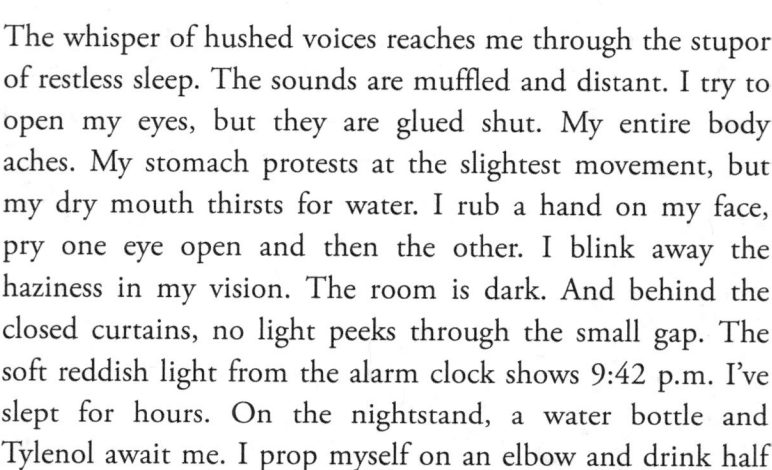

The whisper of hushed voices reaches me through the stupor of restless sleep. The sounds are muffled and distant. I try to open my eyes, but they are glued shut. My entire body aches. My stomach protests at the slightest movement, but my dry mouth thirsts for water. I rub a hand on my face, pry one eye open and then the other. I blink away the haziness in my vision. The room is dark. And behind the closed curtains, no light peeks through the small gap. The soft reddish light from the alarm clock shows 9:42 p.m. I've slept for hours. On the nightstand, a water bottle and Tylenol await me. I prop myself on an elbow and drink half the water and then take two pills, washing them down with the rest of the water.

Light filters from under the closed door. And the whispers sound more urgent now. I drag myself to a sitting position and drop my feet to the floor. The room spins.

My stomach grumbles and reminds me I didn't eat dinner. I'm still thirsty, and my bladder is uncomfortably full. I stand up with my arms out for balance, giving myself a moment to adjust. I take slow steps to the door and listen. Jake and Lynn are talking, but I can't make out the words. I open the door as quietly as I can and spy through the one-inch gap. They are in the kitchenette. I slide through the door unseen and into the bathroom. But when I lock the door, the voices stop.

I turn on the light and immediately regret it. I cover my eyes and wait, peeking through the gaps between my fingers until I can fully open my eyes. I use the toilet, flush, turn on the faucet, and wash my hands, then my face. Brush my teeth. Reach for a towel. Look in the mirror. Gasp at my reflection. My face is puffy, and my eyes are slits behind swollen lids. My hair is a tangled mess. I run my fingers through it. Reach for a brush and tame it somehow. I look at the rest of me. Faded baby blue cotton T-shirt and shorts. Worn soft from many washes.

Outside, they are silent still. Waiting for me. How long can I stay here before one of them comes after me? Five minutes? Ten? I give myself one last look in the mirror and open the door.

Jake and Lynn wait for me at the end of the short hallway. Lynn's wringing her hands. Jake's leaning on the wall, arms crossed. Regret replaces the worry on his face as soon as his gaze lands on me. The neutral cop face is gone. His every thought is clear to see in those mismatched eyes. Sky and sea.

Lynn opens her mouth, but before she can say anything, Jake steps in front of her, and a second later, I'm in his arms. His whole body wraps around me. He lifts me until I'm on tiptoes. His head cradled in my neck, his rough cheek against mine. The heat of his skin warms mine. His familiar scent fills my lungs and shifts the weight in my chest. It's easier to breathe. My arms go around his shoulders, and I fist a hand into his hair and pull him closer. We stay wrapped in each other's arms. Behind us, the sound of soft footsteps walking away is followed by the clicking of the bedroom door closing. We're alone in the hallway now.

He nuzzles my hair. "I'm sorry. I'm so sorry."

I squeeze him tighter. Then pull away so I can see his face. I palm his cheek. Whiskers prick at my skin. I rub a thumb over his lips, and he closes his eyes at the contact. I kiss him. I kiss him because I can't think of a single word that could express how I feel. I kiss him because I need to feel his lips on mine and know that he's real, and despite every horrible thing happening around us and all the obstacles ahead, we have somehow found our way to each other. And if there's no future for us, I can at least have now. And I'll take everything I can.

CHAPTER 37
AVALON

HE PICKS ME UP AND CARRIES ME TO THE LIVING ROOM. Sets me on the couch in a nest of pillows. He dims the lights and grabs a blanket. He sits next to me, pulls my legs over his lap, then covers me with the blanket. One of his hands is around my calf and the other between mine.

His gaze searches my face. I fight the urge to hide. Every emotion is etched on my face, in the puffiness of my eyes and the redness of my skin. I'm raw and exposed. But his gentle touch and searching eyes are a balm to my soul. He's not hiding from me anymore.

Is this it? Is he finally accepting me wholly and fully? Not trying to compartmentalize the parts of me he can accept and tolerate the parts he can't?

I lace my fingers with his. "Tell me what's happening."

His chest expands with a tired breath. "Nothing else to add. We should have the first preliminary autopsy reports in the morning."

"Have you contacted the family?"

"Not yet. They'll be contacted as soon as I have

243

confirmation." There are dark circles under his eyes. The blue and the green are almost the same color in the soft lights.

"That poor family."

His hand on my calf rubs up and down. I don't know whether he's trying to soothe himself or me. "Not knowing is worse."

"Do you think so?"

"I know so."

And there it is. The conversation we never had. Jake's sister.

The hand on my calf stops. "I'm sorry. I'm sorry for the way I reacted before."

"It's okay, Jake."

"No, it's not okay. I—I have a lot of anger about her disappearance. Anger that has been festering for years. And I took it out on you."

I want to offer to help find her, but I don't know how he'll react. If he even wants my help with this.

"She was just fifteen. She was so excited about starting high school. I drove her to the mall to pick out new clothes." His gaze is on the floor.

I bring his hand to my chest. Hold it there. "You were close."

"Very. Even with the age difference. We were always together. Emily followed me everywhere." He smiles now. "The first word she said was my name."

"What happened?"

"She was meeting friends at the mall. It was raining hard that day. I dropped her off at one of the entrances and drove away to park the car. I went to the food court. I got lunch and waited for two hours for her to meet me there. She never came. I called her phone. It went straight to voicemail." He closes his eyes. "I knew something was wrong then. She always answered my calls or texts."

He lets go of my hand and stands. I sit up. I want to reach for him, but I sense he needs the distance.

"I went looking for her. Kept calling and looking. I ran into her friends and asked about her. They told me she never showed up and didn't answer their phone calls either."

He runs both hands through his hair. "I called nine-one-one. Contacted mall security. They weren't worried. She was fifteen. They said that she was probably meeting a boy and lost track of the time. I knew they were wrong."

He looks at me. There's a sheen of tears in his eyes. "I called my parents. They came to the mall, too. Everyone was looking for her. I stayed there until the mall closed, and they forced me to leave. The police interrogated me like I was a criminal and did something to her. My father blamed me. My mother just cried. She couldn't even look at me."

I cover my mouth with both hands. I thought I had no tears left, but I was wrong. They stream freely down my face. "It's not your fault, Jake. You have to know that. Whatever happened to her, it was not your doing."

"No? I drove her to the mall. I left her alone. Someone took her. She had to be terrified. And I couldn't save her." The anger returns to his voice, and I know it's not directed at me.

"Let me help you."

He shakes his head. "What if . . . what if knowing is worse than not knowing?"

His answer rips a hole in my heart. It's all so clear to me now. He's afraid to know—and afraid of not knowing. He holds on to the anger because it's easier to be angry than to live with guilt. I can't believe his family turned on him. They lost one child and threw the other away. That's the reason

Jake's a cop. That's the reason he does what he does. Catching this guy is more than a job. It's redemption.

I stand and wrap my arms around him. Hold him tight. He doesn't hold me back. His arms at his side, his head tilted back. He tries to blink away the tears. I press my head to his chest. My ear over his heart. I close my eyes and listen to his heartbeat. I breathe slowly and evenly and try to infuse both of us with a calm I'm far from feeling. But I do it anyway. Call for it. Ask the universe for help and healing. For Jake. For the missing women and their families.

His arms come around me, loose and tentative. His lips press to the top of my head, and he releases a breath. His arms tighten around me then. And we stay like this for long minutes. Not talking. Not thinking. But finding strength in each other. I make a silent promise to find his sister. One way or another. I'll give Jake the gift of closure so he can be free of the self-inflicted shackles he wears.

He rubs my back and then my arms. Takes a step back. I tilt my face up and find his gaze. We meet halfway into a kiss so gentle it's a whisper of lips, an exchange of breath, a promise of more to come.

He kisses my forehead and lingers there. Inhales. "Apples. You always smell like apples." He takes a step back and then another. Breaks contact. Cold air rushes between us. I shiver.

"I have to go. I'll call you."

I hug myself and nod. "Okay. Get some sleep and be careful."

He smiles, but it doesn't reach his eyes. "I will. You, too. Don't go anywhere alone. Or at night."

"I won't. I'll drag Lynn with me everywhere. Besides, I owe her some girl time." My attempt at a joke fails and only serves as a reminder of how much time I've spent on this case. "And I'll let you know where I am."

He nods. "Lynn will like that." He takes another step back, finds the door, and opens it. With one last look back, Jake leaves. The soft click of the door closing gives way to silence.

CHAPTER 38
AVALON

I WAIT IN THE APARTMENT LOBBY AT JAKE'S INSISTENCE. This has become our routine for nearly two weeks. We jog every morning and meet for lunch or dinner every few days. But chaste kisses are as far as we have gone during this time. His refusal to deepen our relationship and to let me go back to the station is grating on me.

This early in the morning, there's no one around. I see Jake through the glass doors and step outside to meet him. He's wearing his usual loose shorts, but today he gifts my eyes with a sleeveless shirt. I step into him and go on tiptoes to kiss him. Make sure to put my hands on both of his arms to steady myself. His muscles flex under my touch.

He returns the brief kiss and looks over my head and around us. The parking lot will stay quiet for a few more hours. Not many people like to wake up at five in the morning during summer vacation.

"Good morning. Anything new?" I greet him with the same question I have asked every day since we found Victoria's body in the woods.

He shakes his head, still scanning the parking lot. "Ready?"

"Yes." We walk to the track that flanks the beach. A few solitary fishermen brave the early morning in search of a catch.

Jake and I fall into a steady jog. We don't talk for the first couple of miles. This is when I get past that first resistance and find my rhythm. Past the voice telling me to go back to bed and sleep some more. This voice sounds exactly like Lynn. We run another mile in silence, taking the long loop that will drop us alongside the beach. I'm glad he's jogging with me every morning. A part of me is worried this guy could come after me on one of my runs. There are plenty of spots for someone to hide along the track as it cuts through the reserve.

As the final mile approaches, I slow down, and Jake matches my steps. "You okay?"

"Yes. Can we walk the rest of the way?"

"Sure."

We reduce our speed to a leisurely pace, and when our breathing is no longer labored, I make my plea. "I want to look at the rest of the evidence."

He stops in his tracks. "No. It's too risky. I don't want you anywhere near the station house."

"It's no riskier than jogging with you every day. Whoever's going to see us together already has."

His hands go to his waist. "It's not the same."

"I need to see the rest of the evidence. It's been ten days—"

"I don't want you there."

I turn and put my hands on my hips. "Well, tough. Because I'm going anyway. I'll walk in, and they will wave me right through like they did before, and then I will knock on your door."

He shakes his head. "No, you won't."

"I know you're trying to protect me. You're here but keeping me at arm's length. You think that not allowing us to get closer will keep me safe. But it doesn't work like that. I don't need protection—not from you. I'm already fully invested and don't want to wait or waste any more time. I need you, all of you. And I can't have you until we find this guy."

A muscle ticks in his jaw. "Ava . . ."

"I'm not hiding, Jake. Not when I know I can help. I have to go in and find out where he dumped the other bodies. It's already the middle of July, and I have to go home in another few weeks. We are running out of time." In more ways than one.

He removes his sunglasses, wipes his face with the hem of his shirt, and gives me a fantastic view of his abs and obliques. Too soon, he drops the shirt, and the glasses are back on. "Did you see anything about him dumping another body?"

I turn toward the beach, trying to hide the blush I know is coloring my cheeks. "No. Nothing since that day."

He steps into my line of view. "You can't know for sure you'll see anything."

"No, not for sure, not until I'm back in there and look at the other stuff. But I think I will."

"How can you know?"

"Do you know when you feel someone is watching you?"

He nods.

"It's kind of like that. They are all watching me and waiting for me to make a move. I need to go back. Today."

"They?"

I shrug.

He tilts his head back and looks up at the sky as if it could give him a way to prevent me from going to the police station. "I'm not going to be able to stop you, am I?"

"Nope, not a chance."

"Okay. I'll clear my schedule this morning and get the stuff ready."

"I'll be there at ten. But don't take anything out until I get there. I want to try something different."

I'm at his door at nine-forty-nine. The chief of police tracks my every step, hands on his belt. I nod at him and knock on Jake's door.

Jake opens the door, sees his boss watching me, steps aside to let me in, then closes and locks the door behind me.

"Will you get in trouble with your boss?"

"Probably not." He doesn't sound very sure.

I walk past him and to the cabinets where he keeps the evidence. Run my finger over each drawer, slow and deliberate. There's pressure on my back like multiple invisible hands pushing me forward. I heed their call and stop by the third row. That pressure is now a buzz in my ears and all around me. I face the metal cabinets, my hands hovering a breath away from the gray metal. I feel a tug from below and lower myself to kneel on the floor. The bottom drawer sizzles under my fingertips. "This one. Open it."

Jake pulls a set of keys from the drawer in his desk, unlocks the cabinet, and pulls it open for me. I stop him before he can reach inside, then look at the contents and point to a bag. "This one."

Jake removes the bag and sets it on the floor in front of me. I sit cross-legged and reach for the clear plastic bag. Inside it is a single blood-stained shoe. As soon as I touch it, the images start. Images I've seen before. "A woman is dragged through a forest, dirt and leaves, a dense canopy." The old images fade and new ones start. "A clearing and a path. An old hunting cabin. A well or waterhole. Deer grazing in the distance. A rock wall or slope." The images are confusing and disjointed. "A body being tossed into a dark hole. Water splashing." I open my eyes. "This shoe. This was not on the table the last time I was here."

He looks at me, eyes wide. "No. A hiker found it two days ago. He heard about Victoria and thought it might be a clue. He reported it to the park rangers. They collected it, then dropped it off yesterday. We thought it may have belonged to Victoria, but it's the wrong size. Too small for her. We're waiting on a DNA match for the blood now."

"This shoe belongs to Alice."

His eyes widen. "You sure?"

"Yes, I'm sure. I think it got lost when he moved her body."

"I'm confused. How is that possible? You said objects hold the energy of their owners, what they see and feel. If he moved her body after she died, how can the shoe show you where he took her?"

I shake my head as understanding filters through all the disjointed images. "It's not the shoe. It's her. She's showing me what happened after. I think the shoe is just a way to connect. A tool. Like a CB radio or cell phone. Something to create a link to her."

He squeezes the back of his neck. "Anything else?"

The door to his office opens, and the chief of police strides in. Closes the door behind him, leans on it, and crosses his arms. His size rivals that of a pro basketball player, head shaved, and hands like bear paws. "Anyone care to tell me what's going on here?"

CHAPTER 39
JAKE

I FREEZE. AND ON THE FLOOR, AVA'S EYES GO WIDE. I know I locked the door. The chief also has the code, but not the updated one. Even so, I never imagined he'd just walk in.

"Chief?"

He pushes off the door and comes to stand next to my desk and gets a full view of Ava sitting on the floor—evidence bag in her hands.

He narrows his eyes at her and then looks back at me. His glare like a punch to the jaw. "You can start talking any time now, Knox. I'm dying to hear what you have to say." His Southern drawl gets thicker with his annoyance.

I swallow, look at Ava on the floor and back at my boss. When I open my mouth, nothing comes out. I can't betray her. And I have no idea how to explain what we're doing. He can see a lie a mile away. There's no excuse or lie that could convince him.

He hooks both thumbs in his belt loops and rocks on his heels. The casual stance makes him look even more menacing. One wrong word and my job is gone. "Still waiting."

Ava hands the evidence bag to me. She stands up, wipes her hand on her shorts, and holds it out to the chief. "I don't think we've been formally introduced. I'm Ava."

I want to shrink away and hide like a little kid caught with his hand in the cookie jar, but Ava doesn't flinch.

He takes her hand, shakes it, then lets go. "Chief Malone. I've heard a lot about you and your frequent visits to my detective. And since he seems to have lost his ability to speak at the moment, perhaps you can explain what you're doing here and why you are touching *my* evidence bags."

Ava gives me a quick look, and I want to shake my head to stop her from saying anything, but I'm still frozen under the chief's glare. Only one man who scares me, and he's standing three feet away from me and about to rip me a new one.

But Ava takes it all in stride. She's calmer than I expected, given the circumstances. A flashback to the first day we met and her telling me she dealt with much bigger assholes than me comes to mind. And right now, I believe her.

She shrugs. "Well, Chief, I could tell you, but that would be a breach of confidentiality. Being a man of the law, I'm sure you understand."

"Oh, I understand all about the law and confidentiality. I was a criminal lawyer before I was a cop. And one thing I've learned in all my years, and believe me, Miss Ava, it's been a lot of years, there're only two sides to the law. The right side and the wrong side. There's only one way this can play out in your favor."

Ava crosses her arms and tilts her head up. "Yeah? And what way is that?"

"You can tell me the truth, or I can throw you in a nice

little cell out back. You probably won't mind since you like to visit so often."

She tilts her head to one side and then the other like she's giving it serious thought. "You could do that. Throw me in that jail cell. But we both know you have nothing to hold me over, and my lawyer would get me out in an hour or two. Just a lot of paperwork no one wants to deal with."

The chief smiles, and I swear he's enjoying the verbal sparring with Ava. "You got me there, and God knows I hate paperwork. That's why I quit being a lawyer. Just too much paperwork."

"I hear you're a damn good chief, so it was for the best."

"Yeah, but see, now we are at an impasse. I don't like not knowing what's happening in my house right under my nose. And maybe I can't throw you in jail or scare you into talking. But I sure can hurt your friend here." He nods in my direction, and for the first time, doubt crosses Ava's face. The chief latches on it like a leech, and he'll suck every bit of information out of her.

I try to intervene. "Chief, let her go. I take full responsibility."

"Oh, you will. But first, I want to know what the hell is going on."

Ava sighs and looks at me. In that moment, I know she'll tell him everything. To protect me. She'll sacrifice her secrets for me. "No, Ava, you don't have to do this."

The chief raises a hand. "Hush, boy."

She keeps her gaze on me. "It's okay, Jake. I mean, if I can't trust the chief of police, who can I trust?"

She steps toward me and takes the evidence bag with the shoe from my hands. She wobbles, and I reach for her, but she puts a hand up and closes her eyes. Shit. She's having another vision, and the chief is getting a front-row seat for it.

She opens her eyes and fixes her gaze on me. "I need a map. I know where he dumped Alice's body."

I make eye contact with my boss, and for the first time ever, I see surprise on his face.

He takes half a step back. "Your informant is a fucking psychic? You hired a fucking psychic?"

"No, I didn't hire her. It's not like that."

He pounces on me. "You? Of all people—"

"Shut up, the both of you!" Ava's voice rises. "Get me a damn map right now. A fucking paper map. Not digital crap."

We both look at her, mouths agape for a second. "I don't know if I have a paper map."

The chief walks out the door. "Hold on."

I look at her. "Ava?"

She smiles. "That's okay, Jake. I got this."

The chief returns a minute later, making sure the door is locked. He opens the map of New Hampshire on my desk and Ava approaches it. "Help me position myself in relation to the map. Which way is the shore?"

I look at the map, but before I can say or do anything, the chief turns it a quarter of the way. "The shore is to your right, that way."

Ava hovers a hand over the map starting at the seaside and moves it across. She closes her eyes. "Show me. Where are you?" Her voice is no more than a whisper. Her hand stops, and she points down, her index finger pressed against the map. "Here. She's here. There's a clearing and a path, not a trail. A wide path that leads to a well or a water hole. He dumped her into a hole. There's water, but not deep. You'll need ropes or some kind of climbing equipment or a winch to retrieve her."

The chief looks at the map, grabs a pen, and makes a circle around the spot Ava pointed at, then turns to me. "Look up the area on the computer and see if you can get a more detailed map."

I can't believe he's going along with this. I log into my computer and go to Google Earth.

"I want an aerial view so we can get an idea about the terrain."

The two of them hover over my shoulders as I compare the paper map to the screen and try to figure out the exact location. But there's no way. "No. Too many trees and it's in the middle of the state park."

Chief Malone crosses his arms and stares at the screen. "I'll get a team together to search the area."

"No!" Ava and I say at the same time.

He frowns at us. "And why not?"

I take charge. "This information, how we know it, cannot leave this room."

He scratches the back of his head. "I wasn't planning on calling a press conference to inform the town folk we got a psychic on the payroll."

"No one is paying me. I volunteered to help, with the condition that no one—and I mean no one—knows of my involvement. If you go out there and get a team to search for the body, there will be questions. They'll do the math and it won't take long for them to come for Jake and me for answers."

"Are we at another impasse, Miss Ava?"

"No, Jake and I will go. And once we find the body, he'll call dispatch. I'll be long gone before anyone shows up."

"I don't like this. Not one bit. We can't get a civilian involved in the investigation. It breaks just about every rule in the book."

"Is there a rule against going for a walk in the woods in a state park?"

He rubs at the scruff on his chin. "Miss Ava, something tells me you're trouble."

Ava shrugs. "Heard that before."

"Let us go, Chief. When she finds the body, you'll be the first one I call."

He looks at her. "You're certain you can find the body?"

Ava looks past him toward the door like she can see someone there. "I am. I have a question. Why do you believe me? You didn't question any of this, not once."

"Ah, my family is from St. Louis. My mother is a Hoodoo priestess, as my grandma was, and her mother before her. I have an entire family line going back generations and I've seen things."

If I wasn't already sitting, I would fall on my ass. And what's Hoodoo?

Ava smiles. "I would very much like to meet your mother one day. We could have some very interesting conversations."

He nods. "I'll hold off on the search party. You two can go."

Relief floods me. I can't believe the chief's letting us go this easily. "Thanks for understanding, Chief."

He smiles, and it's all kinds of wrong. "But I'm coming along."

CHAPTER 40
AVALON

WELL, THAT'S UNEXPECTED, AND YET I'M NOT SURPRISED. Chief Malone can be charming and scary as all hell. But I don't scare easily. Never did. On the other hand, Jake doesn't look happy at all with the chief tagging along. "Okay. Let's go then. We should drive separately, though." I look from the chief to Jake. "I can follow you there, and once I locate her, I'll leave it to the two of you."

Jake nods, but his frown tells me he doesn't like my suggestion.

Chief Malone walks to the door and stops with his hand on the handle. "We'll all drive separately. Jake, you can lead. Miss Ava will follow you, and I'll be behind her. Meet you two outside in five."

Then he's gone, and it's just Jake and me, alone.

He puts the evidence bag away and locks the cabinet. "I'm sorry. I never imagined that something like this could happen."

"I think my secret is safe with him. I doubt he'll say anything about it to anyone."

"Still. I hate that he just walked in here."

"Did you know he had the access code?"

He shakes his head. "Yeah, but I change the code every week. I changed it just this morning and hadn't given him the new code yet."

Wow. "Really? Why?"

He shrugs. "Safety? To make sure no one comes in when I'm not here."

That bothers me. "You think someone would do that?"

He runs a hand through his hair, leaving it in disarray. "I don't know, but I don't want to take the chance. There are no security cameras in this hall. Call me paranoid. It's just that I have trust issues."

I hold in a huff. Don't I know it? But I keep that thought to myself. I get closer to him and comb his hair with my fingertips. His gaze locks on my face. "There. Better. It doesn't look like a bird is trying to make a nest on your head anymore."

He leans in, kisses me with a soft brush of lips, and pulls back. Then Jake grazes the back of his hand on my cheek. "Let's go before he comes back and drags us out."

A prickle at the back of my neck follows me all the way down the hall, through the personnel door, and across the reception area. I don't look back. Something tells me I shouldn't make eye contact, and it lingers until we leave the place and are outside.

Chief Malone is already in his SUV. I get to my car and wait until Jake exits the parking lot, then follow behind him with the chief on my tail. Unease builds in my chest, the pressure mounting like a weight slowly growing. I need a distraction.

"Hey, Siri? Call Lynn."

The phone rings twice before she answers. "Hey, there. What's up?"

"Talk to me. Tell me what you're up to."

There's a moment of silence, but she doesn't ask me why I'm calling her with my odd request. "I got my nails done. And I'm getting a pedicure right now. Afterward, I'm going for a massage. Did I tell you that the Kayak instructor is also a masseuse?"

I laugh. "No, you didn't. For real?"

She sighs dreamily. "Ah, yes. And he's also a yoga instructor. Imagine how flexible he must be."

I can picture her waggling her eyebrows. "You kidding me? That's a lot of jobs."

"That's what I said. But apparently, being a kayak instructor is something he only does during the summer. The yoga and massage thing are his year-long jobs."

I smile. "Are you going to take his yoga class?"

"Girl, I'm going to take everything he has to offer. You remember those abs, don't you?"

"How could I forget? You have shown me that picture at least a dozen times."

"You exaggerate."

"I woke up yesterday with you holding your phone and that picture on my face!"

"Sharing is caring."

Thank heavens for Lynn. I'm laughing so hard that there are tears in the corners of my eyes. "Oh, Lynn, what would I do without you?"

"Be bored and turn into a recluse."

"Probably." The laugh dies away, and silence fills the car. I take a deep breath. "Jake's boss caught us—"

"Having sex in his office!"

"No! Oh my God, Lynn, no. Although that might have been better."

"What do you mean?"

"He caught me reading some evidence."

"Oh shit. How bad is it?"

"Not as bad as I thought it would be. He believed me. Or at least I think he did. Maybe he's just testing me. He looks like the kind to give you enough rope so you can hang yourself."

"Why do you say that?"

"I know where Alice's body is, and the three of us are driving there now."

"Wait, are they all listening to me right now?"

"No, silly. I would never do that. I'm driving alone. Following Jake with Chief Malone following me."

"Why are you all driving separate cars?"

"Chief's idea. I'll find the body and get out of there before they call dispatch, like last time."

"Not like last time. I won't be there to get you. I don't have a car."

"It's fine. I can do it."

"I don't like this one bit. You shouldn't be alone."

"It will be okay, trust me. I can feel it and it won't be as bad as Victoria."

"You always say that, but you pay for it later."

She's not wrong. "I'm getting better at it. And I think I've turned a corner with Jake."

"About time! I don't know how much more proof he needs."

Ahead of me, Jake slows down and turns off the highway. I glance in the rearview mirror. The chief is still behind me.

Up ahead, signs to the park tell me we're close. "I have to go. We're almost at the place."

"Okay, make sure to call me when you leave there."

"What about your massage?"

"Call me anyway. If you don't get me, leave a message. Let me know where you are, and I'll call you back."

"Sounds good."

Jake slows down in the parking lot and waves me up to come up next to him. I roll down my window. "Any idea which way from here?"

I look around, getting a feel for the area, and wait for the tug at my chest to direct me. "Yeah, follow me."

I drive to the end of the lot, around orange cones, and past a sign that says, 'Service Road. Park Rangers Access Only.' If anyone comes after me, I have two cops to get me out of trouble. But no one else comes. I guess the chief's big SUV with *Police* written on it gets me a hall pass. I drive slowly for another five minutes, going up a narrow two-lane road that winds up and around until I reach a small clearing, then pull to the side. Beyond, the forest is dense—a living wall of green and brown. I exit my car and lock it. Jake and Chief Malone park on either side of my car.

Jake is the first to reach me. He takes my hand and gives it a squeeze. Let's go when his boss comes around the bumper of his SUV.

"What's next, Miss Ava?"

I take in a deep breath. Situate myself and open my awareness all the way up. The pull is like an invisible hand reaching inside my chest and dragging me into the woods. I grab my phone from my pocket and open Google maps.

Jake peers at my phone. "What are you doing?"

"Dropping a pin for this location. I want to find my car when I come back."

He frowns. "What do you mean?"

"We'll be walking into these woods for a while. My sense of direction sucks and I don't want to get lost on the way back."

Jake scowls. "I'm not letting you walk back to your car alone."

The chief also looks at my phone. "You know where you're going, but not how to get back?"

I don't look at him when I answer. "To go in, I have a guide. Let's go. The faster we find Alice, the faster I can get out of here."

CHAPTER 41
AVALON

I WALK INTO THE FOREST, THE MEN ON EITHER SIDE OF me. Chief Malone is half a step behind us. The temperature is cooler under the dense canopy. All around us, there's life. Birds singing and foraging for food. Insects buzzing, and squirrels flicking their tails as we approach.

The farther we go into the woods, the stronger the pull gets. We walk in silence. The only sounds are those of the forest and our feet crunching leaves and twigs as we make our way. We pass what looks like the ruins of an abandoned log cabin.

"How much longer?" The chief's voice is labored, so I guess he's not a runner like Jake and me.

I check my watch. We've been walking for twenty minutes, and the trail is going up the side of a hill. "Not much longer, I don't think."

The chief wheezes. "How do you know?" His voice is not without suspicion.

I look at the ghostly figure I'm following. "Alice told me."

Chief Malone trips, rights himself, and curses. I catch a smirk on Jake's face. He didn't react when I said Alice told me. Is he getting used to this stuff or hiding it well because of his boss?

Alice stops about twenty-five feet ahead. *"Be careful now. Watch your step."*

I stop, and both men do the same. Jake's hand goes to the small of my back. "You okay?"

"Yes, I'm fine. We should go slower and watch our steps. I'll go first, and you two follow me."

"The hell you say. I'll go first." Jake steps in front of me.

I grab his arm. "Stop. This is the exact opposite of what I said. I have to go first. Unless you've suddenly developed some psychic abilities you didn't tell me about. Have you?"

Jake presses his lips together for a few seconds and then steps to the side. The chief chuckles under his breath. I walk to where I last saw Alice and stop. Both men are on my heels. An overwhelming sense of dread overtakes me. I lock my knees to keep from falling and breathe slowly and evenly. There's absolute quiet now, and a wrongness hangs thick in the air. Alice is gone. I no longer see or feel her presence. The body must be near.

I put a hand up. "Stay."

I take two steps forward and stop, walk in a small circle, and then close my eyes. A flash of an image comes, but it's too fast for me to grasp. I crouch down and put both my hands on the ground. "Show me."

A faint tug comes from my left. I look over my shoulder, and through the dense foliage, I see it. A crop of rocks covered in vivid green moss. I stand up. Look at Jake and Chief Malone. Then I point at the spot. "There. She's over there. Be careful. Go slow. Don't fall in. There's a hole there somewhere."

Both Chief Malone and Jake hold their guns pointing at the ground. The two of them take measured steps toward where I pointed. I don't move. The ground in this area is damp, with water trickling down the rocky formation. Ferns and arrowwood grow all around the area, so dense in some spots the ground is not visible beneath them.

"Chief?" Jake puts a hand up. "Watch my back." He holsters his gun, walks to a tree, breaks off a long, skinny branch, and uses it to move the foliage around.

Alice comes back. She's flicking in and out just a few feet ahead of Jake. She points at what looks like a rock ledge. And disappears again.

"Jake."

He stops and turns around to look at me.

"There, see those rocks piled on top of each other?"

He looks at the spot I'm pointing. Nods once. The chief circles closer, his gaze darting everywhere. I could tell him it's just the three of us here, but I know he'd still be on alert.

Jake uses the branch to move the ferns growing all around the rocks. "There's a hole."

He grabs his phone, turns on the flashlight, and shines it down. "I see something. Wait." He takes a step closer, moves the ferns out of the way with his foot, and squats to get closer to the opening on the ground. For a minute, he shines his phone flashlight in the cavity again. Then, he drops his head, stands up, and turns off the light. Putting his phone in his pocket, Jake walks to my side. "There's someone down there. Maybe ten feet down."

The chief looks from me to Jake and back then goes to the

edge of the hole. He grabs a small flashlight from his pocket and looks into the opening. "Holy shit." He puts the flashlight back in his pocket, takes several steps away from us, stops, and when he turns, he's pointing his gun at us.

CHAPTER 42
JAKE

WHAT THE FUCK. NEXT TO ME, AVA FREEZES AS WE STARE at the barrel of a Glock 22. "Chief? What are you doing?"

He doesn't waver. "Funny thing. I was about to ask you two the same question."

I raise my hands slowly and take half a step to the side, putting myself between the gun and Ava. "You know what's going on. You saw it in my office, and we told you what Ava can do."

The chief wags his head to the side. "Miss Ava, why don't you take a step to your left, so I can see you both and keep those hands up while you do it."

"No." I shift again. "Ava, stay behind me. Chief, put the gun down."

He pulls his cell phone out.

My heart booms in my ears. "What are you doing?"

"First, I'm calling for backup. Then I'll sort this mess out about how you two knew where the body was."

"We fucking told you how. You saw yourself and you said you believed her."

"Bullshit! All I saw was my detective and some out-of-towner walk straight to a hole in the middle of nowhere and find a body. A body that's so well hidden it could have gone forever in that hole and never been found. That's what I saw. Try proving otherwise."

"She wasn't even in the country when Alice went missing."

"But you were."

My blood runs cold. He thinks I did this. Him, of all people? He who fucking failed to find Emily's kidnapper and knows how much I struggle with it. He knows the only reason I became a cop was to solve the case myself. I've resented him for years for not finding her. And he knows it. And now he's turning on me. "You know I had nothing to do with the disappearances. You know my reasons for becoming a cop, for staying in this town when my entire family left. How can you think that of me?"

He shrugs. "Your family didn't go far. They're in the next town over. I could never understand how she disappeared like that without a trace. You were the last one to see your sister alive. For all I know, you did it."

Something breaks loose inside me, and I advance on him, one deliberate step at a time. I fist my hands in anticipation of smashing his face in. I don't fucking care that he's my boss. I don't fucking care he's got five inches and some seventy pounds on me. I don't fucking care I'll lose my job and spend time in jail for assault. All I care about is shoving his words back down his throat.

"Stop or I'll shoot. I'm not kidding, Knox."

"Jake! Stop. Stop." Ava runs in front of me and slams her hands on my chest. "Stop. He's baiting you. Can't you see it?"

I'm blinded by fury, and pain, and loss. I push against the

hands on my chest, and Ava wraps her arms around me and locks me into an embrace. Her heart beats wildly against my chest. Apples. It's the smell of apples from her shampoo that finally reaches me. I close my eyes and try to focus on what she's saying. I hear the words, but they don't register. She's saying the same words again and again. The cadence and the sounds are the same. I drag in a breath. My chest is tight, and my head is pounding.

"Stop. Stop. Jake, stop."

I stop and hold Ava to my chest, inhale deeply, and find a measure of comfort in her scent. Jesus, I could have gotten us both killed.

I force myself to hold still, breathe, and relax. When I look up, Chief Malone is about ten feet away, gun still trained on us. I put my hands on Ava's shoulders and detach her from me. Her eyes are wide. I try to move her behind me again, but she resists. She turns in my arms and faces my boss.

Ava takes a small step away from me, but I keep my hands on her shoulders. She takes a deep breath. "Chief, I understand why you'd think Jake and I are involved in this murder. It took me weeks to convince Jake of what I can do. And believe me, spending my vacation time tracking a serial killer is the last thing I want to do. But I cannot just go about my life as normal when I know this man will kill again if Jake doesn't stop him."

She has a point. Had I been in the chief's place, I would have reacted as he did. "Chief, she's telling the truth. She's my informant. Not because she knows anything about the crimes, but because she can see what happened when she touches the objects in the evidence locker."

Ava holds her hands out to him. "Let me prove it to you. I can do it right now."

The chief narrows his eyes at her. "How?"

"Give me something to read. The wedding ring on your hand would work."

He's silent for a long time. Then digs into the collar of his shirt and comes up with dog tags on a chain. Pulling it over his head, he tosses it to Ava.

She catches it in the air and immediately closes her eyes. The tags pressed against her palm, the chain dangling.

"Duane. This belonged to Duane. Your twin brother."

Chief Malone's mouth goes slack.

Ava tilts her head. "You have worn this since the day they gave his belongings to your family. You two were extremely close. I see you through his eyes. He was so proud of you and how much you accomplished by going to college and becoming a lawyer. He always believed in you. That's why he went into the military. There wasn't enough money to pay for two tuitions, so he told everyone he didn't want to go to college."

It's humbling to see a man as big and proud as my boss cry. He wipes his face, but the hand holding the gun is steady.

Ava smiles now. "You two had a secret language you created when you were kids. No one else knew this. You two never shared it with anyone else, and you continued to use it into adulthood when no one else was around. I can hear it but don't know what it means."

"What else?" Chief Malone's voice is a whisper.

"It was supposed to be his last tour. He was weeks away from retiring. An IED killed him. He . . . didn't die right away. He bled out. But he wasn't in pain. He was conscious, and he wasn't scared. He said something. But the medic who came to his rescue couldn't understand him."

The chief takes a step closer, and the arm holding the gun

drops to his side. "What did he say? Do you know what he said?"

Ava opens her eyes, her soft gaze on him. "I can repeat the sounds, but I don't know what they mean."

"What was it?" There's urgency in his voice.

Ava takes a deep breath and closes her eyes again. *"Si laith ven dantothe. Miy ayr vi ven. Si vick."*

He gasps, and the gun drops to the ground. I hold still and fight every instinct to race and grab it. Ava opens her eyes, takes a step closer to the chief, and opens her hand. A faint imprint of the tags is on her palm. "He loved you more than anything in the world. I hope you know that."

The chief swallows, then nods. In two minutes, he went from arrogant and confident to a shell of himself. He takes the chain, puts over his head, and tucks it under his collar again.

Ava hugs herself. "Did the words I said make any sense to you?"

He nods again. "They did."

"Can I . . . can I ask what they mean?"

The Adam's apple in his throat bobs. "I love you, brother. So proud of you. I win." His voice cracks on the last word.

"I win?" Ava repeats.

He looks around, but it's like he's not really seeing anything. His gaze is distracted, as if in a world of his own. "We had this silly game since we were kids. Whoever said the last word won."

"Oh . . ." Ava says, her response nearly soundless.

The chief blinks, and his eyes find her face, focusing. Wherever he was, he's coming back now, returning to himself, the chief of police mask sliding in place.

He lost a brother, and I lost a sister. He should know better. He should understand where I'm coming from. The fire that fueled my anger is flickering awake again. I tamp it down. He forgot all about his gun. I walk to the spot where he dropped it, pick up the Glock, and make sure the safety is on. I give it back to him, handle first.

He holsters it. Wipes sweat from his forehead and runs a hand over his shaved head, then turns in a circle as if trying to situate himself. "How the fuck am I going to explain any of this?"

Ava takes a step closer to him. "I can't be involved. My name can't be on any reports. That was my only condition to helping Jake, and it still stands. I will help in any way I can, but it can't be tracked back to me."

"With that, I agree. I don't want to explain any of it to the DA."

Ava's shoulders drop, and she releases a breath. "Thank you."

He looks at me. "And that's how you found the other one."

It wasn't a question, but I answer anyway. "Yeah, now you know why I've kept tight-lipped about everything."

He reaches for his phone. "We have to get the boys in here and search the area."

"Wait. I'll walk Ava to her car first. Let me get her out of here, then you can call dispatch."

She shows me her phone and points at a spot on a map. Her car pin.

"If you think I'm letting you walk alone in these woods, you're crazy."

"I'll stay here," the chief says. "And Miss Ava?"

"Yes?"

He nods once, hands on his waist. "Thank you."

She smiles, and I think he has a crush on her now.

How is he finding them?
I left no clues. Nothing to follow.
I don't like this game anymore.
Time to clear the entire board.

CHAPTER 43
AVALON

I GAZE AT THE OCEAN, THE DEEP GREEN WAVES ROLLING onto the beach and erasing footprints. Everything is temporary. The waves of time erase all things.

The sea breeze ruffles my hair, and I push it off my face. "Do you have a hair tie?"

Lynn digs into her huge beach tote. "Found it."

I adjust the beach chair to an upright position and move it under the shade of the umbrella. Then, put my hair in a ponytail. "Thanks."

I go back to the book on my lap, but after reading a page and not remembering a single word, I set it on my towel. Digging my feet into the sand, I stretch my back and shoulders.

Next to me, Lynn adjusts her beach chair to match mine. "Want to talk about it?"

I look around the beach and the open space around us. Closer to the water, two kids make sandcastles under the watchful eyes of their mother. People are scattered around, but the beach is surprisingly empty, even for a mid-week summer day.

I sigh. I've been putting this off for four days now, and I've had enough time to process everything. "Yeah. I do." I'll feel better after I share the rest of the story with her. "So, where do I start?"

"You already told me about Jake's boss walking in on the two of you and the three of you going into the park."

I rub sand off my bare legs and adjust my bikini top. "Walking into the woods and finding her was easy. I may as well have had a GPS to follow. What happened after, well, that I never saw coming."

Lynn shifts to face me, her eyes wide in expectation. I tell her the rest of the story, every detail.

"The chief—" Lynn stops, looks over her shoulder, and leans closer. "He pointed a gun at you?" There's rage in her hushed voice.

"He sure did."

"What the fuck. Who is this asshole? What's his name? I want to talk to him."

I laugh, picturing her doing just that, like a Chihuahua going after a Great Dane. "Dude, he's twice our age and three times our size. At least. The man makes Jake look small standing next to him."

She frowns. "I don't care. I have words for that man. Jesus. Were you scared?"

"Yes and no. I mean, the first time you see someone point a gun at you is kind of shocking. I didn't have a chance to react. Jake stepped in front of me."

"Aww, he would take a bullet for you."

Of that, I have no doubt. I tell Lynn the rest, and it somewhat appeases her.

"And that's why Jake hasn't come by in days?"

"Yeah, I think the whole thing about the chief freaked him out. Plus, he wants me away from the station while the dust settles. But at least his boss is taking over all the press stuff, which Jake hates doing."

"When are you going to see him again?"

"Now." The masculine voice has us both jumping.

"Motherfu—" Lynn is the first to recover. "How long have you been there spying on us?"

"I just got here. All I heard was you asking Ava when she was going to see him again. I'm hoping the *him* you're talking about is me."

I stand up and walk around the chair. Jake's sunglasses hide his eyes, but his gaze touches every inch of my exposed skin in the tiny red bikini Lynn made me buy for this vacation.

He kisses me, lingering a little longer than a hello kiss warrants, and then leans closer to nuzzle my ear. "Are you trying to kill me?"

I can't stop the grin that takes over my face. "Hi."

"Hi."

Lynn stands. "You can take my chair. I'm going to take a dip in the water."

"Thanks, but you don't have to go. I don't have a lot of time."

She gestures at his jeans and T-shirt. "You're overdressed." Then frowns. "How did you find us?"

Jake laughs. "I was driving by and someone flagged me down and told me you were at the beach. Pointed straight at the two of you."

Lynn shakes her head. "Damn nosy people." Then she walks toward the ocean and calls out, "I'll be in the water. Carry on without me now."

Jake scans the beach. "We're getting some attention."

I follow his gaze. "They're not even bothering to disguise their curiosity."

He reaches for my ponytail and wraps it around his fingers. "Chief Malone gave me a few days off. Ordered me out of his station, and I'm not allowed back until next week. I was wondering if you'd like to spend some time with me."

I smile, gaze down, and then back up. "What do you have in mind?"

"Maybe meet for lunch tomorrow. There's this nice place out of town I think you'd like."

My heart is doing Olympic-level somersaults in my chest. "I would love to."

He lets go of my hair and traces the contour of my jaw. "Then spend some time at my house . . . maybe stay for the weekend?"

And I just landed gold. "Should I pack a bag?"

"I have an extra toothbrush and some T-shirts you can borrow."

I'm overheating, and it has nothing to do with the sun. The idea of spending a weekend with him, staying in his house, and wearing his clothes is such a turn-on. It's like something a boyfriend would do. I hate to put a label on what we have. Our relationship is complicated. But this feels like a step in the right direction. "Okay." My voice is breathy.

"I have to go, but I'll call you tonight."

I nod expecting Jake to leave without a goodbye kiss because we've garnered even more curious eyes now. But he surprises me by sliding an arm around my waist, pulling my body flush with his, and kissing me like no one's around. His free hand holds the back of my head. The kiss turns intimate and needy. He hardens against my belly, and it takes everything I have not to rub on him like I did in his office. Gosh, how long ago was that? Two weeks? No, more. I want to lock myself in a room with him and make up for all the lost time.

He breaks the kiss and pulls away from me. Every part of my body tingles. I want his hands and lips back on me. But it will have to wait until tomorrow.

CHAPTER 44
AVALON

I GLANCE AT THE GPS MAP ON THE DASHBOARD SCREEN. The restaurant is just ahead.

Lynn's voice comes through the car speaker. "I still think you should have let him pick you up."

"He wanted to, but I want to have my own way in and out. If anything happens and he gets called on an emergency or a case, I don't want to get stuck or have him waste time driving me back. This way is better."

"I guess. You almost there?"

"I'm here, pulling into the parking lot. Found a spot and backing in now. Oh, I see his SUV."

"Good. But I'll stay on the phone with you until Jake's by your side."

"Thanks for riding along with me, even if by phone." We are keeping to our promise to never go out alone. Technically, she's not here with me, but being on the phone for the entire thirty-minute ride makes us both feel safe—me in my car until I meet Jake and her locked in the apartment.

"No way am I leaving you alone with this crazy guy out

there. And yes, the door is locked. I've checked it five times already. The crazy guy would have to be Spiderman and climb the walls to get in here."

"If the crazy guy was Tom Holland, you'd open the door for him yourself."

She laughs. "It's a possibility."

"I'm sorry for abandoning you yet again."

"Pfff. I'm fine. And I'm happy for you. You deserve to be happy."

"Thank you. It will be nice to have a date that doesn't involve meeting Jake at five a.m. to go jogging or meeting him at the police station."

"I want all the details."

"I know you do. Wish I could find the last person, so it could be over, but I don't know when I'll have a chance to go back and look at the rest of the evidence."

"It's only been five days since you found the body. It should settle down soon. Bet you can go back in by next week."

"I hope so. I think this whole thing is getting to Jake. He's divided between wanting to keep me away and wanting me to find out more."

"Well, enjoy the lull and his weekend off before the ghosts come back with more demands."

"I'll sure try. Jake's coming now. Call me if anything happens."

I disconnect the call and turn off the engine and step out of my car. Jake moves his sunglasses to the top of his head and pulls me into a hug before I can say hello. He wraps himself around me and presses me to the side of the car. I return his embrace, the feel of his body against me like coming home.

He pulls back just enough to look at me, then his mouth

is on mine. I melt into him. My body molds to his as I bend to his will. There's a touch of desperation to his kiss—fear blended with want. I miss our morning jogs together but even then we had little chance to be like this. Open with each other because Jake still wants us to keep a low profile while in public. Not that I think it's working that well, especially after yesterday at the beach. I know he's afraid that with finding a second body, the killer will pay closer attention to him. And he doesn't want that attention coming my way. Or Lynn's.

He pulls back and rests his forehead on mine. Our breaths mingle. "I've missed you. Missed kissing you."

His confession surprises me, but I know what he means. The longing for something more, something we can't have. "I'm here now. We have an entire weekend, so let's make the most of it."

He kisses me one more time, steps back, and covers his eyes with his sunglasses. I grab my purse from the car and lock it. He takes my hand, and we walk into the restaurant.

We're taken to a table in a corner behind a booth. Potted plants atop the booth walls add another layer of privacy. We sit across from each other, Jake's back to the sitting area. People have started to recognize him since the press interview on TV. The waiter takes our drink orders, a mango lemonade for me and a beer for Jake. We talk about anything and everything, except the cases.

The hostess brings an older couple to the table across from us. The lady sits, but the man remains standing. "Can we have a booth?"

Jake stiffens when he hears the voice.

I make eye contact with the lady, and her gaze goes to Jake's back. Her eyes widen. "Jake? Is that you?"

His hands fist and then relax. He turns slowly, and the

woman's face breaks into a smile filled with love. The man standing next to her scowls. His face shows only discontent.

Jake stands and walks to the lady, bends down, and kisses her cheek. "Hi, Mom."

Mom? These are his parents? I look at the man and recognize the sneer from my visions from when Jake gave me the rock. He's a hateful sort and reminds me of a rattlesnake.

His icy gaze lands on Jake. "Don't you have a murder to solve?"

I watch a transformation, like invisible armor, slide over Jake. He goes from an open and caring man into something else—someone else. The hostess smiles, unaware of the power dynamics at play. "Do you want to sit together?"

His mother's eyes light up at the prospect. His father's sneer grows. Jake ignores him and smiles at his mom. "Sure. We haven't ordered yet, and the table is big enough."

He pulls a chair for his mother, and she sits next to me and across from his father. Jake takes his spot across from me again. His pinky finger touches the sunglasses he removed when we were seated alone. I feel his need to put them back on to protect himself from his father.

I recognize some of his mother in him. Same hair color and eye shape. But he looks nothing like his father, yet there's something familiar about the older man. I try to figure out what without staring at him. An awkward silence falls, but we are saved by the waiter returning with our drinks. Jake's father takes Jake's beer and drains half of the glass in one gulp, and that's when it hits me. He's the drunk man from that night Jake cooked for me. He's the reason Jake had to leave.

"Ava?" Jake taps my hand across the table. "Your order?"

"What?"

The waiter stands there, notepad in hand. "Sorry, I zoned out. I'll have the vegetarian platter, thank you."

The waiter takes the rest of the orders and leaves. Jake turns to his mother. "Mom, this is my friend Ava. Ava, this is my mother, Caroline." There's genuine affection in his voice. "And my father, Bill." The sentiment doesn't extend to his father.

Caroline smiles, and I immediately like her. She's warm and sweet.

"It's so nice to meet one of Jake's friends. He works too much. I always tell him life is short, he should have more fun, but with him, it's work, work, work."

The father grunts. "Stop coddling him. He's not a boy anymore."

The light goes out of his mother's eyes, and her face reddens. I want to punch his jerk of a father. But instead, I ignore him and smile at his mother. "I agree. He works nonstop. Today is his first day off in weeks and it's nice to get him out of his office."

Bill slaps the table. "Don't worry, honey, the cops will survive a day without him."

Jake looks at his father. "Her name is Ava. Not honey."

His father almost recoils when his gaze meets Jake's. Does he really believe there's something evil about his eyes? His father gets up, and without another word, walks toward the restrooms.

The mood instantly lightens. Jake takes his mom's hands in both of his. "How are you, Mom?"

Her eyes mist, and she presses her lips together. "I'm well. Really. He's not so bad. More bark than bite."

"Come live with me, Mom. You have options. I can take care of you."

She glances at me and back at Jake. "You know I can't do that. He'd be all alone."

"He doesn't deserve you."

"I have to stay. It's okay."

I cast down my gaze to give them a semblance of privacy.

"You don't have to do anything you don't want to. I wish you understood that."

"I do. I do. But there's more to our relationship than you know. All you see is how angry he is, but he's not always like that."

"Mom—"

His father is back. "Look how cozy you all are. What did I miss?" He drags his chair back, wood scraping on tile, the screech like claws ripping through my eardrums.

His mother pulls her hands away and fists them in her lap. She toys with a ring on her right hand, turning it over and over, nearly removing it, and then twirling it back in place. She does this again and again.

No one answers him. Caroline lifts her gaze to her husband. "Oh, you didn't miss anything, dear. Jake was just telling me I should stop by and visit him sometime."

"I bet he did." Bill spits the words with such violence that Caroline flinches. And the loose ring on her hand rolls down her lap and onto the floor. She blanches but has no other reaction.

I nudge my fork to the floor. "Oops. Klutzy me." I kneel on the floor, lift the tablecloth, and find the ring. The moment my fingers touch it, the visions start.

Caroline as a young woman. She's beautiful, happy, and deeply in love. A young man gives her a promise ring. Her mother disapproves. Wants Caroline to marry Bill. Her family sets her up on dates with Bill. She continues to meet the other boy in secret. They plan to run away. Bill feels jealous. He proposes to Caroline. She wants to refuse, but her beloved disappeared. She's pregnant. She accepts the marriage proposal and quickly marries Bill.

She has a baby. Jake. A baby with two different-colored eyes, just like the boy who disappeared.

The vision releases me, and I wobble a little. Blink away the tears threatening to fill my eyes.

Bill knows and resents that Jake is not his son. And Caroline's guilt won't let her leave her husband. Little by little, Jake's story unfolds in my mind. The few things he's told me fill the gaps left by the vision. Jake doesn't know the truth about the circumstances of his birth. But he should. It explains so much. He needs to know, but it's not my place to tell him.

I pick up the fork and set it on the table. "Found it."

Caroline glances at me. I smile at her, and when Bill is distracted, I give her the ring under the table. Her hand grasps mine for a second and then lets go. The ring goes back onto her finger, she fists her hands in her lap, and then stretches them. Glancing at me, Caroline gives me a slight nod. Then she stands up. "I need to visit the ladies'."

I stand up as well. "Me, too. I need to wash my hands after touching the floor."

I follow her into the restroom—thankfully empty, but for the two of us—she walks to the sinks and braces herself on the counter, head down, a slight tremor to her shoulders. I don't know this woman, but I feel a connection to her. Without asking permission, I put an arm around her shoulders and pull her into a hug. She sobs and hugs me back. After a minute, she steps away, puts space between us, and wipes under her eyes. "I'm so sorry. I'm usually not this emotional."

"That's okay. Everyone is allowed an emotional day here and there."

She chuckles. "Thank you. Thank you for finding the ring. It's important to me."

"I know."

She frowns. "You know?"

I don't know why I'm confiding in this woman, but I do. "I know about the ring and the boy who gave it to you. I know you loved him—love him still. I know Jake is not Bill's son. And I know Jake has no idea, but he should know. He deserves to know."

Her mouth opens and closes, her eyes wide. "H-how?"

I shrug. "I just know things. And you can trust me. I won't say anything to anyone. But Jake needs to know. His whole life, he's felt unloved by your husband, the man he thinks is his father. Jake blames himself for it. And he blames himself for Emily. He's been carrying this burden for far too long."

"I-I can't."

"You can. And you will. For Jake's sake, you need to. Bill doesn't deserve your protection."

She's shaking, and the tears are streaming down her face now. "I hoped he would never find out. But then Jake was born with the same eyes as my Ethan."

"Jake and his father—his real father—deserve to know the truth. Maybe even have a chance at a father-son relationship. It's not too late."

She looks at the promise ring on her finger and nods. "Okay. I will. I'll go see Jake when Bill is away. He likes to go hunting and is gone a week at a time. I'll go to Jake then. I promise."

CHAPTER 45
JAKE

So much for a day off and spending time alone with Ava. I didn't mind seeing my mother. It's him I can't stand seeing. His every word is an attack, and every look is condescending. My mother should have divorced him years ago. She could have met someone else and been happy. I don't understand why she stays with him.

Lunch was awkward and would have been a disaster if not for Ava telling stories about her travels and her job. They are gone now, but the heaviness from my father's presence still lingers. Now that it's past lunchtime, the restaurant is almost empty, and our table is cleared. I move to sit next to Ava and take her hand. "I'm sorry you had to witness . . . I don't even know what to call it. The disaster that's my family."

She squeezes my hand. "It's not a disaster. Everyone's family has people who are less than pleasant. I like your mother. She's a sweet lady."

I nod. "She is and she liked you, too. She whispered in my ear that I should keep you."

Ava's face turns pink, and she smiles. "She did?"

"Sure did. And Mom has never said that about anyone before."

The waiter paces behind us. "I think that's our cue to leave."

"We should go then."

My gaze lingers on her. What I want and what I should do are two vastly different things. We stand up at the same time, and I walk Ava to her car.

She nibbles on her lower lip. "I'm following you back to your house, right?"

I tuck a lock of hair behind her ear. "I want to spend the weekend with you. Are you sure you want to stay with me?"

Ava lowers her gaze and then meets my eyes. "Yes, I think you still owe me a dance."

Her cheeks go red when she says that. "I liked dancing with you very much. I would like to dance a lot more."

"What's keeping us from dancing then?"

I can add the word dance to the list of things that will give me automatic hard-ons from now on. "My job and the mess that comes with it. I never imagined it would get this complicated and I don't want to expose you to that. To a serial killer."

She lifts a shoulder. "It is what it is."

"Whoever this guy is, he's watching."

"Everyone has already seen us together, Jake. We've been seen at the police station a dozen times, at least. And how many times did you come to my apartment? Jogging, the boardwalk, the beach. People have seen us. I have to go back home soon, and I don't want to waste any more time away from you."

"It's risky—"

"Maybe it is and maybe it's not. But I'm safe when I'm with you."

"Are you sure?"

"Yes, I've waited fifteen years for this. For you, and I don't want to wait another day."

I kiss her then. I kiss her because I have to. But I rein myself in and stay on the right side of indecent exposure. She molds her body to mine and grasps at the hair on the back of my head. It takes everything in me not to break a bunch of laws right now.

I pull back, and she whimpers. "Okay. Let's go to my house. But I'll follow you." I want to keep her in my sights the whole time.

She sighs. "I really regret driving separate cars right now."

The drizzle that started ten minutes into the drive turned into a storm. The rain comes down so hard I can barely see Ava's car ahead of me. My phone rings, and I tap the screen on the dashboard to accept the call. "Hey."

"Hi, just making sure you're still behind me. I can't see anything with this rain."

"I am. We're almost there. Take the next right and the first left after that. Stay on the phone until we get there."

"Okay."

We're both silent as the rain hits the windshield with such a fury that the wipers can't keep up. She slows as she turns into my driveway. I follow, parking next to her. I try to look at her through the passenger window, but it's like looking through a waterfall. The sound of her laugh comes through the speaker. "Well, this will be fun. Ready to race to the door?"

"I am if you are." The chilly rain might cool me off and ram some sense into me.

"All right. Let's hang up. You count to ten slowly and then go."

I hang up, turn off the engine, and start counting. I make it to four when Ava opens her car door and fights the wind to close it again. She dashes past the front of my SUV before I have a chance to get out. I run after her, and by the time we get under the cover of the porch, we're both soaked.

She's laughing and holding her belly. "Oh my God. I'd be less wet if I jumped into a pool."

"You cheated. You didn't count to ten."

She wipes wet hair off her face. "I didn't cheat. I never said I'd count to ten. I said you should."

The little cheater. She's soaked, her blue blouse clings to her skin, the jeans miniskirt is glued to her ass, her hair is a mess, and she smiles at me like she's never been happier than at this very moment. "You're beautiful."

Her eyes widen, and her laugh dies. She lowers her gaze, and her cheeks go pink. "I don't know about that. I'm sure I look like a drowned rat."

"The most beautiful drowned rat I've ever seen." I kiss her. Her lips part for me, an invitation to go in. And I do. She shivers, and I remember that we're still very wet and still outside.

I pull away. "Let's go inside and get dry."

CHAPTER 46
AVALON

WITHOUT HIS TOUCH, I'M COLD. MY SKIN PEBBLES. A chill runs down my spine. He opens the door and ushers me in. We stop just inside the door, and a puddle grows at our feet. Kojak comes from around the corner and with a disdainful look and sniff, turns his back on us and walks away, tail held high.

Jake toes off his sneakers. "I'll grab some towels."

I take my sandals off, and the cold hardwood floor under my feet adds to my discomfort. Jake comes back with a fluffy towel and a change of clothes. "Go in there." He points to the powder room. "Take everything off and dry yourself. Here's a T-shirt and sweatpants. Bring the wet stuff out and I'll put them in the drier."

I fight with my wet clothes—they stick to me like glue. I quickly dry myself and get dressed. Jake's clothes swallow me. I bury my face in his T-shirt and inhale. Fresh clean laundry and *him*. The long-sleeved T-shirt goes well past my thighs, and I have to roll the waist in the pants several times. Tucking my wet clothes and underwear into the now damp towel, I wonder if I should have kept my panties on, but they are just as wet as the rest of my clothes. Combing my hair with my fingertips, the curls fall in soft waves around my face. The reflection in the mirror shows bright eyes and flushed skin. My stomach flutters with anticipation. I take a deep breath to still myself and open the door.

Not far away, Jake waits. His clothes match mine—a long-sleeved, black Henley and gray sweatpants. He's barefoot, too. "Better?"

"Yes, thanks. Your clothes fit me perfectly. I might have to borrow them more often."

His gaze travels from the top of my head to my red-painted toes. He looks like he wants to eat me. "You can borrow them any time you want."

"I'll hold you to that."

He points at the bundle in my hands.

"Ah, yes. Where's your drier?"

He tilts his head toward the laundry room, and I follow him.

"Just put everything in the washer, and I'll start a load."

His clothes are already in the washer, so I add mine and close the door. Washing our clothes together is strangely intimate. Jake takes my hand and leads me to the living room. We sit on the couch and watch the rain through the bay window. It's the middle of the afternoon, but it looks like evening. "I should call Lynn and let her know I'm here and check on her, too. But I left my purse and phone in my car."

"You can use mine. Let her know you won't have your phone for a while. She can call mine if she needs you."

I take his phone. "Thanks."

"I'm going to make us a hot drink. What do you want? Coffee, tea, or hot chocolate?"

"Tea would be perfect, thanks."

He disappears into the kitchen, and I call Lynn.

"What's wrong?" Her voice is urgent.

"Nothing's wrong. It's me. I left my phone in my car, and with this rain, I don't want to go back and get wet again."

"Jesus. You gave me a heart attack."

"Sorry? I just wanted to check with you and let you know I'm okay. I'm at Jake's house. Everything good on your end?"

"All is well. I'm watching TV. The door is locked. I'm staying inside." She yawns.

"Good, I'll get my phone when it stops raining. In the meantime, call me here if you need anything."

"And interrupt the love fest? Never! You call me. I'm not going anywhere. Have fun and do all the things I would do." She laughs and hangs up before I can say anything else.

Jake comes back with two steaming mugs as I set the phone on the coffee table. "Thanks, all is well with Lynn. She's all tucked in and said she's not going out."

He gives me a mug, and I laugh when I read the quote on it.

Feel safe at night. Sleep with a cop.

"Is this some kind of subliminal message?"

He smiles. "Would you believe me if I said I didn't even notice?"

I take a sip of the tea, and the heat warms me up. "Maybe. Where did you even get it?"

"It was a gag gift. We had one of those secret Santa things a couple of years ago, and that's what I got. You're the first person besides me to drink from it."

His response reveals a lot. Not many people visit his home. He has said as much before. "I'm honored to be the first." I salute him with the mug.

Jake takes the spot next to me, his thigh pressed against mine. I lean into him, and he puts an arm around my shoulders, then tugs me into him. We sit quietly for a while, drinking our tea and basking in each other's touch. I finish my tea first and set the cup on the table in front of us. Jake does the same.

I tilt my face toward his, turning into his arms with a silent invitation. Jake's gaze fleets all over my face and lingers on my mouth before meeting my eyes again. "Are you sure?"

My response is to straddle him and arrange my legs around his thighs until I'm perfectly positioned over his crotch. He inhales, his hands going to my hips. He adjusts me over him and lifts his hips. That bit of friction is a tease, and I want more. So much more. I take charge and kiss him. Nibble on his lips, then invade his mouth with my tongue. Jake lets me lead for a while, his hands firmly on my hips. I press down into his hardness and move.

His hands leave my hips, graze my sides then my shoulders, and then gently fist my hair. He tilts me and deepens the kiss, hungry, demanding, desperate.

I run my hands down his chest and slide them under the hem of his shirt. His stomach muscles contract at the first touch of my fingertips on his skin. I move my splayed hands up his chest, touching as much as I can, learning him. I grab the hem of his shirt and drag it up. He breaks the kiss just long enough to help me pull the shirt off.

His hands mimic mine and do the same, slip under the shirt he gave me, and in one move remove it. We're both bare from the waist up now. His gaze takes me in and lingers on my breasts. He doesn't touch them as I expected—not yet. Instead, he pulls me to him, our chests flush, and kisses me again. My bare skin on his bare skin is almost more than I can take. My nipples are so hard, they hurt. The brush of the hairs on his chest adds another layer of sensation.

He pulls away from me, our breath rapid and erratic. "You're still sure?"

"Yes." I don't hesitate. "I have never been surer of anything in my life."

He turns and moves to lay me down on the couch and comes on top of me. "Hmm, déjà vu."

I laugh. Yes, three weeks ago, we were in this exact same position, but outside instead. I can't believe it's been that long. If we hadn't been interrupted, we could have been doing this all along.

He holds himself off me with one hand and explores my skin with the other. His hand is soft and rough at the same time. He cups one breast and then the other. Then lowers his head and takes a nipple into his mouth while his fingers play with the other. I arch my back and run my fingers through his hair. Pull him toward me. I need more. I need to feel all his skin against mine.

I tug at the waist of his sweatpants. "Jake?"

He lifts his head to look at me and then stands up. Every cell in my body screams its protest as cool air chills my skin. I miss his touch. He takes my hands and pulls me. One second, I'm standing, and in the next, he's holding me, my legs wrapped around his hips, and his hands holding my bottom. From the kitchen counter, Kojak watches us, and I swear that cat is smirking. Jake carries me with ease, his footsteps quiet on the carpeted steps. His bedroom is at the end of the hall, large and open, with slate blue walls and floor-to-ceiling windows. The French doors open to a balcony and the lake beyond, now barely visible through the pouring rain A king-sized bed sits against the darker blue accent wall.

Jake holds me with one hand while using the other to pull back the bed coverings. Crisp white sheets meet my back when he lays me down. I scoot over and make room for him. The waist of my sweatpants unrolls and slides halfway down my hips. I'm nearly naked now. Jake stands at the side of the bed and watches me, his chest heaving with even breaths.

I smile. "You're a little overdressed for this party."

He nods at my pants, just hovering over my pubic bone. "So are you."

I move my hands to the fabric. "I can fix that."

"No, let me." He kneels on the bed, his hands slide up my outer thighs until he hooks his fingers in the waistband, and tugs down. I lift my hips just enough for the pants to get past my butt. He stops and drags a breath in when the fabric reveals more of me. His gaze fixed on the spot between my thighs.

I lie back and watch as his eyes devour me. My skin heats everywhere his gaze touches. He's so beautiful. Messy hair, red and swollen lips, chest heaving, the ridges in his stomach contracting with each breath. The bulge in his sweatpants grows bigger. His gaze finds mine again. Those eyes . . . they're dark with lust. The storm inside him and me rivals the one outside.

He pulls my pants off, steps off the bed, and tosses them on the floor. His thumbs hook on the side of his own pants now.

I go up on my knees. "No, let me."

He stops, and I move closer to him, hook a finger on the

inside of his waistband, and slide it to his hip. Do the same with the other hand. I pull the band out and down to free his erection. It bobs once and juts out between us. I slide the pants down his thighs, and gravity does the rest.

My turn to drink him in. Lean muscles and taut skin, abs I want to lick, and the dips of the V point directly at his cock. And it's a thing of beauty. I never thought of a penis being beautiful before, but I can honestly say his is.

I take him in my hand—the moment my fingers wrap around him, he closes his eyes, and a little moan escapes his lips. He pushes into my hand, and I stroke him. Once, twice, three times.

His hand covers mine and stops me. "This party will be over before it starts if you keep doing that. I'm about to embarrass myself like a green boy. Lie back down, please."

I pout but scoot back and lie on my side. Jake lies down next to me. We reach for each other at the same time. I lean back, while he hovers over me, and we kiss. Not as hungry as before, but just as intense. There's a calm and gentleness to him now, like all doubts have vanished, and we are secure knowing this is right. We danced around our attraction and the ethics of getting involved for weeks. Now, the doubt is gone, and this is the moment we give in.

His mouth moves down my jaw, neck, and collarbone, leaving a trail of kisses. He nuzzles and kisses the space between my breasts. I reach for him, smoothing my hands over every inch of skin I can reach. I rake my nails through his hair, neck, shoulders, and back. His muscles flex when I scratch his sides. He trails kisses down my body, over my belly, hips, and more until he settles over my center. His shoulders push my legs apart as he makes room for himself.

I hold my breath in anticipation, but what I crave doesn't

happen just yet. Jake teases me with kisses and nibbles on one thigh, then the other. He brushes his cheek into the spot above where I want him the most, the scrape of his whiskers over my sensitive bud creating sensory overload. His breath comes in hot, and then, just when I'm about to scream in frustration, his lips find me.

CHAPTER 47
JAKE

I INHALE HER. I TASTE HER. I DEVOUR HER. Outside, the rain drums on the roof and runs down the windows, but that can't muffle Ava's moans when I finally get my lips and tongue on her, in her. It's the sweetest of sounds.

Under me, her hands grasp the linens and twist them. Her hips undulate under my touch. She doesn't wait for release to come to her. No, she hunts it down. I'm the giver, and she's the seeker. We meet halfway in this game of give and take. And I can't wait to make her scream.

She's frantic, her hips moving faster, harder. Her husky voice murmurs my name incoherently. I hold her thighs and latch on.

She explodes on my tongue. Her back arches, her hands fist the bedding, her mouth opens into a silent scream, and her entire body goes rigid. I hold on, giving her more and more. Wave after wave racks her body until, with a final cry, she falls back into the bed and goes completely still. Her body is spent and relaxed. Her chest rises and falls with the force of her breathing, and tears stream down the corners of her closed eyes.

I make my way up Ava's body, kissing her belly, and the valley between her breasts until I'm hovering over her with my face inches from hers. I brush a lock of hair from her damp forehead, and she opens her eyes. A satisfied smile greets me.

She cups my face and traces my mouth with her thumb. "That was . . . I have no words for it."

I nibble her thumb and smile. "I thought I was going to have to call an exorcist."

She covers her face with both hands and dissolves into laughter. "No priest needed. Maybe a little holy water."

"Hydration is important." I love this. Love how her body responds to me. How she laughs in the middle of sex and plays along.

She runs a hand through my hair. "Please tell me you have protection."

I take her hand and kiss it. "I do. Are you still sure you—"

"Jake, if you don't put a condom on and get inside of me right now, I'm—"

I shut her up with a kiss, then reach over to the nightstand and remove a condom from the box I bought a couple of days ago. She watches me as I slide it on. I move over her, and we kiss again. I lower myself on top of her, skin to skin. She tilts her hips up, and I slide in, slowly, inch by inch.

She gasps.

"You okay? Did I hurt you?"

"No, it feels so good."

That's all the incentive I need. I slide in all the way—her

heat all around me, her scent in my nostrils, her taste on my tongue. I'm surrounded by her, and it feels like coming home.

I hold still, savoring the moment, committing it to memory. I want to come back to this moment when she's no longer here. I open my eyes and meet her gaze, see the wonder in her eyes, and something else, too. Something I dare not name for fear of jinxing this. Whatever it is, I'll take it.

She squeezes around me, and I groan. Her legs come up and lock around my hips, and I slide in deeper still. "I could stay here forever."

She nibbles at her lower lip and tilts her hips again in a silent invitation. I move then. Slowly at first, relishing the feel of her. She moves too and matches me stroke for stroke. But the urge to go faster takes over, and I let go of the reins.

Ava rises to the challenge and keeps up with me. Our breathing comes faster, shallower, and the sounds we make are more animal than human.

I'm so close. "Ava?" My voice is rough with lust.

"Jake . . . don't stop, don't stop, don't stop."

And then she's coming, contracting around me, squeezing so tight, I let go and follow her, slowing down until I can't move another inch. I nearly collapse on top of her but hold myself off to the side.

Our breathing slows after a while. I slide off of Ava, walk to the bathroom, get rid of the condom, and wash my hands. When I come back, Ava is in the same spot, eyes closed and unmoving. I lie next to her, tug her close, and pull the covers over us. She turns on her side and molds her body to mine. Her breathing evens out.

Outside, the storm rages on. And inside, a storm of a different kind takes place in my heart.

CHAPTER 48
AVALON

My eyes flutter. The steady drum of rain is a lullaby, and I have to fight to keep from falling asleep again. I try to stretch, but something at my back restrains my movements. I freeze. Open my eyes, and at first, I don't recognize my surroundings. It's dark but not yet night.

A muscular arm wraps around my waist and tugs me closer. Warm lips touch my bare shoulder with a gentle kiss. Jake. All at once, my mind is filled with images. Of him and me and all we did. How completely overtaken by lust I was. My face burns with the memories. Gosh. How am I going to look him in the eyes after all that? I was like a cat in heat.

He nuzzles into my hair and inhales. Then, pulls me closer still. The hair on his legs and chest tickles my bare skin. Naked. I'm naked in Jake's bed. And Jake is naked, too.

Did I fall asleep immediately after we . . .

He kisses me on the shoulder again. "Are you okay?" His voice is soft.

I force myself to relax and nod. "Yeah."

The hand on my waist goes to my shoulder, and he turns

me halfway so he can look at me. Even in the dim light, the furrow of his brow is visible. "Do you regret this?"

"No." My answer is immediate. No hesitation. "No, not at all."

He pulls back a few inches. "What is it then? Something is bothering you."

I meet his eyes, and it's not as difficult as I thought it would be. I search for an answer. "I don't regret being with you, and I'm a little embarrassed about how wanton I behaved."

He smiles, and the tension leaves his face. "Nah, not wanton at all. You were perfect."

I turn onto my back to better see him and touch his face, tracing the contours of his jaw. He turns his face into my palm, closes his eyes, and inhales. His chest expands, and he holds still. So much vulnerability at this moment. He's finally unguarded. My heart hurts with the stabbing of a hundred needles for the pain I can sense in him now, and for the pain I'll inflict on him when I leave. But before I go, I'll find his sister for him. If I cannot stay and give him myself, I can at least give him closure for Emily. I'll find her.

He kisses my palm. Tears prickle my eyes, and I close them, so he won't see me cry. I don't know how many of these moments we'll have to steal away, but I vow to make each as perfect as possible.

I give myself a minute to get under control, and when I open my eyes again, he's looking at me with hunger in his eyes. I kiss him. Slow and steady, and without the urgency we had before. This time, each touch is tender, filled with longing and love.

We're no longer driven by lust, hunger, and passion alone.

This is desire in slow motion.

For the first time in my life, I understand the meaning of making love.

This time, it is my stomach grumbling that demands I get up. Jake is lying next to me. The only part of us touching is our fingertips, and yet the connection between us feels unbreakable. Both of us are on our backs, half covered by a sheet, tired, satiated, and happy.

Jake chuckles. "I guess that means I have to feed you." His stomach also grumbles.

"Hmm, glad I'm not the only one needing food." I cover a yawn with my free hand. "What time is it?"

He looks at the digital clock on the nightstand. "Five-o-five. What do you feel like?"

"Mexican food. I could go for a quesadilla or a burrito or some tacos."

Jake sits up. "I know a good taco place. I'll call." He looks around for his phone, but I'm pretty sure he left it behind in the living room with half of our clothes.

"Be right back." He gets up and gives me a fantastic view of his ass. I go up on an elbow to better appreciate it.

I'm still in the same position when he returns, phone in hand, and the shirts we left behind. Kojak is on his heels.

Jake hands me one of the shirts. "I put the wet stuff in the drier."

"Thank you."

Then, he gives me a menu. "They have vegetarian options, too."

As Jake dresses, I read the menu and sneak peeks at him.

It's a shame to cover all those beautiful muscles. I set the menu aside and tell him what I want.

I get dressed while Jake calls the restaurant. He places the order, and his gaze never leaves my body. "Three beef tacos, three veggie tacos, a side of chips and guacamole, and one plain fish taco from the kid's menu, please."

He hangs up. "It will be here in thirty minutes."

I have to ask. "Fish taco from the kid's menu?"

He looks sheepish. "For Kojak. He gets mad if I leave him out."

I laugh. That cat has Jake, this tough, strong man, wrapped around his little paw. Who would ever imagine this? The more I know this amazing man, the more of his soft side I see.

We move to the living room, and I help him set the table. Kojak watches all from his perch on a corner of the kitchen island. His tail swishes back and forth.

When Jake opens the French doors, I follow, and he puts his arm around my waist. Outside, the ferocity of the rain has subsided to a steady drizzle. The sky lights up, and a few seconds later, a rumble overtakes the pitter-patter of rain. "I love storms. Lightning, thunder, wind. It makes me feel alive."

Jake's body tenses. He sighs and then relaxes, his shoulders dropping as if someone cut the strings holding him up. "Emily went missing on a day very much like this."

Oh my God. Here I am babbling about how much I love storms, and Jake is reliving the worst day of his life. I take his hand. "I'm sorry. I didn't think—"

He turns to me and brings both of our hands to his chest. "No. Don't apologize. I didn't say it to upset you and I wasn't done."

I frown. "Not done?"

He brings my hand to his mouth and kisses my knuckles. "Today, you gave me more than your body. You gave me a fresh memory. A better, happier memory."

"What do you mean?"

He tucks a lock of hair behind my ear. "You gave me something else to think about. Next time it rains like this, I'll think of you and making love to you."

I go on tiptoes, put my free hand behind his neck, and kiss him once, looking him in the eyes. This is my chance. He brought her up. He opened that door. It must mean something. I send a small prayer into the universe that what I'm about to say won't upset him and go for it.

"Jake, I want to help you find Emily."

His face goes hard for a split second and then smooths over. There's a battle inside of him. He's fighting blame, guilt, and mistrust. On one side are old habits, self-preservation and resistance to outside help. On the opposite side there's me, my gift, and a need greater than himself to find out what happened.

I wait until his gaze meets mine again. "You don't have to decide now. Think about it. Let's enjoy this weekend together and forget about everything outside these walls. You can let me know Monday when you go back to work."

He nods once, a slow, barely noticeable movement. "Yes, please help me find her."

CHAPTER 49
AVALON

THE MOMENT I OPEN THE APARTMENT DOOR, THE feeling of wrongness slams into me like a rogue wave. Nothing out of the ordinary, and yet, my heart races as fear coils in my stomach like a poisonous snake. I look around, trying to place what doesn't fit. Everything looks fine. Nothing out of the ordinary. I leave the door open and take two steps in, allowing the disturbing energy to settle into me.

My gaze searches every corner, every surface, and finds nothing. I listen, straining to hear anything that doesn't belong, but the only sound I hear is my own heartbeat drumming in my ears.

I take slow steps to the bathroom and peer inside. The open shower curtain and dry tub suggest it hasn't been used for a while. The counter is clean, and our belongings are neatly tucked away into their travel bags.

I walk to the bedroom and stop at the door. Empty. Where is she? Lynn doesn't get up this early, but her bed is neatly made. She never makes her bed. I step into the room and open the closet door. Again, nothing is out of place. Our suitcases rest on the floor. My shoes are perfectly aligned, the same way I left them. And so are Lynn's—all perfectly organized. This is so unlike her. What the hell happened? Did she go on a cleaning frenzy? I talked to her last night, and she never mentioned cleaning up or going out. She said she was staying in to watch TV.

I approach her bed and run my fingers over her pillow. Dread overcomes me.

Lynn!

I rip open my purse and grab my phone and call her—it goes straight to voicemail. Lynn never turns her phone off or allows the battery to die. I hang up as soon as the voice message starts and tap her name again.

And again. And again. I wait and listen to her entire voice message this time, but it's the same as it has always been.

I start a desperate text message asking if everything is okay but stop. Backspace. Each delete tap is like a stab into my chest. If something is wrong and someone has her phone, I don't want to alert them.

I force air into my lungs. And start again.

Me: Hey, where are you? Want to grab breakfast?

I stare at the screen until it goes dark. No response comes. I knew it wouldn't. My entire body shudders. I tap my phone again, open the Life360 location app, and tap Lynn's name.

It says, 'Device off since Sunday, 10:57 p.m.'

I knew it would be like this. He's too meticulous to make a rookie mistake.

I run out of the apartment, slamming the door behind me, and frantically dial Jake as I rush to the stairs. I'm not waiting for the elevator.

"Hel—"

"Jake! Lynn's missing. She's not in our apartment and she doesn't answer her phone. He took her. I know it."

"Where are you? Are you safe?" The sound of a door banging echoes behind his questions.

I fly down the three levels of stairs and burst through the door, nearly trampling another person. "I'm in my building lobby, coming to you."

"No!" His voice is so commanding that I freeze on the spot. "Stay there. Wait in the lobby. Be near other people. Don't go to your room. Don't go anywhere alone."

A sob escapes me. "I can't—I can't just stay here."

"I'm driving to you. I'll be there in five minutes." The sound of a motor starting accompanies his voice. "Stay on the phone with me."

I can't just wait here. I walk to the front door. "He has Lynn. I know it. I know it with every cell in my body. He took her."

"You can't know that for sure." His voice echoes over the hum of traffic and his SUV's engine.

"I do know. She wasn't in our room, and she's not answering her phone."

"Maybe she forgot her phone. Or maybe the battery died." He's trying to calm me down, but his words lack conviction.

"No, he took her." My voice cracks. I notice people looking at me with concern. I step outside and pace the sidewalk. The bright morning sun stings my eyes.

"Did you see anything?"

"No, but I can feel it. I just know it."

"I'm here, parking now."

I search the parking lot and see him jogging my way, phone pressed against his ear.

Relief fills every part of my body. I nearly drop to the ground. I stagger before locking my knees. Then, I'm racing toward him. I throw myself into Jake's arms and shatter. Tears break free. He pulls me closer, one hand on the back of my head as he tucks me into his chest. He kisses my temple and murmurs against my hair, "We'll find her."

He holds me like this until my tears lessen. Then, he pulls back and wipes my face with his thumbs, the gesture so gentle I want to cry all over again.

Jake tilts his head, and his gaze meets mine. "Let's go back upstairs. I want to look for clues."

He takes my hand, and we go back upstairs. I feel disconnected from everything around me except Jake's hand holding mine.

Jake stops a few feet from my door and squeezes my hand. "The room key?"

I blink as if waking from a trance and pull the key from my pocket. Jake takes it, then gently pushes me back a few more feet. "Stay here until I come for you," he whispers. "If you hear any sounds of a struggle, run. Call for help."

At his words, awareness rushes back, and my body trembles. I want to protest, but Jake stops me with a single shake of his head. He walks to the door and pulls his gun from a hip holster concealed by his shirt. My eyes widen.

Jake looks at me, nods, and slides the key into the lock. He nudges the door open with his foot, and holding his gun with both hands, disappears inside. Months go by in the few minutes it takes him to return. He slips the gun back into the holster, and I catch a sliver of golden skin before my gaze meets his eyes again. I walk to him, my feet heavy as if dragging them through wet cement.

As soon as I step back into the room, that dreadful weight settles over me again.

Jake stands in the middle of the living room. "Okay. Tell me everything. What's different? What am I looking for?"

I look around the room, noticing more than before. The place is spotless. "Everything is wrong. It's too clean." I point at blankets neatly folded over the arm of the sofa. "Lynn would never fold the blanket like this. The pillows are perfect. There's nothing on the counters." I walk into the kitchen area. "Not even a dirty glass in the sink. It's all wrong."

"Could she have called a cleaning service?"

I shake my head. "No, we talked last night. She would have said something."

I walk down the short hallway. He follows me. I point at Lynn's bed. "Her bed. She never makes her bed, and if she does, it's never that neat. She just pulls the blankets up and the pillows are never propped like that."

He walks around it but doesn't touch anything. "Could anyone else have made the bed? Maybe she had someone over?"

I shake my head. "No." I glance at the alarm clock on the nightstand. Eight twelve blinks in bright red. "She would never bring someone back here. That's one of our rules. Look at my bed. That's not how I left it, either. Whoever was here made both beds differently. Tucked in the corners, folded the blankets over the pillows."

He walks to the other side of her bed.

I take a step toward him. The closer I get to Lynn's bed, the stronger the evil energy gets. "Someone else was here. I can feel it. There is a presence here, stronger near her bed. It's the same energy from my readings. It is the same man. I know it."

Jake squats near the head of the bed. Tilts his head and his eyes narrow. "There's something under the pillow."

I gasp. My heart explodes inside my chest.

He takes his phone out and takes several pictures from all different angles. "I need to call in to dust for fingerprints. There's no telling what else they may find, but I want to see what's under the pillow before they show up."

My mouth goes dry, and my throat closes on a sob. I can't speak, so I nod instead.

He reaches into a pocket and pulls out disposable gloves. "I keep a box of these in my SUV." Then, he moves the pillow like he's disarming a bomb. Underneath, there's something that shouldn't be there.

CHAPTER 50
AVALON

WE BOTH STARE AT THE FOLDED PIECE OF PAPER, AND I take a step closer.

His hand comes up to stop me. "Did you notice this before?"

I shake my head. "No, I touched the pillow, but I didn't look under it."

He takes more pictures from different angles and opens the single sheet of paper on top of the blanket now. Jake looks at the nightstand, where a notepad and pen lie.

I get closer and lean over the bed to read the note.

The words are so neatly written that they look more like a printed message than handwriting.

Tsk. Tsk. Tsk.

 You've been a naughty girl.

 Playing games you're not invited to and meddling in things that don't concern you. You changed the rules of the game, and now I have your friend.

 She's a pretty little thing, so full of life. I like them like that.

All sunshine and trust. Never seeing the dark side of life.

I don't know how you're figuring it all out. Or how you found that necklace.

You found my little birds. So fast, too. Victoria was a gift. But not Alice. How did you find her in that hole? You took my little bird, and now I have one of yours. It's a fair trade, don't you think? Mine for yours.

A sob catches in my throat and I press a hand to my mouth. Tears stream down my face, and the words on the note blur. I wipe my face with the back of my hands and read the rest of the letter.

The words are not as neat now. They dig into the papers as if that monster put extra pressure into the pen.

But I confess I'm curious. I'll have fun finding out all of your secrets. I'm sure I can make your bird—no, not yours—she's mine now. I can make my bird tell me everything she knows. And then when all of your secrets are mine, I'll come for you, too. I like that. I like the idea of having the two of you.

And maybe I'll even keep her alive long enough to see me play with you. Oh, the games we'll play. It will be so much fun.

Jake wraps his arms around me and pulls me into his chest. There's no holding back now. The sobs and tears come, not in a trickle, but like a tsunami. Wave after wave of sorrow and pain crashes into me. My knees buckle, and his hold on me tightens.

"I'll find her. I promise you—I'll find her."

He carries me away and sets me in the hallway. I'm sitting on the floor, legs pressed to my chest, my arms wrapped around my knees. Jake squats in front of me.

He's tapping on his phone. "I have to call this in. I'll talk to the chief first."

The words reach me like a weak beam of light trying to break through a dense fog. "The chief first?"

"Yes. I want to keep this contained. He'll know what to do. We need a better equipped crime investigation unit. They'll come and check for fingerprints, look for hair samples, stuff like that."

Jake stands up and takes a couple of steps away from me. "Chief? I have a situation."

As he walks a few feet down the hall, his voice becomes fainter. I press a hand to my chest. The pain is so intense, I expect to find a huge hole in the place of my heart.

Jake comes back and kneels in front of me again. "You can't stay here. After they clear the room, we'll take your things and get you to a safe place."

"There's no safe place."

CHAPTER 51
AVALON

I BARELY REMEMBER WHAT HAPPENED AFTER JAKE TOOK me out of the apartment. Other cops came in. A female officer came to sit with me in the hallway. She was older and motherly-looking, her shoulder touching mine as she sat on the floor next to me in silence. Her presence was comforting, even though I don't know her name.

Calling Lynn's family to let them know she was missing was the hardest thing I have ever done. Talking to Grandma didn't help. She said everything would work as intended, but that's no consolation. What does that even mean?

Now, I find myself back at Jake's house, sitting on his couch, a blanket wrapped around my shoulders and a mug of hot tea in my hands. Exhaustion weighs me down like an anchor, and I'm sinking into cold, deep, and dark waters. It's been two days since I last saw Lynn. I spoke with her last night around ten, and she was fine. Whatever happened was between then and this morning. Would it have made a difference if I had stayed with her? Or would he have taken us both?

Kojak rubs against my legs and gives me a pitiful meow. The muffled sound of Jake's voice reaches me, but I can't quite make out his words. Snippets of his side of the conversation break through my idled mind, and I pay attention.

"Trust..."

"Security cameras..."

"Watch her..."

I set the mug on the coffee table and stand up. The blanket drops to the floor behind me, but I can't muster the energy to pick it up. I follow the sound of Jake's voice and find him pacing back and forth in his kitchen, his cell phone pressed to his ear. I cross my arms over my chest and openly listen to his side of the conversation. As Jake turns, his eyes meet mine.

"I gotta go," he says to the person on the phone and hangs up.

His arms come around me. He pulls me into his chest and tucks my head under his chin. "I'm going to find her, I promise you. I'm going to find her."

I want to lash out and ask him how. How will he find her when he couldn't find the others? But I rein in my anger. It's not directed at him. I'm angry at the asshole who took my best friend, angry at myself for not having seen it, for not having found enough information to identify this guy.

I pull back to look at Jake. "Do they have anything?"

He shakes his head. "Not yet."

I take another step back. "Did you check the cameras?"

His arms drop to his sides. "We have a team going over every security video they have, starting from the time last night when you last spoke with her. It's hours of footage from a dozen cameras, so it will take a while."

I cross my arms. "Did you tell anyone about me and what I'm doing?"

"No, of course not. Did you or Lynn say anything to anyone?"

"No. And I know Lynn would never say anything. Not even her mother knows what I do. She's been keeping this secret since we were kids. Could someone have seen the files? Heard the recordings? Maybe the chief said something."

He pulls a stool from under the kitchen island and drops onto it. "I already talked to my boss, and he hasn't talked to anyone about it. No one has access to the files on the cases, and all the evidence is locked in my office. Including the recordings."

"How would he know about the necklace then?"

"I don't know." Jake sounds frustrated. "Maybe he figured the antique shop had it and traced it back to you?"

"I don't see how that's possible, but it's easy to verify. You can go back there and ask. It has to be someone on the inside."

He shakes his head. "I can't imagine a cop doing any of it."

"That doesn't mean anything. Bad people are everywhere, and dirty cops exist in every town. Even here."

Jake nods more to himself than in answer to my comment. "Somehow, he figured it out. The question is how."

"You're not listening to me. It has to be someone on the inside, Jake. It has to be another cop. Only someone with access to the files and information I gave you would be able to connect the dots to link me to the investigation."

He folds his hands behind his neck. "It makes sense that only somebody on the inside would have access to that information, but I know all of them. I've worked with them for years, and I can't think of a single person who would have the personality to do something like this."

I cross my arms. Anger sparks a fire inside me, and I have a hard time keeping it at bay. "Who else, Jake? Who else would have access to the information? To your files? Access to the evidence? He specifically mentioned the necklace in the note. Who else would have access to it?" My voice rises with each question.

He releases a breath. "All requests to access evidence in the lockers go through me. But technically, if I'm not there, and somebody needed something from the evidence locker, the chief could let them in."

"You have any kind of paper tracking? Sign in logs?"

"Yes, I already checked it. There's no record of anyone trying to access those files. But if it's someone on the inside, and they've been able to fool everyone this long, I doubt they would leave a trail behind."

"Could it be the chief?"

He shakes his head. "No, there's no way he'd do anything like this."

"He pointed a gun at us. What if the whole thing was a sham? What if he was setting us up and hearing about his brother got him sidetracked?"

"Did you feel anything that suggests it could be him when you touched the dog tags?"

I deflate. No, and I would have known. "Nothing."

"It can't be him. But now that we know this isn't just a missing persons' case, but a potential serial killer case, there will be a lot more attention. More hands on deck to help."

"Including the killer doing whatever he can to sabotage everything. I have to go back to the station, Jake, and look at the rest of the evidence. I need to touch that note."

"This is not a good idea. We need to keep you hidden and out of the public eye, especially if the kidnapper is a dirty cop."

"I'm not going to sit and hide while this monster tortures Lynn. The longer he has her—" I stop myself, unable to continue that line of thought. "How about cameras? Do you have security cameras that could show anyone going into your office?"

"Not in the back. All the cameras are pointed to the lobby and reception areas. They didn't have the budget for inside cameras."

I walk to the living room and grab my phone and pocketbook. "Let's go."

"Ava . . ."

"I'm not gonna sit here falling apart when Lynn's life is on the line. I need to touch that letter, and I need to do it right now. Then, I need to figure out where he took her."

"There is a lot of heat on this case right now and the chief is talking about getting the Feds involved. I don't know how much longer I can protect your secret or keep you out of this if you show up with me."

"I've shown up with you plenty of times before."

"It's different now. You're linked to the case, and they don't like family or friends showing up and meddling in things."

"But I'm a link to her. In a normal investigation, wouldn't you ask me questions about her? If she met anyone new? If she said anything that could be a clue."

He runs a hand through his hair, a gesture I recognize as a sign of exasperation. "That's true. But if Lynn was taken by a cop, someone in the department, that's even more reason to keep you out of there. And keep your abilities hidden."

I whirl at him. "I don't care. That asshole already knows I'm involved, and it's just a question of time before he figures out what I can do." I walk to the door and yank it open. "I don't care who finds out, I don't care about my job, I don't care about her kidnapper being a cop. I don't care about anything that doesn't involve finding her. Making sure I find Lynn safe is the only thing that matters."

He grabs his keys from the kitchen counter, then his gun, and tucks it into a concealed holster on the inside waist of his jeans. "You're not gonna let it go, are you?"

"I will chase this piece of shit until my dying breath. Let's go, now."

"I'm not sure that's a good idea, Ava. Whoever took her already promised to take you, too. I want to keep you safe and away from this whole mess. But I don't know whom to trust. I don't know where to hide you, or whom to ask for help. I should have never brought you into this. This is one hundred percent my responsibility."

"No, I'm not a child. I'm an adult. I chose to find you. I chose to bring the necklace to you, and I chose to help with the investigation. It was my choice. My responsibility. If anything, this is on me. I brought Lynn into this mess, and I'm going to get her out. Are you going to help me or not?" I don't wait for an answer. I walk out the door.

Jake follows me.

I GOT MYSELF A LITTLE BIRD.
FEISTY LITTLE THING
SO MUCH FIRE IN HER.
I MIGHT HOLD ON TO HER A LITTLE LONGER.
UNTIL I GET HER FRIEND.
IT WOULD BE SO MUCH FUN TO PLAY WITH THE TWO
OF THEM.
I'VE NEVER HAD TWO LITTLE BIRDS AT THE SAME
TIME.

CHAPTER 52
AVALON

SOMEONE LEAKED INFORMATION AGAIN. THE CITY HALL building that houses the police station is in chaos. Press vans are parked along the street with journalists and cameramen loitering about. Jake slows as we approach the metal barriers that block the front of the building. A cop mans the entrance to the parking lot and, recognizing Jake, waves him in. We drive around to the back of the building, and thankfully, there's no one outside.

"We can go in through the back, but wait here for a second."

Jake walks around the vehicle and scans the area. He opens the SUV door, and I hop out. Hands clasped, we scurry through the back entrance where another cop guards the door.

Cops are everywhere, more than usual. Some in plain clothes and some wearing uniforms from neighboring towns. A dozen heads turn our way, and conversations halt. *One of these men has Lynn.* I want to demand every single one of

328

them to allow me to touch them and ask questions, but I keep my mouth shut until we're locked in Jake's office.

The phone on his desk rings before the door closes behind us. He answers it. "Knox."

"Let me talk to her." The chief's voice is loud enough I have no trouble hearing him from where I stand. Jake gives me the phone.

Taking it with a trembling hand, I hold it out a little so Jake can listen, too. "Hello."

"Miss Ava, it's not a good idea for you to be here."

"Try kicking me out and see what happens." My words are fueled by anger and fear.

He sighs. "I will not kick you out, but perhaps we can use your special skills."

"That's what I'm here for. I need to touch that note. And I want to go through the rest of the evidence to see if I can find any other clues."

Jake tenses. Presses his lips together but stays quiet.

"I'll bring the note in for you."

Chief Malone hangs up, and I set the phone down.

Jake's hands go to my shoulders, and he rubs them, digging his thumbs into the growing knots. I take in a stuttered breath. "Should we tell him of our suspicions?"

Before he responds, there's a knock on the door. Jake opens it, and the chief comes in, locking the door behind him.

Hmm. Last time, he didn't knock. Suspicion rears its head again. "Chief, last time I met you here, you didn't knock. You opened the door and walked right in. How did you do that? The door was locked."

His eyebrows rise. "I used the key code."

Jake frowns. "I changed the key code that morning and had yet to give it to you."

"I have the master code."

Jake and I exchange a look.

Jake crosses his arms, looking very casual. "There's a master code?"

"Yes, it's a safety backup."

I sit on the edge of Jake's desk. "If someone asks for access to the evidence locker, do you just give them the code, or do you open the door for them?"

The chief frowns. "I open the door for them, then sign the evidence out myself. But it's been weeks, maybe months since anyone asked for anything. Why do you ask?"

Another look passes between Jake and me.

Chief Malone crosses his arms. The folder in his hands grabs my attention. I can sense evil rolling from it like an invisible spreading stain.

When neither of us answers his question, he tilts his head and puzzles it out for himself. "You think someone on the inside is responsible for the murders?"

I force myself not to look at Jake and bite my tongue. We haven't discussed what to say about it if anything.

Jake takes a step closer. "It's a possibility we need to keep on the table, but I'm not prepared to make it known. If it's one of us, we don't want to alert him."

"What makes you think it's an insider?" To his credit, the chief didn't immediately shut it down.

"The note. It mentions the necklace, and that information was never released. It's in the case file, but no one besides me should have had access to that."

An idea occurs to me. "Does anyone except you and Jake have access to this office or the files?"

"We have office staff that aren't cops, and the janitorial crew. But I can't see any of them being able to break into Knox's office without being noticed. There are always at least two officers here at any given time."

"What about computers? Could someone hack into the computers?"

"I doubt it. Everything is password protected, and all access is tracked via the key log chain on the server." He nods as the picture we painted for him becomes clearer. "One of us? Hell, the press would have a field day with that information."

I point at the file folder. "Is that the note?"

"Yes, don't remove it from the plastic sleeve."

I walk around Jake's desk and sit in his oversized chair. The thing nearly swallows me as I sink into it. I wheel myself closer to his desk, put my hands flat on it, close my eyes, and breathe. In and out, slowly a few times until my heart stops racing. I open my eyes and look at the chief. "I'm ready."

He opens the folder, and the plastic sleeve slides onto the desk. I hover my hands over the note, the words jumping at me to mock my pain. I close my eyes and let my hands touch the plastic sleeve. My palms burn, but I don't remove them. Rage reaches out to me like the tentacles of a sea monster. There's so much anger emanating from the piece of paper. He feels slighted, as if us finding the bodies is a personal offense to him. "He's so angry. He prides himself in always being in control, always being ten steps ahead, but us finding the two bodies days after he dumped them is making him feel . . . inadequate."

"Inadequate?" The question comes from Chief Malone.

"Yes, he's feeling weak and powerless." I'm shaking, my

hands trembling so much, they make the plastic sleeve slide on the desk.

Jake shifts next to me. "This isn't good. People who are angry and feel powerless tend to make harsh decisions."

The chief nods. "He already made a harsh decision. Kidnapping Miss Reynolds doesn't fit with the rest of the victims' abductions. None were taken from their homes."

I close my eyes again and return my focus to the note. Splay my hands over it. "He's writing the note. There's a syringe and a small glass vial on a desk. He hates disorder. He's disgusted by the mess in the apartment." I open my eyes again. "I can't see his face. I see what he sees. He must have drugged her. Lynn would have put up one hell of a fight. I doubt she would go along even if he had a gun."

Chief Malone nods. "In your report, you said the apartment had been cleaned?"

"Y-yes." My voice cracks.

"Just like the car from one of the victims. It was spotless," Jake says.

I slump back into the chair and look at Jake. "I need to see everything you have."

He returns the note to the chief and clears his desk, then brings out a plastic box.

The chief's cell phone buzzes. He grabs it out of his pocket. "Yes."

Jake and I watch him.

"Send it to Knox and me and no one else." He ends the call.

"They found something on the security video and are emailing a copy to you right now."

I get up, and Jake takes the chair, his fingers flying over the keyboard as he enters his password.

As soon as his email fills the screen, he hits refresh. Again. And then again. My stomach twists in knots. A new message appears. The first email attachment shows a man dressed all in black wearing jeans, a baseball cap pulled low over his face, and a hoodie with the hood covering his head. He used the stairs, not the elevator. And by his movements—head down and body slouched—he's well aware of the cameras. He doesn't knock and appears to have a key. The timestamp says 10:24 p.m. The video ends.

I'm shaking so much I have to hold on to the desk. Jake stands up and guides me to the chair.

"Look at the timestamp. This was minutes after I talked to Lynn. And he turned off the locator app on her phone, so the last known location is the apartment at 10:57 p.m."

Both of them frown at me. "What locator app?" Chief Malone speaks first.

I forgot to tell them. I push the heels of my palms into my forehead, attempting to relieve the pressure behind my eyes from turning into a massive headache. "We have an app on our phones so we can check on each other. It started as a way for her to know where I was while I'm traveling. I checked the app as soon as I realized she was missing, and it said her phone was turned off." I unlock my phone and open the app. "Look."

Both of them lean closer to see the message on the screen.

The chief nods. "Was Miss Reynolds' phone at the apartment?"

"No." I look at the computer screen. "What's the other video?"

Jake clicks on the attachment. The video plays. It's a shot of the hallway outside the apartment. The door opens, and the same man from before leaves, but now taking Lynn with him. She, too, is wearing a baseball cap and a hoodie. Lynn stumbles at his side as he holds her up, an arm over his shoulder. Anyone seeing them would think she's drunk. The time stamp on this video is 11:09 p.m. "He was in there for forty-five minutes. She's been missing for nearly twelve hours." The drugs had to have worn off by now. My God, Lynn. Please.

I press a fist to my mouth and hold in a sob. The image blurs as I blink away tears. The man takes her to the stairs, and the video ends. "That's it? No video of him walking in or out of the building. Or the parking lot?"

Chief Malone shakes his head. "No. The security person at the building thinks he used the maintenance entrance and got in through the basement. No cameras there. He had to know the building well enough to know which camera areas to avoid. Except for the hallways. There's no way to avoid that."

"How easy would it be for someone to gain that information? Find out how to get into the building and avoid the cameras?"

Chief Malone rubs his face. "The building blueprint is public information. The cameras would take a little more work, but not that hard, either. He could have walked in weeks ago to scout the place, and there's no way to know."

Jake crosses his arms. "Wherever he's been hiding has to be near the park. He must have easy access to it and is comfortable enough walking in there while carrying a body. Probably at night."

I stand up and pace in the small space behind his desk. "Not necessarily. What if he's hiding somewhere in the park? It would be easy enough for him to get rid of the bodies in the middle of the night."

Chief Malone tilts his head. "In the park? I doubt. Both recovered bodies showed signs of being frozen for a while. He couldn't possibly have a freezer big enough to hide bodies in the middle of the park. How would he get access to power?"

Frustration slams at me. I stare at the door. "Why can't I just go out there and touch something from each of them? Like . . . like their car keys? That would tell me something."

Jake takes a step back.

Chief Malone's eyes widen, and he's the first to recover. "That's not a good idea. First of all, not everyone from the department is in. Some are out patrolling, and others have the day off. If the kidnapper is a cop, going out there would alert him. What if you don't find anything incriminating? And it would, for sure, blow your cover. The press is outside, waiting. They would make a spectacle out of this if someone let that slide."

"How many women have disappeared in total? Was it three you said when we first met?"

Jake hesitates before he answers. "Four. Someone else went missing a couple of weeks ago."

"What? You never said anything about it."

He has the decency to look contrite. "I didn't want to add more stress to an already stressful and demanding situation."

Chief Malone clears his throat. "No, it's only three. The last one turned up yesterday. She had a fight with her boyfriend and was hiding out with a friend. I didn't have a chance to update you."

I sigh. "I'll look for clues in the other stuff then. Thanks, Chief. Jake will let you know if I find anything." Did I just dismiss the chief of police in his own station? Yes, I did.

His brows go up, but he doesn't say anything else before he leaves. It's just Jake and me in his office. And a growing mountain of guilt. While I was with him, Lynn was alone, and this asshole probably knew it. He took her to get back at me for finding the other two women.

I push away the dread. I need a clear mind for this. "Let's look at the rest of the evidence."

CHAPTER 53
AVALON

THE MASSIVE HEADACHE AND PRESSURE BEHIND MY EYES are finally starting to ease. Thanks to the pain meds and veggie burger Jake forced on me a couple of hours ago. I wish Grandma were here. She might be able to see more than me. Which was nothing. Nothing that can aid us in finding Lynn. Just more random images of this asshole charming women and then taking them. How can he be so convincing? They all seem to trust him. All except the girl in the bowling alley. Is it a small-town thing? Are people more trusting? Or is it something else? If he's really a cop, that could be a reason, too. But if he's a cop, I must have seen him more than once. As often as I visit the station, all of them know me or know of me.

I push a hand into my chest and rub at the never-ending ache. If he's a cop, he could be out there right now, laughing at us, maybe even sabotaging our efforts to locate her.

The reflection in the ladies' room mirror as I wash my hands reveals pale skin and red-rimmed eyes. My hair is messy from how often I've run my hands through it. I shake the

337

excess water from my hands and try to tame my curls the best I can.

The bathroom door opens, and Jake enters. He looks me over from head to toe.

I try for a smile and fail. "You're in the wrong bathroom, you know."

He stuffs his hands in his jeans' pockets. "No, I'm in the right place."

"What if someone else comes in?"

Jake shrugs. "I asked Diane to watch the door. No one will come in."

"Diane?"

"The cop who sat with you in the hallway this morning. Do you remember her?"

I nod. My head is still in a fog. It's no wonder I can't see anything of value when I examine the evidence. I can barely remember anything since leaving Jake's house and returning to the apartment. The woman who sat next to me on the floor is only a vague memory.

I grab a paper towel and dry my hands.

Jake leans on the wall a couple of feet away from me. "How are you holding up?"

I muster enough energy to lift one shoulder and try for another smile that doesn't quite make it. "I'm okay."

His lips press into a thin line. "No. How are you, really?"

The sincerity and care in his mismatched eyes reach me and pull at the last string holding me together. My lips tremble, and tears wash down my cheeks like a waterfall.

He comes to me, pulls me into his chest, and tucks my head under his chin. Jake combs my hair with his fingers. "That's it. Let it all out. You don't have to keep it all inside. If you hold it all in, it'll blow up when you least expect. Got to release the pressure now and then."

I hold on to him and let myself fall apart, crying onto his chest until his shirt is soaked, all the while he rubs soothing circles on my back.

"I'm good now." Pulling away, I go to the sink and wash my face. When I look at my reflection in the mirror, I'm not alone. There's also a young woman—a teenager—and her hands move *in a come with me* motion.

"Jake?"

"Yeah?"

"I need to look at the evidence again."

He crosses his arms over his chest. "No, you're exhausted. You went through every piece of evidence multiple times. You need to rest."

"Jake, I need to see Emily's evidence."

He pales. "Why?" His voice is a whisper.

"Because when I find her, I'll find Lynn, too."

CHAPTER 54
JAKE

My chest locks up, and I have to force the trapped air from my lungs. As if I forgot how to breathe, I drag in a stuttered breath. "What makes you say that?"

With lowered eyes, Ava wraps her arms around her middle as if trying to protect herself. When she looks up, there's apprehension in her eyes. "What is it? What are you afraid to tell me?"

She smiles, but there's no joy in it. "Am I that transparent to you now?"

Is she? No, I don't think so. But we are in synch and have been for a while. "You're stalling."

Ava nibbles her bottom lip and meets my gaze. "Emily is here."

A trapdoor opens under my feet and swallows me whole. My vision fades and my heart pounds in my ears like a thousand jackhammers. I sway as if drunk from my overwhelming emotions. No. No. No. I didn't hear what Ava said. It's not possible. Is it not? She saw spirits before. So, why not Emily? Hasn't it been too long? Tears rush to my eyes and blink them away.

Ava reaches for me, but I step back and raise my hands up to ward her off. I can't bear to be touched right now. I stumble back until I hit the wall. I try to speak, but my throat is locked up. I close my eyes, clamp my head between my palms, and squeeze. Try to stop the erratic thoughts and the pounding in my temples.

It's happening all over again. Instantly, I'm back to the day Emily disappeared. The images and emotions, the days, weeks, and months that followed, all coming to me at once.

"Breathe." The sound of her voice is like a sliver of sunlight breaking through a dense fog. My lungs obey her command, and my chest expands with a rush of cool air. I drop my hands to my knees and bend at the waist, sucking in one breath after another. The tension eases bit by bit. The pounding in my ears retreats, and the muted sound of voices outside the restroom make themselves present again.

I stand up, using the wall to support myself, rub my palms over my face, and look at Ava. She stands out of reach with both hands pressed to her mouth. Her shoulders convulse under silent sobs, and a stream of tears wets her cheeks.

I open my arms, and she rushes into them. I press my cheek to the top of her head, holding her tight, taking and giving strength.

"I'm sorry." Her voice breaks into a sob.

My hands rub up and down her back. "Shh, no. Nothing to be sorry about. It wasn't you."

"I shouldn't have told you." Ava's voice is the echo of a whisper.

I push her back a few inches and cup her face in my

hands. I want her to see me and hear me. "This is not on you. This is fourteen years of grief, denial, and hope catching up with me."

She blinks. "Hope?"

"Hope that even though I didn't believe it—couldn't believe—that Emily's soul existed somewhere."

Ava wipes at her damp face. "Why couldn't you believe it?"

I dig up the truth I've never told anyone from a deep, dark place inside myself. "I didn't think I deserved the comfort of believing in an afterlife."

"Why not?"

"I . . . someone I knew back then suggested my family hired a psychic to find my sister. My parents refused because it goes against their beliefs. I insisted and paid for it. The woman fed us lie after lie. The police followed her clues, and days went by, then weeks and months. All for nothing. She was a con artist. She gave us false hope, stole from us, and sent the investigation in the wrong direction. After all of that and seeing how much it hurt my parents, I stopped believing in everything."

Her mouth opens, and a small *oh* escapes. "That's why you were so angry when we first met."

"Yes. It's also the reason I became a cop. To solve her case when the police at the time couldn't. It's been nearly fourteen years since that day, and I'm no closer than they were. And now you're telling me you saw her, and you can find her . . ."

There's a light knock on the door, and after a moment, it opens a few inches, but Diane doesn't walk in, only her voice enters the room. "Just want to let you know the chief is looking for you two."

"Thank you. We'll be out in a minute."

When the door closes, I wipe an errant tear from Ava's face, then rub the wetness from my face.

She smiles. "What a pair we make."

"Yeah, don't we." I pull my sunglasses from my shirt pocket and, for once, the reason I wear them is not the color of my eyes.

CHAPTER 55
AVALON

J‍AKE KNOCKS ON THE GLASS PANE OF CHIEF MALONE'S open office door.

The chief looks up and does a double take. My face is red and puffy, and sunglasses hide the redness in Jake's eyes. Nothing can hide the weariness in his voice.

"Did you want to see us, Chief?"

"Yes, come in and close the door."

We sit across from him, the cluttered desk between us.

"We got another video. This one is from the parking lot. And it's so short it was nearly missed." He taps his keyboard and turns the monitor toward us. Jake and I lean in. The grainy video is no longer than a couple of seconds. It shows a light-colored SUV leaving the parking lot. That's it.

I stand to inspect the now frozen image on his screen. "What makes you think this is related?"

Malone points to the timestamp on the corner of the screen. "The timestamp. This was eleven minutes after the video of him leaving your apartment. That's enough time to go down four flights of stairs and walk to the back of the

344

parking lot. Moving nice and slow so as to not call attention and making sure no one was watching. But more importantly, it was also the only vehicle to leave the parking lot until hours later."

Jake stands next to me. "Do you know the make and model of the vehicle?"

"We think it's a Chevy Tahoe, probably white or light gray. I have a tech working on the video to see if they can get a clearer picture."

Jake points at the screen. "The kid who stole the necklace said he took it from a white SUV. How much do you want to bet it's the same one?"

I drop back into the chair. "Is there anything else that can be done to track the SUV?"

"We're working on that right now. Checking on security cameras from around the area. Unfortunately, with half of the area being on the beach, our options are limited. This guy knows the area well enough to evade the cameras."

I nod.

"Is there anything else, Chief?" Jake asks.

"No, I'll let you know if anything else comes in. We have eyes and ears on the streets."

"Okay. We'll be in my office. There's something else we want to check, but it's too soon to talk about it. I'll update you if we find anything."

We go back to Jake's office, where he grabs a set of keys from a drawer, then we walk to the back of the building where the hum of the air conditioner and our footsteps are the only sounds. Jake unlocks the only door and flips on the lights. Inside are two caged areas with floor-to-ceiling bars. Inside the cages are metal lockers. Cameras are in place above the door and in the corners.

"What's this place?"

"This is where we keep the evidence for cold cases and where we keep extra guns and ammunition."

"I guess that explains the cameras."

Opening the cage on the left, Jake stops near the far wall and kneels down. He unlocks the bottom drawer and retrieves a small, dark plastic bag. "This is the only thing recovered." Keeping the bag, he relocks everything, and we return to his office.

Jake and I sit on opposite sides of his desk. "Give me a minute to center myself." Eyes closed and slow, even breathing, I disconnect from everything else to clear my mind and open my senses.

"Let me know when you're ready."

"Okay, I'm ready now." I hold my hand out, eyes still closed, and Jake places the object in my hand. My eyes pop open and I gasp. "No bag?"

He shrugs. "It's been examined a half-dozen times over the last fourteen years. I hoped each technological advance would find something new, but they never found anything. I've given up on it."

I gaze at the old Motorola flip phone in my hand, so small and cool to the touch. "I had one of these, too." I close my eyes again and wrap both hands around it. *Show me, tell me your story.*

The images come, faint and slow at first. "The phone was a birthday gift. Emily really wanted it. I see her using it to talk to friends late into the night. She liked to send you messages. You two texted a lot, even before texting was a thing. You had a code?" I smile at the sweet memories. "She loved you. You were more than her big brother, you were her best friend, and the person she confided in when she was sad or upset." The more I see, the more I understand how close they were. The two found friendship and comfort with each other when their parents, or rather their father, got drunk and verbally abusive. Jake felt the need to protect her from the brunt of it. He was more of a father to Emily than their father.

The images speed up, snippets of days and months condensed into a multitude of images. "I see her at school and doing homework. Riding her bike, playing with a black and white dog." Then the images flip to that day, the day she went missing. I know this because they are a mirror of what Jake told me. "It's raining. More than raining, it's a downpour. I see you two inside a car. Something's hanging from the rearview mirror. It's a . . . unicorn. She gave it to you."

Jake reacts to what I said with a stuttered breath, like a trapped gasp.

"She runs out of the car and into the mall. She's laughing the whole time while the rain is drenching her. She's walking, and someone calls her name. She smiles. She knows this person. It's a man. He's tall. I can't see his face. He's wearing a navy-blue baseball cap. The cap has a New York Yankees logo. They walk together. She looks at her phone, and he takes it from her. She tries to get it back, but he puts it in his pocket. She doesn't seem mad. She trusts him. He's flirting with her, and she laughs at him. She thinks he's joking. He's not. He tries to put an arm around her shoulder, and she pushes him away. He gets mad but covers it. She keeps asking for the phone back, but he won't give it to her."

No, he wouldn't. He said he wanted to show me something first.

I gasp and open my eyes. And no more than a few feet away from me is Emily. I glance at Jake and back at her.

Jake stands up in slow motion as if his moving could scare her away like a wild bird. "Is she here?" His voice is no more than a whisper.

I swallow and nod. "Yes." My voice is as low as his.

"What did he want to show you?" I ask the space to Jake's left.

He said he bought a gift for Jake's birthday and wanted to ask my opinion about it and I believed him.

"What happened then?"

I don't know. He did something to me. I don't remember what happened until I woke up in the cave.

"In the cave? Where's this cave?"

In the woods.

My entire body is shaking. "Do you know if Lynn is okay?" My voice croaks.

For now. You have to come fast if you want to save your friend.

"Who took you?"

She looks down, so much sadness on her beautiful face. *Jake's friend.*

She disappears. I drop Emily's cell phone on the desk and slump back in the chair. Nausea takes over. I cover my mouth with my hands as my body tries to expel the veggie burger I ate today.

Instantly, Jake is at my side with a garbage pail in his hands. I take it from him, and he holds back my hair as bile coats my throat. The bitter taste burns like poison as it leaves my body.

Jake rubs circles on my back. "You okay?"

I nod.

He gives me a water bottle, and I take a gulp, wash my mouth, and spit into the pail. I do it again and again until the bitter taste is gone. I grab a tissue from the box on his desk, wipe my mouth, and toss it into the pail, too. "I'm sorry."

"No apologies needed." He takes the pail from me before I can protest, ties up the plastic bag inside, and sets it next to the door. Then he kneels in front of me. "What did she say?"

"She said he took her to a cave in the woods. It's the same guy. The man who took Emily is the same one who took Lynn. She said he was your friend. This guy is someone you knew when she disappeared. Someone she knew as well and trusted."

Jake's gaze drifts as he searches his memories. "Did she say his name?"

"No, she disappeared right after. Do you have any idea who he is?"

His face turns into a mask of cold fury. "Yes, I think I know who he is, and if so, you're right. He's a cop."

"Can I touch something from him or something on his desk? I might be able to intuit something."

He takes my hand and opens his office door so hard it slams on the wall. He practically drags me behind him and into the main area of the station. He stops in front of a desk and releases my hand. Then, steps aside. The room is deadly quiet, and all eyes are on us. Chief Malone comes to his door with a frown on his face. I have zero fucks left to give.

I hover my right hand over the desk, and a sting on my palm draws it to the right, over a mug filled with pens and a knife-shaped letter opener. I take the letter opener, and pure evil assaults me. I brace myself on the desk as the images assail me.

Blood, so much blood, all I see is red. He likes to play with the letter opener when he's at work. It's his idea of a joke. He plays with it and relives all the things he did. This is too much. Too much. I don't want to see any more. I open my hand, and the letter opener drops to the desk with a clank. I nod at Jake.

Chief Malone steps into the room. "Into my office, now."

We follow him, and every person in the station watches us as the chief closes his door on all of them.

CHAPTER 56
JAKE

"I'ᴛ's Jᴇꜰꜰ."

The chief's eyes widen. "How do you know?"

"Ava saw it when she checked another piece of evidence."

"I thought she found nothing else in the evidence bags."

"Not those. I gave her Emily's cell phone."

His hands go to his waist. "What?"

Ava takes a step closer. "It's the same person. The man who kidnaped Emily is the same man who kidnapped and killed all the other women."

Chief Malone is shaking his head. "That's one hell of an accusation, and an accusation to which you have no proof."

"But we do. Jeff drives a white SUV, and he lives less than a quarter of a mile from the park. We need to get a search warrant for his house."

"That's circumstantial evidence at best. For a warrant, I need something more substantial to take to the judge." The chief widens his stance. "This will rub the entire team the wrong way."

I mimic his posturing. "And where is Jeff today? Off. I bet

351

if you cross-reference when the women disappeared, it will match to his days off."

"That's easy enough to check." The chief goes to his computer.

His fingers fly over the keyboard, and the printer churns to life. We all watch as the single sheet of paper slides off it.

Chief Malone lays the paper on his desk. "Here's his schedule for the year, and each day he was off."

I run my fingers over the dates. "Here. June fifteenth. That's when Alice Thompson was reported missing. He was off that day and the next two days. March twenty is when Victoria went missing. He was off that day and for two days after. The girl from the bowling alley went missing on January sixteenth." I run my finger across the lines for January. "He worked that day. But look at this. He took three sick days after. For everyone, he was off for three days."

"Son of a bitch." The chief grabs his phone. "This doesn't leave this room. I don't want anyone leaking this information and alerting him. I'll call Judge Marshall and get a search warrant. I don't want our guys in on this. I'll take the two detectives we borrowed from Portsmouth with me."

"Chief—"

"I don't want you in this search, Knox. You're too emotionally involved. You stay put and watch your lady friend. Keep her safe or have you forgotten the threats to her life?"

I'm about to protest when Ava kicks my foot and glares at me with a silent request for compliance.

The chief nods at the door in an obvious order for us to get out, and we leave. Everyone stares at us. We retreat to my office, where I close the door, slumping against it. Every conversation I had with Jeff is rushing at me. "Jeff was always around, even showing up at mealtimes. I never really clicked with him, but I felt sorry for him. His family was an even bigger mess than mine. More than once, he came by with a black eye or busted lip. His father was a mean SOB."

"Having a bad childhood is not an excuse for kidnapping and killing people."

I shake my head. "Of course not. But maybe I should have suspected something years ago."

She palms my cheek. "You couldn't have known, and there's no point in worrying about it now."

I close my eyes and nuzzle into her touch.

Her hand falls away. "Let's go."

I open my eyes. "Go?"

Ava grabs her purse and loops it over her shoulder. "We have two or three hours of sunlight at the most." Then she takes Emily's phone.

I frown. "Go where?"

"To find Lynn. I know where she is. I'll tell you everything on the way there."

I push off the door. "I'll get the chief."

"No." Her voice is harsh. "Sorry, no chief, no other cops. Just us. If you go in full force, he'll see us and take off. We need the element of surprise."

"This is not a good idea. I don't like it one bit. You should stay here—safe—and I can go in with backup to get Lynn."

"That won't work. It has to be the two of us. If anyone else comes along, we'll blow the only chance we have to get Lynn out safely."

Everything in me wants to refuse. "This is a bad idea. It's risky and dangerous. Who knows how far Jeff will go to protect himself and get away? He won't give up easily."

"Jeff is the chief's problem. He will go to his house with

the search warrant and hopefully find Jeff at home. Lynn is my concern. I brought her into this, and I'll get her out. You can come with me or not. Either way, I'm going. And before you say you can keep me from doing it, no—you can't—don't even try."

She stands in front of me, a warrior intent on doing everything she can to save her friend, and I won't let her do it alone.

"I'm coming with you."

CHAPTER 57

AVALON

WE EXIT THE BUILDING THE SAME WAY WE CAME IN AND avoid the press madhouse out front. But this time, instead of the SUV, Jake walks to a black and gray police cruiser.

I hesitate. "What are you doing?"

He unlocks the passenger door for me. "I'm taking my police cruiser."

"Why?"

"Because it has everything I need inside."

I take in the tinted windows, which make it impossible to see inside. Sliding into the seat, I make sure not to touch any of the equipment. There's a laptop on the dash and a CB radio in the middle console.

Jake drives slowly as we approach the parking lot exit. The cop at the parking lot gate in front of the City Hall waves us through. "Where are we going?"

"Back to the park."

He gives me a quick glance and turns right out of the station. "Okay, spill it. Tell me everything."

And I do. I tell Jake everything I saw and what Emily told

me. I tell him about the times I saw his grandfather too. I talk and talk as he drives.

"That's everything. I don't want to keep anything from you. That's the whole truth and nothing but the truth."

His only reaction is his hands squeezing the steering wheel. "Why didn't you tell me about my grandfather earlier?"

"I didn't think you were ready to hear any of it."

He nods, more to himself than me, his eyes fixed on the road. "Do you think my grandfather and Emily are together?"

I don't want to give Jake platitudes, so I take a moment to respond. "Yes, I do. Based on everything I've experienced, not only here, but over the years, and everything I've read about life after death and spirits, I believe they are together. More than believe it, I know it."

He reaches over and squeezes my hand. His Adam's apple bobs with a swallow. "Thank you."

"For what?"

He lets my hand go and grabs the steering wheel to make a sharp turn. "For making me believe again."

It's my turn to touch him, and I squeeze his wrist, then let go.

Jake slows down and drives through the open gates to the park. "Where to?"

"The same area we found Alice."

He raises an eyebrow. "That far in?"

"I'm afraid so."

Jake drives to and parks in the same spot as before. "Let's go."

Jake opens the cruiser's trunk, and then a locked box. Inside are guns, ammunition, and a bulletproof vest. He attempts to slide the vest over my head, but I take two steps back. "No, it's yours, and you should wear it."

His face hardens, and he recovers the distance I put between us. "Either you put this on and do as I say, or we're leaving, and I don't care if I have to handcuff you and drag you kicking and screaming out of here."

Gosh. He would do it too. "Okay, I'll wear it."

He slides the vest over my head and fits my arms through the holes. "It's too big."

"It's adjustable." He pulls the Velcro off the sides to make the vest tighter around my chest, then does the same with the straps over my shoulders. It's still loose but fits better than before.

Jake grabs a handgun from the locker and checks to make sure the magazine is full. Then, holsters the gun to his leg with a strap. Then he checks the gun in his waist holster and slides three extra magazines and a small flashlight into his back pockets. He grabs a shoulder holster and yet another gun. "Ready?"

The weight of the bulletproof vest and seeing Jake arm himself brings home the reality of our situation and hits me like a sucker punch. I answer in a shaky voice. "Yes."

Jake takes the lead and goes up the same trail as the last time. The forest closes in around us and it grows denser with each step. Night insects chirp, making their presence known. Or maybe showing their discontent at our presence. Gray clouds above the trees' canopy lend an ominous feel to the forest.

The rustle of the wind and the insects are the only other sounds. Everything else is quiet. Quieter than one would think in a forest so full of wildlife.

Jake stops at a small clearing near the spot where we found Alice. "Where to?"

I hold Emily's phone to my chest and let my senses take over, then point to the right. "That way, past the hole." I don't have to clarify what hole I'm referring to. I don't think either of us will ever forget what happened that day a week ago.

When we walk past it, I cast my gaze down and avoid looking at it. We walk another five minutes, and I stop to orient myself. The wind stills, as well as the insects. Above us, clouds hover heavy and gray through the frame of motionless branches and leaves. It's like the forest itself is watching us.

Jake puts a hand on my shoulder. He, too, can sense the wrongness of this place.

Then, a twig snaps under a foot, as startling as a crack of lightning.

"Well, well, well, what have we got here?"

We turn at the same time, and twenty feet from us is Jeff. The dog is at his side. Unleashed. Jeff's left hand is in his hoodie pocket, and in his right is a gun—pointed directly at us.

CHAPTER 58
JAKE

I don't enjoy having guns pointed at me, and now it's happened twice in one week.

"Déjà vu," Ava says, her voice as quiet as the forest.

Jeff points his gun at Ava. "Take the gun out of his holster, nice and easy, and toss it over here."

I lift my hands higher, and Ava unstraps the holster at my chest, gingerly removes the Glock by the grip with two fingers, and tosses it onto the ground.

"Kick it closer."

She does as he says. The gun slides through the dirt, and he kicks it into the bushes.

Jeff takes a step closer. "Going for a romantic walk? You picked a beautiful place. It's so peaceful here. So quiet, one could scream for hours and never, ever be heard." He smiles.

The hairs on the back of my neck stand up. "Why are you pointing a gun at us, Jeff?"

"This?" He waves the gun. "Oh, that's nothing. Just a little personal protection. Lots of bodies showing up in these woods lately."

359

He's playing games with us. "What are you doing?"

"Me?" He points at himself with the gun. "Oh, the same as you, going for a walk on this beautiful evening."

I take a slow step to the right, trying to get in front of Ava, who's frozen in place. She seems to wake up then and evades my attempt.

"Why are you here?"

Jeff shrugs. "Funny story. I was going home and imagine my surprise when I saw the chief breaking into my house with two boys from Portsmouth. Y'all sure are busy on my day off. Now, the question is, what's the chief doing in my house?"

"You're gonna have to ask him that. Why don't you go back home and see for yourself?"

He scratches at his neck with the gun. "Nah, I'm enjoying myself right now. But I have another question. What are you two doing here? And so late, too. It will be dark soon and terrible things can happen at night. Lots of predators in these woods."

Ava glares at him. "Funny how this predator only goes after innocent women. I guess he's too much of a coward to pick on someone his own size."

Jeff's face goes red, and he steps closer, his movements agitated. Next to him, the dog whines, picking up on the tension. "They weren't innocent. None of them. They thought they were better than me. They all deserved what happened to them."

Ava shifts next to me. "You mean they deserved what you did to them? It was not something that happened to them. It was something you did. You kidnapped them and you hurt them. You killed them, and you enjoyed doing it."

Jeff's face contorts and the cords in his neck stand out.

"You don't know shit! You weren't there. You didn't see how they acted. Or what they did."

The dog moves forward, placing himself between Jeff and Ava. He whimpers again—his alert eyes shifting between Jeff and us—this situation is so fucked up. We might be able to run and hide and evade being shot, but we'll never escape a trained police dog. And I don't want to shoot it, either.

I hold my hand out and slowly put it on Ava's shoulder. "Ava . . ." I want her to be quiet and not antagonize Jeff any further.

I attempt to get Jeff's attention on me again, keep him talking and get him to relax. Distract and divert. "Isn't it a little hot for a hoodie?"

He looks at himself. "Yes, now that you mention it, I am a little hot." He carefully removes his hand from the pocket.

I tense, but his hand is empty. No, that's not true. There's something on it. His hand is bandaged, thickly wrapped in gauze.

Ava nods in his direction. "What happened?"

"Oh, nothing. Had a minor incident with a bitch."

Bitch. Lynn.

Ava hugs herself. "You got bitten by a dog?"

"Now, why would you call her a dog? She's your friend—"

Ava takes a step forward. "What did you do to her?"

His smile is evil. "Nothing much—yet. I've been waiting for you. Trying to puzzle out how I was gonna get you away from your guard dog there, and here you are. Like a gift dropping at my feet. Thanks, Knox. It was so kind of you to bring her to me."

My hands fist and he notice it.

"Down, boy. Don't do anything stupid. I don't want to shoot you just yet."

I move closer to Ava. "What do you think will happen? You can't get away with this. Drop the gun, turn yourself in, and end this madness."

"And why would I do something dumb like that? Turn myself in? I'll get life, and you know what they do to cops on the inside. It isn't pretty."

"I'll talk to the DA on your behalf. We can cut a deal. Make sure you're safe."

He laughs. "There's no such thing as safe. Ask her friend. She thought she was safe behind locked doors."

Ava's shoulders pull back. Her nails digging into her arms are the only sign his words hit her hard.

He takes two steps to the side and back again. "Besides, no one knows anything. There's no proof. They can search my house all they want, but they won't find a thing."

"There's enough evidence pointing at you."

"Bullshit! There's no evidence, and if there is, it's circumstantial at best. You think I'm stupid? You think you're better than me because you made detective? I was there for three years before you, and they gave you the promotion. You came in thinking you were gonna do what the chief and everyone else couldn't. But you didn't, did you? You failed, too. Where's Emily, Jake? Did you find her yet?" He laughs, and the sound is deranged.

Before I have a chance to react, Ava takes several steps forward. He points the gun at her face. A kill shot.

CHAPTER 59
AVALON

TODAY IS NOT THE DAY I DIE. TODAY IS NOT THE DAY I DIE. Today is not the day I die. I say it over and over in my mind like a mantra.

I don't flinch. I don't react to the gun the bastard is pointing at me. I keep my hands up and stare him down. "You're wrong. We know what happened to Emily. We know what you did to her, and we know where you hid her body."

His face transforms from gloating to rage and back again in the span of a second. He laughs. "You almost had me there. You're good. Great acting skills. I give you that."

His gaze goes past me and to Jake, who's edging toward me, hands in the air. He stops at my side and lowers one hand to the small of my back.

The German Shepherd pushes against Jeff's leg, head down and tail wagging, slow and unsure. He doesn't seem to notice the dog. "You're bluffing. You don't know shit. You'll never find her. Never."

I look at him in the eyes. I don't waver—show no fear. "It was raining the day you took her."

He scoffs. "So? Everyone knows that."

I continue as if he hadn't said anything. "You knew Emily would be there. You overheard her making plans with Jake. And you thought that would be the perfect opportunity to take her."

Jake tenses at my back.

I haven't told him any of this because I didn't know it myself until now. "You didn't plan your first kill very well. In fact, you didn't know you would kill her that day. Oh, you fantasized about it in great detail. But back then, you didn't know if you could do it."

He sneers, his lip curling like a wolf showing its teeth. "You don't know what you're talking about."

"Don't I?" I slowly lift my hand and point to his right. "About a hundred yards that way, there's an old mine, a cave, really. It's been abandoned for over one hundred and fifty years. That's where you put her body. You stuffed her into a large duffel bag, filled it with rocks, and dumped her into a subterranean lake."

He rushes at me, gun shaking in his outstretched arm. "How do you know that?"

Jake moves, trying to shove me behind him.

Jeff swings the gun his way. "Don't move. Don't even think about it. I'll fucking blow your brains out."

Jake halts with his hands up.

Jeff's less than ten feet away from us now. The dog alternates between barking and whimpering as he paces halfway toward us and back around Jeff's legs. "Shut up!" He kicks the dog.

I stop myself from moving toward the poor animal. My every instinct is on alert. I'm pushing Jeff past his breaking point, but there was always the chance that this could happen. I don't know where I find the courage to keep going, to keep talking, but the certainty that this will end now wraps around me like a mantle.

I drop my hands. No longer worried about being shot. "I'll tell you what else I know. I'll tell you everything."

His curiosity will be his downfall. I hope my big mouth isn't mine.

CHAPTER 60
JAKE

WHAT IS SHE DOING? DOES SHE REALLY KNOW WHAT happened to Emily, or is she bluffing? If it's true, why didn't she tell me? She's making him angrier. He'll lose control and shoot us both. I have to stop her. "Ava, no."

"Shut the fuck up, Knox. I want to know everything your little girlfriend has to say." He's shaking, the gun wavering in his hand as he moves it from Ava to me and back again.

There's a calmness about her that radiates in waves, and it only serves to aggravate Jeff more. She's not scared, and she's not cowering. She's not feeding into his need to overpower and control.

"I'll tell you what happened, and you tell me whether I'm wrong or not. How's that?" Her voice is soft and confident.

Jesus Christ, what is she doing? Can't she see how close he is to losing it?

"You took Emily's phone. You lied to her. You told her you wanted her opinion on a birthday gift for Jake. You lured her with her love for him. A love you wanted for yourself but could never have."

366

He pales. The hand holding the gun drops an inch.

"Should I keep going? I think I will. You overpowered her, drugged her, put her in your piece-of-shit car, and that's when it hit you. What you had done. Am I right so far?"

My heart is trying to climb up my throat, and I breathe deeply and slowly as I assess the situation. Ava's making him angry but also doubt himself. She's chipping at his confidence. The cockiness from just minutes ago is waning.

"You panicked. You didn't want anyone to find you with Emily. How could you explain it? She would tell Jake, and you knew Jake would come after you. Maybe not kill you, but he would hurt you because there's nothing Jake loved more than his little sister, and you took her away from him. Because you were jealous. You envied him. You thought he had everything that should have been yours. But instead, you had crap parents who didn't care."

Jeff's panting, his chest and shoulders moving with each short breath. "You can't know that. That's not possible." The hand holding the gun drops halfway. A modicum of relief fills me—the gun's not pointing to Ava now.

"You took her to that cave while she was still unconscious. You freaked out and decided the only way to escape was to kill her. Kill her and hide the body where no one could find it. So, you did. You stabbed her. You were terrified at first. But you liked it. You liked how it felt when the knife broke into her flesh. You liked the metallic scent of blood and how warm it felt on your hands. You loved the rush it gave you and how powerful it made you feel. You were a god. Isn't that right, Jeff?"

The way Ava says his name is a taunt. My heart slams against my chest so violently it hurts. I want to throw up. I want to rip him to pieces. I want to keep Ava safe. I do none of those things. I detach myself as years of training kick in. I hold it together for Ava's sake and mine because not all of us will walk out of this place alive today. Of this, I'm certain.

Jeff snarls like a rabid animal. Spittle flies, his free hand fisting and flexing. He moves erratically, walking back and forth over the same five or six-foot wide area. The dog's hackles rise, his ears flatten, and he sniffs the air, sensing the wrongness in his master.

I inch to the side, away from Ava and closer to Jeff.

Ava keeps talking, baiting him, keeping his attention on her. This is our only chance. If anything happens to her, I'll never forgive myself.

"How am I doing so far? Should I keep going?"

Jeff's injured hand goes to his head and grips his hair as if he will pull it out. He's on the verge of a breakdown.

"And then you stuffed Emily into the duffel bag. Filled it with rocks and rolled her body into the lake. Did you sleep well that night? Did you have nightmares? Did Emily's face haunt you when you closed your eyes? Or was it just another day for you?"

His eyes are red-rimmed, and his face contorted with rage. "How? How do you know?"

"You want to know how I know what you did to Emily? I'll tell you."

He takes a step closer to Ava.

"I know all of this because Emily told me. She's standing right behind you."

He turns, gun wavering in all directions, searching the trees and bushes in the fast-falling darkness. The forest is more shadow than light now. This is my chance, and I take it. I rush him. He turns just before I reach him, arm raised, and shoots.

Ava screams.

The blast is deafening. My ears ring, and I lose my balance for a fraction of a second and stumbled into Jeff. The gun goes off again.

We hit the ground hard. The smell of gunpowder and dust fills the air as we wrestle in the dirt. The dog barks and growls. We fight for the gun, my hand locking around his wrist. He knees me in the stomach and pushes me away.

He staggers to his feet as I reach for the gun at my waist. It's not there. I go for the gun at my leg as Jeff lifts his arm, aims toward Ava, and shoots.

"Nooooo." A strangled shout rips out of me.

Everything slows down.

Ava falls back, her head turning, hair flowing and covering her face, arms stretched out to her sides. She hits the ground and doesn't move.

The eighty-five-pound dog lunges and locks his deadly jaws on Jeff's throat. He falls back, his arms flaying, and the Glock fires again and again. I cringe at the horrible sounds of tearing flesh and cartilage.

The dog lets go. Gurgling sounds come from the bloody, gaping hole in Jeff's throat. He twitches and goes still, his eyes open and fixed on the darkening sky. The dog whimpers and crawls over to Ava, his muzzle covered in blood.

Terrified, I run to Ava's side and brush the hair away from her face as gently as I can. The entire left side of her head is covered in blood. It runs down her face and onto her neck. So much blood it paints my hands red.

I'm sick to my stomach. "No, no, no, God, please, no. Ava? Ava, Ava."

The small moan is barely audible. I check her pulse, and it beats steady against my fingertips. I look over her entire body and don't see any other wounds. Then, my gaze falls to the bulletproof vest. A round grazed the left side but missed her entirely.

I grab my phone and dial dispatch. "This is Detective Jake Knox and I need an ambulance. Now."

I give them the location where we parked and hang up. I have to carry Ava out and meet them by the cruiser.

"Ava, please, can you hear me?"

Her eyes flutter open, and she winces. She tries to touch her head, but I grab her hand. Her eyes widen. "You're hurt and bleeding."

"No, I'm fine. It's not my blood, it's yours. What do you feel? What hurts?"

"My head hurts, and my side aches."

"I called the medics, but I have to carry you out of here."

She winces again. "Jeff?"

"Dead."

"Help me up, please."

"Let me pick you up."

"No, I need to touch Jeff. I need to find Lynn."

I curse under my breath but help her up. She leans heavily on me. "Don't look." I lower her next to his feet, and she reaches for his ankle, hovers her hand for a moment, and closes her eyes before touching him. She flinches the moment she does.

"I know where Lynn is." She swallows and her voice cracks. "And where he kept the bodies. Call the chief."

I grab my phone and dial.

"Knox? We got nothing. The house is clean. I—"

"Shut up and listen." I put the phone on speaker.

Ava gives me a pained smile. "Chief?"

"Did Knox just tell me to shut up?"

"Chief, is there a shed, garage, or something like that on the property?"

A moment of silence before he responds. "Yes, there's a detached garage."

"Lynn is in there."

"We searched it. It's empty. The only things inside are a bicycle, tools, lawnmower, and a refrigerator filled with beer."

"There's an underground bunker, and the trapdoor is under the refrigerator."

"Hold on." The sound of steps and a door opening. "Okay, I'm back in the garage. Hey, you men, move the refrigerator out."

We wait.

"You have to be fucking kidding me."

I squeeze Ava's shaky hand in mine. "Chief? Chief?"

"There's a trapdoor. It has a lock. We're cutting it right now and I have a man going inside."

I hold Ava to my chest. Being careful not to touch her head. There's so much blood, it runs in rivulets down the side of her face and soaks into her shirt and the vest. I'm coated in her blood.

"She's alive. She's okay. We got her."

Ava explodes into tears with wracking sobs as her body goes limp in my arms. "I need to talk to her. Lynn? Lynn?"

"She's alive, and she's okay, no visible harm. But she's drugged. We called for an ambulance. You can meet her at the Bay Center Hospital."

I turn off the speaker mode. "Chief?"

"I don't know how she did it—"

"Chief, listen. Jeff is here."

"Here where?"

"Same place we found Alice's body."

"You arrested him?"

"He's dead."

"Self-defense?"

"The dog killed him."

"What?"

"I'll explain later. I have to go."

He curses. "Secure the area and wait for me. I'll send a team now and be there as soon as I wrap up things here."

"Ava was shot. It looks like a graze wound, but she needs medical care. The medics are on their way, but I have to carry her out to meet them on access the road."

"Jesus Christ. Okay, go. I'll call in for the park rangers, too."

I hang up, and Ava is looking at me. "The dog killed him?"

I nod.

Her eyes widen. "Where is the dog?"

"I think Jeff shot him. He's lying down."

"Where? We need to help him." She tries to stand up.

"We need to get you out of here."

"I need to see him."

I help her to the dog's side. He whimpers, and his tail thumps to the ground when he sees her.

Ava runs a hand through his fur. "We have to take him to a vet."

I grimace. "I know, I want to, but I can only carry one of you out of here."

"I can walk. You carry the dog."

"Ava."

"I'm not leaving without him. He saved our lives."

"I know. But you've been shot, and you're still bleeding."

"I'm not leaving the dog behind. I can hold on to your shoulder if I need to. But you're carrying that dog."

Bullheaded woman. But I admire her loyalty, so I sigh and pick up the dog as gently as I can.

She pats his head. "What's his name again?"

"Duke."

"I think he needs a new name."

"Yeah? What do you want to call him?"

"Hero."

CHAPTER 61
AVALON

By the time we get to Jake's parked cruiser, the ambulance and paramedics are waiting for us. So is Chief Malone with half a dozen officers around him. High beams from the cruisers and other vehicles parked along the way illuminate the rapidly darkening night. It will be pitch-black in another twenty minutes.

A cop rushes to us and takes Duke—no, he takes Hero from Jake. "I'll rush him to the vet."

I stop him with a hand on his arm. "I think he was shot more than once. Please make sure he gets the best care possible. He saved our lives."

"You can count on it." He disappears behind the line of vehicles. As a medic approaches, Jake points to the ambulance. Every step toward it takes more and more effort. My side burns, and pain pounds behind my eyes. I sit at the bumper of the ambulance. Someone shines a light in my eyes, and I flinch in pain.

Jake helps remove the bulletproof vest. "I think a bullet also grazed her side."

The medic whistles. "You got lucky."

"I guess I did."

"This might sting a little." He squirts saline solution on my head.

I wince. It stings a lot.

"God, I need to call Grandma and Lynn's family to let them know she's okay."

Jake rubs my back. "Let the medic do his work. You can make calls on the way to the hospital."

The medic bandages my head. "This should hold you until we get you to the hospital. Let's check your side."

I lift my shirt, and a purple bruise is forming on my side.

"They should take an X-ray and make sure there're no broken ribs. With some rest and pain meds, you'll be good as new in a few days."

He glances at Jake, who's hovering as close as he can without being in the way. "Does anyone else need help?"

"You need a body bag for that asshole."

The medic's brows shoot up. "Give me five, and we'll take you to the hospital."

"Miss Ava." Chief Malone squints at the bandage and shakes his head. "You are a very lucky lady tonight."

"So I've heard." The pain is making me cranky. "What about Lynn? I want to see her."

"You will. They'll take you to the same hospital where she's being checked out right now. I want to thank you, Miss Ava. We would not have found your friend without your help." He looks at Jake. "And you for believing in her in the first place."

Jake nods once. Looks away as if uncomfortable with the praise. "We found Emily, too."

"What?" The chief takes a step back.

"Can you get a recovery team in the morning? Her remains are in a duffel bag at the bottom of an underground lake in the abandoned mining cave."

"Jesus. All this time, it was him?" The chief reaches out and squeezes Jake's shoulder.

I hop down and grimace. That hurt. "I want to go now. Can we go now?"

The medic who treated me appears. "Yes, I'm here. We can go right now. You get back in the bus." He points at the ambulance behind me.

A woman also wearing a medic uniform approach. She smiles at me. "I'm no vet, but I checked the dog, and I think he'll make it. Officer Sherman is taking him to the animal hospital right now. He called in for the emergency vet. They know he's coming."

Jake gives the cruiser keys to the chief. "Can someone drive it to the hospital? I'll go with Ava."

Chief Malone takes the keys. "I'll send someone." Then he leans closer to Jake and whispers, "We found three more bodies in that bunker. He had a walk-in freezer. I think one is the girl from the bowling alley."

Jake's eyes widen. "Jesus."

The chief nods. "That's not all. We found journals and polaroid pictures, too. The bastard liked to keep notes."

***

"Lynn!" I hug myself and walk stiffly to her side. Now that the adrenaline is fading, the pain in my side and head is increasing. She looks so small in the hospital bed with a blanket pulled up to her chin. A red-purple bruise blooms on her cheek, and she has a black eye but no other visible injuries.

Her eyes flutter open, and it takes her a moment to fix her gaze on me. "Ava? You okay? They told me you're okay. They said you're the one who found me."

"I'm good, hurting a little, but okay."

She looks at the bandage on my head, the blood-stained shirt. "What happened to you?"

"I'm fine, just a bump on my head and a scratch on my side, but it feels like Mike Tyson landed a couple of punches on me. What happened, Lynn?"

She smiles, and a bead of blood forms on her cracked lip. I take a tissue, wet it in the water glass, and dab at her lip.

She winces and takes the tissue from me. Presses it into her mouth. "He had a master key to the apartment. I fell asleep on the couch, heard a noise, and when I looked up, there he was."

"Oh my God."

"I knew it had to be him, but I tried to play along. I asked him if he came in with you and Jake, but he didn't buy it. The next thing I knew, he took a syringe and injected me with something. I don't remember much after that, except going down into a cellar, I think."

"It was a bunker. The bastard had a bunker under his garage."

"Did the police get him?" Her voice is hoarse.

Jake steps to my side. "He won't be hurting anyone else."

Her eyes flutter closed. "That's good."

I brush a lock of hair away from her temple, and she flinches. "I'm sorry I dragged you into this mess. It's my fault. If I hadn't—"

"No, if we start blaming anyone, then it's me for insisting

377

you go into that antique store. We aren't doing this. Not today, not ever. The only person we can blame is that asshole."

I nod, my gaze lingering on the ugly bruise on her face. "He hit you."

She smiles, and it's crooked because of her swollen face and lip. "He did that after I took a chunk of his hand."

I frown. "How?"

"He grabbed my face, told me how pretty I was and how ugly I would be once he was done with me. His hand got too close to my teeth. I bit him as hard as I could and held on until he hit me. Then, I spat at him."

I pat her arm. "You got him good. He had a bandage around his hand."

A look of disgust distorts her face. "I tasted his blood. I've brushed my teeth a dozen times and used half a bottle of Listerine to wash out my mouth."

Jake smiles at her. "It's over. He won't hurt you or anyone else ever again."

Her eyes fill with tears, and she rubs at the corners. "I guess you want to ask me questions for your report."

"I do, but not today. You need to rest and recover. We can talk in a couple of days."

I snort. "The chief will love that."

Jake shoves his hands in his pockets. "It's my case and the chief can kiss my—"

"The chief doesn't want to hear the rest of that sentence," says the man in question as he gives Jake the keys to his cruiser. "It's parked in lot B, row eleven."

Lynn squints at him. "I remember you. You're the one who cut off the zip ties. You got me out of that place."

"Not me alone. It was a team effort, and you can thank Miss Ava. We searched the entire place and were about to leave when she called. We'd never have imagined he built a bunker under his garage."

She looks at me, her eyes drooping. "Best friends forever."

A nurse comes in then. "Our patient needs to rest. Everyone must go. Say your goodbyes. You can come back in the morning. Visiting hours start at nine."

I kiss Lynn's forehead. "I love you. I'll see you in the morning."

"Love you right back," she mumbles as she falls asleep.

CHAPTER 62
AVALON

I CLICK THE SEAT BELT ON. "I WANT THE PAINKILLERS they gave me, a hot shower, and food. In that order."

"That can be arranged. I have a shower with hot water, and food is just one phone call away."

I shift to look at Jake. "You're taking me to your house?"

He backs out of the parking space and glances at me. "I won't be able to let you out of sight for a while. And I don't think you want to go back to the apartment and be alone there."

I get shivers just thinking about it. "No, I don't. And I don't think Lynn wants to go back there either."

He squeezes my knee once and grabs the steering wheel again. "I can drive you over tomorrow, help you pack, and bring everything back to my house. I have three guest rooms. She can take one of them."

I smile. "And the other guest room is for me?"

We stop at a red light, and he leans in for a kiss. "There's plenty of space for you in my bedroom."

"I like the way you think."

As Jake opens the door to his house, an orange blur races to the door and climbs up Jake's jeans and shirt.

"Ouch, sharp claws, Kojak." He holds the cat, belly up like a baby. Kojak purrs his contentment and tries to rub his face on Jake's. "He's never done that. Do you think he knows? Did he sense that something could have gone terribly wrong today?"

I reach over and scratch under Kojak's chin. "Yes, animals can sense when something is off, for sure. There are records of animals running away minutes before major disasters strike, like earthquakes and tsunamis. It's not a big stretch to speculate that they may sense something bad happening to their owners."

Jake puts Kojak over his shoulder, and the cat wraps his paws around his neck. My heart melts. What is it about a man holding a cute animal that hits all the spots?

Jake walks to the kitchen, and I follow him. "Let's get you some food. How about some canned salmon today?"

He feeds the cat, washes his hands, and turns to me. "Your turn." He opens the fridge, gets a bottle of water, then grabs the painkiller bottle from his pocket and shakes a pill into my hand.

I swallow the pill with half of the water. "Thank you."

He holds my hand and takes me upstairs. "Now, for that shower. I would very much like to assist with that." He looks at my bandaged head. "I can help wash your hair and bandage your head again."

"Is that so?"

He smiles, but it doesn't quite reach his eyes. "Full service."

He's pushing the day away by keeping his emotions at bay. His grief over his sister and finally finding out what happened is something to deal with later. I know he'll have questions. But just not yet. For now, we both need a respite and sleep. I'm grateful for that. I smile back, tiredness hammering at me. My entire body aches.

Jake turns on the shower and kneels in front of me, removes one sneaker, and then the other. My socks follow. Then he unbuttons my jeans, pulls down the zipper, and works the denim over my hips and thighs, all the way down to my feet. I step out of them. He pulls my blood-covered shirt up and over my head, being careful with my bandages, then tosses it in the garbage. He gasps at the purple bruise on my side that spreads to under my breast.

"Doc said I was lucky because both bullets grazed me. I didn't get the full impact on my side. If I did, I would have broken ribs for sure."

"I'm sorry. You should have never been there."

"Yes, I should. Lynn would be dead if I hadn't come with you. You would be dead. We can talk about it later. Where's that full service you offered?" I turn my back to him, and he unclasps my bra. My panties follow. He kisses the back of my head, neck, and shoulder, then stands in front of me. His gaze heated. I tug at his shirt and remove it. His shoes, socks, jeans, and boxer shorts follow. Steam billows around us. He offers me his hand, and we step into the shower.

Pink water runs down the drain, removing the last physical evidence of what happened today. Jake's gentle beyond measure as he runs soapy hands over my neck, arms, and torso. My hair is next, and his touch is a balm to my soul. I've never had anyone wash me before. His hands miss no part of me, and while his touch is not sexual in any way, it's sensual all the same. He can't help his body's response to my nakedness, even if he's not expecting sex. But I am. As the meds dull the pain and the hot water washes away blood and dirt, all that could have gone wrong races through my mind. I need to be closer to him. I go on my tippy-toes and wrap my arms around his neck, our naked, wet bodies flush. The scent of lemon soap fills the steamy air. I kiss him, slow and demanding, as the water falls over us.

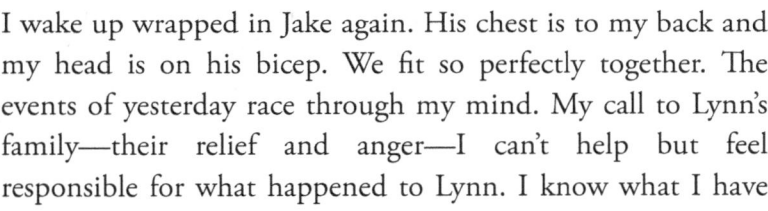

I wake up wrapped in Jake again. His chest is to my back and my head is on his bicep. We fit so perfectly together. The events of yesterday race through my mind. My call to Lynn's family—their relief and anger—I can't help but feel responsible for what happened to Lynn. I know what I have to do, but I don't want to.

Jake shifts behind me and stretches, his body arching into mine. He kisses my shoulder. "Hungry? We never ate last night."

"Now that you mention it, I'm starving."

"How about we go to your apartment first so you can get clean clothes, then we can go for a breakfast burrito on the pier. After that, I'll help you pack and drive you to the hospital to see Lynn."

I try to swallow the knot forming in my throat. "That sounds perfect." But my voice cracks.

He turns me to face him. "What's wrong?"

I can't lie to myself anymore, and I can't delay the truth to him either. "Yesterday, when I called Lynn's mom, she said they are coming today to see her."

Those beautiful sky and sea eyes search my face. "I take it Lynn's leaving with them."

Tears fill my eyes. "Yes."

"And you're leaving, too." It's not a question. He knows.

"I have to. I can't let her go back and stay here." The tears fall freely now. "I wish I could, but I can't."

He nods and releases a heavy breath. "I understand."

"We'll stay long enough to answer any questions you or the chief may have, but then we'll go back to New York."

He wipes at my tears and kisses my forehead. I want to break into a thousand pieces. The cage of his arms is the only thing holding me together now. I wish I didn't have to leave, but I've known all along we would end like this.

CHAPTER 63
AVALON

I SHOULD BE HAPPY, EXCITED EVEN. THIS TRIP IS THE pinnacle of my life's work. But I'm adrift, following the current because that was set for me months ago. Spending three months in Greece assisting with a dig is something I've wanted to do for years. And this is a real chance to be a part of it. Firsthand discovery, right along with the archeological team. I should be riding the high, but instead, my feet are lead weights I dragged to the airport and through customs, and finally onto the business class section of British Airways flight 1642.

The dreamer in me wants to exit the plane, run through the airport like the heroine in a movie, get into my car, and drive back to New Hampshire. Then, I'd tell Jake I'm there to stay. But that town holds too many terrible memories, and even if we were all safe in the end, I don't know that I could live there. It's been four weeks since I last saw Jake, and I couldn't go back to see him again after we left. Phone calls and texts are a poor substitute for building and maintaining a relationship. As much as Lynn says she's okay and seems to be

385

completely recovered, there are times when I see a flash of fear in her eyes—fear I have never seen before—and I know she's right back there, in that hole zip-tied to a chair.

The realist in me wants the plane to take off, so I can recline my seat, close my eyes, and sleep all ten-plus hours of this overnight flight. Perhaps with the aid of a large glass of wine.

The seat next to me remains empty for now, and I hope it stays that way. I'm not in the mood to be pleasant or social. I keep my gaze locked on the window and avoid making eye contact with the other passengers. In the aisle, someone adds their luggage to the overhead compartment. Damn it. I guess I'll have a seatmate after all. How rude would it be if I raised the wall between us right now?

The person takes the seat next to me. "I've never been to Greece before, but I'm looking forward to it."

My heart stops and my breath locks in my lungs. The man's voice sounds like Jake. Jesus, am I hallucinating his voice now? I dare not look. I dare not hope. It's impossible.

"I'm hoping to find a guide to help me get around. Do you know anyone?"

I turn slowly, moving my head toward the man and hoping against hope that Jake's sitting next to me and yet not believing it is possible.

Mismatched blue and green eyes greet mine. "Hi."

"Jake?" My heart is a wild thing trashing about in my chest.

"Ava." He smiles, his gaze searching my face.

I reach for his hand. "What are you doing here?"

"Heard Greece is beautiful this time of the year."

Tears prickle my eyes, and I realize he's not joking. "Jake!"

He leans closer to me and cups my face in his hand.

"There's this woman I fell madly in love with. She opened my eyes to an entire universe I didn't know existed. She gave me peace and a part of myself I thought was long lost."

"You love me? And you're going to Greece with me?" There's no holding back the tears now.

"I do. I was always going to follow you. Even when I fought myself because I was so set in my ways and petrified of leaving everything I know behind."

I lean into his hand. His solid touch is proof I'm not dreaming. "You were scared?"

"I was terrified, Ava. I dedicated the last fourteen years of my life to finding Emily. My entire identity revolved around being a cop and solving crimes. Who was I if not a small-town detective?"

"And now?" Hope blooms in my chest.

"And now I'm not scared anymore. I'm curious and excited to find out who I am without the burden I put on myself. And I want to figure it out at your side—with you—if you'll have me."

I sob. I don't know what to say.

He wipes my tears with his thumbs. "Please say yes, or it will be really awkward sitting next to you for the next ten hours."

"Yes, oh my God, yes. I love you. I have loved you since the day you fished me out of the sea and saved my life—"

He kisses me then. Telling me with the touch of his lips and tongue how much he loves me.

The sound of someone clearing his throat interrupts us. The flight attendant leans closer. "Sorry, we are getting ready for takeoff and you need to put your seat belts on." He then lowers his voice. "But as soon as we hit cruising altitude, feel free to lift the partition for some privacy." He winks.

We sit back, and Jake holds my hand as the plane races down the runway and lifts off. "I have so many questions."

He turns my way. "Ask away."

"How did you know where to find me? And how long can you stay with me?"

"For your first question, the answer is Lynn."

"That explains why she was acting weird this last week. She was asking me all kinds of questions about my flight and seat numbers and the dates of my flights."

"Yes, she called me, said you were leaving for Greece, were staying there for three months, and I'd better get my ass in gear before you got away."

I try to keep the disappointment that Lynn had to call him from showing on my face. He's here, and that's all that matters.

"I didn't come because she called me. I had quit my job but had a few loose ends to tie up. Her calling gave me the chance to make plans to travel with you. I would have come either way."

"You quit the police? What did Chief Malone say?"

"He said, 'go get her'."

I swallow the growing knot in my throat. Gosh, I hope I won't spend the entire flight crying. "Jake, I love you, and I love that you're here with me, but I hate that I made you quit your job—"

"Don't. The only reason I became a cop was to find Emily, and you found her for me. Nothing is holding me to that job or that town. I'm glad to leave it all behind and start fresh with you."

"Kojak! What about Kojak? And Hero?"

He smiles. "My mom has both of them."

"She has Hero, too?"

"Hero retired as a police dog with honors, and I adopted him. My mom is divorcing her husband and living in my house now. She told me the truth about my real father. She said you told her she needed to tell me and I thank you for that."

"Oh, Jake. I'm sorry I never said anything to you. I didn't think it was my place, but she promised she'd tell you."

"She did. And she located him, too. I met him." Jake laughs. "I look exactly like him, down to the two-colored eyes. He's never married or had other kids. After all these years, I think they are getting together again. And I thank you for that, too."

"I don't know what to say. I'm so happy for you, your mom, for your real dad."

He nods. "We had a ceremony for Emily after you left. A proper burial. It was the closure I needed. And it gave my father—Emily's father closure, too. He apologized and thanked me for finding her killer. But that was before Mom dumped his ass, so he's probably blaming me for that now." He laughs without humor.

"He may never have been a good father to you, but you were always a good son to him."

"I don't know about that."

"You were. That first day in your house, when we got interrupted, it was him, wasn't it? He was drunk, and they called you to take him home. Someone else might have let the cops send him to jail to sober up. But you took care of him, knowing he wouldn't do the same for you."

"I did it for my mother to save her the embarrassment and trouble of getting him out."

"Still. You're a good son, and you were a wonderful grandson. Your Pops told me so."

The corners of his eyes crinkle with his smile. "You're incredible, you know?"

"I don't know about that." I lean in and give him a quick kiss. "What are you going to do now?"

He shrugs. "I have options. I could join the NYPD. I know people there. Or I could start my own private investigation firm. I know this girl who could be my partner."

I smile. "Is that so?"

His beautiful eyes search my face, unhidden by sunglasses. "It is."

My heart flutters like the wings of a thousand butterflies. "How long can you stay with me?"

"What about forever?"

I hope you enjoyed reading this book. If so, please leave a review. It doesn't have to be elaborated or long. Reviews help authors, and readers like you find more books to love.

Amazon
Goodreads
BookBub

BOOKS BY ERICA ALEXANDER

Riggins U Series

Because of Logan
Because of Liam
Because of Dylan

Stand Alone Books

Courage, Dear Heart
Seventeen Wishes
In Her Eyes
One Wild Night
(Part of the Dissent Anthology)

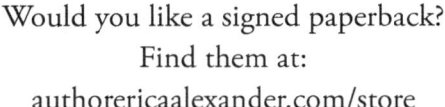

Would you like a signed paperback?
Find them at:
authorericaalexander.com/store

ACKNOWLEDGMENTS

While writing is a solitary endeavor, there's a host of people in the background that makes it possible. Among them, are:

Nicole McCurdy from Emerald Edits, thank you, not only for the fantastic feedback, but also for your support and friendship over the last few years. We may have an ocean between us, but our love for words is a bridge that connects us.

Thanks to my fellow authors, Erika Kelly, Mia Kayla, and Lisa Suzanne. For your support, friendship, and laughs. I wish we didn't have so many miles between us.

Thanks to my good friend Giseli Vargas. We started our friendship over our shared love of books, and it has become so much more. I can't thank you enough for the gorgeous paintings you created for me. I look at them every day. I could not love them more. When are you moving to NJ?

Thank you, Paula Judith Johnson, for your support, suggestions, and friendship.

To the three boys in my life: my husband and two sons. I love you more than life itself. I'm so grateful to have the three of you in my life.

And to you, the reader: none of this would be possible without your love for books—a love we share.

RIP YOUR HEART OUT ROMANCE

Erica Alexander is known for crafting emotional stories filled with complex characters, a touch of angst, and just the right amount of humor. She loves taking her characters—and readers—on a journey that may be bumpy but always ends with a well-earned happily ever after.

Happily married to her husband for over 30 years, Erica is a proud mom to two amazing kids who inspire her every day. When she's not busy catering to the small feral cat colony she cares for—or tending to her two rescue cats and loyal pup—she's likely reading, baking something delicious, or binging Netflix and Prime marathons.

Erica lives in New Jersey with her family and her menagerie of furry friends.

You can find Erica at:

www.ingramcontent.com/pod-product-compliance
Lightning Source LLC
Chambersburg PA
CBHW072108250626
47159CB00007B/2351